Praise for Peter David

"David's best-known style—light, breezy, and chock-a-block with well-chosen pop culture references—is rarely so well employed as in his Knight novels. His Arthur is a true treasure of light fantasy, fully human and yet a walking legend both, full of foibles and yet the sort who could lead battalions into Hell. His cast of returnees from Camelot, reborn into the modern era, are true to themselves, though the outcome now is generally happier (or more harmonious) than it was in the age of myths . . . Anyone looking for a delightful Arthurian tale set in the here-and-now will enjoy David's trifecta of enchantment. It's not your father's King Arthur—but it might be the one you share with your kids. Recommended." —*SFRevu*

Praise for
One Knight Only

"This irreverent romp impartially jousts at White House staff pomposity, the inanities of today's press corps, Congressional antics, and mismanaged U.S. foreign policy. Some of the goings-on are belly-laugh funny . . . a wild mix of ancient legends." —*Publishers Weekly*

Praise for
Knight Life

"A fun spin on that Mark Twain classic. A mix of classic Arthurian fiction and satiric commentary about the nature of today's politics. Engaging." —*The Monroe (LA) News-Star*

"A rollicking urban fantasy in the manner of Neil Gaiman or Christopher Moore. Lots of humorous incongruities, as Arthur's old-fashioned ways meet contemporary absurdities such as politics and television." —*Science Fiction Weekly*

Ace titles by Peter David

HOWLING MAD
KNIGHT LIFE
ONE KNIGHT ONLY
FALL OF KNIGHT

LOGAN-HOCKING
COUNTY DISTRICT LIBRARY
230 E. MAIN STREET
LOGAN, OHIO 43138

Fall of

Knight

PETER DAVID

ACE BOOKS, NEW YORK

THE BERKLEY PUBLISHING GROUP
Published by the Penguin Group
Penguin Group (USA) Inc.
375 Hudson Street, New York, New York 10014, USA
Penguin Group (Canada), 90 Eglinton Avenue East, Suite 700, Toronto, Ontario M4P 2Y3, Canada
(a division of Pearson Penguin Canada Inc.)
Penguin Books Ltd., 80 Strand, London WC2R 0RL, England
Penguin Group Ireland, 25 St. Stephen's Green, Dublin 2, Ireland (a division of Penguin Books Ltd.)
Penguin Group (Australia), 250 Camberwell Road, Camberwell, Victoria 3124, Australia
(a division of Pearson Australia Group Pty. Ltd.)
Penguin Books India Pvt. Ltd., 11 Community Centre, Panchsheel Park, New Delhi—110 017, India
Penguin Group (NZ), 67 Apollo Drive, Rosedale, North Shore 0745, Auckland, New Zealand
(a division of Pearson New Zealand Ltd.)
Penguin Books (South Africa) (Pty.) Ltd., 24 Sturdee Avenue, Rosebank, Johannesburg 2196,
South Africa

Penguin Books Ltd., Registered Offices: 80 Strand, London WC2R 0RL, England

This is a work of fiction. Names, characters, places, and incidents either are the product of the author's imagination or are used fictitiously, and any resemblance to actual persons, living or dead, business establishments, events, or locales is entirely coincidental. The publisher does not have any control over and does not assume any responsibility for author or third-party websites or their content.

FALL OF KNIGHT

An Ace Book / published by arrangement with Second Age, Inc.

PRINTING HISTORY
Ace hardcover edition / June 2006
Ace mass-market edition / June 2007

Copyright © 2006 by Second Age, Inc.
Cover art by Tristan Elwell.
Cover design by Annette Fiore.
Interior text design by Kristin del Rosario.

All rights reserved.
No part of this book may be reproduced, scanned, or distributed in any printed or electronic form without permission. Please do not participate in or encourage piracy of copyrighted materials in violation of the author's rights. Purchase only authorized editions.
For information, address: The Berkley Publishing Group,
a division of Penguin Group (USA) Inc.,
375 Hudson Street, New York, New York 10014.

ISBN: 978-0-441-01506-1

ACE
Ace Books are published by The Berkley Publishing Group,
a division of Penguin Group (USA) Inc.,
375 Hudson Street, New York, New York 10014.
ACE and the "A" design are trademarks belonging to Penguin Group (USA) Inc.

PRINTED IN THE UNITED STATES OF AMERICA

10 9 8 7 6 5 4 3 2 1

If you purchased this book without a cover, you should be aware that this book is stolen property. It was reported as "unsold and destroyed" to the publisher, and neither the author nor the publisher has received any payment for this "stripped book."

YE OLDE PRELUDE

✝

HERE WAS NEVER more than one unicorn. No matter what you may have read elsewhere, there was neither a first nor a last. There was only one, because that was all the world needed and all it would allow. Just as there was never more than one God, but He/She/It had many names and was seen by many different people as being many different things, either splintered into multiple facets or unified as a whole. One unicorn. One God.

This is what happened to the one unicorn . . .

There once was a great warlord who lived thousands of years ago, a master of many lands and many tribes, all of which bowed down to him and pledged fealty. By the standards of what would be his far more civilized descendants, he was very fierce and brutal. He wore metal ornaments interspersed with memorabilia removed from the bodies of the greatest of his opponents. These included anything from their fingers to the skulls of their youngest sons, depending upon his mood.

The warlord . . . whose name is lost to posterity, and a very small loss it was, we should add . . . was determined that nothing and no one in his land should be stronger or braver or faster or smarter than he. To that end, if he ever saw any of his soldiers becoming a potential threat, he would "reward" him by sending him off to head up his conquering troops in a distant land, then taking steps to make sure the soldier never returned. A small bit of poison dropped into a cup during a meal, or a fast dagger in the night . . . whatever means were convenient.

There were giants in those days, as well as creatures of myth, except they weren't referred to as "creatures of myth" but instead as "prey." The warlord was one of the more active predators, and whenever he or his hunters would bring down some particularly fantastic being, there would be a great feast during which the warlord would drink the blood of his conquest and devour its heart. The rest of the creature would be cut up and served raw, since it was firmly believed that scorching the meat with fire only ruined the flavor.

Now the warlord had a son, Lailoken, who often participated in these hunts. But the son held a terrible secret close to his heart, and that secret was that he found these indulgences repulsive. In fact, he had little taste for battle at all. Not that he was incapable of engaging in the fine art of war; he could and did as needed. He was neither as tall nor as powerful as his father, which was probably for the best since gods only know what the warlord would have done to the young man had he seen him as a threat. Lailoken fought in the name of his father, and he fought in the name of his people. He disliked taking life, however, and he certainly despised taking it needlessly.

Whenever they would embark on a hunt for a fantastic creature, Lailoken always made certain to be nowhere nearby when the killing stroke was required. He saw it all as a needless cruelty and wanted no part of it if he could at all avoid it.

Whether his father noticed this reluctance and set matters with the unicorn hunt into motion deliberately, or whether it was mere happenstance that things turned out the way they did, no one will ever know. What is known is this:

Word reached the warlord through his spies and lookouts that the only known unicorn in the world had wandered into his territory. The creature was occasionally referred to as the King of the Unicorns, which angered the warlord greatly, for he himself was not a king and it rankled him that this animal—fantastic or not—sported such a title when he, the mighty warrior, did not. It further irritated him since there were no other unicorns in existence for the creature to be king *of,* and what point was there in being a king if there were no followers?

So the warlord marshaled his best hunting party and, with Lailoken at his side, went out after the unicorn.

There was a mighty forest not far off, and it was believed that the Unicorn King had taken up residence therein. So the warlord and his followers stormed into the forest, beating the bushes furiously, unleashing their hounds and sending them careening wildly through the woods accompanied by even more beaters (not to mention footmen, soldiers, scouts, spies, and whoever else was available for this great hunt).

They spread out through the forest, breaking up into groups of three, two, and even—in Lailoken's case—one. Lailoken made his way through the woods, easing past bushes and trees and broken branches. His long black hair kept getting in his face and it was a constant chore to push it out of his eyes. In the distance he heard the sound of dogs and eager pursuit; all the while he kept his ears strained for the sound of the unicorn. But none came, and he began to hope that maybe the reports of the creature's presence were exaggerated.

Then he thought he heard something not too far off. The barking of the dogs changed from eagerness to sudden fear. There were shouts of men blending in with the howling of the hounds. Lailoken could tell even from this distance that some sort of battle was going on. Some of the dogs were outright screaming, which was a terrible sound because Lailoken didn't think dogs were actually capable of screaming. He was amazed how human they sounded in their distress . . . and, by contrast, how much like animals the human voices came across.

More crashing, more screams and howling until Lailoken could not separate animal from man, and was even moved to wonder if—deep down—there was all that much difference. His heart thudded viciously, and he felt completely paralyzed by the moment. He knew that he should go and help. He carried no sword, but he had a long, elegant spear clutched tight in his hands. The shaft was dusky brown hardwood, strong but supple. The head was leaf-shaped, flared at the bottom and slightly wavy along the blade edges. Twin half-moon-shaped cutouts were inset into the lower section of the head. The blade gleamed in the glare of the sun, and Lailoken stared at it fixedly, as if the sun itself was trying to convey some sort of message to him.

What Lailoken kept waiting to hear—and what did not reach his ears—was the sound of some other beast . . . possibly the one they were hunting or perhaps something else. Certainly whatever it was, he would be able to distinguish its cry from that of hounds and men. If it were a unicorn, as they were hoping to find, it would undoubtedly make some sort of whinnying, horselike sound, wouldn't it? And if it were something else—a phoenix bird, perhaps, or some other fantastic creature—it would likewise have its own unique sound, correct? Yet Lailoken was hearing nothing like that, and it almost made him wonder if instead of a creature, the dogs and men had encountered something far more down-to-earth. Attackers from another tribe, perhaps, or maybe cleverly hidden traps that were mowing them down while he, Lailoken, remained frozen in the woods . . .

"I must help them," he said forcefully, gripping his spear so tightly that his knuckles turned white. "I must help them before—"

That was when he heard the mighty crashing in the woods, almost right on top of him. He jumped back and cried out in fear and alarm, even as he leveled his spear and braced himself for whatever it was that was coming at him.

The beast stumbled out into the clearing nearby him, and Lailoken gasped in wonderment. He didn't lower his spear, but he felt as if his eyes were going to burn out of their sockets.

It was not white, as he had expected it might be. Instead the unicorn was dappled and gray . . . or at least it had been. Now its hide was stained with red, dozens of wounds covering its magnificent body. A long, thin tail with a bushy end whipped around, and its head was long and elegant and also had wounds upon it. Its eyes were the most extraordinary blue orbs that Lailoken had ever seen. To say that the eyes looked human would have been to understate it. They were human . . . more than human. There was a transcendent human soul within the body of that astounding beast.

Most astounding of all was the horn. It was not a simple, straight white cone. Instead it looked like two separate bones, or perhaps hair so hard that it was akin to bone, for they were intertwined like braided hair. One "strand" was purple, the other pink.

The unicorn's right leg was broken. It was nothing short of miraculous that the beast was still able to walk. Whatever divine ability was keeping it upright deserted it the moment it stumbled into Lailoken's presence, and the unicorn crumpled to the ground not five paces from the astounded young man.

The tip of Lailoken's spear trembled as he aimed it at the unicorn. The creature lay there, looking up at him, and there

was something in the beast's eyes that looked like nothing
so much as recognition.

The others were coming, and Lailoken knew that he had
to act quickly. He was prepared to lunge forward, driving
the spear deep into the unicorn's heart, or at least where he
approximated that the heart might be. But he found himself
unable to do so. His feet were rooted to the place, and he
cursed himself for his weakness of spirit and his cowardice.
So instead he retreated a few steps, drew back his arm, and
prepared to let fly with the spear. He very quickly discovered that he could not do that, either.

The unicorn, with what seemed to be great effort, lifted
its head.

And it spoke.

To Lailoken's shock, the creature's mouth moved, but no
words came out. Nevertheless, he heard the beast's voice inside his head. It sounded both old and young at the same
time, and even though it was one voice, it sounded like many.
Like a hundred, no, a thousand voices speaking in concert.

You must kill me.

"No," whispered Lailoken, realizing that he had no choice
but to admit the weakness within him. "No, I . . . I can't . . ."

*I am the Unicorn King, and I am done for. But it is not meet that
I die at the hands of such as they. Only one such as you is worthy.*

"I'm not." He looked desperately in the direction of the
oncoming hunting party. Perhaps sensing that their prey was
helpless, was dying, the hounds were pursuing with renewed
vigor. The soldiers were shouting to each other, drawing in
the tight circle of pursuit. "I'm as nothing. Ask my father,
he'll tell you . . ."

*Your father is as nothing. You have a destiny. You must do this
thing.*

"But . . ."

Do you love me?

He looked into the eyes of the unicorn, deep into those

eyes, plummeting forever into them, and even though it took barely seconds, he knew the answer. "Yes. I love you as I do the full moon on a soft winter night. You fill my soul with the knowledge that there are still things in this world worth marveling at."

Then honor me . . . by taking me out of it. Now. Please, now.

Lailoken felt hot tears running down his face even as he held tight upon the spear and charged forward. He couldn't bring himself to throw it. It would have seemed dishonorable. Instead three, four quick steps, and he thrust forward, putting his full weight behind the spear. It slammed into the heart of the unicorn, cleaving it in twain. The creature jolted from the impact, throwing its head back, and for the first and only time it let out a cry of anguish. It did not sound like any sort of animal noise at all. Instead it sounded like the blowing of a ram's horn, except much louder. The ululation was so overwhelming that the trees and ground shook, and leaves blew off as if whipped from the branches by a powerful wind. In the distance Lailoken heard the hunters cry out and the dogs bark in anguish, their sharp hearing no doubt receiving the most assault from the unicorn's death cry.

And with all that, still the beast was not done. Its head, having thrust upward, had fallen lifelessly, and the soul was departing its eyes; yet, for all that, its voice still sounded within Lailoken's head.

Now yourself. Mix our blood. Hurry.

Lailoken didn't hesitate. He yanked out the spear and stared in wonderment at the thick blood that was upon it. Twisting the spear around, he drew the bloodstained blade across the palm of his hand. Blood welled up, and he drew the flat of the blade across the palm, intermingling his own blood with that of the unicorn.

You have your destiny now . . .

The words echoed within him, and he cried out in agony. He thought the world was exploding around him, but it turned out not to be the case. Instead it was simply a massive eruption of white, directly behind his eyeballs, and there was intense heat coursing through his bloodstream. He collapsed, howling, begging for it to stop, and he curled his legs up into the fetal position and flung his arms around them, drawing his knees almost up into his chin. "Make it stop, make it stop," he moaned repeatedly, and even as he did he kept wondering what in the world the unicorn could possibly have meant in saying that he was worthy of this, that he had a destiny.

The next thing he knew, someone was shaking him violently. There were shouts from all around him, and he looked up to see that his father was looking down at him, a mixture of awe and annoyance upon his face. "Do you hear me? Are you awake?" He roughly slapped Lailoken's face, and Lailoken nodded.

He pointed at the carcass of the fallen unicorn and said, "Did you do this?"

Lailoken couldn't tell what the right answer could possibly be. That was how contradictory his father's tone sounded. Finally deciding that the truth was the preferable way to go, he took a deep breath, let it out slowly, and said, "Yes. I did."

The warlord grunted upon learning this. He asked nothing of Lailoken's condition, apparently thinking that it wasn't of all that much consequence. He stepped back and walked over to the unicorn. He prodded the beast's body with the toe of his boot, then kicked it more forcefully. The unicorn didn't move.

"It's smaller than I expected," he proclaimed, which surprised Lailoken since the beast looked large enough to ride. Then, managing to set aside his disappointment, he declared, "Come. Let's take it home, to the banquet hall."

"Father . . ." Lailoken managed to say, as a couple of the hunters helped him to his feet.

The warlord turned and stared at him. "What?"

Are you proud of me? I finally killed something for you. Did I do well? Will you speak my name with love? Do you have anything to say to me? Are you finally satisfied, you bloody bastard, you . . .

"Nothing. It . . . is nothing, father."

"Good," said the warlord, and he marched stiffly away while his beaters and huntsmen and aides began to tie the unicorn, just above its hooves, so that it was dangling from a long pole suspended at either end upon the shoulders of burly men.

"Good hunt, sir," one of the hunters said. Another patted him on the shoulder in a gesture that would have been unthinkably familiar for Lailoken's father but was acceptable to the young man.

"Let me take that for you, young lord," said one of the spearbearers, and he reached for the spear that Lailoken was holding.

Lailoken instantly pulled the spear away from the bearer, and his face twisted in anger. "You do not touch this," he said. "No one touches it."

The spearbearer immediately stepped back, raising both his hands in a palm-forward gesture indicating that he was not looking for trouble. "Yes, young lord. I mean, no, young lord. Whatever you say, young lord. I was merely doing what I thought I was supposed to do."

Allowing himself to calm after his initial, slightly crazed reaction, Lailoken simply nodded, and said, "Yes. Yes, of course. I can . . . sympathize. We all do what we are supposed to do . . . and let the gods sort out the rest."

AS THE FULL moon, like a great unblinking eye, rose in the night sky, there was massive celebration in the warlord's banquet hall. The warlord sat on his throne, basking in the reflected glory of his hunters. To hear the story as it was being told and retold, it had been the warlord himself who had struck the fatal blow to the great horned creature. It had merely stumbled through the woods, fighting the inevitable, and collapsed dead right at Lailoken's feet.

Still, there were women draping themselves over Lailoken as he reclined against an assortment of pillows beneath him. Only the warlord was upon a chair, upraised so that his servants would bring food to him. Everyone else was seated on pillows scattered upon the floor around the low-slung table.

The main course, naturally, had yet to be brought out. Lailoken made distant, disinterested small talk with the women, courtesans all, jockeying for attention of the warlord's son. The reason was obvious: to gain something for themselves. Riches. Title. Position. Lailoken would be a superb acquisition for an ambitious young woman, and he knew that all too well. Consequently, he trusted none of them and despised them all. Nevertheless, out of a sense of courtesy that his father would no doubt have found absurd, he tried to put on a positive face and tolerate them.

"What was it like?" one of them chirped.

The question caught his attention. "What was what like?"

"Killing the beast. Killing the unicorn." The other women were wide-eyed as the one doing the asking leaned forward, hanging on Lailoken's shoulder. "What was it like?" she inquired.

He couldn't even bring himself to look at her, fearing that he would lose his temper and strangle her so that no further stupid questions could emerge from her throat. "It was like murdering the better part of myself," he said.

"Ooooo," said the girl, then pondered it a moment. "What does that mean?"

"If you have to ask," replied Lailoken, "you will never understand."

At that moment a roar went up as the carcass of the unicorn was hauled in by several servants. It had been dressed up a bit, the blood cleansed from its hide, but it was still hanging upside down. Staff holders had been erected at either end of the table, and the long rod from which the unicorn was dangling was set into them, first one end, then the other. There were "ooos" and "ahhhhs" from everyone present, for only a few of them had actually been out beating the bushes or a part of the hunt. A couple of females actually swooned into the arms of their men, although Lailoken cynically suspected that it was merely an act in order to gain attention and sympathy.

The unicorn's eyes remained open, although they were now opaque. It was like a thick fog had rolled in over an ocean, making it impossible to see the roiling blue waves. Its tongue was hanging out slightly from its mouth. Lailoken was seized by an urge to reach over and try to bring its eyelids down over its eyes out of respect. But he resisted the impulse, unable to bear the thought of what his father would say in response to such an action.

Stepping down from his throne, the warlord walked with that unmistakable swagger that indicated to Lailoken that his father had already consumed more mead than was probably good for him . . . and as the evening was young, it was terrifying to think what he was going to be like by the end of it.

"Bring me my chalice," called the warlord, "and the weapon!"

Lailoken's eyebrows knit, unsure what weapon the warlord was demanding to see. Moments later, however, he understood, and his blood boiled in fury. He knew the warlord's chalice only too well. It was wooden, but ornate and rimmed with jewels . . . a magnificent vessel that he'd acquired from some plundered hoard somewhere, ostensibly from some manner of secret society who'd fought to the last man to protect it. It was a drinking vessel that the warlord saved only for special occasions such as this. But Lailoken's spear was also being brought forward, stains of the unicorn's blood still visible upon it.

Before he even knew what he was doing, Lailoken was on his feet and pointing angrily. "That's mine!" he cried out against all better judgment. "You had that taken out of my chamber!"

The warlord stared at him placidly as the cheering and shouting from all around instantly subsided. His voice was very quiet when he replied, which was always dangerous. When he roared with anger, much of it was for show. When he spoke softly, that was when the recipient of his words was in the greatest peril. "All that is in this place," said the warlord, "is mine. Even that which is yours is mine, and merely something that I let you have at my sufferance. It is debatable whether you contributed anything to the successful conclusion of the hunt. However, I am doing you the courtesy—the honor—of making you a symbolic participant in this ceremony by utilizing your spear. Do you have a problem with my extending that honor to you?"

There is no honor in this. What we've done—what I've done—dishonors us all. We all deserve to die. Those were the words that hammered through his mind, but he dared not speak them. Instead, his teeth gritted, he replied, "No, father."

"Are you quite certain?"

"Yes, father."

The warlord still made no move, the air crackling with tension. Then, as if his son had not spoken, he swept his arms wide in a theatrical manner . . . the spear in his left hand, the cup in his right. Addressing the entirety of the hall, he cried out, "Behold! The creature known as the King of Unicorns! A king without followers; a lord without a land. See how I have laid him low! See how this moment will remain a message for all those who think that they are truly greater than they are!"

He jabbed the spear forward toward the base of the unicorn's throat and, with practiced ease, pierced a large vein. This movement prompted a cheer from the onlookers, even though Lailoken flinched involuntarily when the spear penetrated.

Blood immediately began to pour out of the gash, and the warlord brought the cup around and down. The blood was thick and slow, which was to be expected since the beast had been dead a few hours. It didn't gush so much as it dripped in a thick, steady stream. The warlord held the cup steady, grinning, and there were continued whoops and cries from all around.

Lailoken had not sat back down. Instead he stood there, his fists clenched. Without even bothering to look at his son, the warlord tossed the spear in his direction. People on either side scattered as the weapon wafted through the air. Lailoken twisted sideways, just to make sure he was avoiding the spearhead, and caught the shaft one-handed.

The warlord watched with fascination as the cup filled with blood. It filled nearly to the top, then the warlord stepped back and held the vessel high, ignoring the slow stream of unicorn blood that continued to spill upon the floor. "To the unicorn! Gods willing, he's learned his lesson!" He tilted the cup to his lips and began drinking the blood.

Watching with disgust, Lailoken's lips twitched convulsively, and a deep nausea began to rise up from his stomach. Concerned he was going to be sick, he gripped the spear firmly and started to turn away.

That was when he heard something he'd never heard before . . . that no one in the warlord's court had ever heard: the sound of the warlord screaming.

He had just drained the cup, and there was still blood on the edges of his thick beard and mustache. Suddenly he let out a screech, and his eyes went wide with terror. Everyone was taken aback as he continued to howl, grasping at his throat. Stubbornly, even amazingly, he was still clutching his golden chalice. He tried to speak words, and they might have been cries for help, but it was impossible to be sure.

Lailoken strode quickly forward, not sure what he could or should do. The warlord saw him coming and staggered toward him, reaching out without even looking as if he was aware of what he was doing. The cup began to slip from his fingers and, reflexively, Lailoken caught it.

The instant he did so, he felt as if some sort of incredible current of energy was passing through him. It was unlike the burning sensation he'd experienced before at the time of the unicorn's death. Instead it was far more powerful, unlike anything he would have thought remotely possible. Once, many years ago, he had witnessed a great, dark funnel of wind and fury descend from on high and go crashing through a forest, uprooting trees and boulders alike. High above it in the sky, blinding illumination had crackled across the clouds, and Lailoken knew that he was seeing the untrammeled fury of the gods unleashed. As horrifyingly fascinating as it was, he hoped he would never witness anything like that again.

In this case, he wasn't witnessing it at all. He was feeling it firsthand.

Blinding flame erupted from both the chalice and the head of the spear. It was no natural color, but instead a combination of pink and purple, not unlike the unicorn's horn. The two jets of fire did not go straight up. Instead they crisscrossed directly in front of Lailoken, merging and forming a massive fireball that would have blinded him if he'd looked directly at it.

People were running, screaming, falling over each other, and even killing each other to try to get away. The warlord's mouth was still open, but no noise was emerging from it. Instead he was standing there, arms out to either side, convulsing wildly, and Lailoken saw a last, desperate look in his eyes. Lailoken would spend the rest of his existence wondering what exactly that look was supposed to signify, or even if his father had the faintest idea that his son was standing in front of him.

Then, from the fireball that was roaring directly before Lailoken, a new stream of fire—larger and even more powerful—emerged. It slammed into and through the warlord, and the warlord went up in flames. It spread outward like a spider's web, infusing everyone else in the chamber. It leapt to the walls, the tapestries, the ceiling. Everything and everyone was suddenly aflame, and burning most furiously of all was the trail of unicorn blood that had come from the beast's dripping corpse.

Courtiers and courtesans, servants and flunkies, none were spared. Everyone was burning, his or her skin blackening and turning to ash far faster than any fire could have, or should have been able to accomplish. Even as they fell, they came apart, their bodies unable to retain cohesion, and their corpses blew apart into free-floating cinders the instant they struck the floor.

Lailoken had been screaming as loudly as his father, but now, mysteriously, a strange sort of peace settled upon him. He realized that he hadn't actually been in any pain. Something was protecting him from the fury that he was channeling, making him merely a vessel for the ravaging power. He could have thrown down the chalice, tossed aside the spear. Instead he simply stood there and watched, no longer afraid.

And then he began to see the events from outside his body. It was as if a third eye of some sort had opened within the back of his brain, enabling him to see things that no one else was capable of perceiving. He saw himself from a great height, standing there with the spear in one hand and chalice in the other, while he was completely surrounded by the fire. Everything was aflame. Even the body of the unicorn was burning now, and as for the people themselves, the ones who were in their final, dying spasms . . . well, he knew he should feel something for them. Pity. Sadness. Mourning. The nubile women who had been courting him, the hapless servants who really didn't deserve to be annihilated. Even his father . . . gods, his father was dead, mere gray specks whipping around in unearthly winds being generated by who-knew-what?

He knew all the emotions he should be feeling. Unfortunately—or fortunately, depending upon one's point of view—he felt none of them. He was indifferent, as if watching the death throes of an ant colony that had been flooded out by a passing squall. Lailoken wondered, in that same distant manner, whether he was simply in shock and therefore not processing the information correctly, or if they just really, truly weren't worth getting especially upset about.

You will learn and understand came the words. Lailoken didn't comprehend their origin; they appeared to be coming directly from the blaze itself.

Teach me, Lailoken asked.

I shall, said the blaze, and the flames converged upon him.

RESIDENTS OF THE nearby village had come running when they saw the plumes of smoke in the air. They arrived and stood helpless, watching the great house of the warlord go up in flames. Even as they watched, they knew that they were seeing something that was not of this Earth. The colors of the flame were simply not right.

Not only that, but there should have been a charnel-house smell emerging from the place, the stench of burned flesh. Certainly many had died within, which was fairly obvious by the lack of escapees in the vicinity. But there was no smell. What sort of flame could possibly have been so vicious, so hot that the corpses would have been incinerated rather than simply cooked.

Helpless to do anything to stop it, the villagers stood around, praying that the wind would not blow the flame in the direction of their homes. And there was much muttering about demon involvement. That either the gods from above or below had looked upon the activities of the warlord and intensely disliked what they had seen, and had meted out appropriate punishment.

There were cries and shouts as the high towers of the castle gave way and collapsed upon themselves, landing on the lower sections and crushing them. There was even more muttering then, for the villagers truly had no idea how to react. None of them were huge admirers of the warlord, who was cruel in his moods and vicious in his temper. On the other hand, his reputation had served to protect them, and they were grateful for that and apprehensive about what was going to happen now that he was most definitely dead.

So the villagers did what all simple folk do in such instances: They began to pray. The village priest, seizing control of the situation, led them in continued supplications to the gods, asking them for strength and guidance. A small goat was brought forward from a nearby farm and promptly sacrificed as an offering. This continued all through the night and into the morning hours without let up, until dark clouds coalesced above and began to pour rain down upon the uncanny conflagration.

There was a steady hiss as the water streamed down, and soon there was nothing but a vast haze of smoke hanging in the air, and it was damned near impossible to see anything. The villagers had ceased their prayers once the rain began, instead falling back to the shelter of the woods and watching from a safe distance until the last of the oddly colored flames was extinguished. Then they began chattering with one another, each asking the other what should be done, and naturally none of them had a better idea than the others as to what the best way to proceed was.

"Look!" one of the villagers, a sharp-eyed farmer, suddenly cried out, pointing in the direction of the castle ruins.

Others looked to see where he was indicating, and there were gasps from all over as they slowly verified that their eyes were not deceiving them.

From deep within the mist that was now hanging over the castle, an individual was emerging. No one could quite make out who or what it was, for he was covered with soot. His hair was long and thick, hanging down around his face, which in turn was grime-besmeared.

In his right hand, he was carrying a spear. In his left, curiously, was a cup. Tucked into his belt was something that was an odd combination of purple and pink. It bore a resemblance to a spike of some sort, but no one could quite make it out beyond that.

He made his way through the rubble, stepping gingerly over the debris. He was wearing a long cloak around him that was very singed and as covered with ash as he himself was. Finally, he emerged from the outermost edge of the castle and stood there, a bizarre and even frightening sight, as the first rays of the sunrise began to creep over the distant hilltop.

"Well?" he said impatiently. "What are you all staring at?"

And with that, he turned away from them. They said nothing to him, unsure of what it was they were facing. If he'd been one of the warlord's court, his current filthy state made it impossible to determine who precisely he was. Or perhaps he was a demon incarnated, spat up by the eldritch flames they'd all witnessed.

Finally, a small boy stepped forward, his eyes wide with curiosity. "Are we supposed to worship you?" he asked with genuine curiosity.

The sole survivor of the inferno that had consumed the warlord's home stared down at him for a long moment, and then said, "Yes. Yes, why don't you go ahead and do that. Be certain to let me know how that turns out for you."

And with that, he turned his back to the villagers, strode off into the forest, and was never seen by any of them again.

PARTE THE FIRST:

Revelations

CHAPTRE
THE FIRST

✟

ARTHUR PENDRAGON, LORD of Camelot, former mayor of New York City, former president of the United States, and son of Uther, awoke to a day that promised to be very much like the previous one, and the one before that, and the one before that. He could not for the life of him decide whether that was a good thing or a bad thing.

The boat's gentle rocking woke him, as it usually did. There was a soft sighing of contentment next to him, and even in the darkness of the cabin, he could see the general outline of his wife—Gwendolyne Queen Penn, or Gwen Penn as he occasionally liked to needle her—cuddled next to him. Gwen's flesh pressed up against his, but there was nothing seductive about the movement. The sheet had simply slipped off, and she was seeking the closest source of warmth . . . which just so happened to be a thousand-year-old king who, in turn, just happened to be her husband.

A small stream of light was filtering through the curtains covering the nearest porthole, and Arthur propped himself up on one elbow, taking in her sleeping form. She was so beautiful, and he loved her so deeply, that sometimes his heart ached with the intensity of the adoration he felt for her. Perhaps that feeling was heightened by all that they had been through and the times that he had nearly lost her.

Gwen. His Gwen.

Her strawberry blond hair, streaked with some gray here and there, had fallen in her face. It was longer than he'd ever seen her wearing it. And why not? There was no one around to cut it. He was a legendary king, not a barber or a beautician. He had told her any number of times that she didn't need to primp herself or care about such things when it was just the two of them, and she had taken him at his word. When she breathed, strands of it blew up and down. He watched the steady rise and fall of her chest, and it brought him a peace he had always thought he was incapable of experiencing.

So why am I so damned bored?

He regretted the thought almost as soon as it occurred to him, and he wanted to take it back. Then he realized the absurdity of such a notion. One could not govern one's thoughts; they went where they wished. As long as one didn't say everything that popped into one's head, then that was sufficient.

We worked hard. We overcame monumental challenges: Terrorists. Ancient kings. The Basilisk. We've earned this. We've earned our happily ever after.

The only thing that Arthur kept coming back around to, though, was that "happily ever after" was a self-contradictory statement, like "jumbo shrimp." How was "ever after" supposed to be happy?

What did one do when boredom set in?

One kept his big mouth shut, is what one did.

Arthur slid out of bed, padding naked and noiselessly to the head. There he attended to business, then stopped to study himself—really study himself—in the mirror for the first time in several months. Since they'd embarked on their extended two-person ocean voyage to nowhere aboard a forty-six-foot motor-sailing yacht that could operate under wind power or with a motor as the occasion dictated, Arthur hadn't been working especially hard on his tonsorial upkeep. His brown hair was shaggy, and his beard had lost its fine line and was looking decidedly unkempt.

"Not exactly royal, is it," he muttered to himself.

He hesitated a moment, then scrounged around in the small bathroom area until he found his straight-edged razor. Briskly applying some cream, he carefully went over the edges of his beard until he had trimmed them into a fine line once more. He congratulated himself on doing so without once cutting himself. Once upon a time, the steady rocking of the ship would have been more than enough to guarantee that he'd likely slit his own throat.

Not that he was inexperienced in seafaring matters. As Lord of Camelot, he had had a navy at his disposal, and more than once had taken command at the helm of a warship. Plus, as a lad, he'd undergone a couple of lengthy voyages and thoroughly learned his way around the fundamentals of seamanship. That knowledge had not left him, even after all these centuries. In fact, he felt almost guilty over how much easier it was managing this vessel—which he'd dubbed the good ship *Malory*—than the ones he'd cut his sailing teeth on. Still, it had taken him a little while to reacquire his sea legs, but he'd managed. He'd always managed.

He wiped off the last dabs of shaving cream and tossed on a pair of shorts and a light shirt before heading up to the deck. Since it was just he and Gwen, clothing wasn't really a requirement. But there was enough of what Gwen referred to as "old school" thinking in him that he couldn't bring himself to just trot around buck naked all the time, or have Gwen similarly unattired. "What fun would it be when the intent is to have fun?" he had asked Gwen when she had broached the subject. She had simply laughed, called him quaint, and never mentioned it again.

The salt air of the placid Pacific Ocean hit his nostrils as soon as he got topside. He stood in the prow, his hands upon his hips like a latter day Peter Pan, and breathed it in. The ocean spread around him like a sheet of blue-green glass, with no one around for as far as he could see.

He clambered up and over and began to unfurl the sail. Having checked the compass to ascertain their whereabouts, he sent the ship cruising east. There was a small, underpopulated island where the natives were always happy to see them. Arthur and Gwen stopped by every now and then when they felt like talking to someone other than themselves. The natives' English wasn't especially good, and they had never seen either a television or newspaper, so they didn't especially care about the fact that the former president and first lady swung by once in a while. Still, it was a nice time to interact, not to mention stock up on freshwater.

And it was pleasant.

Pleasant.

"That's my life now. Pleasant," said Arthur to no one. He rolled the word around on his tongue, said it very slowly. "Pleeeeeasaaant." It rhymed with "peasant," which he wasn't especially happy about.

He stood next to the harpoon gun for a long moment, fingering it longingly, his eyes seeking something that he might be able to use it on. A passing shark, perhaps. That would be nice. A big one, something that could give him a bloody challenge. Hell, if he saw one, then, just to make it interesting, he could run back down, fetch Excalibur, leap into the water, and take the creature on in its own environment. That seemed more sporting somehow, rather than standing safely upon a deck and letting fly with a spear from a distance. Granted, it would give Gwen fits, since she'd be petrified at the thought of Arthur's being devoured by sharks, leaving her to fend for herself single-handedly on a yacht in the middle of nowhere. But even so . . .

It was moot, in any event. He saw nothing. Nothing challenging, at any rate, or available to him. A school of dolphins was passing in the near distance, but he ignored them. He'd learned that lesson the hard way, nailing a passing porpoise early in their cruise and hauling it in, only to have Gwen fairly screaming at him, "You killed *Flipper?*" That put an end to that.

Stepping away from the harpoon, he unspooled a fishing line and tossed it into the wake of the ship. Then he flopped down onto his fishing chair and waited to see if something would come along and grab the bait. They had fruit and various breadstuffs for breakfast, but the sportsman in him fancied the notion of catching something for whatever meals he could.

He lost track of how long he sat there. All he knew was that time passed, and some more time, then the footfall from behind him told him that Gwen was approaching him. He glanced over his shoulder and smiled at her as she approached, drawing her white robe tightly around herself. The weather was balmy, but the breeze was stiff, and could be cutting this early in the morning.

Gwen brushed her hair out of her eyes and came up behind Arthur as he turned his attention back to the fishing line. "Morning, love," she said, draping her arms around him.

"Morning."

She kissed him on the cheek. Her lips remained there for a brief time, longer than an ordinary kiss would require, and he heard her mutter a thoughtful "Hunh."

"Are you all right?" he asked her.

"Yes." She straightened up and went to the railing, staring out at the same balmy vista that he had been studying.

"Sleep okay?"

"Slept fine. Everything's fine."

He cocked an eyebrow. "Are you quite certain?"

"Yes," she said.

Which, as Arthur knew all too well, meant no. He knew his wife, however, and was certain that she would get around to telling him what was on her mind sooner or later. It was just a matter of which one it would be.

As it happened, it was later.

Gwen had gone through most of the day in a mood that wasn't exactly unresponsive, but neither was it especially chatty. Arthur informed her that he had made an executive decision and had set their ship in the direction of Bogo Pogo, which was the name she'd come up with for the island. He expected they'd arrive there within two to three days, presuming the weather held up. Gwen, wearing a white two-piece bathing suit and stretched out on a towel, sunning herself, displayed little to no enthusiasm, but simply said, "Okay, that's fine."

When he did wind up catching some fish, Gwen took them down to the galley without comment. She had developed quite a bit of expertise when it came to scaling and gutting fish, and she prepared their midday meal with her customary expertise. Arthur complimented her repeatedly on the meal, but all she did was smile slightly and nod, and nothing much beyond that. Arthur sighed inwardly and continued to wait with the patience of someone who literally had nothing better to do *but* wait.

At one point an airplane, a twin-engine prop job, appeared over the horizon. "Gwen!" Arthur called, and had to repeat her name a couple of times before she awoke, having dozed off while sunning herself. She propped herself up on her elbows and looked at him questioningly, but then heard the distant buzz of the airplane. He didn't have to say anything further. She immediately gathered her gear and went down into the cabin, out of sight. Arthur continued to fish as if nothing was unusual. The plane passed by, never coming closer than a mile or so away. Still, better safe than sorry.

"All clear!" he called to her.

She came up from below, wearing her robe once more. There was a look of resolve on her face as she walked over to Arthur and dropped down cross-legged onto the deck. She looked up at him, and said, "You're bored. Bored and frustrated."

"I am neither!" he protested.

Gwen laughed at that, shaking her head. "You know . . . you always made such a point of stating that you didn't lie. I always figured that it was this major moral imperative on your part. Now I don't think so. Now I think it's simply because you completely suck at lying."

"I do not suck," he said with that archness that always sent Gwen into hysterics whenever he used coarse vernacular. This time, at least, she managed to restrain herself somewhat. "You do so suck at lying. Ohhh, don't feel bad"—and she ran a hand across his cheek—"that's a good thing. If you were skilled at lying, you wouldn't be the Arthur I've come to know and love."

"I shall take that as a compliment," he told her.

"Well, good, because it was intended as such." She pulled on his hand, indicating that she wanted him to join her on the deck. He made sure the fishing line was secured and did so, crossing his legs in imitation of hers. It wasn't easy, though, and he felt a bit of stiffness in his thigh. He rubbed the cramp out as best he could. "Arthur," she said, resting her hand upon his, "don't even bother to deny it. I know you're bored."

"Not with you. Never with you."

"I know that," she said confidently. "But Arthur . . . my God, you're a warrior king. A world leader. You're built for quests and conquests. You're made for great things."

"And is this not a great thing?" asked Arthur. "This, here. You and me, together, at peace."

"You strike me as the sort who believes that 'at peace'

should be saved for when people really are 'at peace.' As in 'rest in.' Know what I'm saying?"

"That's true to some degree," he admitted. "But Gwen, you have to understand that—"

"What? What do I have to understand?"

He turned his hand around so that it was atop hers. "Gwen . . . I sat in a cave for centuries, *centuries*, recovering from the wound I sustained from my bastard son, Mordred. And in all that time, even as I was reading and studying and healing, and surviving decade after decade thanks to Merlin's magic . . . in all that time, I wasn't thinking about world leadership. I wasn't thinking about quests. I was thinking about you. About the Gwen whom I had left behind and knew that I would never see again. And then I returned, Merlin releasing me and sending me into New York City to seek out my political fortunes. And I found you. My Gwen, reincarnated, her spirit living again within you. Finding you again . . . that was the *true* miracle of my life. Then, after I became president, and that damnable terrorist sniper cut you down with his cowardly attack, I thought I'd lost you a second time and was damned near ready to die myself."

"And you found the Holy Grail," she said. "And healed me."

"I did that, yes. Well . . . I had some help . . ."

"And now . . . what?" Gwen asked. "Where do we go from here?"

"I told you. Bogo Pogo . . ."

"Arthur!" She reached over and stroked his chin, her gaze fixed upon the lower sections of his face. "Did you think I wouldn't notice. You trimmed your beard."

"What of it? I did it for you. You shave your legs for me, so I trim my beard for you. What difference does it make? It's no major thing . . ."

"I know. It's a minor thing. But it suggests major things. It suggests that . . ."

"That what?"

"That you want to return to the world. Be of it rather than simply in it. That you want to find a way back to bigger and better things. You know . . . the things you were meant to accomplish."

"That claptrap is Merlin's song, Gwen, not mine," he said. "He's the huge believer in my having a major role to play and being put on this Earth to accomplish great things. Me, I believe in free will, along with the right to accomplish only that which I desire to do. Let others run their lives as if they are guided by destiny. Not I. Without free will, what else is there?"

"Bullshit, my love. You're King Arthur, for God's sake. If King Arthur doesn't have a destiny steeped in greatness, what hope does *any* of us have?"

"I appreciate your vote of confidence. But honestly, Gwen, what would you have me do? I can't return to being president, or politics. Frankly, I don't know that I have the stomach for it anymore. Plus there's the practical matter of, well . . ."

"Me?"

"You," he agreed. "Do you have a solution to that?"

"No," she admitted with a heavy sigh.

"No. Nor do I. So I don't exactly see the options open to me other than this."

"But don't you see the problem then? Instead of this"—and she gestured around the ship—"being our . . . our well-deserved reward after more hardships than a reasonable God would have provided for one lifetime . . . this becomes our prison. Our Elba. Our place of exile, from which there's no escape. You just said it yourself. Without free will, what else is there?"

He grunted in annoyance at the well-made point, but had no ready answer. Nor did she. So they agreed to table the matter for the time being and discuss it further when either or both of them had some sort of workable solution.

They relaxed on the deck of the yacht that evening, stared up at the stars for a good long time, and eventually went to bed.

It was about one in the morning when they awoke to sudden, churning waves so forceful that Arthur thought they must have sailed into the middle of a storm. But there was nothing else happening to indicate a storm . . . no fierce winds, no hammering of rain, certainly neither thunder nor lightning. Just the waves in the normally calm Pacific Ocean that were becoming more and more violent with each passing moment.

"What's happening?" Gwen cried out, jostled violently awake by the ship's shaking.

"I don't know!" Arthur struggled into a pair of sweat shorts as he scrambled toward the stairs leading up to the deck. "I'll find out!"

"Arthur, you can't! There's a—"

"We don't *know* what there is! And I'm not about to cower down here."

He threw open a long, narrow cabinet and pulled out Excalibur. The redoubtable blade gleamed in the darkness of the cabin.

"What do you think you're going to do with that?!" Gwen cried out. "Stab the ocean to death?"

"If it annoys me, yes." With that, he charged up onto the deck, keeping the sword gripped tightly. Gwen watched him go, hesitated, and then leaped out of bed and proceeded to pull on clothes herself. She wasn't about to stay hidden below if her husband was risking his neck up above.

By the time she scrambled to the deck, she discovered water lapping over the edges of the yacht. Arthur had gunned the motor to life, and was now trying with all his might to steer the *Malory* away from . . . what?

She saw it clearly now, a huge bubbling of water, as if something gargantuan was surfacing from below. Gwen had no idea what it could be. Actually, that wasn't strictly true. It was just that what she was coming up with sounded daunting, even for the wielder of Excalibur. A blue whale, perhaps, that had decided for some reason that the yacht presented a threat? Maybe a submarine, although she couldn't begin to guess what a submarine would be doing cruising around there. Or a giant kraken, perhaps? Granted, the creatures bordered on legendary, but then again, her husband had crossed that border ages ago, so who was she to judge?

Arthur, bathed in the light of the full moon, wildly gesticulated toward the cabin, shouting, "Get below! I *order* you to get below!"

"You *order* me?" She staggered across the rocking deck and grabbed his arm. "Who do you think you are, ordering me!"

"The bloody king!"

"Yeah, well, I'm the bloody queen, so get *over* your bad self!"

"My self is *not* bad!" he shouted over the roaring of the waves. It was starting to look as if the vessel might be swamped.

"It's an expression, you medieval doofus!"

"How about this expression: Get below! Now!"

"If we die, we die together!"

*"How about you do what I say, and we don't—oh, **bugger this**!"*

He released the wheel, and it spun violently on its own as the waves pushed the yacht to the starboard side. What was truly insane was that, for all the violence erupting around them, the skies continued to remain cloudless and full of moonlight. He turned, grabbed Gwen, and tossed her over his shoulder in a fireman's carry.

"Let me go!"

Arthur started toward the entrance to the cabin, with the intention of tossing Gwen into it and bolting the door from the outside if necessary. Suddenly he stopped in midstep, his eyes going wide. He almost dropped Gwen as the deck rocked wildly beneath him, and he grabbed on to a trailing rope from the sail and held tight.

"*What's going on? Is something behind us? Turn around, for crying out loud!*"

Gwen twisted her neck to see where he was staring, and her jaw dropped.

"Oh my God," she whispered.

A massive vessel was rising from beneath the waters directly behind them. Gwen remembered the first time, as a youngster, when she had sat enraptured in a movie theater as *Star Wars* unspooled upon the vast screen. She would always remember that opening shot, where the gigantic space vessel appeared overhead and kept going and going for what seemed an endless amount of time.

That was how she felt now, staring in shock as the vessel continued to rise higher and higher. Long strands of seaweed and not a few dead fish fell to either side, and it was thirty feet high, and then forty, and it kept going. Gwen shook her head in disbelief.

The entire thing was made of wood . . . dark, gleaming wood, covered with what appeared to be pitch to reinforce the exterior. It was a gargantuan ship, fifty feet high, eighty feet wide, and almost two football fields in length. It almost seemed to leap out of the water before settling back down, and great gouts of water came blasting down the deck of the yacht. Arthur staggered but continued to clutch Gwen closely to him. Gwen, for her part, coughed up water, then reached down into her cleavage and pulled out a small, flapping striped fish that she quickly tossed overboard.

It took a while for the ship to settle down, then a small figure could be seen moving at the prow of the ship. Then a second figure joined it. Even with the full moon gleaming above, they couldn't make out at first who it was. But that didn't stop Arthur and Gwen from being able to take an educated guess, considering the circumstances.

"*Ziusura!*" Arthur shouted. "Is that you?" And then, anticipating what Gwen might say before she said it, he warned her in a low voice, "Don't call him the other name. He *hates* the other name."

"Of *course* it's me!" shouted the aged Sumerian. "Who the hell else would it be in a giant ark? Did we interrupt something?"

It was at that point that Gwen realized Arthur was still holding her slung over his shoulder. "Put me down, please," she said in a low voice, then louder she called, "Nothing at all, Noah! We were just, you know, floating here and wondering if someone might show up and nearly capsize us because things were too quiet!"

"Gwen, please, don't antagonize him," the second dark figure spoke up.

As Arthur eased Gwen to her feet, he called, "Percival?"

"Yes, sire!"

"What are you doing on a giant submersible ark?"

"Yeah, and now that I think about it," Gwen shouted, taking a step forward, "how the hell did you submerge it?"

"Would you like to see for yourself?" Ziusura asked, sounding like the picture of innocence. "We could go under again, then surface directly beneath you . . ."

"You wouldn't dare, Noah," growled Gwen.

"Arthur . . ." Ziusura said warningly.

"Gwen, please . . ."

"How did you submerge it?" Gwen repeated, apparently oblivious to any potential danger. "It's made of wood!"

"So?" replied Ziusura.

"Wood!"

"Yes, we've established that."

"Wood floats!"

"Obviously."

"It doesn't sink!"

"Right again."

"So how do you go cruising around underwater?"

There was a long silence, then Ziusura said, "I don't understand the question."

Gwen threw up her arms in exasperation and turned to Arthur. "I give up. *You* talk to Captain Nemo."

"More gladly than you can possibly believe." He stepped around in front of her, and shouted, "Percival . . . Ziusura . . . it is, of course, wonderful to see you. It's been ages. Would I be vaguely close to correct in hoping that this is merely a social call? A chance to catch up on old times?"

"Actually, Highness, not even close," said Percival reluctantly. "World matters have taken an unexpected shift, and we've come to warn you."

"Are we entering an ice age? Or a season of massive monsoons? Is the ocean draining, perhaps? I don't see how any other change in world events could possibly be of any relevance to us . . ."

"Trust me, Highness," Percival said grimly, "when you've heard what I have to tell you . . . you're going to find yourself wishing the ocean *was* draining."

Arthur sighed heavily, and said to Gwen, "Just so you know . . . you were correct. About everything. I was bored and desirous of something to do. Are you happy that you were right?"

"Actually," Gwen replied, sounding no happier about it than Arthur, "as it turns out, I'm almost never happy about being right. Doesn't that stink?"

"I couldn't say," said Arthur. "If I should ever chance to be right about something, I'll be sure to let you know how it feels."

CHAPTRE
THE SECOND

R ON CORDOBA, CHIEF of staff to the president of the
United States, sat behind his desk and braced himself,
knowing that he was going to be receiving a visit that he really wasn't looking forward to.

Over the past year, his blond hair had started thinning
out with exceptional speed that he could only credit to the
nature of the job he was doing. He had to believe that he was
the first person in history to go bald as the result of metaphor, since he made a point of only figuratively tearing his
hair out on any given day rather than literally doing so.
His slender body was still in whipcord shape, and for that he
was grateful. After all, he reasoned, how else would he be
able to bend over backwards to accommodate everyone if
he didn't possess that flexibility?

He had just endured a frustrating ten-minute meeting
with the White House press secretary, venting over not being
able to have anything remotely resembling a coherent answer
for the questions that the press were throwing at him. There
were only so many times in the course of one conversation

that Ron felt comfortable with saying "I know" without having anything substantive he could offer.

Ron Cordoba had been part of Arthur Penn's life—or Arthur a part of his—for about as far back as he could remember. He'd gone from being a public relations genius who had helped guide Arthur to a win as mayor of New York, to becoming his chief of staff during his presidency, to an insane adventure that had brought him to an island where resided a race of immortals ruled over by Gilgamesh, of all damned people, and finally back to the White House, resuming his position as chief of staff to Arthur's successor, President Terrance Stockwell.

He'd led the sort of life he could only have dreamt of, back in the days when he was a bookish young man who read tales of King Arthur and his knights under the covers of his bed at night, squinting with the illumination of a flashlight. Ron had grown up and suddenly discovered himself battling side by side with—

Ron shook his head, leaning back in his chair and rubbing the bridge of his nose in exhaustion.

The door to the right of his desk opened. Only one person came through that door. It was the one that connected to the Oval Office, and Ron forced himself to stand and cast a weary but determined eye upon his boss. "Good evening, Mr. President," he said.

"Evening, Ron," said President Stockwell, gesturing for Ron to sit back down. Nevertheless, Ron remained standing and only sat once the president had taken a seat opposite him. Ron had always been struck by the toll that the office of the presidency took upon its occupant. He was watching for some signs of this rapid aging process on Stockwell's face, but there was very little to see. Stockwell's face was almost triangular, his dark eyes a bit too closely set together and a bit too recessed. His black hair was cropped closely, nearly to a buzz cut, and a sharp widow's peak extended down past the edge of his otherwise receding hairline. Basically, he looked exactly the same as he had when he'd first taken on the position over a year ago. The last president that Ron could recall who displayed so little sign of aging was Richard Nixon, who seemed to thrive on power like a leech. Which admittedly made him slightly nervous about Stockwell, but he knew that the trust issues really didn't have any actions by Stockwell himself as a source. It was just free-floating anxiety, really, and nothing that Stockwell could reasonably be blamed for.

Stockwell rocked back in the chair for a moment or two, then said briskly, "So, Ronald. We have a bit of a situation here."

"Well, I'm juggling about six situations, Mr. President. Is there any one in particular that you wish to focus on—?"

"Here's a wild thought, Ronald. How about we focus on"—and his voice suddenly dropped to a lower register as he leaned forward with fearsome intensity—"the one that CNN is focusing on. And MSNBC. And the *New York Times*, the *Wall Street Journal*, and—oh, this just in—the covers of *Newsweek*, *Time*, and *People*. I'm speaking of Penn . . ."

Ron, his voice measured but willed with warning, said "Former. President. Penn. Sir." He added as an afterthought, "With all respect."

Stockwell looked as if he was about to make an issue of it, but obviously decided that his energies would best be spent elsewhere. He tilted his head slightly in acknowledgment, and said, "I'm speaking of former President Penn . . . and the international sensation that the former first lady has caused."

"Might I point out, sir—"

"What is he?"

"Sir?" Ron raised an eyebrow. "I don't . . ."

"What is he? Who is he?"

"Sir, I don't understand the question."

The president considered the response, then leaned back and drummed his fingers on the chair's armrest. "Ron," he said slowly, "when you said you needed to take a brief leave of absence in order to aid former President Penn on some sort of initiative, I didn't ask you a lot of questions. And I would certainly have been entitled to, what with my being commander-in-chief and all . . ."

"Yes, sir, you did not, and I appreciate that."

"And do you know why I didn't, Ron?"

"Well, I—"

"I'm going to provide the answer for you, Ronald. You don't have to strain yourself."

"Thank you, sir."

"I did it because I trust you. The fact that you asked was good enough for me. The fact that you came back not too long after was also good enough for me. And when you told me that the first lady was 'doing better,' and were vague about the details, I didn't ask for specifics because I assumed that if there was a seriously significant change in her condition— something that I really needed to know about—you would tell me. You wouldn't leave me with my ass hanging out in the wind. Well, guess what, Ron. I've suddenly come down with a severe case of drafty ass."

"I didn't think—"

"No! You didn't!" thundered Stockwell, dropping any attempt to rein in his temper. "You didn't think! The last anyone knew of Gwendolyne Penn, she was in an irreversible coma! And now that appears not to be the case, and everyone wants to know why, including me! Except I should have been the first person to know, not the one who's playing catch-up to twenty-four-hour news channels and celebrity magazines! Or do you think I'm wrong?"

"You're not wrong, sir, no," said Cordoba. "But it's . . . complicated. You see, I made promises to former President Penn, and—"

"You also made promises to me, Ronald. You serve at the

pleasure of the president. Not the former president. Me. This president. And you don't get to have divided loyalties in that capacity. Not at this level. Not at any level, really, but certainly not at yours. You tell me right now what the hell is going on, or—"

"The Holy Grail."

Stockwell stared at him.

"I'm sorry I interrupted," said Ron. "You go ahead, sir. Finish your—"

"The Holy Grail," Stockwell repeated slowly. "The cup of Christ. The one that he drank from at the Last Supper . . ."

"Or that caught his blood when he was crucified, yes, depending upon which version you believe in. Although I suppose it could have been both."

"All right, but . . . I'm asking you about the former first lady . . . and you're talking to me about objects out of myth and legend? You understand that I'm not seeing the connection . . ."

Ron took a deep breath and plunged into it. "Gwen is alive and well and hearty because we—Arthur, I, and some others—went to a remote island that was the hiding place of the Holy Grail. In fact, the island actually turned out to be the Grail. The Grail has four forms—the cup, the sword, the belt, and the land. And the land was being ruled over by Gilgamesh, the ancient Sumerian hero. He and Arthur had a throw down and, long story short, Arthur won, acquired the Holy Grail, which transformed back into a cup, helped Gwen drink from it, and she completely recovered. And that's what happened."

Stockwell didn't move from the chair. Ron waited a while for his boss to make some sort of response, or ask a question, or something. Instead, Stockwell merely stared at him. "I know," Ron said tentatively, "that none of that sounds like it makes any sense . . ."

"Actually," said Stockwell, "considering that all the explanations I came up with made little to no sense . . . that one actually comes closest to holding together. The Holy Grail . . ."

"Yes, sir."

"Ronald . . . I don't know if you remember, but a year or so ago, I looked you in the eyes and I asked you about the whole business with Arthur Penn identifying himself with the Arthur of legend."

"I remember it well, sir."

Stockwell shifted in the chair. "I looked you in the eyes, and asked you if it was all part of some massive campaign stunt . . . grandstanding in order to entertain potential voters . . . and I asked you if he was King Arthur . . ."

"No, sir."

"Ronald . . ."

"No, sir, you did *not* ask me that," Ron said firmly, slapping his palm on the desk. "You asked me if he was suffering from some sort of psychosis. You asked me if he really, truly thought that he was King Arthur. And I said to you, 'I've known Arthur for a long time, and I can assure you: He is not suffering from a delusion about being King Arthur.'"

"And you left out the part about his actually *being* King Arthur."

"You wouldn't have believed it."

"I don't believe it *now*!" Stockwell stood up, and Ron automatically began to do likewise. Noticing it, Stockwell gestured in irritation for Ron to take his seat again, which he promptly did. Stockwell shoved his hands into his suit jacket pockets and walked back and forth, shaking his head as he did so. "I mean . . . it's just impossible, what you're saying."

"Well, sir, obviously it's not impossible, because it's the case. Either that, or you're going to have to factor in that the top medical experts in the world told you of a certainty that Gwendolyne Penn would never recover from her wounds. Ever. Faced with that impossibility, I think you'll have to

agree that we'd better begin downgrading from impossible
to highly improbable."

"You're asking me to believe that Arthur Penn is a five-
hundred-year-old king?"

"No, sir. First of all, from my understanding, it's closer to
a thousand years, and second, I'm not asking you to believe
anything. I'm just telling you what I know to be fact. What
I've seen with my own eyes. Whether you believe it or not is
up to you."

"I suppose that's true enough." He considered a moment.
"This is why Arthur declined any and all continued protection by the Secret Service, isn't it. He didn't want anyone
else seeing that Gwen was alive."

"I tried to convince him that he was being overcautious."

"It took a damned act of Congress to have his guards removed, Ron. I remember him addressing all those congress-
men. 'Where I will go will be far from the eyes of man. I ask
you, as a token of respect, to honor my wishes for privacy.' I
thought he was going to commit suicide or something."

"He wasn't being insincere. In some respects, Arthur Penn
is the most solitary individual I've ever known."

Placing his hands on the chair back, Stockwell looked as
if he was physically bracing himself. "Tell me what you've
seen. All of it."

Ron proceeded to do so, describing the entire sojourn to
Pus Island, renamed Grail Island for obvious reasons. He
described the confrontation with Gilgamesh, and Arthur's
wielding of Excalibur in the final confrontation with the
king even more ancient than he. He told of their last-minute
escape from the island through the intervention of Ziusura,
another ancient being from Gilgamesh's time who had been
rewarded with immortality by his gods (at least, so he said)
and was very likely the prototype for Noah. For good measure, he threw in the entire business with the Basilisk and
the final, awful fate of terrorist leader Arnim Sandoval.

Throughout all of it, except for the occasional interruption seeking clarification, Stockwell remained silent. He didn't move from the spot, staying behind the chair and gripping it firmly. When Ron finally finished his narrative, Stockwell let the silence continue for a time, then said, "And if I asked your wife . . . she would tell me much the same story?"

"You mean Nellie?"

"Unless you have another wife I should know about."

"No, that's the one I've got, sir," said Ron with an amused smile. "And yes, she would. As Gwen's personal aide, she was there for the whole thing. That was the series of escapades that really brought us close together. We wound up getting married a few months after returning."

"All right," Stockwell said. "Here's what we're going to do, Ron. You're going to pick up the phone, call Nellie, and simply tell her to come here. When she arrives, I am going to ask her to describe the same incidents you described to me . . . after you assure her that you've already told me. If her narrative doesn't match up with yours, then I'll know that you're lying to me, and we're through. Does that seem reasonable to you?"

"Not especially, sir, no. But if that's what you want, that's what we'll do. It begs the question, though, of what exactly will happen if what she says does match up with what I've told you. If so, what then?"

"I swear to God, Ron, I haven't the faintest idea. I do know this, though: Arthur and Gwen have to be told about this. They have to know what's happened."

"Yes, sir." Ron nodded. "I'm on it."

Stockwell looked at him suspiciously. "How, exactly, are you 'on it'?"

"I sent Percival and Ziusura to find them. I've no doubt they can track them down."

"I see. You dispatched Noah and the Grail Knight to find King Arthur."

"Yes, sir."

"All right, well . . . keep me apprised of how that goes."

"Yes, sir."

"Now pick up the phone and call Nellie."

"Yes, sir."

As Ron did so, Stockwell thought about it, then said, "You know what, Ronald? I think I liked it better when you lied to me."

"Most people do, sir."

CHAPTRE
THE THIRD

ZIUSURA LOOKED AROUND the cabin of the *Malory* in disgust. "You call this living accommodations? You can't be serious. I wouldn't let animals live in such confined quarters. It's astounding you haven't gone completely mad."

Arthur paid him no mind. Instead he was staring at several glossy photographs spread out before him on the narrow table. He was slowly shaking his head as Gwen sat nearby with her face in her hands, moaning softly. "I have so screwed this up," she moaned.

"You've screwed nothing up, my dear," Arthur told her patiently, even as he continued to study the photos. There was no denying the contents: Gwen and Arthur on the deck of the ship, Gwen looking quite fetching in a bikini and Arthur comically wrestling with a swordfish he'd just landed. "At least you weren't photographed sunning yourself topless."

"I might as well have been. Couldn't make things much worse."

"Actually, I tend to disagree," said Arthur. He looked over at Percival. Percival was as immortal as Ziusura, but whereas the smaller, elderly man with the white beard looked ancient—although obviously not as truly ancient as he was—Percival still appeared ageless. The Moor remained powerfully built, with broad shoulders and muscular arms. And ever since the large black man had taken to shaving his head, thus shearing away the vestiges of gray therein, he might have appeared anywhere from thirty or sixty to the unknowing eye. No one would have pegged him as being a thousand years old, thanks to the effects of drinking from the Holy Grail.

Arthur had recognized the Grail instantly, of course, when he saw it hanging at Percival's side. It had resumed its form of the sword, and Arthur never forgot a sword that had been wielded in an attempt to kill him. Personally, he preferred the Grail's form of the cup, and still didn't understand why the damned thing kept changing shape. He'd asked Merlin, but Merlin had declined to explain it to him, which was typical. As far as Arthur was concerned, it was a toss-up who was more inclined to ignore an order of his: his wife or his sawed-off mage advisor.

Percival Moor looked distinctly sympathetic to the frustration of his liege as Arthur continued, "And these were taken via a satellite, you say? Because we've been very cautious. Whenever there's the slightest sign of others—passing airplanes, boats, what-have-you—we've always made sure to keep Gwen hidden below."

"Via satellite, yes. You were photographed from orbit."

"The things people can do now," Arthur muttered, shaking his head. "Do we have any idea whose satellite it was?"

"No. The pictures simply showed up everywhere late last week. The AP, CNN, every major news outlet. They were greeted with skepticism at first, naturally. Fakery is so easy these days when it comes to photography."

"Oh for the days," Ziusura said, "when seeing was believing."

"True. Speaking of which, how did they know that these were recent photographs? They could have been taken anytime when Gwen was 'officially' alive, and simply never been published before."

Percival reached over and tapped one of the photos, one that had clearly been taken from a higher altitude. "This one. The ship's name and registry are clearly visible. The Associated Press checked it through and confirmed that you purchased the vessel after the shooting, not before."

"Wonderful."

"This is my fault."

Arthur turned toward Gwen, his face darkening. "Gwen, could you *please* stop saying that . . ."

"Merlin suggested that we just take up residence in your magically protected home at Belvedere Castle in Central Park!" she pointed out. "No amount of modern technology would have been able to find us there! But me, no, I had to say that I'd feel claustrophobic living out the rest of my days there. That I felt as if we had to stay out, move around, see what we could of the world without it seeing us. And look what happened."

"Gwen, there's nothing we can do about it. What's done is done, and indulging in recriminations is simply an unproductive waste of time. What we really have to ask ourselves is: What now?"

"Why does there have to be anything now?" said Gwen. "So the word is out that I'm up and around. So what? So people will call it a miracle, and eventually they'll move on to something else. Why do we have to be concerned about this at all?"

"Don't be an idiot," said Ziusura.

Arthur shot an angry glance at him. "With all respect to my elders, Old Man . . . I will not have you addressing my wife that way."

"I wouldn't address her that way if she weren't being an idiot."

The king started to rise from the table, but Gwen put a hand on his, and said gently, "Arthur . . . it's okay. He's right. I *am* being an idiot. At the very least, I'm being self-delusional."

"No, you're not," he said, even as he sat back down.

"Yes, I am, and I love you madly, darling, you know that. But feel free to verbally slap me around sometimes, because I deserve it." She took a deep breath and let it out slowly. "We can't just ignore this because everyone and his brother is going to want to know how it happened."

"I know," Arthur admitted.

Percival looked extremely disturbed about the notion. "Ron is already feeling the heat back in Washington. Stockwell, too. People are screaming 'cover-up.'"

"People like to scream," Ziusura said dismissively. He glanced around. "Do you have any cookies?"

Gwen stared at him. "Why?"

"I like cookies."

"Oh." She pointed to a cabinet, and Ziusura went over, pulled out a bag of chocolate-chip cookies, and proceeded to pop them in his mouth one at a time. Gwen looked at Percival incredulously, and continued, "There is genuinely sentiment that there's some sort of government cover-up? How could people come to that conclusion?"

"Because Americans don't like to hear the words 'I don't know' from their leaders," Arthur said grimly.

"They'd rather think that their leaders were lying to them?"

"Why not?" shrugged Percival. "They're used to that. They figure that political leaders lying to them is a cost of doing business."

"Arthur hasn't lied to them."

"No, I simply quit on them and went into hiding."

"You didn't go into hiding!" When he looked at her with a raised eyebrow, Gwen amended, "Okay, you did go into hiding. But for me."

"And what about Ron? And Terrance? Don't I have some degree of obligation to protect their interests?" He turned back to Percival. "How likely is this to turn into something ongoing and major?"

"There's no point in discussing likelihood. It's happening. And you certainly can't be surprised by it, Highness."

"No, I'm not. Not at all. The citizens of the world had an emotional investment in Gwen's medical condition. Now they see her fully recovered. With a lack of information, a vacuum will exist into which any manner of misinformation can seep."

"What sort?" asked Ziusura between crunches, wiping some crumbs off his face. "I'm curious. I've been rather insulated for the past millennia or so, and really don't have much of a clue what passes for human reasoning these days."

Arthur began to tick off possibilities on his fingers. "They might think that the entire shooting of Gwen was some sort of hoax."

"That makes no sense."

"Yeah, well," Gwen pointed out, "there are still people who think that the moon landing was faked on a sound stage in Area 51. It's—"

"Wait," Percival interrupted, looking at Arthur with curiosity. "I just realized. You were president. You had access to Area 51 and information about it. What's the deal with that? If you don't mind my asking, Highness, what *is* in Area 51?"

"Oh. A casino."

Percival stared at him unblinking. "A . . . casino."

"Yes. A very big one. Massive, really. Very festive." He paused and added matter-of-factly, "It's in Nevada, Percival. What *else* would be there?"

"But . . . sire . . . it's one of the most tightly secured, secretive locations in the country!"

"Well, of course, Percival. It has to be that way. What happens in Area 51 stays in Area 51."

The Grail Knight leaned back, his expression doubtful. "What I find most disturbing about this, Highness, is that you don't lie."

"That's correct. Don't ask questions, Percival, if you don't truly want the answers."

"Could we get back to me, please?" asked Gwen.

"Yes. Of course. So . . . hoax," Arthur again started counting off possibilities on his fingers. "That's one. And since, as Percival's question indicates, people are so enamored of conspiracy theories, they might believe that Gwen was truly injured—"

"Which I was . . ."

"—and the government performed some remarkably secret, daringly experimental procedure upon her that cured her completely. A procedure that could no doubt be utilized on other poor devils who are in vegetative states."

"Except, of course, the government is holding out on its citizens," said Gwen.

"And that's just off the top of my head," said Arthur. "I'm sure there are others. The point is, this is going to leave the president and Ron in a no-win predicament. Either they'll be seen as completely ignorant of the forces behind Gwen's miraculous recovery, in which case they'll be considered uninformed and ineffective. Or else they'll be seen as trying to cover up the facts of the matter, and thus working contrary to the interests of Americans. Either way, they'll be terribly weakened politically. It will hurt their ability to govern in terms of the public's faith in them."

"Which doesn't even begin to take into account," Gwen added, "the inevitable hearings and investigations that

Congress is going to launch in order to play to its constituents. But if we go back . . ."

"If you go back," said Percival, "the spotlight is going to be straight on you."

Arthur smiled thinly. "And here, Percival, I would have thought your mission in all this was to talk us into going back."

"I would not presume to try and talk you into anything, Highness. The truth of the matter is that I'm here at Ron's instigation, in order to apprise you of what's happening. But I wouldn't dream of influencing—"

"Bluntly, Percival, what happens if we don't go back?"

"Ron's ass is grass."

"That sounds painful," said Arthur, who then gave it a moment's more thought and decided, "Actually, that simply sounds strange. Then again, I was living in a cave for nearly a thousand years, so I never pretended to understand everything that everyone was talking about. Still, when all is said and done, Ron has been a loyal friend and aide, as was his wife, Nellie. I don't see how Gwen and I can, in good conscience, spend the rest of our lives carefree if it means that Ron's buttocks will become transformed into a lawn."

"So we have to go back?" asked Gwen.

He looked to his wife. "Do you disagree? Tell me now. Because if you do, I am willing to overlook the dictates of my conscience for—"

"You know what, Arthur?" she laughed. "You can't lie to a soul on this planet . . . except yourself. You really think that you would be able to 'overlook the dictates' of your conscience? You can't set aside your morality any more than you can set aside your need to breathe. Oh, you could manage it for a brief time, I suppose, if you felt you were doing it on my behalf. But sooner or later, the pressure would get to you, and we'd be on our way back to Washington."

Ziusura pointed languidly in Gwen's direction. "This one's smarter than I would have credited her, Arthur," he said.

"Thanks a lot, Noah."

Ziusura put down the cookies and said, "That's it. You want an up-close and personal view of a flood, young woman? Your wish is granted . . ."

"Easy, Wise and Aged One," Arthur said soothingly. "She meant no disrespect."

"Oh yes I—"

"Gwen!"

"Fine, fine, fine. I'm sorry about the 'Noah' thing." She frowned. "There is one possibility we're not considering."

"Dropping you into the ocean?" suggested Ziusura. "Let's see them make a case if they can't find you . . ."

"What the hell did I ever do to you?"

"Your getting shot led him," Ziusura indicated Arthur, "to seek out the Grail, which ended up putting an end to the nice, peaceful, island-bound life that I'd gotten very accustomed to, thank you very much."

"A terrorist shot me! What was I supposed to do!"

"You've never heard of ducking?"

"All right, that's enough. Gwen," said Arthur, "what's the possibility we're not considering?"

"That I simply go myself. Leave you out here. Leave you out of it."

"Why in the name of the gods would I agree to something like that?"

"Because," Percival said, comprehending, "she'll be more willing to lie than you."

"Right. I'll lie like a rug. I'll come up with some sort of cover story. Faith healer down in South America. Aliens in UFOs. Elvis cured me. Something like that."

"We're not going to do that, Gwen."

"We're not? Are you sure?"

"I'm sure. This is a situation that needs to be addressed, and I'm not going to send my wife in my stead. I'm going. Now if *you* wish to remain behind—"

"That's not happening."

"Very well, then." He glanced at a navigational chart on the wall. "Percival, I assume you have a means of contacting Ron . . ."

"Absolutely. You wouldn't believe the communications system Ziusura has on his boat."

"At this point in my existence, Percival, there's very little that I would have difficulty believing. So . . . contact Ron. Tell him that in"—he made some fast calculations—"approximately four days we will arrive in Pearl Harbor. If he could smooth the way in arranging for a ship or two to escort us in, speed along our ship getting docked, and having a plane there to meet us . . ."

"Air Force One?"

"I'd settle for something that serves peanuts and some free drinks. Oh . . . and you may want to tell Ron that he should go ahead and tell the president who I really am, if he hasn't already."

"Do you think that's wise, Highness?"

"I haven't the faintest idea if it's wise or not, Percival . . . but I think he's going to have to absorb a lot of information once we arrive, and the less we dump on the poor bastard at one time, the better."

"What about Merlin?" asked Ziusura. "The little runt seemed to have a good head on his shoulders. Perhaps he might be useful in this matter."

"I'm still not certain that Merlin has forgiven me for re-signing and derailing his plans for my monumental destiny," said Arthur wryly. "He goes where he wishes. I very much suspect that, if he chooses to become involved in all of this, we'll be hearing from him soon enough."

CHAPTRE
THE FOURTH

✝

T̲H̲E̲ ̲A̲U̲D̲I̲E̲N̲C̲E̲ ̲A̲P̲P̲L̲A̲U̲D̲E̲D̲ wildly for the magician on the small stage as he stepped back and took a bow, smiling pleasantly and bobbing his head in appreciation. There were about a hundred or so patrons in the club, grouped around small tables that accommodated anywhere from two to four people. Some had ordered food, everyone had ordered drinks. But the Magic Shack wasn't renowned for its cuisine, and the drinks were notorious for being over-priced. Instead the unassuming venue was the premiere spot for magicians in the Los Angeles area who excelled in sleight of hand and close-up magic. No huge, theatrical boxes to be sliced and diced, or vanishing motorcycles, or other such non-sense. This was gasp-out-loud, staring right at it, "How the hell did he do that because I never looked away for a second" magic. This was for the hard-core only. More often than not, half the audience was made up of other magicians who were eager to see what the up-and-comers had up their sleeves, as it were. If you impressed this crowd, you were *gooooood.*

Merlin Junior impressed them regularly. More than impressed: He baffled them.

Junior was a gawky, eight-year-old boy, with skinny arms and legs, ears that stuck out almost at right angles to his head, and silky brown hair that hung down to the back of his neck. One would have wondered what in the world an eight-year-old was doing in such a place. Certainly his parents would have something to say about it.

But if Merlin Junior had parents, no one knew anything about them. He had simply shown up one evening at the Magic Shack, strode up onto the stage during a brief dead period, and before the manager could haul him off the stage, started doing magic. Astounding magic. Wearing a tank top so that his arms were completely exposed, he snatched cards out of the air with machine-gun rapidity. As he did so, he created a three-story house of cards, whipped a handkerchief out of the air, dropped it over the house of cards—which, despite all reason, actually *supported* the handkerchief rather than collapsing—made a mystic pass, whipped away the cloth, to reveal a house of cards transformed into an actual dollhouse. This naturally prompted an explosion of applause, which became more thunderous when he tossed the cloth over it once more, did another mystical pass, and transformed it back into a house of cards.

The manager, after congratulating the self-billed Merlin Junior on his brilliance, informed him that he couldn't come back. That having such a youngster working his place just opened up too many problems. Merlin Junior nodded, said he understood, and then showed up the next evening and did exactly the same thing. Not exactly: This time he had an entirely new act that was even more dazzling than the previous. Word about him began to spread and, by the end of the week, when people were showing up and asking whether Junior was going to be working that night because he was who they had come to see, the manager was visibly sweating and pulling at his lower lip (one of his most typical nervous habits). Relief flooded through him when Merlin Junior strode in to great applause, and when Junior and the manager locked eyes, the latter knew that he had to bow to the inevitable.

The only line he drew was that Merlin Junior could not sit at the bar. "We got people watching this place," he told the youngster. "The instant your butt hits a barstool, I lose my liquor license, and this place goes belly-up. So that's off-limits. Understood? I'm not kidding: It's really out-of-bounds. Got it?"

"Got it," Merlin Junior said calmly, and there seemed to be a world of amusement in his eyes. The manager was pleased to see, as weeks went by, that Junior stuck to their agreement, never risking the Magic Shack's liquor license. He paid Merlin Junior a nominal sum for every appearance, plus free food and all the nonalcoholic beverages he desired. Every so often he would sit down with Junior and, asking casual questions, would try to get him to open up about his past. Junior never took the bait. Never discussed his parents, never revealed anything about himself. Eventually, the manager stopped asking.

This particular night, Merlin Junior took his customary seat near the back of the Magic Shack. There were a few small tables in the rear of the bar area: Not actually *at* the bar and therefore not out-of-bounds. It was at these tables that Merlin usually seated himself after he performed, since they were in the shadows and nobody noticed him there. He offered a tired smile up to the waitress as she placed a glass of water in front of him. "Thanks, Flo," he said.

"You killed tonight, honey," Flo told him.

"I've killed in the past, but not tonight."

She laughed at that and patted him affectionately on the shoulder. "You're something else, honey," she told him, and headed over toward other customers.

"You have no idea," said Merlin. He extended his index finger, touched the surface of the water, and smiled as it transformed into wine. He took a sip and sighed deeply.

He heard the young woman before he saw her, the chair scraping across the floor, being pulled from a nearby table (since he only had the one chair at his). Looking up across the table, Merlin blinked owlishly at the young woman who was now seated opposite him.

She was a stunner, he had to admit that much to himself. It had been quite some time since Merlin had looked at any woman in that appraising sort of fashion. He'd had far more important things on his mind, and besides . . . he looked like an eight-year-old, for God's sake. Nevertheless, he took in her long blond hair, her eyes that were a curious mixture of blue-green. Unlike so many Los Angeles women who looked like walking skeletons, this one's face was actually full, with a healthy red glow to the cheeks. Her lips were wide, her nose small and delicate. She was wearing a blue dress that tied behind her neck.

"Devil with the blue dress on?" he inquired, one eyebrow raised.

"You were amazing tonight," she said.

"I know."

She laughed at that. "Not exactly the modest one, are you."

"Modesty is overrated."

"I bet." She extended a hand. "I'm Vivian. Vivian Mercer."

Merlin stared at her for a moment, regarding her suspiciously. Then he shook the extended hand curtly. "Merlin," he said.

"Not 'Merlin Junior'? That's how they bill you."

"I know how they bill me. It was my idea. See a child billing himself 'Merlin,' and it's preposterous. Everyone knows Merlin is an elderly man with a long white beard. But I call myself 'Merlin Junior,' and that makes it seem more reasonable to people somehow."

"And do you care what people think?"

"Not particularly. Or . . . at all, really."

"Then why . . . ?"

"Because it pleases me to do so," he said, sounding a bit cross. "I'm not accustomed to having to explain myself. Now did you come over to harass me or . . . ?"

"No! No, not at all!" She looked concerned, but then smiled widely, and Merlin had to admit to himself that she did indeed have a dazzling smile. "I was just . . . well, see, I'm a bit of an amateur magician myself, and I was just wondering if you might give me the slightest hint of how you did some of the tricks you performed tonight . . ."

"Ah! Well, wonder no more."

"You will?"

"Not if you were the last woman on Earth . . . which, by the way, wouldn't be that much of a hardship if you asked me."

"Wow." Vivian sat back in her chair. "You don't seem to have a high opinion of women."

"I'm eight years old. I'm not supposed to. Although, for what it's worth, I don't have much of a high opinion of practically anybody."

She suddenly reached over and took his hand, staring at his palm. He tried to pull away, greatly irritated. "What the hell do you think you're doing?"

"You have an amazing life line," she said, her eyebrows raised so high they were practically intersecting. "It's what I thought."

"What is?"

"You have a very old soul."

Merlin yanked his hand away, shaking it off as if he'd shoved it into something unpleasant. "Leave my soul out of this. In fact, leave me out of this."

"Hey, Junior!" It was Flo, and Merlin had never been so happy to see the waitress in his life. She was standing next to Vivian, scowling, as she addressed her comment to Merlin. "This lady bothering you, kid?"

"Yeah. She is, actually."

Her hip outthrust, Flo said tartly, "You got nothing better to do than bust a kid's chops, sweetheart? Don't you think maybe you should pick on somebody your own size . . . or generation, for that matter?"

"I wasn't meaning to pick on him," Vivian assured her. "I'm just an admirer."

"Well, he's a little young for you, sweetheart, so I think it'd be better if you admired him from afar, okay?"

"But I was just—"

"Okay?" Flo repeated in a way that indicated any answer that was other than what she wanted wasn't going to be accepted.

Vivian looked as if she was going to offer further protest, but then simply nodded, and said, "Okay." She rose, put out a hand, and said to Merlin, "It was a pleasure to meet you."

"Thank you," said Merlin, raising neither hand from the table to shake hers.

Her hand dangled there in midair for a moment, then she lowered it and forced a smile. Her gaze wandered over to Merlin's glass. "By the way," she said loudly enough for Flo to hear, "I don't think the authorities would approve of you serving alcohol to a minor."

"What?" Flo demanded. "What are you talking about? What are you trying to start? I gave him water."

"Looks like wine to me."

"Junior, let me see that."

Merlin had quickly scooped up the glass in his hand when Vivian spoke. He muttered something under his breath and then handed Flo the glass. Flo stared at it for a moment, then looked at Vivian as if she'd lost her mind. "Lady, I've been slinging drinks for twelve years now, and I have to say, in my expert opinion . . . that's a glass of water."

Vivian stared at the glass of clear liquid, then half smiled as she looked back to Merlin. "Yes. Yes, of course it is," she said, and turned and walked out the back of the room.

Flo let out a heavy sigh and placed the glass back in front of Merlin. "I swear to God, I don't know what gets in some people's heads sometimes. Junior, if anybody else tries to bother you, you let me know immediately, okay?"

"Sure thing, Flo," said Merlin. But he wasn't looking at her. Instead he was looking at the door through which Vivian had departed. "Vivian. She had to be named Vivian. Damn, this is ill omened."

"Why, honey?" asked Flo.

Merlin looked her up and down for a moment, clearly trying to decide what to say. Finally, he shrugged and said, "'Vivian' is one of the variant names of 'Nimue.'"

"I'm not sure how you get 'Vivian' from 'Nim-way,' but all right, I'll bite," said Flo good-naturedly. "Who, or what, is 'Nim-way?'"

"Nimue is the true name of the Lady of the Lake," replied Merlin. "One of the wild cards of Arthurian legend."

"Arthurian? You mean like King Arthur and Camelot?"

"Just like."

"Which I guess you'd have an interest in, what with your name being Merlin and all."

"You'd guess right," said Merlin dryly, swirling the water around in his glass. "On the one hand, she was responsible for getting the sword Excalibur to King Arthur. On the other hand, she seduced the wizard, Merlin, stealing magiks from him, including a spell of imprisonment that locked him away in a cave for cen—" He stopped and cleared his throat. "Forever. Then again, what else can you expect from a creature of the water. Her passions and loyalties ebb and flow as do the tides, moving in and out and acted upon by forces mere mortals cannot begin to comprehend."

"How you *do* go on." Flo laughed. "You're certainly passionate about this Merlin and Arthur business."

"I was passionate about it. But then my passion . . . waned."

"And why's that?"

"Because," Merlin said, staring into the glass, "there came a time when Arthur simply didn't need his Merlin anymore. When their interests no longer overlapped. When Merlin was . . . irrelevant. Merlin gave Arthur's life magic, don't you see. But Arthur turned his back on it, wanting other things from his life. A life that Merlin had no place in. It was a tragedy, and I've little use for pointless tragedies."

"That's very sad."

"It is, rather."

"But honey"—and she shook him by the shoulder—"cheer up! It's all just stories, when you come down to it. Stories aren't worth getting *that* upset about."

"You're right, Flo. They're not."

She nodded in approval, walked away, and didn't even notice as Merlin casually transformed the water back into wine. "And it's all just stories after all . . . isn't it." He tossed back the glass and drank the wine in one swallow. It burned pleasantly as it went down his throat, but other than that, it didn't make him feel any better.

He hated having no one to talk to. That was the truth of it. For all the times that he had harangued and berated Arthur, he despised the notion that Arthur had absented himself from their relationship. That he had chosen Gwen and a life of fleeing the greatness of his destiny, trading it for a voyage to nowhere that was a remarkable symbol of the wasted opportunity that was Arthur's great legacy.

This business with Merlin's hanging about the Magic Shack—entertaining the audiences using magiks that were so simple they weren't remotely worthy of a mage of his talents—it was just a way to kill time. Time granted him by being practically immortal.

He watched people in Los Angeles rushing about and trying to do everything they could to stave off the ravages of time. Plastic surgery with its nips here and tucks there, drawing tight the skin upon their faces and bodies as if they were trying to fix a drumheads. And all for what? So they could look younger for a little while longer?

Well, he was there to say that looking young for a while longer could be a tremendously overrated business.

"Cheer up, kid," said one of the club's regular magicians as he wandered past. "You always look so serious. You know what they say: Youth is wasted on the young."

"Tell me about it." Merlin sighed.

CHAPTRE
THE FIFTH

✝

RON CORDOBA HAD no idea at all how the press caught wind of Arthur and Gwen's return. Technically, that wasn't actually true. He had some idea, all right. Someone with a mouth the size of the Grand Canyon had blabbed about it . . . probably someone at Pearl Harbor who had leaked the news to someone else who had in turn fed it to someone else further along the food chain. All he knew was that he had a full-blown security breach and media event on his hands, when all he'd really wanted to do was try and get some solid footing in the situation.

He reasoned that it was too late to start crying about it now. The word was out, and the press secretary was fielding so many questions, so fast and furiously, that Ron felt the need to walk into the pressroom—much to the shock of all concerned, since it was something he rarely if ever did—and announce that this line of inquiry was not only at an end but so were the regular press conferences. He then pulled the press secretary out and ordered all the lights in the pressroom shut off, just to show that he meant it.

This naturally earned him an earful from the press secretary, who pointed out, not unreasonably, that the best way to handle the story was for the White House to control it. But Ron shook his head, and retorted, "Wake up and smell the leak. We're no longer controlling. It's out there, like a burning factory fire. In my opinion, all we can do right now is try not to spill more fuel on it. And I can assure you, that's all the press conferences are going to be."

"But Ron—"

"No buts! The lid is on until further notice. If I see a single off-the-record quote showing up in the *Washington Post* that could be remotely traced to you, you'll be gone so fast no one will remember you were ever here."

He wasn't exactly sure what that meant, but the secretary simply nodded, and echoed, "The lid is on."

Every once in a while, Ron loved having power.

Still, power was only relative. Right now he was seated in the room that was the epitome of power in the country: the Oval Office. Stockwell was behind his desk, shuffling through papers and reading reports, shaking his head in a way that indicated he wasn't exactly thrilled with what he was reading. Ron was seated alertly in one of the more comfortable chairs, and asked tentatively, "What's that you're going over, sir?"

"Reports detailing the success rates of small businesses over the last five years," said Stockwell, without looking up.

"How's that going?"

"Eighty-five percent crash and burn every single year."

"Well, one has to admire the consistency."

Stockwell afforded him a brief glance. "Indeed."

One of the president's aides opened the door partway, and announced, "Sir. He's here."

There was no need to explain who the "he" was. Stockwell was immediately on his feet, as was Ron. The aide, with no further preamble, opened the doors wide. Arthur Penn, with

Gwendolyne at his side, entered. Coming in directly behind them was Percival. He was dressed in black and was wearing the exact kind of long, flopping brown duster that Secret Service agents tended to despise since they could conceal anything from a pistol to a rocket launcher. Indeed, the agents stationed just outside the Oval Office were eyeing Percival with open suspicion. If Percival noticed that he was being singled out for that kind of scrutiny, he didn't let it show.

"Mr. President," said Arthur, and Stockwell responded in kind. They shook hands firmly. Gwen extended her hand as well, and Stockwell shook it, smiling warmly. Percival contented himself to incline his head slightly from a short distance away, which suited Stockwell fine. Stockwell had never known quite what to make of Percival, never fully understanding what his involvement with Arthur was. He'd always suspected, deep down, that Percival was some sort of muscle who did Arthur's dirty work for him.

Then Arthur and Gwen turned toward Ron, and their greeting for him was a bit less formal. Arthur wrapped both of his hands around Ron's outstretched one and shook it warmly, while Gwen simply disdained handshakes of any kind and instead embraced him. In this case, Percival did approach him and shook Ron's hand warmly. The two men had shared a life-and-death adventure together, and that sort of escapade always served to forge a bond that was not easily broken.

"It's great to see you again," Ron said.

"Indeed. In the case of Mrs. Penn, one would almost say it was miraculous," said Stockwell, gesturing for Arthur and Gwen to sit. They did so, and Stockwell sat as well. He interlaced his fingers and rested his hands on his desk. "So, Arthur . . . it seems we have ourselves a bit of a situation."

"It does indeed."

"One for which—and I don't say this accusingly, but merely as a statement of fact—a number of people in my administration are getting their heads handed to them, both by the press and the general public."

"It's such hypocrisy," said Gwen.

Stockwell glanced at her, his face puckered with curiosity. "Hypocrisy?"

"Arthur showed me the cards, the letters, the communications from all over the world while I was in a coma. And nine out of ten of them—maybe more than that—said the exact same thing: 'We're praying for a miracle.' With that many people praying together, is it so impossible for us to say, 'Guess what? It was a miracle. Let's be thankful,' and move on?"

"On a logical basis, Mrs. Penn, no, it's not impossible at all. As a matter of practicality," the president said grimly, "it is completely impossible. Miracles are what you pray for. Results are what you get. And although I've no doubt there are a number of people out there who are perfectly willing to accept your recovery as divine providence, end of story . . . there are far more who see it only as the beginning of the story. Your medical condition was too widely disseminated in the media. The damage done to you by the assassin's bullets was examined by medical experts in excruciating detail, all on the world stage. Doctor-patient confidentiality? Forget it. That ship sailed the moment pieces of your head exploded."

"I'd forgotten how you have a way of putting things, Terrance," said Gwen.

"I'm the leader of the free world, Gwen. I don't have time to mince words. This has to be attended to, and I'm looking to know what it is that you're going to do about it. And I need to know . . . if it's true."

"It?"

Nothing was said for a moment, then Ron loudly cleared his throat. "Arthur . . . I, uhm . . . I felt he deserved to know about your true background. Where you really came from. Who, uh . . ."

"Who I am?" Arthur said gently.

"In so many words: Yes."

"It's all right, Ron. The development is not unantici-
pated. How did he take it?"

"About as well as could be expected."

"I'm sitting right here," Stockwell pointed out.

"Very well, Terrance," Arthur said reasonably, turning to
Stockwell. "How are you dealing with the revelation, as it
were?"

"It's . . . a lot to process, Arthur, I have to admit. The entire notion behind myth and legend is that that's . . . that's
all they are. Fantasies. Epic tales that get passed along from
one generation to the next. They're bigger than life. And
now I'm being told that, here you are, King Arthur, seated
right in front of me."

"Do you believe in God, sir?" Percival suddenly spoke up.

"Of course I do," Stockwell said unhesitatingly.

"So why should believing in Arthur Rex be that much of
a problem?"

"Because he's not God. He's a man, flesh and blood."

"As was the Christian savior, as I recall. If he walked in
here now and proclaimed that he had returned, would you
believe him? Or would you figure him to be a madman."

"Truthfully, probably the latter."

"I don't know about you," Gwen said, "but I find that
kind of sad. That we've reached a point in our society
that . . . I don't know."

"Men cling to faith as their reason to believe in God," said
Arthur, smiling sadly. "Sometimes it seems to me that their
faith also prevents them from believing as well. People have
no trouble handling the divine . . . as long as it's a safe distance away. How are we to aspire to be closer to God when, if
He comes closer to us, we head in the other direction."

"Are you now saying you're God?" asked Stockwell.

"Hardly. On the other hand, if He presented himself to me, I would certainly be more inclined to give Him the benefit of the doubt than to dismiss Him out of hand."

"Fair enough. But the fine line we walk, Arthur, is that those who claim to be nearer our God tend to get on the wrong side of the American people, since everyone wants to believe that they themselves have their own personal connection with the almighty. Ron is telling me stories about the Holy Grail, and I'm not certain how to—"

"You could try showing them this," suggested Percival. He reached deep into his coat, and when he withdrew his hand, there was a gleaming goblet in it.

Stockwell gaped at it for a moment. Then he started to reach for it before reflexively pulling his hand back. He stared at it with uncertainty. "Are you saying . . . that's it?" Percival nodded. "May I . . . ?"

Percival glanced at Arthur, who nodded slightly. The Grail Knight strode forward and, rather than handing it to Stockwell, placed it in the dead center of his desk. He took several steps back as Stockwell just stared at it.

"Breathe, Terrance," Arthur said gently.

Stockwell exhaled heavily, not realizing until that moment that he'd been holding his breath. Slowly, his hands trembling in spite of himself, Stockwell reached out and took the Grail carefully, balancing it with both hands. Then he experimentally shifted the cup from one hand to the other. "It's . . . colder than I expected," he said finally.

"Did you think it would be scalding to the touch?" asked Arthur.

"I'm . . . not sure. I'm not sure what I . . ." He shook his head and placed the Grail gingerly back down on the desk. "I thought it would be . . . revelatory in some way. That I would hold it and—"

"Be instantly nearer to Jesus?" asked Percival.

"I suppose that sounds ridiculous."

"It doesn't sound any one way or the other. Your expectations are what they are. No one's going to gainsay you."

Stockwell nodded, although it was hard to know whether he'd actually heard what Percival had just said. Instead he said, "I was skeptical of everything Ron told me. Then we brought in Nellie, and she told me practically the exact same story. Just enough variances to make the differing point of view believable, but in all the major aspects, the stories matched up."

"So you believe, then."

"I would say, Arthur, that I'm perhaps eighty percent of the way there. My concern is this: If it's this much effort for me to believe, how in the world are we going to convince the American people? Or the world? How are we going to say that Arthur Penn was truly King Arthur, and that he found the Holy Grail and used it to cure his wife?"

"First of all, Percival found the Grail," Arthur corrected him.

"Well, that solves the problem then," he said sarcastically. "That small clarification is just going to do wonders for the way this will play in Paducah."

"I'm not concerned about how this will 'play,' Terrance. I'm concerned about the truth."

"And I'm concerned about all of it, Arthur. Are you actually suggesting that we go public with the entire story?"

"Absent anyone innocent getting hurt by it, the truth is generally the preferable way in which to approach all matters," Arthur said.

Even Gwen looked uncertain at that notion. She reached over and took his hand. "Arthur, are you sure?" she said worriedly. "I mean, I know we discussed it, but—"

"It seems to me the only option. I am, naturally, open to whatever other possibilities the president may have."

Stockwell drummed his fingers on the table. "Ron, you

were a hell of a PR man before you became chief of staff. What's your take on it?"

"Some people will believe; some won't," Ron said. "Some will think it's a desperate attempt to cover up something else; but there are enough others of a fanciful—dare I say it, faith-oriented—state of mind that they might accept the notion. Either way, at least it allows us to spin the story."

"Does it?" asked Stockwell, not sounding convinced. "Or does it just make us look like idiots? Look, we're shooting in the dark here," he continued, before Ron could respond. "If we're seriously talking about going public with this, we have to run this by Mahoney." When he saw Arthur's quizzical look, he said by way of explanation, "Tyler Mahoney. My press secretary. He knows everyone in the White House press corps . . . how they think, how much they'll swallow. If anyone can give us a reading of what we can expect, it's him." He tapped his intercom. "Terry. Get Tyler up here, would you?"

The door promptly opened and Terry, the president's aide walked in, looking extremely concerned. "That may not be possible at the moment, Mr. President. There's a situation that's just developed that Tyler's dealing with."

"What sort of situation? Something involving us?"

"No, sir. It's David Jackson of the *Daily News*. He was in Tyler's office, having a real shouting match with Tyler because the press conferences have been closed down, and he just collapsed."

"He who? Tyler or Jackson?"

"Jackson. And there's blood coming out his ears. They don't know what it is. The medics are on their way."

"They won't be needed," Arthur said abruptly, standing. "Percival. Come with me. We'll settle this right now."

Instantly, both Stockwell and Ron were on their feet, Ron instantly realizing what Arthur was intending, and Stockwell a few seconds behind him. "Arthur, we have to discuss this—!"

"No, Ron. We do not. Gwen, remain here, please. I don't need you being assaulted by reporters until we have a more controlled situation." He threw open the door, and there were two Secret Service men just outside. "Stand aside," he ordered, and they instantly did so. Percival had retrieved the Grail from the desk, and seconds later they were heading down the corridor, Ron bringing up the rear.

Stockwell sagged back into his chair, rubbing his forehead and trying to control the dull roar that he was hearing. He could have ordered the Secret Service men to try and stop Arthur in his tracks, but the thought of a former president being manhandled was not one he wanted to entertain. To say nothing of the fact that he wasn't certain Arthur and Percival together couldn't fight their way past the agents, which was even less desirable.

"God help me," he muttered.

"God help us all," echoed Gwen, choosing not to dwell on the notion that if God did show up to help, He probably wouldn't be able to get past White House security.

REPORTERS BEING THE type of creatures that they were, they were flocking from throughout the building upon hearing that Jackson had collapsed. There were so many trying to crowd into Tyler Mahoney's office that Tyler—an exhausted man in his thirties who was convinced his hairline had receded two inches since taking this job—was moved to shout at them, "Jesus, people, you're like sharks at a feeding frenzy! Give the man some room!"

Not that Jackson looked like he needed it. Seeing him lying helpless upon Mahoney's floor was shocking in and of itself, because he was a young man with thick black hair that was now matted with blood. His eyes, usually so eager and focused on whatever story he was working, were staring off into nothingness. Mahoney was crouched next to him, saying softly, "Don't worry, Dave. It's going to be fine," and not having the slightest idea whether or not Jackson heard him. "*Where the hell are the damned paramedics!* This is the goddamned White House! We should have crash carts coming out our asses!"

"Stand aside," came a commanding voice that, although none of them had heard it in over a year, everyone within proximity recognized instantly and obeyed without hesitation.

Former President Penn strode forward with a large black man behind him who looked to be a personal security guard. The reporters immediately began to shout questions, but the black man turned and leveled a gaze at them of such fearsome intensity that it caused every one of them to lapse into silence. Arthur extended a hand to the black man, who in turn handed him a large, sparkling gold cup. "You," Arthur said briskly, snapping his fingers and pointing at Tyler. "Your name again?"

"Tyler Mahoney, Mr. President. It's an honor."

"Yes, it is. That water, there," and he pointed to a bottle of Poland Spring water that was on the edge of Mahoney's desk. "Give it here, please."

Uncomprehending, Mahoney did so. Arthur promptly upended the bottle and poured its contents into the cup. A few droplets splashed out of it and landed in the pot of a dying plant that Mahoney had on his desk.

"The paramedics are here!" someone shouted from behind.

"Thank them for their efforts," said Penn, who by that point had knelt next to Jackson and was pouring the contents of the cup between his slack lips. Jackson continued to look at nothing with his unfocused eyes.

"Coming through!" came the shout of the paramedics, and that was the exact moment that David Jackson suddenly sat upright, gasping for breath.

It was so abrupt that everyone watching jumped back, except for a TV cameraman who had filmed the entire thing.

"You'll be quite all right now," Arthur assured him.

"What . . . happened?" Jackson gasped. "I was . . . I don't remember, what . . . ?" Then he focused on Arthur for the first time, and his eyes widened. "You're the former president!"

"That," Arthur said, "is only the beginning of the story."

"Oh my God. Is everyone else seeing this?" It was the cameraman who had spoken, and he'd shifted his focus to the plant on Mahoney's desk . . . which had suddenly gone from being nearly dead to blooming and in full health in seconds.

"It's a trick!"

"Has to be!"

"Couldn't be—!"

Questions and words were flying all over as the bewildered paramedics stood there and wondered why in the world they had been summoned.

Then Arthur raised his hand for silence and immediately the crowd hushed. "It is no trick," Arthur said with calm solemnity. "Come. We shall go to the pressroom. I shall talk. You will listen. And then . . . we'll see what we shall see."

CHAPTRE
THE SIXTH

†

MERLIN'S APARTMENT WAS nothing fancy, and that was by his choice. In his lifetime, he had resided in everything from castles to the White House, and had never felt completely at home in any of them. Something deeply rooted within him despised the entire notion of such ostentation.

So the place that he had chosen to dwell was a third-floor walk-up in the seedier section of downtown Hollywood. Whereas others would certainly have found the location less than desirable, there was a certain rattiness to it that Merlin found quite appealing. If nothing else, he didn't have to worry about nosy neighbors inquiring as to the whereabouts of his parents. There were children in the area roughly his age and even younger who were more or less left to fend for themselves, thanks to their parents being off and involved with prostitution, drugs, and—most repulsive of all—auditions. As a result, Merlin's fending for himself wasn't about to raise any eyebrows.

He trudged up the stairs, feeling more tired than usual. He had to think that the centuries were beginning to wear on him, the legs of his eight-year-old frame bending under the weight of millennia of emotional baggage. Passing other residents of the building, he greeted them with the most perfunctory of nods, barely acknowledging their existence, before he finally got to his door. He snapped his fingers, and the inner locks unlatched. The locks were there to deal with the more mundane intruders who might endeavor to gain entrance; he'd erected mystic wards to stave off anyone who might be more problematic than a run-of-the-mill burglar.

The door swung open before him, and he strode in. It was a studio apartment, cloaked in shadow, which was how he liked it. He was certainly no vampire, but the daylight held little attraction for him. He was built for residing in darkness.

He put together an indifferent dinner of warmed-up pizza, having ordered a pie three days ago and parceled out a couple slices each night since then. It was economical, which wasn't all that much of a consideration to Merlin since he could literally pull money out of the air. Lately, though, as his surroundings indicated, he simply hadn't cared that much about money, or sustenance, or his environment . . . or anything.

Merlin did, however, at least give a damn about personal hygiene. After eating the pizza and wiping the crumbs from his mouth with an accommodating shirtsleeve, he walked into the bathroom and started the water running. The bathtub was the one thing in the entire apartment that he found pleasing; it was large and heavy, with big claw feet that raised it a few inches above the floor. It had class and style and personality . . . more so, Merlin felt, than some persons he knew.

A television sat in one corner of the apartment. It had been there when Merlin first moved in. He'd put it on once or twice, but was so filled with indifference over everything he saw on the screen that he hadn't bothered with it since.

The pizza box being empty, Merlin bent it in half and shoved the container into the garbage can. Then he stared into the trash can and saw there a metaphor of himself.

Shoved aside. Shoved away. Bastard.

He knew that Arthur had not done it deliberately to hurt him. For that matter, what if Arthur had invited him to come along with them? What then? Arthur, Gwen, and Merlin, the fifth wheel, sailing around the Pacific on a yacht? The very notion was ludicrous. He had come to tolerate and even slightly respect Gwen after a fashion, although he still tended to blame her when it came to questions of Arthur's not properly reaching his potential. Even so, the notion of being one-third of an uncomfortable threesome, always feeling that Arthur and Gwen were eyeing him and wondering what the hell he was doing there . . . repulsive. Repulsive and unworthy.

Yet he felt abandoned.

It angered him because it was such an irrational way to react. In the end, he knew, all of us are responsible for our own lives. We make our choices and we live with them. Arthur had chosen to walk away from his position as a potential world leader. He had chosen a life of quiet with Gwen over a life of activity with Merlin . . .

Well, that was the rub of it, wasn't it.

It wasn't just that Arthur had chosen Gwen. It was that he had left Merlin behind.

"You're acting like a child," Merlin scolded himself in his childish voice.

Suddenly there was a splashing in the direction of the bathroom. Perhaps a rat had fallen into the tub and was drowning; it certainly wouldn't be the first time.

Merlin picked up a broom, prepared to bring it crashing down on the skull of the rodent; it wasn't worth even the smallest expenditure of his magic. Striding into the bathroom, he started to bring the broom up over his head, then froze in position.

Something was emerging from the water. There was a soft glowing dead center of the tub that was becoming brighter and brighter, then Merlin stepped back as slowly, majestically, the attractive blonde named Vivian who had come up to him at the Magic Shack rose up from the water like Venus on a clam shell, gloriously naked and covered only by strands of her long golden hair.

She smiled at him teasingly. "Remember me?" she inquired.

Merlin smacked her with the broom.

Vivian jumped back, skidded, and landed heavily on the floor of the tub, sending water cascading everywhere. She sat up and sputtered, "What did you do *that* for?"

"I thought you were a rat," he replied sanguinely.

"You did not!"

"Well, you are. By the way, next time you're going to emerge from a body of water, might I suggest the toilet. Since it's full of shit, you'd be right at home." He tossed the broom onto the bathroom floor, reached over, and turned the water off. "And for the sake of all that's unholy, pull on some gossamer. If you think you're going to be able to seduce me again, then clearly you're not paying attention to matters at hand."

He strode into the living room and flopped onto a chair, listening for the sound of Vivian's wet feet as they splashed onto the floor. Moments later she entered, wearing a veil of gossamer as he had suggested. "I cannot believe you're still upset with me."

"Of course I'm still upset with you, and what were you playing at in the Magic Shack? Did you think I wouldn't recognize you the instant I saw you?"

"You didn't recognize me."

"Of course I did."

"Hardly. If I hadn't given you that clue of my name . . ."

He waved her off dismissively. "I had already figured it out. You changed your appearance, as is your habit. At this point I'm wondering if you even remember what you originally looked like. It doesn't matter, Nimue."

"Merlin," she said in that wistful tone that sounded like waves lapping gently against a shoreline. She sat at the foot of the chair, curling her legs up underneath herself. "I thought that we'd settled the score. After all, when you returned and summoned me, did I not immediately restore Excalibur to Arthur? Do you think that was fun for me?" She shuddered at the recollection. "Central Park Lake is not exactly the most attractive environment for one of my stature. Tossed cans, spare tires, muck everywhere . . . it was ghastly. But I did that for you, Merlin. I did that to make up for—"

"For betraying my trust? For trapping me? For seducing me into a damned cave for a thousand years?"

"Well . . . yes," she said, sounding a bit petulant. "Are you saying it wasn't enough?"

"How could anything be enough, you neurotic naiad?" he demanded. "Yes, you performed me that one service. Did you seriously believe that somehow evened the score? That anything could even the score? You could perform services for me from now through the end of time, and it wouldn't be enough."

She stared up at him sadly. "I'm sorry that you feel that way."

"Well, honestly, Nimue? How am I supposed to trust you? I mean," he said in frustration, "you're looking at me now with those same sad, wet eyes that you used on me a millennium ago to stick me in that damned cave. I trusted you then and wound up much the worse for it. So on what grounds could I possibly trust you again? For that matter, I don't even know what it is you're doing here. You play games with me at the Magic Shack, you pop out of my bath. What's going on, anyway?"

"What's going on, Merlin, is that you forget who I am and what I am. I am one with the ebb and flow, not only of the world's water, but the world's fate. I know when things are happening and the currents of destiny are shifting."

"The Basilisk told me much the same. She was always boasting of being able to sense when 'the wheel was turning.' What is it, anyway, with females of myth and legend and knowing of what's to come? What makes the lot of you so bloody ponderous?"

"I know nothing of what the Basilisk might have been talking about," said Vivian, "but I know what I've been sensing, and I came to warn you."

"Ohhhh, you came to warn me." Merlin laughed. "Warn me, who lives his life backwards. Who has the most highly developed sense of that which is to come in the entire history of magic. You, of all people, have come to warn me, of all people."

"Save your boasting, Merlin," Vivian said. "Claim to have the sight all you want, but let's face it: You haven't been exactly one hundred percent in foreseeing the challenges Arthur had thrown at him. For someone who purports to be omniscient, your record is less than impressive."

His lips thinned into two very narrow lines. "Fine," he snapped. "Tell me what you've come here to say."

"I don't truly know whether I should even bother now . . ."

"Dammit, woman—!"

"All right, all right," she said with faux exasperation. "Something's going to be happening with Arthur."

"Something's always happening with Arthur."

"It's more than that. Something big. Something global."

Curious in spite of himself, Merlin sat up a bit straighter and cocked an eyebrow. "Really," he said, keeping his voice sounding bored.

"Yes. And it's going to involve the Holy Grail."

"I see. Are you sure that you've got your facts on a timely basis, because he's already . . ."

"And the Spear."

That brought Merlin bolt upright. His voice dropped low and sounded nothing like the voice of a young man. Instead, it rumbled with power and implicit threat. "You had best not be joking, milady, or—"

"I would not joke about matters of such consequence, Merlin," Vivian told him. "The Spear Luin is in the mix."

"The Spear *cannot* be in the mix," Merlin said. "We both know the danger that it represents."

"Yes. You and I both do. But there are other forces involved that either don't know . . . or else don't care."

"What other forces?"

She shook her head. "I don't know."

"Don't know or won't tell."

She smiled elusively at him. "Couldn't say."

Quickly she began to backpedal for the bathroom. Now Merlin was up on his feet, clenching his fists. "Blood and thunder, Nimue! Stop playing games!"

"*You* should have been nicer to me," she said carelessly. "I am the Lady of the Lake. I go where I wish and help whom I choose. If you mind your manners better in the future, I might choose to help you."

"*Nimue—!*"

He called out an incantation even as he heard splashing in the bathtub. He charged in just in time to see energies swirling around the bathtub and the waters therein surging about. Of the Lady of the Lake, there was no sign.

"Damn you, Nimue! Get back here!" He shoved his hands into the water, splashing about furiously, soaking both his shirtfront and trousers, not to mention whatever sections of the bathroom floor hadn't already been doused. But there was no sign of her. She had completely dissolved back into the water and from there could have gone just about anywhere in the water-based alternate plane of reality called the Clear.

He thumped his fist on the edge of the tub, his mind racing. Something happening with Arthur? Something huge, global even? What was the best way to find out what that might be? What spell would be the most appropriate means of . . .

"Oh, of course," muttered Merlin, and he went to his television set. He turned it on and, plopping himself down in front of it, proceeded to channel surf to see if there was anything going on with Arthur in the world. It took him less than ten seconds to discover a news story that was being covered by every news program on every station. They went with different angles, different reporters, different interpretations of the day's event, but essentially they all boiled down to the same thing:

ARTHUR PENN, FORMER president, had returned to the White House, accompanied by his wife, who had previously been as good as dead, except now she was hale and hearty. The reason he was giving for her miraculous turnaround was—according to a press conference held right in the White House—that he was truly the Arthur of Camelot fame. This was not the first time he had made such a statement. He had once claimed to be the legendary king during his run for mayor of New York after accused by a political rival of harboring such beliefs. At the time, it had been seen purely as a political strategy and been embraced as such by New York voters.

Now, though, he had taken it to new levels. Levels that were making it harder to overlook the claims or ascribe them to political gamesmanship. It was Arthur's contention that Gwendolyne Penn had been cured through the magic of the Holy Grail . . . an assertion given stunning weight with not only the presence of Mrs. Penn, but also an impromptu demonstration of the alleged cup of Christ in resuscitating a stricken journalist.

Merlin moaned loudly and sagged back in his chair. Reactions were flooding in from all over the world, but none of them mattered to him. All that mattered was that he had never so wanted to throttle King Arthur as he did at that moment.

YE OLDE INTERLUDE

April 30, 1945

STURMHAUPTFUHRER (CAPTAIN) WILHELM Wagner
sprinted through the underground bunker, doing the
best he could to ignore the explosions coming from the Allies inevitable, and infuriating, march upon the Reich
Chancellery above them. There, in the center of Berlin, the
forces of the Fuhrer were making their last stand. Wagner's
troops had been damned near wiped out by the advancing
Soviet troops, and the captain would have far preferred to
die with his men.

Instead fate had apparently spared him for something else
entirely. He had pulled his men back to full retreat in the face
of the Soviets, and Wagner himself had barely gotten out of
there. His impulse was to go back and fight, but his orders
had been very specific: *Fall back to the Chancellery and report to
the Fuhrerbunker where Field Marshal von Greim will meet you.*
The specifics of what he was supposed to do upon encounter-
ing von Greim had not been presented him. That was, of

course, acceptable. His was not to question orders, but merely to follow them.

His uniform was filthy with the blood of his men along with the dirt and grime of the battlefield. Buildings had collapsed into rubble around him, and dust was everywhere, including having coated his lungs. Every so often he had to stop, lean against whatever he could find, and cough heavily and repeatedly in a desperate attempt to clear his breathing passages. He wondered if that alone was going to kill him.

Wagner had no idea how matters had come to such a pass. His belief in the Fuhrer's vision for a Germany that could stand up tall and proud in the world, never to be pitied or conquered again, had never wavered. He had been absolutely certain that theirs was the Master Race. How in the world could it be that here, in the center of their own capital, they could be hunted, under attack, on their last legs.

There had to be a plan. That's all there was to it. The Fuhrer had to have some sort of plan. Perhaps what he was planning to do was lure the Allies to some prearranged point in Berlin, then spring a trap on them. That would certainly be the sort of devious, brilliant planning for which the Fuhrer was noted. And perhaps . . . perhaps Wagner was to be a part of it. What a notion. What an honor!

Wagner had never met the Fuhrer; he'd merely seen him from a distance during occasional rallies. He wondered if the opportunity would be presented him now. He wondered what he would say.

The walls of the underground passage suddenly rocked from another blast overhead. Wagner staggered, catching himself before he fell over, and he snarled a curse at the on-coming Russian army . . . not that they could hear him, of course.

He arrived at a checkpoint in the tunnels and was amused to see a lieutenant sitting at a desk. He had papers neatly arrayed in front of him; amazingly they had not been tossed around by the shaking from overhead. Either that or he had managed to sort them back into order very quickly. He looked as if his presence there in the tunnels, illumination provided by a series of lanterns, was the most natural thing in the world. He looked up quizzically, and said, "Yes?"

"Heil Hitler," said Wagner immediately, thrusting out his hand.

"Heil Hitler," echoed the desk lieutenant, responding to the salute in a casual fashion. "How can I help you?"

"Sturmhauptfuhrer Wagner, reporting as ordered."

"Ah. Yes." He glanced at a particular paper on his desk, then reached down and picked up a field phone. He cranked it up for a moment, then lifted the receiver and announced that Captain Wagner had arrived. He nodded in response to whatever was being said on the other end, then replaced the phone and looked up impassively. "Walk down that way, turn right. You will be met."

"By Field Marshal von Greim?"

"You will be met," was all he said in response.

Wagner nodded, tossed off yet another salute, got the required response, then headed down the corridor as instructed. Once having turned the corner, he felt another coughing fit coming on. He leaned with his back against the corridor and proceeded to cough so violently that small spots of blood and—he thought—a piece of one of his lungs emerged from his mouth.

"Are you ill?" a rough voice asked from nearby.

Wagner began to respond, then he saw who was asking him. It was not von Greim. The man who approached him was cloaked in an aura of death, and wore that cloak proudly. His head was square, his forehead high, and his eyes narrowed into a perpetual squint of suspicion.

Captain Wagner immediately slammed the backs of his heels together and saluted. "Herr Bormann! They had . . . told me to expect Field Marshal von Greim . . ."

"He is indisposed," said Martin Bormann, the right-hand man to the Fuhrer himself. "This particular duty has been given me by the Fuhrer himself. Do you understand?"

"Of course, Herr Bormann."

"Follow me, then."

As they headed down the corridor, Bormann spoke in a low, gravelly tone. "The Fuhrer selected me for this assignment as a little joke, you see. He knows the one point of opinion from which I diverge with him is on matters of Christianity. So, naturally, he puts me in charge of attending to this . . ."

"This what, Herr Bormann, if I may ask. And why me?"

"The Fuhrer likes your name."

Wagner wasn't quite certain he'd heard him correctly. "My *name*, Herr Bormann?"

Bormann nodded. "The Fuhrer was particularly influenced by the Wagner opera *Parsifal*. When a list of available officers for this particular duty was presented him, your name leapt out at him. It is a method of choice steeped more in superstition than logic, but our Fuhrer has his superstitions, and none can gainsay him on them," he noted with a shrug.

"But . . . Wagner's first name was Richard."

"Actually, Wagner's *middle* name was Richard. His first name was Wilhelm."

"Oh," said Captain Wilhelm Wagner, now understanding. Except . . . he didn't quite. "With respect," he said as they continued down a gradually darkening corridor, "I am still a bit confused. I mean . . . *Parsifal*? The opera about the legendary Grail Knight? Am I being put in charge of the Holy Grail?" He was unable to keep the amusement at the very notion out of his voice.

To his amazement, Bormann stopped, turned, looked him straight in the eye, and said, "Something like that."

Directly in front of them was a huge vault door. Nothing short of a Howitzer could have penetrated, and perhaps not even that. Bormann stepped in front of it and worked the series of combination locks upon it. There were three, and despite the continued sounds of explosions overhead, Bormann never once appeared hurried or concerned.

The last tumbler clicking into place, Bormann stepped back and pulled the door wide open. There was nothing but darkness within, at least insofar as Wagner could see. But Bormann reached in with confidence and withdrew a large black canister. It was buckled in several places along the side.

"You should at least see what it is you are being entrusted with," said Bormann.

He knelt next to the canister and undid the fastenings. Then he carefully opened it, and Wagner found himself staring down at what appeared to be some sort of spear.

"I do not—?" He looked questioningly at Bormann.

"This," said Bormann, "is the Spear of Destiny." He looked up at Wagner, waiting for some sort of reaction. Wagner just stared at him and shrugged slightly. "The Spear of Destiny," repeated Bormann. "The Holy Lance. The Spear of Longinus. Spear Luin, as the Irish call it. Does any of that mean anything to you?"

"Should it, Herr Bormann?" he asked politely.

Bormann chuckled slightly. It was an odd sound, coming from this man. "I suppose not necessarily. When one is with the Fuhrer as much as I, and hears about such relics as often as I have, one just tends to assume that everyone knows about them. The Spear of Destiny, Captain Wagner, is the Spear wielded by the Roman soldier Gaius Cassius Longinus . . . that was used to pierce the side of the body of Christ."

"You mean . . . Christ on the cross?"

"Where else would he be?" Bormann asked sarcastically.

Wagner looked at the Spear with shocked reverence. The concept that he was beholding, with his own eyes, an artifact traceable to the savior himself . . . it was almost too much for him to contemplate.

"The Fuhrer," Bormann continued, "has intense fascination with such objects. He has gathered as many as he can. He considers this Longinus Spear to be the crowning glory of his collection."

"Does it . . ." Wagner wasn't quite sure what to say. "Does it . . . possess any particular . . . you know . . . properties?"

"Properties?"

"It is said . . ." Self-consciously Wagner lowered his voice, even though there was no one around to hear it. "It is said that the Fuhrer seeks power through these . . . these items. And I was wondering . . . if I am not overstepping myself . . . ?"

"What sort of power this Spear has?" He shrugged. "Frankly, Captain, the only power I know of that this Spear possesses is the power to convince others that it has true power. Other than that, aside from its value as an antique, it has nothing to recommend it other than the power generated by one's belief in it. Since I have no such beliefs, it has no power over me. You are, naturally, invited to draw your own conclusions."

"Am I correct in assuming, Herr Bormann, that you are not showing me this artifact simply because you thought I would be interested in its historic value."

"A safe assumption, Captain." Bormann proceeded to put the Spear back into its case. "You know of the Russians' progress. There is every likelihood that they will make it down to here, the heart of the bunker. Should that occur, they would doubtless take whatever is in it . . . and that would include the Spear. The Fuhrer absolutely does not want possession of the Spear to leave the hands of the Reich."

"I am sure he does not . . ."

"You don't understand, Captain," Bormann said, snapping closed the case. "He is convinced that to lose possession of the Spear is tantamount to a death sentence. At least, that is what the superstition dictates. Whosoever has the Spear, if they lose it or it is taken from them, is doomed. At least so the Fuhrer believes, and neither you nor I am in a position to convince him otherwise." He stood and handed the case to Wagner. "You were born and raised in this section of Berlin, yes? You are familiar with it?"

"There is no back road, no alleyway, no path that is unknown to me, even with the city as devastated as it is," said Wagner proudly.

"Good. Then it will be your job to avoid all invading troops, and take this to—"

"It doesn't matter."

The voice that echoed through the corridor was completely new to them, and Wagner's Luger was instantly in his hand. *"Who goes there!"* he shouted into the darkness.

For a moment, nothing stirred. And then, seemingly from the very shadows themselves, something or someone separated from them and presented itself. It was a man, or at least bore the general shape of one. He was cloaked and hooded, making it impossible to see any specifics of his face or build.

He was, however, clearly holding something. There was a spear in his right hand. Even in the darkness, Wagner could see that it was an exact duplicate of the Spear of Destiny.

"Lower your weapon immediately," said the man in the darkness.

Wagner had no intention of doing so. There was only one reason that he had not discharged his weapon instantly, and that was because—in the interest of security—he wanted the answer to his next question. "How did you get down here?"

"I got down here because down here is where I desired to be. Now put your weapon down."

"That is no answer!"

"It's all the answer I intend to provide."

"Shoot him!" shouted Bormann, thoroughly unnerved.

As far as Wagner was concerned, that was the end of the

discussion. Taking deadly aim, his finger began to squeeze tightly on the trigger.

But when the gun fired, it jerked wide of its target. That was because a knife had come slicing through the air, thrown so quickly by the shadow man that Wagner had never even seen his hand move. All he knew was that one moment he was taking aim, and the next a knife had buried itself in his shoulder up to the hilt. Wagner cried out, staggering, and dropped his gun. He tried to reach up and pull the knife from its new sheath in his body, but before he could, the shadow man was right in front of him, and he delivered a fierce punch right to the knife handle. This caused such a shock wave of pain through his body that he collapsed, crying out and feeling weak and unmanned because of it.

"Here is what is going to happen," said the shadow man. It was difficult to get a read on his voice. He was speaking perfectly accented German, but Wagner suspected it was not his native tongue. It was impossible to determine, though, just what his nationality might be. Then again, with blood welling up from the brutal wound in his shoulder, Wagner wasn't exactly at his best at the moment. "You," continued the shadow man, pointing at Bormann, "are going to switch the spear I am holding for that one. I will then depart, and you will leave the fake spear to be found right here in the bunker. I assure you, this replacement is so close that it will take them years to discover this one is a fraud, if they ever do."

"And you will return the Spear of Destiny to us?" Bormann asked carefully, still not sure what he was dealing with.

"What? Oh . . . no. No, that won't be happening. I will be taking it to its true . . . destiny, if you will. Or even if you won't, as the case may be. Now step back from the case."

Wagner tried to get to his feet, but the pain was overwhelming. Bormann backed up slowly. It was curious that the intruder had not told Bormann to keep his hands raised.

It was as if he didn't consider Bormann a threat and didn't care what Bormann did.

The shadow man opened the case and withdrew the Spear of Destiny.

"That," Bormann said coldly, "is the property of the Third Reich."

"Believe me," replied the shadow man, "the Third Reich's losing the Spear is going to be the least of your problems. Unless, of course, you believe that losing the Spear is the final nail in the coffin of the Third Reich, but I leave that to others."

"Put it down."

"You have no right to it."

"I said," Bormann warned him, "put it down!"

He reached into his coat with the clear intention of pulling a gun. It was a foolish move, prompted more by loyalty to his Fuhrer and to the Reich than anything remotely approaching common sense. The shadow man, however, did not hesitate. He swung the Spear of Destiny around and jammed it right through Martin Bormann's chest. It went in at an angle, slammed through, and came out his back, pointing toward the ceiling.

Bormann let out a terrified scream as the shadow man lifted Bormann off his feet as if he weighed nothing. The Spear didn't bend in the slightest.

"You wanted to know if the Spear bore any special properties," said the shadow man in a shockingly casual manner to Wagner. "This should answer that."

Wagner started to lunge for his fallen gun, but then he stopped, paralyzed with horror, as he watched Bormann's skin begin to blacken and crisp, as if he were being incinerated from the inside out. There was no heat, no stench of burning flesh, a smell with which Wagner had become all too familiar in the past years. Bormann was roasting from a fire that was not of this Earth.

The screaming had stopped almost immediately; perhaps Bormann's vocal cords were the first things to go. All Wagner knew was that, within seconds, Bormann's flesh was completely gone. All that was left were the tattered remains of his skeleton, held together by a few stray bits of flesh, muscle, and sinew that had miraculously avoided the fate of the rest of the body.

The shadow man casually angled the Spear downward and the remains of Martin Bormann slid off and onto the floor. He turned and looked toward Wagner, who still couldn't make out any details of his face.

"Do you wish to share his fate?" asked the shadow man very quietly.

Wagner knew this was to be one of the defining moments of his life. His reaction in the face of such otherworldly danger would be the measure of the kind of man he was. He knew he wanted to spit out defiance, to tell this . . . this creature . . . to go to hell.

Instead the words that came out of his mouth were, "No. No . . . I don't."

"You are wise beyond your years, Captain," the shadow man told him. He sounded slightly amused. "A pity that you allied yourself with a losing cause. You could have accomplished far more with the winning side. Then again . . . none of us chooses our destiny, I suppose."

He had, by that point, inserted the fake spear into the container and snapped it shut. Then he gently tossed it over to Wagner so that it landed near him. "Farewell."

"Who are you?" demanded Wagner.

The shadow man laughed. "An admirer," he said. "An admirer of ancient artifacts. One who knows the way of things. I have been looking for this weapon for quite some time, and once I found it, I merely awaited the right moment to come and claim it. That moment is now. And now . . . the moment is passed. Again . . . farewell."

He began to step back toward the shadows that had spat him out, and Wagner—trying not to moan from the blood loss—clutched at his shoulder, his hand already red with blood, and said, "But . . . what are you going to use it for?"

"Well," said the shadow man, "I was thinking about perhaps destroying the world. We'll have to see how that works out, though."

With that, he stepped backwards in the shadows, bowing once again as he did so, and vanished.

CHAPTRE
THE SEVENTH

✝

CARDINAL FRANCIS PATRICK Ruehl had never liked Arthur Penn. Not when he was president and certainly not now.

As far as Ruehl was concerned, Arthur's entire approach to politics was to act as if he was completely different from all other politicians. In Ruehl's experience, those who made the greatest point of emphasizing how different they were from all the other guys were the ones who were the most alike all the other guys. Thus, in his estimation, Arthur was very likely a massive hypocrite. Since Ruehl despised hypocrites, it meant he cared little for Arthur Penn or the way he had gone about doing his job.

Granted, his likes and dislikes were not of tremendous importance. His job wasn't to decide whom to like. It was to perform the wishes of His Holiness, the Pope. And in this case, those wishes could not be clearer:

Bring the Holy Grail home.

Ruehl was prepared for a fight. That was normal, though. Ruehl was always prepared for a fight.

Of all the cardinals who operated out of the Vatican, Ruehl had a nose that held the record for most times broken. Ruehl was a scrapper, by both nurture and nature. This stemmed from his formative years growing up in some of the rougher sections of Brooklyn. He'd gotten into a lot of street fights and taken any number of poundings although he prided himself on giving as good as he got. Sometimes he didn't like to think about where he would have wound up if his parish priest hadn't intervened and guided him down the proper path to salvation. Then again, sometimes . . . he did like to think about where he would have wound up. Certainly, whether he'd lived or died, either way it would have been simpler than the life he now led.

Ruehl had a big, open face, with a lantern jaw that was perpetually thrust outward as if daring someone to take a swing at it. His hair was red to match his occasionally fiery disposition, and his eyes were dark and displayed piercing intelligence. Ruehl, for all that he believed in tolerance, did not suffer fools gladly, as any number of fools who had crossed him had discovered to their dismay.

He was feeling both jet-lagged and a bit cranky as the limousine angled up the main driveway of the White House. This was certainly not his first time visiting the seat of American executive power. He'd been meeting with American presidents regularly, in various capacities, for the last twenty-five years. They didn't intimidate him. Why should he be intimidated? Whatever power they wielded, it stemmed from responsibilities ascribed them by mere voters and citizens. The man whom Cardinal Ruehl represented answered—as the old commercial went—to a much higher authority. This enabled him to look at those whom he encountered, no matter how powerful they were, with a certain degree of superiority. He knew that this wasn't a charitable way to view the world. That he was even self-aggrandizing when by rights he should be self-effacing. Nevertheless, he was who he was, and he'd been around too long to start changing.

He knew that the White House was designed to intimidate visitors and remind them where the true seat of power was. But since Cardinal Ruehl knew where the true seat of power was in the grand scheme of things, naturally that did not work on him.

"We're here, your Eminence," said the driver, as the limo slowed.

"I can see that," replied Cardinal Ruehl, peering out the window. "You can keep the engine running if you want. This shouldn't take long."

T HE MAN SIMPLY doesn't like me," Arthur said in irritation as Gwen straightened his necktie. "He doesn't like me, and neither does the Pope."

"The Pope loves everyone. It's in his job description somewhere."

Arthur chuckled at that. Then he frowned. "Why is he coming here again?"

"Arthur, why do you think?" She stepped back, checking her handiwork and nodding approvingly. "You've gone public with the Holy Grail. Do you seriously think that's not going to set off a few bells at the Vatican?"

"I suppose." He paused a moment, then said, "What do you think I should say?"

"About what?"

"When he wants to take it."

She sighed. "Do you think that's what he's coming here for?"

"Of course. Don't you?"

"It's entirely possible," she admitted. "What are you going to tell him if he does?"

"I could swear I just asked you that question."

"You don't need to ask me what to say to people. I'm sure you have your own thoughts on the matter."

"Yes, well," and he straightened the lapels of his dark blue jacket. There was amusement in his eyes. "I was probably going to tell him to sod off."

"You can't do that, Arthur." She pointed around them at the Lincoln Bedroom. "In case you've forgotten, we're guests here. You're no longer in residence. The last thing we need to do is cause Terrance problems by you bitch-slapping Cardinal Ruehl around."

"Any man with a name like that deserves a little slapping, don't you think?"

"No, I really don't. And the press is going to be there as well, so for God's sake, don't you think a little decorum would be appropriate?"

"All right," Arthur said reluctantly. "But just a little."

THE MEETING WAS scheduled to be held in the Mural Room, and a selection of the press corps was already set up there. It was Arthur and Stockwell's mutual decision that the interview with Ruehl should not be held in the Oval Office. To all intents and purposes, Arthur was acting as a private citizen, even though he was a guest in the White House. Stockwell didn't want to give anyone the impression that the things he had been saying, or the claims he'd been making, were in any way endorsed by the office of the president.

Indeed, Stockwell had been walking one hell of a tightrope ever since Arthur's return and various announcements. The natural question that was being posed to him was, "Do you believe that Arthur Penn is truly King Arthur? Are you supporting his claim that Gwendolyne Penn was cured by the Holy Grail?" Mahoney had dodged the question for as long as he was able to—which wasn't all that long—until finally Stockwell came out himself and said, in as straightforward a manner as he could, "I believe that former President Penn believes it, I have tremendous respect for him, and I have no intention of disputing him in this matter." Which was, of course, a long and roundabout way of saying, "I don't want any part of this."

Consequently, when the call came from the Vatican, Ron Cordoba made damned sure that the president's schedule required him to be the hell out of Washington, DC, when the Cardinal made his appearance. As far as Cordoba was concerned there was no advantage, none, to Stockwell's being there. Later, when the public meeting between Arthur and the Cardinal came completely unraveled, Ron's decision would be seen as uncannily prescient, instead of what it was: familiarity with Arthur's ability, through his imperiousness and annoying tendency to say exactly what was on his mind, to take any potentially incendiary situation and transform it into a full-blown incident. Ron's respect for Arthur as a man—and for that matter, as a king, accustomed to everyone doing exactly what he said when he said it—was second to none. But he was all too aware of Arthur's limitations. The very attributes that made him a great king served, in Ron's opinion, to make him a problematic president.

If the United States had been at peace, God only knew what sort of difficulties Arthur would have had. But because America was under a state of siege, the people and Congress had rallied around him, a state of affairs that was ideally suited to one of Arthur's peculiar talents. And although Ron would never, in a million years, have wished Gwen's trauma upon her, part of him thought that—in the final analysis— Arthur's departure from power couldn't have come in a more timely fashion. Except he felt so guilty feeling that way that it had been partly what motivated him to accompany Arthur on his insane, albeit ultimately successful, quest to revive the fallen first lady.

But Ron knew Arthur, and he also knew Cardinal Ruehl—
a pugnacious individual with a stubborn streak almost as
wide as Arthur's. Initially Ron had wanted the meeting
between the two to be in private, but the Cardinal stated
that the Pope wanted all communication between his envoy
and the United States to be open and aboveboard. Arthur
had made similar sentiments known, leaving Ron no wiggle
room. He likened the entire upcoming encounter to walking a tightrope smeared with butter, with broken glass as a
safety net. He was going to do his damnedest to prevent
things from getting out of hand by being present to ride
herd. If he failed, then it was merely the chief of staff screwing up. His place in the affair would be forgotten in short
order. But if the president were present, his "failure" would
be a part of the story, whatever the story was and however
long it perpetuated. It would make him look weak, and that
was exactly what Cordoba wanted to prevent.

So it was that that day in the Mural Room, the president
was off inspecting some well-timed tornado damage in Wis-
consin when Arthur Penn sat down in a chair opposite Cardinal Ruehl. Gwen was seated next to him, and Ron was
standing nearby. He was standing mainly because he felt that
it afforded him a slight position of power by being able to
look "down" at the two men who were eyeing each other
warily. They shook hands as cameras flashed. It reminded
Ron that the tradition of handshaking developed from a
time when it was the best means for two suspicious men to
make sure the other wasn't holding a weapon to stab him. It
underscored for Ron just the type of environment that had
forged Arthur. In the twenty-first century, it was simply a
traditional hand greeting. In Arthur's time, it was the potential difference between life and death.

"I have," Cardinal Ruehl said with his customary stiffness, "a message to read from His Holiness." He reached into
the folds of his robes, and it was at that moment that Ron

saw Percival standing off to the side. He hadn't even noticed the Grail Knight enter the room. It was amazing how quietly such a large and occasionally menacing-looking man could move. He had his White House security tag hanging around his neck, so the Secret Service hadn't challenged him. Ron had a feeling that that was a good thing: If the Secret Service tried to go up against Percival, there was every chance they would come up on the short end of the confrontation.

Ruehl placed a pair of reading glasses on the end of his nose and peered at the letter. "We extend greetings to former President Penn, and heartfelt congratulations over the recovery of his lovely wife. In this day and age of cynicism and skepticism, it is comforting to see an indisputable example of a miracle in our midst. The subsequent resuscitation of the gentleman of the press presented even further proof, for the many doubters and strayed among us, that the hand of our lord and savior, Jesus Christ, is present in our day-to-day lives. However," and Ruehl paused just a heartbeat, peering over the tops of his glasses before continuing, "although faith is a part of our everyday lives, and we accept the words of our savior as faith, we regret we cannot accept that pure faith to the words of mere men. We leave your claims of immortality and ancient pedigree to others to investigate. But we find your claim to be in the possession of the cup of Christ to be so monumental that we believe the full resources here at the Vatican must be brought to bear to explore it. There is, needless to say . . ."

"And yet he says it anyway," Arthur commented softly. Ron saw Gwen nudge him slightly.

". . . a great deal of interest from every quarter of not only the Catholic Church, but the whole of Christendom," continued Ruehl as if Arthur hadn't spoken. "Therefore, it is my request—" Again, Ruehl paused, and this time he lowered the paper and said with slow clarity, as if (to Ron's mind, at least) he was addressing a simpleton, "I wish to emphasize that the 'my' refers, not to me, but to His Holiness himself . . ."

"Yes," said Arthur with a tight, restrained smile. "Even a thousand years ago, we had a thorough grasp of pronouns."

This prompted a ripple of laughter from the assembled press. Ruehl's face, however, remained slightly pinched. He returned his gaze to the paper. "Therefore, it is my request that the reputed Holy Grail be transferred into the possession of my emissary, Cardinal Ruehl"—and he tapped himself unnecessarily on the chest—"to be transported immediately to Rome. There it will spend the next year being investigated and examined by a wide variety of experts, both theological and scientific. It will be subjected to a rigorous battery of tests to determine its authenticity. If, after that time, we have reason to believe that your claim is genuine, then we assume you would have no objection to the cup of Christ remaining on permanent display in the Vatican. After all, should it be the genuine cup that our savior drank from at the Last Supper, or that caught his blood when he was crucified, it would naturally be the single greatest find in the history of the Church, surpassing even—in my opinion—the Shroud of Turin or claimed pieces of the cross.

"Although naturally we cannot and would not endeavor to force you to accede to our request, please note that we judge you to be a good and fair man who would certainly agree that this presents the best course of action insofar as the reputed Grail would be concerned."

Cardinal Ruehl then carefully folded the missive and replaced it within his robes. Then he carefully interlaced his fingers, resting his hands upon his lap, and said, "May I have the cup, please."

In retrospect, Ron would conclude that it was the way he said it—as if the cup coming into his possession was a foregone conclusion and Arthur was simply a messenger of the Pope's will—that sent the train clattering calamitously off the rails. If the Cardinal had been deferential, or unassuming, or even (don't laugh) humble, there was a possibility that maybe, just maybe, things would have gone differently.

As it was, Arthur sat there for a long moment, one eyebrow raised, as if he were studying some new and intriguing bit of mold that had presented itself on a sandwich. Then, very calmly, he said, "The Grail is not mine to give."

"I beg your pardon?"

"I said," Arthur repeated, adopting the same tone that Ruehl had used earlier when clarifying who "me" was referring to, "it is not mine to give."

"I don't understand," said the Cardinal, his voice tinged with disdain. "You claim to be a king. If that is the case, then I'd think a king could do whatever he wanted to do."

"In theory. I, however, am a civilized king," replied Arthur, "and thus tend to recognize the rights of others."

"Mr. Penn," said Ruehl, looking as if he were fighting to keep his temper in check, "let us be . . ." He glanced uncomfortably at the cameras, clearly wishing that the reporters were not in the room recording every word that was being said. "Let us be candid here. It is in your best interests to cooperate."

"Is it now?"

"Yes. From my understanding, you are in dire need of all the friends you can acquire. The Senate is holding hearings into the specifics of your election, with the contention that if you are who you say you are, then your election to the presidency represents a massive fraud. Furthermore, I noticed when I arrived the gathering crowds in front of the White House. These are people who are making—there is no other word for it—pilgrimages. The sick, the dying, crawling out of their deathbeds and coming here in the vain hope of drinking from the Holy Grail and cheating death."

"Former President Penn is more than aware of that, as are we," Ron spoke up.

"What sort of cruelty, then, is it to these people that you are offering them false hope—"

"I'm not offering anyone anything," Arthur said a bit heatedly. "The Grail was obtained as part of a quest in which good men and women risked their lives in pursuit of a higher purpose. I did not seek to publicize either the Grail's existence or its restorative powers. These came about thanks to the fact that modern technology deprived us of our privacy. The fact that there are now people seeking the Grail's aid is not . . . unforeseen by me." He hesitated and looked slightly pained. "The problem is obvious. It was one thing to act quickly when that reporter was stricken. But if we begin a policy of treating some, then we must treat all. People must be discouraged from gathering outside the White House, because if they are not, they will come from all over the globe in a never-ending stream. Washington will shut down. And I will spend the rest of my life doing nothing else but ministering to the ill. Were I a saint, I suppose it might be an endeavor I would undertake. But I am not. And furthermore, there is a simple aspect that is being overlooked: The Grail is not mine."

"Not yours?" said the Cardinal. "I don't understand . . ."

"The statement is self-explanatory. The Grail is not mine. It is his." And he gestured toward Percival to come forward. Percival took several strides forward, looking as if he was gliding as he did so. "You may have read about him in literature. This is Percival. He is one of my knights."

Immediately flashes began going off as the reporters started snapping pictures. Percival winced against the barrage of lights but remained stoically silent. Several reporters were calling out asking to check the spelling of his name, since there was some confusion as to whether it was Percival, Parcival, or Parsifal.

"Gentleman!" Ron shouted above them, quieting them. "You are here with the understanding that you will pose no questions unless invited to by the participants. You are being allowed here because of the historic importance of this meeting. We will not have this degenerate into a free-for-all."

"This is ridiculous!" the Cardinal said, as if Ron hadn't spoken. "There were no black knights of the Round Table!"

"Oh, you're an expert in that field now, are you?" Arthur asked in amusement. "Have a good deal of first-person experience?"

The Cardinal sputtered a moment, then calmed himself by taking a deep breath and forcing a smile that looked like something a pit bull would display, presuming dogs could smile. "So not only are you King Arthur, but you have one of your knights of the Round Table with you as well. How . . . impressive. Very well. Should I address you as 'Sir Percival'?"

" 'Percival' will be fine," rumbled Percival. Ron could tell that the Grail Knight was deliberately pitching his voice lower to sound even more impressive. Inwardly he grinned at that. Percival had been around long enough to witness the slow, steady battle for equal rights that had been the legacy of blacks in America. So here he now was, in the White House, with everyone including an emissary from his Holiness waiting to hear what he had to say.

"Very well. Percival. Your . . . liege here . . . would that be right?"

This generated some more guffaws from the press until Percival said with complete sincerity, "That would be right." The seriousness with which he addressed the clearly sarcastic question of the Cardinal silenced all the laughers.

"Your liege has said the Grail does not belong to him. That it is, in fact, yours."

"Were Arthur to order me to present it to him, I would do so. But he would never do that. He has far too much respect for me."

"And I'm sure it's well earned," the Cardinal assured him. "But let's get down to it, then. Since the alleged Grail belongs to you . . . and presuming you heard the directive from His Holiness . . ."

"I heard it," Percival confirmed.

"Then you would certainly have developed your own answer, yes?"

"Yes."

"Excellent!"

"And the answer is no."

The Cardinal was out of his seat when Percival said it, and this time he made no effort to restrain himself. "How dare you!" snapped the Cardinal. "How dare you dismiss a request coming directly from His Holiness in such a disrespectful manner!"

"To be fair, your Eminence," Ron said quickly, trying in futility to stave off complete disaster, "I saw nothing disrespectful in Percival's tone."

"It isn't his tone! It's that he's saying 'no' at all! The Catholic Church—"

"I don't trust the Church, sir," Percival said quietly. "I have a few more years of existence than you. I am a Moor, sir, and I have witnessed firsthand the brutality that organized religion—particularly yours—can inflict upon people. I risked life and limb to obtain the vessel, and I see no reason to entrust it to a sanctimonious institution that has a history of inflicting torture and death upon innocent people."

The Cardinal was across the room, boiling mad, ignoring the TV cameras and the bevy of reporters, ignoring Ron's frustrated efforts to get him to sit back down and take a moment to calm himself. "I won't stand here and be libeled by you!"

"Slandered. Libeled is written," Percival said, his calmness seeming to grow in inverse proportion to the Cardinal's rising anger. "Moreover, it's neither if the statements in question are true."

"You're referring to matters of ancient history . . ."

"I know you have no offspring, Cardinal," Percival said

quietly. "Nevertheless, I'm sure you can comprehend how parents can look at their adult children and, to them, it's only yesterday that they were infants. Decades of time pass in a subjective eyeblink. It's much the same thing. The Crusades, the Spanish Inquisition, the Borgias, hundreds of other incidents big and small, many of which have been lost to the history books . . . they're like yesterday for me, Cardinal."

"You cannot possibly be insinuating that the positions taken by the Church or popes in those times remotely reflect the thinking of the Church now. And to focus only on the evils that can be laid at our door without taking into account any of the great things we've accomplished to benefit mankind . . ."

"I don't deny that your church has also done good works," Percival said diplomatically. "And the current Pope, whom I've never met, may be a perfectly decent agent of your God's works on Earth. But you're suggesting that I turn the Grail over to the Church permanently. I know what I'm talking about when I say that forever is a long, long time, and a lot can happen. If I am to accept the proposition that where the Church is now does not reflect where it once was . . . then certainly you have to admit that where the Church is now likewise does not necessarily reflect where its policies will be a hundred, two hundred years from now. And if those policies are less than beneficent, and you have the Grail in your possession . . . well, let's just say that I feel more comfortable with the Grail in my hands rather than yours in the long term."

One of the reporters could no longer contain himself. "How did you become immortal? Did you drink from the Grail too?"

There was an outside chance that Ron might still have managed to avoid complete chaos if he'd moved quickly enough to head off Percival's reply. But even as he tried to say, "We'd rather not go into that at this time," Percival spoke over him without hesitation: "Yes."

"It doesn't just cure you?" said another reporter, and a third called out, "It makes you live forever?"

"No!" shouted Ron.

"It can," said Percival.

At that moment, Ron would never have believed that matters could possibly get worse as he tried to slam shut the floodgates that had burst open because of Percival's flat admission. Everyone was talking at once, shouting out questions, and Ron was barking orders that the room was to be cleared while reporters were starting to push forward, each one bellowing questions one over the over.

Yet they did become worse, and that was because Cardinal Ruehl, raised in the rough streets of New York, was accustomed to making himself heard over the most raucous demonstrations. So despite all likelihood, when it seemed that all the voices were blending into one vast cacophony, Ruehl's voice managed to get above all of them as he bellowed, *"If that cup can do what you say it can do, it belongs by rights to the Church because it acquired its powers through the might of our lord, Jesus Christ!"*

To make matters even worse than that, it so happened that Percival was capable of being even louder than the Cardinal. *"Bullshit! Not only do its powers predate Christ, but it's entirely possible that he acquired whatever abilities he might have had by drinking from the cup!"*

At which point it was no longer necessary for anyone to shout. Both exchanges had been easily heard, and a deathly silence fell upon the room. All that kept going through Ron's head at that moment was *Thank God POTUS isn't here, thank God POTUS isn't here . . .*

"Are you telling me," the Cardinal said slowly, as if he were weighing the notion of declaring a sentence of death upon him, "not to mention the millions of Christians throughout the world . . . that our lord Jesus Christ—"

It was entirely possible that Percival might have said something else, something far more severe, except that Arthur himself interrupted Percival before he could continue. "He is not telling you anything," Arthur said. His jumping in prompted a glance from Percival, but the obedient knight instantly silenced himself in the face of his liege lord's taking back control of the situation. "He is simply suggesting possibilities. I will grant you that these are possibilities that the Church may find upsetting, even blasphemous, to contemplate. Then again, once upon a time, the Church found it similarly blasphemous to suggest that the sun did not revolve around the Earth. Those who have suggested notions unpopular to the Church have faced everything from excommunication to torture and death, and yet subsequent generations decided their claims had merit and were true. So perhaps, just for once, the Church might want to keep an open mind before trying to destroy someone with an unpopular opinion."

But the Cardinal wasn't buying it. "We are not speaking of a forward-thinking notion that was subsequently proven true via science. We are speaking of a concept that is core to our very faith. The divinity of Jesus Christ can, must, and does come from his divine father who art in heaven. You cannot possibly suggest otherwise."

"Were you there?" demanded Arthur.

"Of course not. That changes nothing."

"The only thing that remains unchanged is humanity's stubborn insistence on refusing to consider that which is beyond what is already accepted dogma." Arthur shook his head in disappointment. "What in the world does it take to get people to look beyond themselves? When are we going to reach a point as a species where 'What if?' are not the two most profane words that anyone can utter?"

Gwen, who had kept so quiet that some had practically forgotten she was there, put a hand on Arthur's arm. "He doesn't understand, Arthur. They'll never understand. And maybe it's better. The last thing you want to do is challenge the beliefs of—"

"Why not challenge beliefs?" Arthur replied. "How else will new beliefs ever develop if the old ones remain sacrosanct? How will people learn? Grow? How else will they learn to—"

"To what?" demanded the Cardinal. "Learn to leave their God behind? Learn to abandon their faith? And who are they supposed to turn to, sir. *You?* Is that what this is about? Are you trying to create a cult of Arthur?"

"All I was trying to do was live a quiet life," said Arthur. "Apparently that wasn't enough."

"So instead you return. How like a king."

"I cannot say I appreciate your attitude," Percival spoke up, and there was unmistakable menace in his voice. "Or your sarcasm."

"And I do not appreciate this . . . this theater! This farce!" The last bits of the Cardinal's more stately demeanor crumbled away as his street-warrior persona broke through the veneer of reserve. "This is just idiocy! Some sort of ridiculous game! A con! That's all it is. You people are trying some sort of con game, and you don't want us to have the alleged Grail because you know that you'll be found out and exposed as liars and hypocrites!"

Arthur, who had seated himself at Gwen's urging, exploded to his feet, standing with such fury and force that Percival—who'd been moving forward—stopped where he was. *"How* dare *you impugn my honor, sir!"*

"Well, then why don't you do something about it?" sneered the Cardinal. "Why don't you strike me down with Excalibur!"

Instantly Arthur's hand was at his side, and both Ron and Gwen shouted "No!" at the same time. It made no difference. Arthur gripped the invisible pommel of the sword that always hung, unseen, at his side. Enchanted by Merlin's magiks, it was never visible unless it was withdrawn from its scabbard. That was exactly what happened as Arthur pulled the sword free from its sheath. It made almost no rasping sound as the blade left its sheath, but when Arthur whipped the enchanted sword around, it hummed through the air with the sound of a thousand angry bees. The mighty sword glowed with power, and swung straight at the Cardinal as if it were hungry to plunge itself in to him.

The Cardinal let out a most undignified yelp, but didn't budge an inch. Instead he remained frozen as the blade came to a halt more than two feet short of him. Despite the fact that the sword never came near him, the menace was unmistakable.

Arthur, however, spoke with no trace of anger, as if wielding a lethal blade was the most routine thing in the world for him . . . which, Ron Cordoba knew, it very much was. "I would think that you, a man of prayer, would know the power of wishes . . . and that they should be used judiciously. Which is a roundabout way of saying that you should have a care what you wish for, lest you get it. Now . . . I believe that you have been given your answer. You will be departing this place without the Grail. You will, however, have a gift of far greater importance: Something brand-new to think about. My people and I have no intention of trying to diminish your god. On the other hand, we see no reason to lie about certain truths that we have in our possession, merely to spare your feelings or the feelings of your followers. If your beliefs are good and true, they will sustain you no matter what anyone says. If they are insufficient to sustain you, well . . ." and with one smooth move, Arthur reversed the sword and slid it back into its scabbard. As was always the case when the mighty blade was sheathed, the entire weapon hanging upon his hip disappeared. This action brought gasps from the assembled press corps, who were having a difficult time believing what they were seeing.

". . . that," continued Arthur, "is hardly my problem now, is it." Without waiting for the Cardinal to reply, Arthur looked at the reporters, said, "I believe this audience is now at an end. I will answer no questions, if for no other reason than that I believe they've already all been answered. Good day gentlemen, ladies."

As they exited the Mural Room, with Percival and Gwen directly behind him, the sound of the reporters shouting practically with one voice, throwing a blistering barrage of questions at Ron, filled the air. As a frantic Ron tried to sort through the chaos, Arthur said with remarkable cheer, "*That* went well, don't you think?"

"Do you think so, Highness?" Percival asked casually.

"You still have the Grail, don't you?"

"Yes."

"Well, that's your answer there then, isn't it."

As they made their way briskly down the hallway, Secret Service men in front and behind them, Gwen said, "Arthur, you don't seriously think that went well, do you? My God, you just dissed the entire Christian world!"

"I dissed no one. I simply said what I knew to be true . . ."

"You don't know it to be true!" Gwen protested, as they walked into the Lincoln Bedroom. "You think it to be true! But you don't know for sure. No one knows for sure!"

"It's true."

They stopped and stared in amazement. Merlin was seated in a chair at the far end of the room.

Seeing that an intruder had apparently materialized out of nowhere, despite the apparent youth of the person in question, the Secret Service quickly advanced on Merlin. "These boys must be new," Merlin said with a smirk, and he raised a hand.

"Merlin, no! Gentlemen, I know this lad. Back off, please."

They ceased heading toward Merlin, but one of them turned to Arthur, and said, "Sir, regulations clearly state—"

"What do regulations say about you being turned into squirrels?" Merlin asked innocently.

"That's enough, Merlin. On my authority, gentlemen, please."

The Secret Service men eyed Merlin suspiciously, then left the room without ever looking away from him . . . as if they expected him to pull a weapon out of his pocket at any time. The moment the door was closed, Arthur placed his hands on his hips, and said to Merlin, "I thought you were out of my life forever."

"And what gave you that idea?"

"Probably," said Gwen, "it was the way you said to him, 'I'm out of your life forever.'"

"Did I ask you? Did I?" Merlin nodded in acknowledgment toward Percival. "Evening, Percival."

"Hail and well met, Merlin Demonspawn."

"See?" said Merlin approvingly. "Some people still know how to greet a wizard."

"Yes, because the standard, 'Oh God, please don't transform us into jellyfish' lacks a certain charm," said Gwen.

Merlin fired her an annoyed look, but Arthur walked between the two of them and actually smiled down at the boy mage. "You give me more grief than any ten other men, but damn, it's still good to see you, Merlin. What brings you here?"

"I go where I wish and do as I wish. It's a privilege I've earned through time, learning, and sheer tenacity. I'm here because you, oh King, are going to need counsel. My counsel."

"Is Arthur in trouble?" Gwen said, and before Merlin could respond, she added in a slightly pleading tone, "Merlin . . . I know you've never been a big fan of mine. I mean, yes, there have been times when you've tolerated me more than other times . . . especially when I saved your life . . ." He made a face when she said that, not wishing to be reminded of it or even to acknowledge it if he could help it. "The point is, when all is said and done . . . we both care about Arthur, and both want the best for him. So please . . . tell us what's going on?"

For a long moment, Merlin was quiet. Then he shrugged, and simply said, "I've been paying attention to the news. I saw this conflict brewing. I knew there were going to be some problems. So I decided I'd best be served here instead of anywhere else. That's really all there is to it."

Arthur had never been more certain that Merlin was lying. But he had nothing upon which to base that other than vague suspicion, and so he simply extended a hand, and said, "It's good to have you back then, Merlin."

Merlin put out his own, much smaller hand, which seemed to disappear into Arthur's palm. "It's good to be back, Wart." Then, as if annoyed by the sentiment, he pulled his hand away and shoved it into his pocket. "And by the way, what I said before was true: I do know that the Grail predates the Christian savior. Of course, if you think I'm going to be stupid enough to step in front of an army of reporters and make such pronouncements, you can simply forget it. I'm a wizard. I'm all about subtleties. There's nothing remotely subtle about being part of a declaration that ends with the phrase, 'Film at eleven!' And frankly"—and he stabbed a finger at Arthur—"I think you were dumb as a post to share your opinion on this matter—valid or no—with the world at large. You have absolutely no idea of the firestorm you've unleashed."

"I've survived firestorms before, Merlin."

"Actually, you've been mortally wounded by them. I take it you have no overwhelming desire to go back to healing in a cave for a thousand years."

"Not especially, no."

"Then prepare yourself, Arthur. Because matters are going

to get far worse before they're going to get better . . . presuming they ever do."

"But why?" Arthur demanded, eyeing Merlin suspiciously. "I keep thinking there's something you're not telling me."

"Of course there are things I'm not telling you. The sheer volume of things I know that I don't tell you could sink an ocean liner. I'm doing you a favor, Wart. I'm declining to subject you to everything that I have to deal with. Now try being grateful for once."

Arthur nodded, but nevertheless his every instinct warned him there was more going on in this business then Merlin's standard contrariness. There were other forces at work, forces that Merlin clearly did not want to bring up. There was only one reason that he could truly discern for that: Merlin, like any wizard, was superstitious. He believed that the mere mention of certain things . . . especially powerful and deadly things . . . could engender bad luck and disaster, and hasten the arrival of whatever it was one was trying to stave off. So if there was something that Merlin was reluctant to discuss . . .

. . . it was because he was afraid of it.

CHAPTRE
THE EIGHTH

✝

ARTHUR COOPERATED FULLY with the Senate hearing investigating his claims, and naturally his cooperation only made it harder for them, not easier.

The problem was that the committee handling the investigation couldn't decide what side of the question they wanted to come down on. There was concern that, if they took his assertions and demonstrations at face value, they might come across like madmen to the many skeptics who still believed that Arthur was trying to have off the American people for some bizarre reason. There were definitely skeptics. It didn't matter how many times the "Excalibur footage" was aired. It didn't matter that many specialists—from film special effects experts to Las Vegas magicians—went over the footage of the vanishing sword practically molecule by molecule, and still couldn't come to any sort of consensus. Some maintained it was a hoax for no other reason than that they couldn't figure out how it had been "faked." They rejected the fundamental notion that it was genuine magic with a genuine relic and instead became obsessed with discovering how the entire procedure had been a sham.

In short, no one wanted to be the ramrod in investigating—with all seriousness and a straight face—the alleged scam perpetrated by Arthur, King of the Britons, upon the American voting public that had no idea it was electing a mythical ruler for its president.

On the other hand, if Arthur's claim was to be dismissed out of hand, then it begged the obvious question: What the hell were they investigating? If Arthur had simply lost his mind and was making demented claims, then certainly that wasn't the business of the United States Congress. Rather it was the personal business of his immediate family to seek out psychiatric help. Since Arthur was serving in no official capacity for the United States government, there was no basis upon which to investigate him further.

Nor did the aspect regarding Gwen's amazing recovery offer any guidance. Words such as "miraculous" and "inexplicable" were bandied about by an assortment of experts. But not a single one was prepared to state uncategorically that the only way Gwen could have recovered was through something as divine as the intervention of the fabled Holy Grail. The closest they came was the head of traumatic injuries at Washington General, who simply shrugged, and said, "Makes as much sense as anything else."

The result was that when it came to questioning both Arthur and Gwen, the committee was cautious to the point of complete ineffectiveness. They shied away from pressing Arthur on matters of his past and did not push for details when he explained about the "great quest" through which he—or more correctly, Percival—had come into the possession of the Grail. The press howled that details stemming from the investigation were sketchy at best, pathetic at worst. Editorial cartoonists had a field day, depicting such images as the committee lobbing actual powder puffs Arthur's way.

Percival was never called at all. The committee wanted no part of the notion of calling a large black man a liar and a madman.

Meanwhile the situation outside the White House began to spiral out of control, so much so that a furious President Stockwell was called in to meet with the joint chiefs in the Situation Room. Stockwell was already fuming as a result of the calamitous press conference with the Cardinal. He was hearing about it from every church head and every leader of every country in the world where the predominant religion was Christianity. As he took a seat at the head of the table in the Situation Room, he felt as if he had turned into a broken record. He had run out of different ways to say that he did not agree with Arthur's position, that he himself had absolute faith in the divinity of Jesus Christ, and that his own belief in the savior and God had never wavered in the slightest. Which was, of course, a gargantuan lie. Stockwell had lost count of the times when witnessing the evils that men were capable of perpetuating upon each other had led him to wonder how any sort of benevolent deity could allow such atrocities. His own faith was actually hanging by the thinnest of threads. But it was hardly the time for candor.

The reports he was getting from his people were hardly cheering news. It seemed to come at him from all sides, rapid-fire descriptions of impending doom.

"All major traffic arteries into DC are clogged . . ."

"No hotel or motel space to be had anywhere. People are camping out. Waste disposal is becoming a problem . . ."

"Massive security risks . . ."

"Flooding in through the airports . . ."

"People are walking along the Beltway to get to the White House . . ."

It wasn't as if they had to describe it to him: It was all right there, up on the screens. Footage taken from news feeds and satellite photos. With cars sitting piled up and unmoving, people were approaching on foot, threading their way through stopped cars like something out of a doomsday-themed movie. There was no longer a crowd outside the White House. It was an assemblage that made the Million-Man March look like an elementary school outing. The National Guard had been called in, and barricades had been set up of necessity, since some people had tried to clamber over the fence and nearly gotten themselves shot by the Secret Service for their trouble. Still, the Guard was outnumbered by a thousand to one, and if the crowd made a dedicated and determined push—if they became desperate enough or greedy enough or whatever—there was little doubt that they could overwhelm all security. At least, they could do so initially. But when they came stampeding across the White House lawn, they would be met with everything from sharp-shooters to machine-gun fire.

"We could have a bloodbath on the front lawn," Stockwell said tonelessly, scarcely able to believe what he was being faced with.

The Joint Chiefs nodded as one. "That is what it could come to, Mr. President—"

"The hell it will," Stockwell said. "I am not about to see photographs of the military mowing down United States citizens being circulated throughout the world. Gentlemen, there's an obvious answer to this. For as long as former President Penn is here, they're going to keep coming. But if he leaves, they leave."

"Where do we take him, sir?" asked one of the Joint Chiefs. "As you can see . . . his home is not an option."

Sure enough, one of the screens was showing the situation outside Arthur's home in Avalon. It was not dissimilar from what was going on in Washington: people trying to get there in anticipation of Arthur and Gwen's return so that they could seek their own miracles from the Holy Grail. The only saving grace was that there was just one major road leading to Arthur's seaside residence, and the military had already moved in and cut it off. No one was able to get within a mile of Arthur's home.

But it was impossible to determine just how long that situation would last as well. What if people got the bright idea to try and approach from the ocean? It was only a matter of time before navy vessels patrolling the waters would wind up shooting on, and sinking, desperate people.

"The terrible truth is simple, which is what makes it so terrible," Stockwell said as if talking to himself. "This country is filled with desperate people. People who feel they have absolutely nothing to lose. The prospect of going up against our own military personnel isn't going to deter them. Which means we're going to be asking soldiers—twenty-year-old kids—to open fire on soccer moms. I don't know which would be worse . . . if they carry out the order, or if they don't. In the end, this could blossom into the single largest incident of Americans killing Americans since the Civil War. And call me crazy, gentlemen . . . but unlike the president who oversaw that little showdown, I don't think I'm going to be having any monuments erected to me to honor my participation."

"So what are you saying, Mr. President?" asked the secretary of defense. "I mean, we can't just put President Penn back on his yacht and let him sail off to sea. Now that the world's eyes are on him, other sailing vessels will track him down. Potentially hostile vessels."

"Wasn't that a risk when he was sailing around with no Secret Service protection?"

"Yes, but an acceptable risk. As you know, we were

keeping tabs on him despite the public denials. There were regular flybys, monitoring devices hidden on the ship to keep tabs on its whereabouts. We all knew that Mrs. Penn had recovered, but we simply kept it quiet as an issue of national security."

"Is it possible that the photos came as a result of some sort of leak in our own security system?" Stockwell demanded, but before anyone could respond, he shook it off. "Forget that. It doesn't matter right now. We've plenty of time to check the open barn door to find out how the horse escaped. For now . . . you're right," he reluctantly admitted. "If the last thing we need is Americans firing on Americans in a riot situation, the second-to-last thing we need is a former president being taken prisoner by a hostile country . . . or, knowing him, pirates or something. He can't stay here. He can't go to his home. Camp David would just generate the same sorts of mob scenes." He drummed his fingers and stood. Everyone else naturally sprang to his or her feet. "Gentlemen, I don't care where we stash him at his point. Find someplace yourselves. Hell, ask him if you have to. But find a place."

"Mr. President . . ."

It had been Ron who had spoken up. He had remained silent for the entire meeting, probably because he knew that he had assumed a prominent place on Stockwell's shit list. Like an angry lizard, Stockwell turned and fixed an unblinking stare upon him. "Yes, Ron?"

"I believe . . . I know of a place that's secure."

"Really. And why haven't you mentioned it sooner?"

"Because," Cordoba admitted, "I wasn't entirely sure you'd believe me."

Slowly, Stockwell sat back down. Everyone else did as well. Stockwell, leaning forward, interlaced his fingers, and said, "Right now . . . you'd be amazed what I'd believe. Try me."

* * *

THE MOOD IN the Lincoln Bedroom was grim. Arthur, Gwen, and Percival watched CNN in silence as the scenes of growing insanity were portrayed in glorious and nauseating detail.

"Shut it off," Gwen said finally, lowering her gaze so she wouldn't have to look at it.

"To what end?" asked Percival. "If we turn off the set, we'll just hear the noise outside. It's a clear night; sound is carrying nicely."

"We have to get out of here," said Arthur. "That's all there is to it. We have to leave the building."

"Like Elvis."

"Yes, Gwen. Just like Elvis," Arthur agreed firmly, then cast an inquiring glance toward Percival. Percival shook his head slightly, and mouthed, *I'll explain later.*

There was a knock at the door and, moments later, a distinguished and affable-looking black man in his early fifties entered the room, pushing a rolling cart with several covered plates upon it, along with a bottle of wine and a carafe of water. "Good evening, Brady," Arthur said.

"Good evening, Mr. President," replied Brady. He had been one of the head stewards for as long as anyone could remember, reliable for his impeccable service and discretion. He went about setting up the food.

"Things getting a bit exciting outside, aren't they, Brady," asked Gwen.

"Yes, ma'am. They are."

Brady continued on about his business, and his surprisingly taciturn manner caught Arthur's attention.

"What's Merlin's feelings on all this?" asked Percival.

Gwen shrugged. "The great mentor and advisor has been locked in his room meditating."

"So Merlin shows up . . . and then vanishes?"

"Yup. Guess it's a wash."

*N*IMUE!"

Merlin was shouting into the full bathtub, and when he got no response, turned and bellowed into the sink that he'd also filled with water. For good measure he'd also filled up the bidet and a washing basin, plus naturally he also had the toilet to bear his wrath. "Nimue!" he kept calling, moving from one container of water to another to another. "Stop playing around! This is serious business! You can't just show up out of nowhere, drop a warning about the Spear, and vanish! If you care at all about Arthur or me, then you'll give me more information than—"

"Is . . . everything all right in here?"

He turned and saw a couple of Secret Service men standing in the doorway of the bathroom, looking around suspiciously. They hadn't drawn their weapons, but their hands were hovering in the general direction of the inside of their jackets.

"Why wouldn't everything be fine?" Merlin demanded. "Who the blazes are you?"

"Agents Castor," one of them indicated himself, and then the other, "and Pollux, sir."

"We heard you shouting," said Pollux. "We thought perhaps you weren't alone."

"Well, obviously, I am. That's the problem, isn't it?"

"Did you lose something?" The Secret Service men clearly weren't sure how to address Merlin. His size and apparent age certainly seemed to indicate the inevitable slight condescension adults normally use toward children. But there was nothing remotely childlike in Merlin's manner or deportment, underscoring the feeling of "wrongness" that people invariably got when interacting with him for any length of time.

"Not something. Someone." With a sigh of exasperation, Merlin said to them with the full knowledge that they wouldn't have the slightest notion of what he was talking about, "I'm trying to find the Lady of the Lake. But she's not showing herself."

"There's no lake in here, sir," said Castor.

"Yes, I know there's no lake here," Merlin said pityingly. "She can show up out of any body of water."

"Well then, sir, you might be better off checking the Potomac."

It was difficult for Merlin to tell whether the agent was yanking him around or not. "Not likely. She tends to prefer more stationary bodies of water rather than anything with a strong current."

The two agents exchanged a look. "The Reflecting Pool?" said Pollux.

"Just what I was thinking. The reflecting pool near the Washington Monument."

Merlin's mouth opened, then shut without saying anything at first. He stared at them for a moment more, then said, "My God . . . that's . . . a good idea. That's . . . extraordinarily good."

"Thank you," said Castor. "Unfortunately, we're in a state of lockdown at the moment. Under normal circumstances we could escort you there, but these are far from normal circumstances."

"Then again," Pollux suggested, "you could no doubt transport yourself there through . . . what?" He turned to the first Secret Service man. "A simple self-relocation spell?"

"That would do it, I'd think."

Merlin's incredulity was growing. "How did you become so familiar with sorcery?"

"Sir," Castor said stiffly, "you don't seriously think you're the first guest, or even resident, of this building who is conversant in the mystical arts, do you? Our experience with the occult is hardly limited to the occasional first lady's ouija board. We have to be ready for anything in our line of work."

"Gentlemen," Merlin said with complete sincerity, "I don't often say this but . . . I'm impressed."

"We're Secret Service, sir," said Pollux. "We're trained to be impressive."

CHAPTRE
THE NINTH

✦

WHAT I DON'T understand," said Percival, pouring a glass of wine for himself in the Lincoln Bedroom, "is that Merlin and I spoke about the Grail ages ago . . . and he claimed to know almost nothing about it. Now he purports to know all about it. Which is true?"

"Probably all of it . . . and none of it," said Gwen. "That's how wizards, or at least this wizard, acts most of the—"

"Brady." Arthur interrupted Gwen, which was unusual for him since generally his conduct when it came to his wife was the height of courtesy. At this point he simply wasn't listening to what she had been saying, since his attention had been focused elsewhere. Brady had been involved in setting out the food that he'd brought in, doing so briskly and efficiently as was his wont. But Arthur, even though he was seated across the room, had perceived that something was out of kilter in the man's demeanor, and now he was on his feet and crossing the room. His actions naturally captured Percival's and Gwen's complete attention. "Brady . . . is something wrong?"

Brady, normally the most convivial of gentlemen, clearly could not bring himself to look directly at Arthur. "Nothing's wrong, Mr. President . . ."

"With all respect, Brady . . . I think you're not being entirely candid with me."

"I just . . ." With an effort, he turned and looked at Arthur. "I . . . don't think it would be appropriate for me to—"

"Devil take propriety. You're a good man, Brady. You've done nothing except live an exemplary life of service to this nation's leaders." He squared his shoulders. "If you're upset with me about something, or want to tell me that you think I'm mad as a hatter, you should not feel any reticence to—"

"Upset?" Brady looked at him in confusion, and then flashed a small smile at the notion. "Mr. President, I have . . . as you say . . . served quite a number of our leaders. And I'm not trying to blow smoke up your skirt when I say that, of all of them, you are the single most decent man I've ever encountered. The most scrupulously honest, the most . . ."

Abruptly emotion overwhelmed him. It was as if the strength went out of his legs, and Brady was suddenly sitting before he even realized that he was going to be doing so. It was only through Arthur's quick movement to slide a chair under him that prevented him from sinking to the floor. "Brady," he said softly, "what's really happening here?"

"It's not appropriate for me to discuss it with—"

"Brady, I'm ordering you to tell me. Not that I'm entirely sure my orders carry any weight, but still . . ."

Brady shook his head, and now Gwen came forward and crouched so that she was at his eye level. "Brady," she said, one hand resting upon his shoulder, "Arthur's just trying to help. And he wouldn't be asking you if he didn't want to know."

"It's just . . . ma'am, in all the years I've been doing this job, I have never—ever—asked anyone for a single favor.

And I've been in the presence of a lot of powerful men who could have granted a lot of powerful favors. So I don't see that it's right for me to start now . . ."

"The Grail," Percival spoke up tonelessly. "This has to do with the Grail."

Brady nodded without responding.

"Brady . . ." Arthur prompted him.

At first, Brady didn't reply. But then, before Arthur could speak again, Brady said with an unmistakable tone of bitterness, "I'm a religious man, sir. Go to church every Sunday. Pray to our Lord. Ask for nothing except His love. Tried the best I could to conduct myself in His teachings, as He would want. Can't say that I lived a totally blameless life. What man has? I've tripped up here and there, but still, I think the scales tip more in my favor than against when it's all tallied up. I've tried to obey all the commandments." His voice trailed off, but no one in the room urged him to speak, certain that he would continue on his own. They were right. "My wife is dying, Mr. President. Stomach cancer, eating her from the inside out. My Linda is the sweetest woman in the world . . ."

"I remember her. I met her once."

". . . and she's never done anything to deserve anything like this. She keeps saying that God tosses you only as much as he thinks you're capable of dealing with. She says there's some sort of grand plan to all this. But I'm thinking that if this is a plan, then it's a damned bad one. You know the commandment about worshipping no other gods . . . ?"

"Of course," said Arthur.

Brady looked up at him with quiet passion reflected in his face. "I would be willing to throw aside that commandment. I would be willing to worship you, Mr. President, and throw all my prayers and supplications to you, and sing you hosannas and praise you in the highest. Because in the past six months I've been doing that with the God I've been worshipping all my life . . . and I'm tired of his answer to my prayers being 'no.' I need to worship someone who gives a damn, and I think that's you, not Him."

"I'm not looking for worship, Brady."

"That may be, Mr. President. But I'm looking for a miracle. And I wasn't going to ask you, and swore to myself over and over again that I wouldn't. Guess I don't have the world's best poker face," he added ruefully.

There was silence for a moment, then Arthur said, "Percival."

"Yes, Highness?"

"Do you have the Grail?"

"Of course, Highness." Percival produced the Holy Grail seemingly out of thin air. Arthur wasn't sure just how Percival managed to do that, and he wasn't entirely certain he wanted to know.

Brady's eyes widened when he saw it. "Is . . . is that . . . ?"

"It is. Where is your wife?"

"She's at Johns Hopkins in Baltimore . . ."

"Then that is where we're going."

"Arthur," Gwen said nervously, "the White House is locked down. They may not be willing to just let us head off to Maryland."

"Then we'll find a way," Arthur told her. "Come." With the utter confidence that stemmed from being a warrior king, Arthur headed toward the door. But before he made it halfway across the room, the door opened abruptly to reveal Ron Cordoba and several Federal agents.

"Ah! Ron! Excellent timing," said Arthur briskly. "We have a situation—"

"Yes, sir, I know."

"We need to get to Johns Hopkins . . ."

He was astounded when Ron shook his head and realized that there had never been an occasion when Ron Cordoba refused him anything. "That's not going to happen, sir. We have to get you out of the White House, and we have to do it in a highly visible manner."

"I know that. I'm not blind, Ron. Circumstances outside have become untenable, and if I don't get out of the capital soon, things are going to go very badly. But first thing's first. Brady's wife—"

"I know the condition of his wife, sir . . . Brady, again, my condolences," said Ron, and Brady nodded in acknowledgment. "But right now, the only thing that matters is getting you to a secure location."

"Where?" demanded Percival.

"The only place that's not connected with the US government, but that we can be certain no one will be able to find you."

Gwen looked blank, but Arthur understood immediately. "Of course," he said, and when Gwen turned to him in bewilderment, he simply said, "The castle."

"Of course," she echoed him.

Percival was still confused. "Castle . . . ?"

"Later, Percival. Trust me: Later. Ron . . . there will be plenty of time for that. But first . . ."

"Sir," Ron said sharply, "you don't understand. There is no 'first.' There's no bargaining. There are no side trips to anywhere except to your destination. That's all there is to it."

Arthur's eyes narrowed, and a sense of danger crackled in the air. "You . . . are dictating terms . . . to *me*?"

"Sir . . ."

"*To me?* How dare you . . . !"

"*Arthur! What do you think you're going to do, huh? Draw Excalibur and cut your way out of here? Kill them? Kill me?*"

No one moved. Arthur glared at Ron with such fury that Gwen wasn't sure whether her husband might indeed yank out his invincible sword and bisect his former chief of staff.

Ron spoke first, visibly fighting to restrain himself.

"Arthur . . . there's no choice here. None. This order is coming straight from President Stockwell. He wants you out immediately."

"If it came straight from him, then I will go straight to him and convince him otherwise."

"He doesn't want to see you."

"Unfortunately, the feeling is not mutual. Take me to him immediately, or I'll find him myself."

"How do you plan to do that? Hack your way into the Oval Office? Do you want to be the first US president who was shot down by his own Secret Service agents?"

Arthur was about to respond when a gentle hand rested upon his forearm. He turned and saw tragedy in Brady's eyes. "Mr. President," Brady said, and his voice was quavering, but there was firmness in it yet. "Mr. President . . . I . . . I can't let this happen. Because there's people out there"—and he pointed in the general direction of the crowds outside the White House—"who are just as deserving as Linda. Maybe . . . I don't know . . . maybe even more so. It's not right for me to play upon your sympathy . . ."

"You played upon nothing, Brady."

"Yes, I did, Mr. President, even if you're too much of a gentleman to admit it. I should never have said anything. I shouldn't have put you in this . . . this impossible position. The bottom line, sir, is . . . I'm an American. And my commander-in-chief has given an order that Mr. Cordoba and these agents are trying to carry out. If I'm responsible in any way for them not doing that . . . I just . . . I can't allow that to happen."

"Not even to save your wife? You don't think she'd want that?"

"With the greatest of respect, sir . . . was your wife happy that you resigned your office because of her?"

Arthur and Gwen exchanged a long look. They both knew the answer, recalling when she had faced him after coming

out of her coma and chewed him out for making such sacri-
fices on her behalf.

"Arthur," Ron began imploringly.

But Arthur put up a hand, and simply said, "Ron . . .
would you give us a minute, please."

Cordoba hesitated, but then said, "Of course, sir." He
gestured to the Federal agents, and they backed out of the
room, closing the door behind them.

Gwen wasn't sure what she was expecting . . . some kind
words from Arthur to Brady, perhaps. Some comments of
encouragement.

Instead, Arthur moved as if galvanized into action. "Percival, the Grail. Now."

Without question, Percival handed it to him, but there
was clearly concern on his face. Gwen knew exactly what was
going through his mind: He was wondering if Arthur was
planning to hand the Grail over to Brady. Percival was far
too dedicated a knight to offer protest if that was Arthur's
decision, but it was obvious to Gwen that such a move on
Arthur's part would be crushing to Percival's spirit. He had
vested far too much of himself into the Grail. If it left his
possession once more after he had finally reacquired it,
Gwen didn't doubt that—despite his immortality—he
might well fade away and die.

Arthur apparently knew what Percival was thinking as
well. "Trust me, Percival," he said with a brief smile.

"As ever, Highness."

Arthur crossed quickly to the table that Brady had rolled
in. He took the bottle of wine, headed over to the sink, and
upended it, draining the contents. Then, setting the bottle
down, he picked up the decanter of water with his left hand
and held it over the goblet. "I have absolutely no idea if this is
going to work," he said. "But I figure a slight chance is better
than no chance at all." Slowly he poured the water into the

Holy Grail, filling it nearly to the brim. Then he looked at Gwen and tilted his head in the direction of the wine bottle.

She understood and started to move toward it, but Brady was faster. He picked up the Grail and, ever so carefully, reverently, he expertly transferred the contents from the Grail into the wine bottle. For good measure, Arthur repeated the procedure twice more, and Brady twice more poured it over until the wine bottle was nearly full. Then Arthur put the water decanter down, picked up the cork to the wine bottle, and handed it over to Brady. Brady shoved the cork back into the bottle as best he could.

"I wish I could do more for you, Brady . . . give you more . . ."

"You've given me hope, Mr. President. That's all I can ask."

"All right, then. Guard that with your life. And you have to swear to me that you will not drink from it yourself. At least not while you're in good health."

"I swear, sir."

"Because we're dealing with strange powers. Powers that are far beyond our understanding. They are not to be meddled with lightly."

"Yes, sir. I won't drink from it, I swear. I would never in any event. Because if drinking a portion of this somehow cures my Linda . . . I'll want to make sure to keep some of it around in case there's some sort of relapse."

"I believe you, Brady." He gripped him firmly by the shoulder. "Don't be too much in a hurry to leave. Don't act as if you have some sort of contraband in the wine bottle. Remember, you are doing nothing dishonest. Godspeed to you, then."

Then he turned and handed the Grail back to Percival. Gwen noticed that Percival made a little, relieved sigh as he took it from his king and tucked it back into his coat.

Arthur straightened his jacket and said, "Percival . . . Gwen . . . I believe it's time to go."

"What about Merlin?" asked Gwen.

"We'll pick him up from his room before we leave. Whatever meditating he's doing will simply have to wait."

But Merlin was not in his room, nor any of the rooms nearby. This caused a certain degree of consternation among the Secret Service, who were obviously not sanguine about the notion of the strange young boy with the mysterious relationship to Arthur just casually wandering around the White House somewhere. But with minutes ticking by, it was finally decided that Merlin could always be removed at a later date. Right now the main thing was to get Arthur out of there, and as conspicuously as possible.

So it was that the thousands of people gathered outside the White House, waiting for their shot at a miracle . . . waiting for an appearance by their latest savior . . . were surprised to see a large helicopter, a Sikorsky VH 3D, lifting off from within the White House grounds. It stayed relatively low as it glided forward, and as it hovered above the crowd, the powerful beating of its propellers caused all manner of shouting and confusion below. Hats blew away, people struggled to keep their coats wrapped around themselves against the brisk night air, and errant newspapers and discarded trash swirled about.

Then the side door of the Sikorsky slid open and a cry went up as Arthur Penn appeared in the opening. It was easy to tell it was he, because the army personnel who were keeping the people back had sweeping searchlights swinging through the night sky, and one of them was trained on the copter. This hadn't occurred by happenstance. The men on the ground had been informed of what they were to do because the people in the White House wanted to make damned sure the people on the ground knew that Arthur was aboard the chopper.

He was locked into place via tethers, and he addressed the crowd through a loudspeaker.

"My friends . . . as you can see," he called down, "I am departing the confines of the White House! Therefore, I am now asking you to return to your homes! No good will come from your extending your stay here! Someone will get hurt, and I would not wish that for all the world!"

The crowd was not uniform in its response. There were some who waved signs that said, ANTICHRIST! and CHRISTIAN HATER! and BURN IN CAMELOT! plus more that were even more emphatic in their condemnation of him. He supposed he couldn't blame them. He had openly challenged their core beliefs. After the mess of a press conference, he had told Gwen that he had simply been asking questions, nothing more. To which Gwen had replied that maybe there were some questions that shouldn't be asked, ever . . . because not only could they not be answered, but people didn't want to know the answers in the first place. He had thought at the time she'd been wrongheaded in her thinking, but now he wasn't so sure.

Nevertheless, interestingly enough, the supplicants vastly outweighed the Arthur-haters in the crowd. Their voices quickly overwhelmed those who were shouting abuse, and some of them even knocked the protesting signs out of the hands of the critics.

And those people shouted up at him. "Save us!" they cried out. "Help us!" "Cure us!" Children were thrust into the air, clutched in the hands of their desperate parents. Arthur looked down and saw them all, with all manner of defects ranging from a baby with no eyes to a toddler with horrific burns upon his body.

There were others as well. Not babies, but adults, all of them in various stages of walking decay. In his time as king, he had toured leper colonies. In his time as president, he had inspected and investigated areas where the poor congregated.

He had witnessed firsthand their frustration and misery. On those occasions when a natural disaster had arisen, Arthur had been the first one on the ground to help provide aid and succor wherever he could . . . a tendency that his supporters had labeled heroic, his critics had dismissed as grandstanding for the TV cameras, and his security people had called "aggressively suicidal" since they were never able to secure fully the environments into which Arthur was thrusting himself.

But he had never, in all his days, encountered anything like this. Truly pitiable, they had come in wheelchairs and wagons, on crutches or on dialysis. The sick, the needy, the wanting, the dying. So many pleading for his help and far too many to help . . . and no absolute certainty that aiding them would do the least bit of good. For every one that he helped, there were a hundred more. It was the same old problem as before: He couldn't help everyone, and so he was frozen into impotence, unable to aid anyone.

So many were shouting and screaming his name that they all blended together in a cacophony of desperation. Looking back into the chopper, he made a circular gesture with his pointer finger. He could hear the disappointed roars from below. They were crying out to him, raising their voices in entreaty.

They were doing in actuality what Brady had said he would be willing to do in theory. They were praying to him, begging him to help them make their lives better. They were treating him as if he were some sort of god who could, with a wave of his hand, make their lives better somehow.

Except . . . well . . . wasn't he? He knew he was no god, to be sure. Despite his long age, despite the two worlds of magic and mundane that he straddled with moderate success, he was still human. Still capable of being killed just as easily as any other man.

Then again . . . so was Joshua, son of Joseph, otherwise known as Jesus. Wasn't he? Wasn't that the entire point?

With no other idea of what else to say, Arthur bellowed through the loudspeaker, "Return to your homes! Await my instructions! If you believe in me . . . do as I say! I shall return," said the king, "but not to here. Go home and wait for my word! Bless you all!"

Arthur stepped back into the helicopter, and the door slid closed. As one of the crew helped Arthur off with the rig, he saw that Gwen—belted into a large, reasonable comfortable chair—was staring at him. "Don't say it," he warned.

" 'Bless you all? Wait for my word?' "

"You know, once upon a time, when I told someone not to say something, they bloody well didn't say it." Arthur sighed.

"Don't you think you sounded just a *touch* messianic there?"

"What's messianic about 'bless you'? It's what people say when someone sneezes."

"No one was sneezing down there, Arthur!" she pointed out. "They were looking for . . . I don't know . . . a sign or something. You blessed the crowd! All you needed was a balcony and some robes."

"And a large funny hat," Percival added. "It doesn't work without the large funny hat."

She fired him an annoyed look. "You're not helping, Percival."

"True. But then again, I wasn't trying to, so it doesn't bother me too much."

"Gwen, I had to say *something* to them," Arthur said reasonably as he belted himself in. One of the flight crew checked to make sure that Arthur was secured and, once he was satisfied, gave a thumbs-up to the pilot. The helicopter had, until that moment, been moving very slowly. But once the pilot knew that Arthur was safe in his seat, the Sikorsky angled away quickly, embarking on its journey. "My entire purpose was to get them to leave the White House. To leave Washington and go home . . ."

"And wait to hear your word."

"To await my word, yes. A common enough term."

"Arrrrthur," she moaned, covering her face with one hand, "don't you see how it's going to sound? How it's going to come across? You meet with a representative of the Pope, you practically come right out and say that not only is everything the Church knows wrong, but you've got the smoking Grail to prove it . . . and then you wind up preaching to your followers from on high and telling them that you will return to them!"

"Well, wasn't that in a book about me? *The Return of the King*?"

"That wasn't Arthurian! That was *Lord of the Rings*!"

"Oh. Was it?"

"*Yes!*"

"I think you're confusing it with *The Once and Future King*," Percival said helpfully. "That one was you."

"Really. Which one had the little people with the hairy feet?"

"*The Return of the King.*"

"Ah. All right. My mistake, then."

"Arthur, this isn't funny," Gwen admonished him. "You're setting up a situation that's, at the very least, incendiary." Her eyes narrowed as she looked at him suspiciously. "And, frankly, I'm not entirely sure that you're unaware of that."

"What is that supposed to mean?"

She leaned back in her seat and closed her eyes. "I don't want to discuss it now, all right? Please?"

"As you wish."

"I'll tell you one thing, though: As soon as he turns up, Merlin's going to chew your ass over this."

Arthur chuckled. "This is one of those moments where I'm relieved to have picked up some of your vernacular. Otherwise, that would have summoned for me a most disturbing image." He looked out across the rapidly receding landscape of DC. "I hope he catches up with us soon."

MERLIN GLANCED UPWARD and saw a helicopter flying low over the city, angling upward and gaining altitude with every second. It struck him as a curiosity, but nothing more than that.

The Washington Monument stood strong and proud against the moonlight. Merlin had never quite understood the design point; it was a touch too phallic for his tastes. Still, even he had to admit that, at certain angles, it could look impressive. Amazing what mere mortals were capable of accomplishing when they put their minds to it.

Part of him thought that he was wasting his time as he approached the Reflecting Pool. This was a long shot at best. Still, he had to admit that the Secret Service agents might well have had a point. It was the exact sort of body of water that the Lady would have preferred. Flat, unmoving, almost like a vast sheet of glass. As was always the case with her, the fact that it was only a couple of feet deep would have made no difference. There were mystical forces at work when the Lady of the Lake chose to make her presence known, a warping of space and time. The truth was even though they had been lovers an age ago, there was still much about Nimue that Merlin didn't fully comprehend. He supposed that that was as it should be. The oceans that covered three quarters of the world remained an endless mystery, and women as a gender were mysterious as well. Nimue was the incarnation of both, so her nature demanded that she be damned near unfathomable.

"The Lady of the Lake. Unfathomable." This prompted Merlin to laugh slightly at his own inadvertent joke. But then he wiped away his amusement and faced the Reflecting Pool. *"Nimue!"* he called out to her, and there was more than just the speaking of her name in the summons. There was the feel of magiks that were old when the world was young. "Nimue, I summon you here! I summon you to this place, at this time! In the name of the unnamable, by the power and presence, I summon you! I summon you!"

He waited.

Nothing. Not a ripple.

"Nimue! Get your flabby ass out here, now!"

That did it. The center of the pool suddenly began to roil fiercely, to bubble and foam. Merlin was sure that he heard the faint sound of trumpets in the distance. He folded his arms and waited, and the water seemed to peel back upon itself, folding and twisting, then there she was, lifted up dead center with her arms outstretched in a most dynamic pose. He hated to admit it, even to himself, but she was certainly a splendid creature. The last thing he wanted to do, though, was give any hint that he thought that.

There was vast annoyance in her face, and she placed her hands on her hips, her head tilted slightly.

"Flabby?"

"I needed to get you here . . ."

"Flabby?"

"You told me about the Spear, but you didn't—"

"You want my help and you're calling *my* ass *flabby*? My ass is taut, Merlin—"

"As I know from personal experience, Nimue. I just said it to get your attention, and by the way, considering how you've been fiddling with me, it was as much as you deserved."

She looked as if she were about to shout at him some

more, then her ire evaporated and she smiled with thin lips, as green as seaweed. "Well, aren't you just the little trickster. And I suppose I have been a bit naughty . . ."

"Just a bit, yeah," Merlin said sarcastically.

"Still . . . you could at least apologize for—"

Merlin threw up his hands in exasperation. "I apologize, all right? Satisfied?"

She walked across the water to him, her feet making little *splish splash* noises as she did so. "It's a grudging, half-hearted apology, but I suppose for you, that's better than nothing. All right, Merlin, you're forgiven."

"I'm relieved. Now will you please, in the name of all that's unholy, tell me what—if anything—you know about the Spear? And how do you know it?"

She stopped a few feet away from him. "You don't have to sound so huffy about it, Merlin. If you hadn't lost the thing in the first place, you wouldn't be in this situation."

"And if you hadn't imprisoned me in the second place, I'd have had a thousand years or so to find it again."

"A valid point," she admitted. "That was rather mischievous of me, wasn't it."

"It's in the past. Forgive and forget, that's my motto."

Nimue laughed at that, and the water beneath her foamed in sympathy with her. "Since when is that your motto? I would have thought it would be 'lie in the high weeds and seek revenge.'"

"That's my backup motto. Nimue—"

"Very well, very well." She sighed. "The Spear . . ."

"Yes. The Spear."

"The Spear of Destiny is in the hands of a very powerful necromancer. Not just a necromancer . . . an alchemist."

"An alchemist?" Merlin made a face. "One of those fools obsessed with transforming lead into gold?" He made a dismissive wave. "Penny-ante tricksters, dime-store charlatans, the lot of them."

"This one is far more than that, Merlin, and he's thinking about a good deal more than transmuting chemical elements."

"Really."

"Yes, really."

"All right, Nimue, I'll bite. What is he thinking about, then?"

"Basic elements. Purity. Purifying things through basic elements."

"Do you *have* to speak in riddles, woman?"

"I don't have to, no. But it amuses me to do so, and it's kind of fun to watch you squirm every now and then."

"Really. And how *fun* do you think it would be," Merlin inquired, "to suddenly find yourself laboring under a spell of absolute veracity? They're not a lot of fun, Nimue. They tend to split the mind open like an overripe cantaloupe, and the person subjected to it doesn't always quite return to normal. And if you think your status as the premiere water elemental of this sphere somehow renders you immune to it, I am perfectly willing to show you that you are tragically mistaken."

"My"—and she arched an elegant eyebrow—"aren't we the cranky young man tonight."

"Nimue—"

"The world, Merlin. He wants to destroy the world. He wants to sweep the entirety of the surface in purifying fire, cleansing it of the disease known as humanity. Transform the world from the leaden presence of people into the gold of nature . . ."

"Nature that's been incinerated?"

"What was burned will eventually regrow." She regarded him thoughtfully. "You seem concerned about it. I thought you believed an alchemist was a penny-ante charlatan."

"Even a penny-ante charlatan can wreak havoc if he's given the mystical equivalent of a nuclear warhead. Still"—Merlin stroked his chin and reminisced briefly about the days when he had a beard. It gave him a sense of gravitas that he sorely missed—"the Spear of Luin can only do so much on its own. It's powerful, yes . . . but it can't destroy the world."

"Can it kill a sorcerer?"

"I should think so, yes."

"Too bad," she said.

Merlin thought that was a curious thing for her to say, and suddenly he staggered forward. He looked down in utter shock as he saw the head of the Spear Luin, the Spear of Destiny, protruding through his rib cage.

He opened his mouth in surprise and there was blood trickling from between his lips. Then, before he could say or do anything, he was being lifted off his feet. He thrashed about, trying to find purchase, unable to do so. With dull horror, he realized what was happening: Someone was behind him, had rammed him through with the Spear and was raising him up as if he were a piece of struggling meat.

He couldn't turn around, but he saw a brief reflection in the pool before him. It was a man, cloaked in darkness, a broad-brimmed hat drawn low, a black cape sweeping out around him.

"Suffer not a wizard to live," growled the shadow man from behind him.

There were few people in existence who knew precisely what the Spear was capable of, and of those few, Merlin had the clearest idea. He felt an energy surge beginning that, he knew, would skeletonize him in a matter of seconds if he did nothing about it.

Through bleeding lips, he spoke a name. A secret name, one that had not been uttered in centuries.

Instantly the Spear of Destiny shivered, and energy ripped from the head and down the shaft. It knocked the shadow man back, and he lost his grip on the Spear. It sent Merlin crumpling to the ground. He grabbed at the Spear, just below the head, and he knew there was no way to push it back out the way it had come. The Spearhead would rip apart what was left of his torso if he tried it. There was only one option. He gritted his teeth, shut his eyes tight, bit down fiercely on his lower lip to contain the inevitable screams of agony, and yanked as hard as he could. He both succeeded and failed. He succeeded in pulling the Spear all the way through his body, out the front rather than through the back. He failed in managing to contain his suffering. He let out an ear-shattering, long, sustained, agony-filled scream that did not sound like anything an eight-year-old boy would ever have been capable of generating. It was an aged scream, a full-grown man in more pain than he had ever known in his endless life.

Desperately he tried to maintain his grip upon the Spear, but the anguish was so overwhelming that he was in no shape to resist when the shadow man came in from the side and kicked Merlin in the face. Merlin fell onto his back. His entire chest was so thoroughly soaked in blood that his shirt looked as if it were made of scarlet-colored material. He tried to speak, but he felt as if his throat were thick with foul-tasting liquid.

The shadow man advanced on him, holding the Spear with the point downward. "Not bad for a penny-ante charlatan, eh. A poseur. A pretender. When the book on you is finally closed, note well who closed it . . . and whose story was finished."

He lunged forward, slamming the Spear point down as hard as he could. Merlin, summoning his last dregs of strength, pushed hard with his right foot and it sent him rolling over and into the Reflecting Pool. The Spear drove into the concrete border that surrounded the pool and wedged there. The shadow man let out a frustrated yell and tried to yank the Spear back out. It stubbornly refused to budge. The shadow man pulled yet again, and this time it came clear, sending pieces of rubble rolling about.

He moved forward quickly and drove the Spear down and into the Reflecting Pool, the water already red where Merlin had fallen in. He leaned forward, putting sufficient strength into the thrust so that he could slam the Spear through Merlin's body, this time finishing him off. Consequently, he almost fell forward, completely off-balance, because the Spear didn't go through its intended target. Instead it simply struck the bottom of the pool and, once again, embedded itself into concrete. The only thing that stopped the shadow man from tumbling into the Reflecting Pool was the Spear itself, for he leaned on it to prevent himself from falling in.

All during the altercation, the Lady of the Lake had stood a few feet away, watching the struggle in silence. Her face was impassive, her alliances impossible to discern.

"Where is he?" the shadow man roared. He yanked the Spear out of the water, not without effort. He jabbed downward again, this time with less force, content to use the Spear as a means of finding Merlin first so that he could apply the coup de grace. Even in that application, however, he failed. There was no sign of the young sorcerer. The red-tinted water was the only indicator that the wounded mage that fallen into the water at all. The shadow man whirled to face the Lady of the Lake, and he was holding the Spear in an outthrust, challenging manner. *"Where is he?"* he demanded once more.

"I hope you're not intentionally pointing that thing at me," Nimue said. "I can't say I do especially well with weapons being bandied in my direction."

"Is this"—and he pointed to the area where Merlin had been, but no longer was—"your doing, Nimue?"

"Merlin is perfectly capable of popping in and out on his own," Nimue reminded him. "After all, you're talking about someone who vanished from within the most tightly guarded building on the face of the planet. What makes you think that he couldn't vanish himself from the bottom of two feet of water?"

"Because he was mortally wounded!"

"If he was mortally wounded, then why are you worrying about him at all?"

"A mortal wound," snarled the shadow man, "is not necessarily the end of the road for one who is immortal. A higher standard of death is required to dispatch such a foe."

"You mean something higher than stabbing him in the back?"

He scowled at her. "Do we have a problem, milady?"

"A problem?"

"Between the two of us." He was no longer holding the Spear pointed right at her, but he was still cradling it in his hand with a purpose. "I had thought we were of one mind on this matter. You're not thinking of . . . reneging . . . on your loyalties, are you?"

She smiled fetchingly and came right to the water's edge. She spread wide her arms, and purred, "Of course not."

He stepped toward her, and she enfolded him in her embrace. She kissed him passionately, so much so that the water in the pool began to bubble furiously. Then she released him and said teasingly, "A boy should never be sent to do a man's job."

"I know of many a pedophile in this sad, pathetic world who would strongly disagree with you," replied the shadow man. "It is for the likes of those and many others of a similar sick mind that this world must be cleansed. You still understand that."

"Of course I do. The concept is fairly straightforward."

"Good. That's all that matters."

He stepped back from her, bowing as he did so. "Thank you for your aid in this matter, as you have provided in all other matters, my Lady of the Lake."

She pressed her palms together and returned the bow. "To a better world . . . for both of us. A world without Merlin . . . without Arthur . . . without people in general."

"What a wonderful world it would be." The shadow man sighed, as the Lady of the Lake sank beneath the water's surface. Within moments all traces of her presence would be gone.

CHAPTRE
THE TENTH

✝

AFTER THE HELICOPTER landed at JFK, Arthur and the others made their way through the darkened streets of New York toward Central Park. Very little was said once they were in the unmarked, nondescript sedans. Arthur watched the lights of the city that he had once ruled as mayor, during a time that seemed a lifetime ago. The lights of the skyline, the lights of the streetlamps as they whizzed past. It was near three in the morning, so even the city that never slept was very light on traffic, catching its breath and resting up for the start of a new day.

Gwen was dozing lightly, her head resting against his shoulder. Percival sat across from them on the facing seat and said nothing. He wondered what was going through Percival's head. It wasn't all that long ago that Percival had been a hopeless derelict, living in the streets of New York City and not even living, but simply existing in a state of helplessness and hopelessness. Blessed and condemned, all at the same time, by having taken a draught from the cup that he so zealously maintained in his keeping. If there was ever a love/hate relationship in the world, it was Percival and the Holy Grail.

Then the driver of the sedan called back, "We're here, sir," as the car glided to a halt. Arthur knew without even checking that the other cars were stopping as well in perfect synchronization. A moment later, the doors were opened for them on both sides by the Secret Service. Their heads were moving back and forth like conning towers, trying to look in all directions despite the lateness of the hour and the fact that Fifth Avenue, which was where they had pulled up, was deserted except for them. This was the exact sort of situation the Secret Service despised. They preferred to have a minimum of a week's time to secure an area, not mere hours. But they were accustomed to doing what they were told, and so they simply worked with the resources they had on hand.

Arthur drew his greatcoat around him against the chill night air. Truthfully, he'd known much colder weather in his youth and shrugged it off, but lately he was feeling the cold more in his bones. He wondered why that was, and decided that perhaps it would be best not to dwell on it.

"Do you know where we're going, Cook?" Arthur asked the nearest Secret Service man. Joshua Cook had been with Arthur that awful night when Gwen had become prey to the bullets of a would-be assassin. He was a heavyset black man—albeit with fairly light skin—a shaved head, and thick eyebrows.

"My orders are to escort you to Belvedere Castle."

"That's correct. But do you know why?"

"No, sir."

Arthur extended a hand to Gwen, who was blinking the sleep out of her eyes. She smiled and nodded toward Cook, who returned the gesture. Percival emerged from the other side of the sedan. "Do you have any children, Cook?"

Cook blinked in surprise, clearly not having expected the question. "A little boy, sir."

"Ah. Good. Well, when the little boy grows up and has children, the things you see this night will be the sort of thing you tell your son's son."

"We're Secret Service, sir," Cook said stiffly. "We don't tell others what we see."

"Trust me . . . you'll tell him about this. But fear not: He won't believe you."

With that, he gestured for Cook and the others to follow him. He needn't have done so, since they were going to follow him anyway. The Secret Service wasn't about to let a former president go wandering into Central Park in the middle of the night all by his lonesome . . . although Cook secretly had little doubt that Arthur could handle anything they might encounter.

They made their way along the path until eventually they were standing before Belvedere Castle. As always, it retained its timeless quality. What Arthur was about to do had once been his most closely guarded secret. But word was out about him now, so there was little point in skulking around.

Arthur walked slowly around to the far side of Belvedere Castle. The others followed him. Gwen was smiling, knowing that he was looking for a certain portion of the wall. She didn't offer her aid; generally speaking, she tried to keep out of the way of his pride whenever possible. "Just think, Gwen," Arthur said as he walked the perimeter. "If we'd come here in the first place, we could have kept your return secret and no one would have known."

"You said you didn't want that for us. That it would have gone from being your home-away-from-home to your prison."

"And yet here we are anyway."

Finally, he found it: a small cylindrical hole in the wall toward one stone corner. He withdrew Excalibur, reveling as always in the heady sound of steel being drawn from its sheath. The Secret Service men took a step back reflexively upon the appearance of the weapon, and he noticed that Cook's hand even moved automatically toward his gun. But then Cook overcame the reflex and let his hand dangle by his side.

Arthur took Excalibur and, holding the hilt in one hand and letting the blade rest gently in the other, he slid the point into the hole.

With a low moan and the protest of creaking, the section of the wall swiveled back on invisible hinges. There were audible gasps from the Secret Service men, and Gwen murmured, "I never get tired of seeing that."

"Magic," whispered Percival. "Merlin?"

"Yes," said Arthur. "Merlin." Before him was a stairway, the top of which was level with the ground in front of him, the bottom of which disappeared down into the blackness that was the castle—or at least an aspect of the castle. "Yes, it's . . ."

He stopped and leaned against the door, suddenly feeling dizzy and disoriented. Realizing something was wrong, Gwen touched his arm in concern. "Are you all right?" she asked.

He turned and looked at her, and his face was pale. "Just now . . . when I was talking about Merlin . . . I got the . . . the oddest feeling. Standing here, now, in a place so redolent of magic . . . something's wrong . . . Gwen, we have to go back."

"Go back?"

"To Washington."

"Sir," Cook said urgently, "that's not really an option. The president . . ."

"Hang the president. We're talking about Merlin. When the president's gone to dust and no one remembers his name anymore, the name of Merlin will still—"

Abruptly another agent, who was wearing a headset, suddenly looked up. He was far too well trained to reflect any alarm he might have felt, but he said, "Agent Cook, we have a situation."

Cook, who had his own headset, immediately transferred his full attention to it. "This is Cook. Immediate sitrep." He listened for a long moment, then said to Arthur, "Mr. President . . . people are coming."

"People . . . ?" Arthur shook his head.

"We were spotted somehow," Cook said tightly. "It could be anything, from a leak at JFK to someone just happening to spot us heading into the park and calling a couple hundred of his closest friends. But there's a crowd of people heading this way, and they're chanting your name."

"My God, it's like something out of a horror movie," muttered Gwen. "They'll be wanting to eat our brains next."

"Sir, you have to go . . ."

"But, dammit, Merlin . . ."

"Sir!" said Cook, and there was a look of cold frustration in his eyes. It was obvious he despised what was going on. Apparently he was barely able to wrap his mind around most of it, and circumstances were changing so fast that he was having trouble keeping his mental footing.

Arthur could hear the sounds of people in the distance, heading in his general direction. For just a heartbeat, he imagined fighting his way past the Secret Service men, enlisting these oncoming followers into a great cause and holy quest to get back to Washington, to see what had happened to Merlin, to . . .

"Arthur!" It was Gwen, looking at him pleadingly, and he suspected she knew everything that was going through his mind just then.

He looked to Percival. Percival simply stood there, arms folded, and he said, "Your call, Highness." Cook looked at the unflappable Percival, and Arthur knew that whatever decision he made, Percival would back him up.

But even if he did it—fought his way past these Secret Service men, enlisted the aid of this unknown crowd—then what? This wasn't ancient Britain, and he wasn't king. He was a former president, the United States was gargantuan, and the chances were he wouldn't even make it out of New York. And then what? Criminal charges for assaulting Federal agents? Disgrace? Prison?

He longed for the days when he was an authority unto himself, but those days were not these, and he knew that, at least for the moment, he was going to have to play the hand he'd been dealt.

"Percival, Gwen . . . in," he said, with a nod. Without hesitation, they did as they were instructed, dashing into the darkness of the doorway. He called after them, "And be careful of the—"

He heard an alarmed shout, and stumbling, and falling bodies, and then a flurry of profanity from both Percival and Gwen.

"—stairway, remember it's a bit difficult to maneuver in the dark . . ."

"No shit!" Gwen's voice floated from within.

He grimaced apologetically to Cook. "Sorry. The first lady displays an occasionally colorful word choice . . ."

"Yes, sir, I remember."

Arthur stuck out a hand and shook the agent's firmly. "Godspeed, Cook."

"Same to you, sir," said Cook. Arthur started to turn away, and suddenly he couldn't because Cook was still gripping his hand. Arthur looked back at him with an eyebrow raised quizzically.

"Agent Cook!" called one of the agents nervously. The sounds of the people were getting louder.

Ignoring the oncoming crowd, Cook said in a low, tight voice, "Are you really him? Are you really who they say you are?"

Arthur looked him in the eye, and there was a glint of steel in his gaze. "Yes. I am."

Cook nodded, and Arthur could see that there was something in his face that was unreadable. He shoved a small white card into Arthur's hand, and said, "Don't make us wait so damned long for your next return, all right?"

Arthur turned the card over. It was a business card, with Cook's private number on it. "That's a promise, Cook," Arthur assured him.

With that, Cook released his grip on him, and Arthur stepped back into the entryway. The door swung closed once more, and when the crowd of Arthur worshippers finally arrived, the Secret Service men had melted into the shadows and there was no sign of the object of their adoration or hatred, depending upon each one's particular point of view.

PARTE THE SECOND:

Idols of the King

CHAPTRE
THE ELEVENTH

✝

EUGENE FRANCIS BRADY drove toward his home on a bright, warm Tuesday morning, and was working on fighting back tears. The tears, however, were tears of joy . . . something that he never would have thought likely that he'd be shedding. He had anticipated only tears of loss on behalf of his wife, Linda, over a slow, long, agonizing death that she had not remotely deserved. More than that: It was the sort of death that the most evil, wicked creatures on Earth really did deserve, but never seemed to receive. Instead they went on about their wicked, wicked ways, never being brought to task, while others suffered.

He drove past his local church and snorted derisively at the statue outside. He had been over and over it in his mind. It could be argued that his prayers had wound up bringing Arthur to him, or him to Arthur, and so therefore all of it was part of the Lord's mysterious plan.

But . . . what if what Arthur had said was right? What if he'd spent his entire life worshipping, not the origin of miracles, but merely the lucky beneficiary? In which case . . . what?

Brady had no answers. He was not a man who was prone to deep, philosophical considerations. He was a simple, honest, hardworking man. He had his faith and his wife. With the loss of the latter such an imminent possibility, the former—which had served him through everything from his stint in Vietnam through to the loss of his only son to a hit-and-run driver—had taken a major hit.

He didn't know what to do with the tattered remnants of his faith, but he did know what to do with his wife.

He was taking her home.

Brady kept looking at her, and the tears in his eyes mixed with laughter as he looked at her again and again, unable to believe that she was there with him, hale and healthy.

"You feeling okay, Linda?" he asked the slender black woman with the graying hair seated next to him.

She laughed and dropped her head back against the headrest. "I'm so glad you asked for the hundredth time, Gene. Because, you know, the first ninety-nine times you asked, I wasn't absolutely for certain positive that you cared. But this last time, this was the one that sold it."

"All right, all right. I'm sorry."

His hands were on the steering wheel, and she reached over and placed one hand gently atop his. "Don't apologize. I'm teasing. I think it's sweet. And I'm just happy to be home."

So was he. It was remarkably ironic. Here they'd saved up all this money to go on a world tour . . . and then her cancer had left him beating himself up because they'd never have the opportunity to embark upon it. When her miraculous cure had occurred, Brady didn't even have to think about his next move: He booked the trip that they'd dreamt of for much of their lifetime. He had then informed the White House that he would be departing for three months and fully expected that he would be let go as a result. Instead no less a personage than the chief of staff had told him not to be ridiculous and to attend to his wife.

They had gone everywhere they had ever wanted to see. They'd also stopped at one particular place that Brady had become interested in during his reading, following the events in the White House. In the charming English countryside, Brady and Linda walked through the ancient construct known as Stonehenge. What had intrigued Brady was that, according to legend, Merlin himself had created this marvelous ring of stones for some unknowable reason. He regretted that he hadn't had a chance to ask either Arthur or Merlin if it was true. He'd encountered the young man in the White House who was supposedly the ancient mage, albeit a child of around eight for some reason, but Merlin had said nothing to him beyond an occasional grunt. And the night that Arthur had departed the White House, the alleged Merlin had likewise vanished, apparently under his own power.

He wished he'd had more time to talk to him. To them. To all of them. But he hadn't. And now they were gone, God knew where.

So Brady settled for standing in the middle of an alleged ancient source of power, the use for which had never been determined for certain by any archaeologists, and trying to commune with the spirits of those amazing and aged beings.

For the rest of the trip, his thoughts kept returning to Stonehenge, a place of hoary miracles . . . probably because the modern miracle of his wife's recovery was right there by his side as a reminder that magic still lived in a world that seemed far too mundane for its own good.

Now they were returning home, having retrieved the car from the friend who was watching it for them and turning over the motor once a week. Linda was watching the familiar passing scenery with the air of someone who had gotten

a second lease on life and had every intention of never forgetting that.

"It looks wonderful," she whispered. That amused Brady
a bit, since she had never been wild about the neighborhood,
calling it dreary and unpleasant. Apparently nothing in-
creased one's appreciation of one's surroundings quite like
being under the threat of having to depart those surroundings for good.

"That it does," he replied diplomatically, as he eased the
car into the driveway.

They went into the house and settled in. Linda, understandably feeling jet lag, went up to her bed and lay down.
Brady unpacked their suitcases, then sat down and started
going through the mail. As he did so, he heard the front
doorbell ring and headed over to answer it. He figured it
was one of the neighbors stopping by to say hello and welcome them back.

What Brady saw upon opening the door was not remotely what he was anticipating.

A man was standing there in a gray suit that was on the
verge of becoming a bit too tight for him thanks to an expanding waist. He had round cheeks, thinning hair, and a
stubbly beard that was desperately in need of a trim. Standing at medium height, he had a voice that was inversely
proportional in size, for when he opened his mouth, he spoke
in a deep, booming voice that suggested he was speaking to
someone in an unseen balcony.

There was another fellow next to him who came up to
about his shoulder. He was thinner and a bit sallow, with
short-cropped red hair and a slightly pinched look as if he
were perpetually sucking on a lemon.

"Mr. Brady," he said, reaching out a hand to shake Brady's.

"Yesss," said Brady, taking the hand and wincing slightly
at the power in the grip.

"Barry Seltzer at your service. This is my assistant, Sal. Do you think maybe we could come in?"

"What are you selling?" Brady said warily.

In response, Barry boomed a loud laugh. "I like you," he said, waggling a finger at Brady. "You're a funny guy and, more important, you get straight to the point."

"And the point will be that I'm closing the door in your face unless you—"

"Your wife drank water from the Holy Grail. Am I right, or am I right?"

He still had the jovial expression on his face, but there was a trace of savvy and cunning as well. Brady was taken aback, and the shocked expression on his face told the story even though he had not yet said anything.

"I'm right. I'm always right." He shook a fist mockingly at the heavens. "Curse me and this infuriating thing about my always being right! What kind of curse is that to live under, I ask you." He paused, then said in amusement, "You don't know what to ask first, do you. How do I know? Did someone tell me? Did I figure it out on my own? Am I going to be blackmailing you now, or perhaps get you arrested for . . . I don't know . . . drinking water without a license. Something like that, right?"

"Something like that," echoed Brady.

"Again, do you mind if we—"

"Come in," Brady said, feeling as if he'd been kicked in the teeth.

Barry and Sal entered, Sal keeping his expression fixed and forward while Barry looked around the house with so much enthusiasm that one would have thought he'd entered the Taj Mahal. "Very nice. *Very* nice. How long you folks lived here?"

"Long time," said Brady as he closed the door behind them. "What do you want?"

"Not going to offer us any tasty beverages or . . . ?"

"What do you want?"

Barry smiled sadly as he eased himself into a rocking chair. It made him look like all he needed was a shawl and some knitting. "Mr. Brady . . . may I call you Eugene . . . ?"

"No."

Without missing a beat, Barry said, "Okay. Mr. Brady, then: There's something you need to know straight up. I'm not here to blackmail you. I'm not here to do anything to you. I want to do something for you. For everybody. And, hey, let me make it clear straight up: I'm not a philanthropist. I'm not a do-gooder. I'm just a small-time businessman who wants to make himself an insanely rich businessman and needs your help to do it."

"In exchange for which . . . ?"

"You'll become insanely rich too."

"Soooo . . . you don't want to take money away from me. You want to give it to me."

"Exactly."

"Uhhh . . . huh," said Brady, making no attempt to hide his skepticism. He remained guarded, although he did take the time to sit down opposite Barry and wait to hear what he had to say. "So before we go any further . . . tell me how you knew about my wife."

"Yes, well . . . that's thanks to diligence and resourcefulness on the part of Sal here." And he gestured toward his assistant. The aide took a step forward and inclined his head. "Sal? Care to run it past Mr. Brady . . . ?"

"It was a long shot," said Sal, who spoke with a soft, almost whispery voice. "But not too long a shot, obviously. When King Arthur made the presence and nature of the Holy Grail known—"

"Wait. You believe that he's . . ."

"Oh, Sal and I are firm Arthurians," Barry Seltzer said eagerly.

"Arthurians? You mean like . . . worshippers?"

Barry laughed aloud at that. "I think 'worshipper' might be too strong a word. I mean, hell, even in my days in Hebrew school, I wasn't what you would call a worshipper of God so much as I would just sit there during services and pray, 'Please don't find some exciting way to hurt me.' And now along comes Arthur, and I have to admit, I love watching the gentiles running around screaming at each other because he's challenged their notions about their Jesus. You remember Jesus. Nice Jewish boy, went into his father's business." Barry laughed again at his own joke, then settled back down. "Point is, I was never comfortable with the whole God thing. Not ever. Felt like there were too many things unanswered, too many things we're supposed to take on faith."

"Well, it's hard to argue that, since faith is a major component of religion."

"Maybe. But Arthur, though . . . he's the real deal. Everyone knows it. To my mind, there are two kinds of people: people who have admitted that to themselves and people who are in denial. Hopefully they'll come around. In any event, we've kind of wandered away from the path . . ."

"What sort of business do you do again?" Brady asked.

"We'll get to that. Sal . . . ?" And he gestured to his assistant.

Sal nodded and picked up where he'd left off as if there'd been no interruption. "When King Arthur made the presence and nature of the Holy Grail known, it was not only predictable that a member of the White House staff would seek his aid to save the life of a loved one, but it was practically inevitable. And it was equally inevitable, knowing Arthur's loyalty to those who surround him that he would be unable to resist aiding them, even if it was against his better judgment. The names of White House staff are hardly secret. So we simply began by making a list of those staffers whose jobs made them the most likely to come into direct contact with King Arthur while he was at the White House, and started investigating which of them had a close relative who was dying some sort of slow, lingering death . . . the exact type of situation for which the Grail would be the most useful."

"Your wife's name came up, as you can imagine," said Barry.

"You invaded my privacy," Brady said angrily. "You had no business—"

Barry put up his hands in surrender. "I know we did. I'd love to apologize, I really would. But it got us the results we wanted and needed. I feel bad that you're upset, but honest to God, I'm not at all sorry I did it."

"Then," continued Sal, "we simply kept monitoring those patients to see if anyone had a miraculous recovery."

"Which your wife did," said Barry. "And I couldn't be happier for you. Really. Except her recovery occurred a few days after Arthur had already departed Washington."

"And the hospital records indicate that you were the sole visitor. Which means that either King Arthur or Percival, the Grail Knight, managed to sneak in unobserved, have her drink from the chalice, and then get out, again without being noticed . . . or . . ."

"Or something else happened." Barry leaned forward, and there was sincerity on his face. "Mr. Brady . . . I'm going to ask you a question. I would very much like you to give me an honest answer. If you do so, I'll tell you my vision. At which point if you want me to leave, Sal and I will pick up, head out that door, and I swear to you that not only will your secret be safe with us, but you will never see or hear from us again." He paused, then added, "Unless of course we, you know, run into each other in the supermarket or something. I mean, I can't control the laws of chance . . ."

In spite of the seriousness of the situation, Brady found himself chuckling at this odd fellow. "Fine, fine. Ask your question."

"All right." He took a deep breath as if about to vault off a precipice. "Did Arthur pour water into the Grail . . . and then pour the contents from the Grail into another perfectly normal container . . . and the water from the second container is what your wife drank, healing her?"

"That's more like three questions than one . . ." He saw that Barry was sitting there expectantly, waiting, looking hopeful, then he sighed and said, "Yes. That's exactly what happened."

"*Yes!*" Barry was on his feet, pumping the air with such triumph that one would have thought he'd just scored the winning touchdown in the Super Bowl. "Yes! It'll work! I knew it! I knew it would work!"

"Congratulations, sir," Sal told him, never losing his cool.

"This is incredible news. Incredible!" Barry was walking back and forth, as if his mind was racing, and his body was sprinting to keep pace with it. "If we can pull this off . . . if we can find him, get him to agree . . . the benefit for humanity, the profits for us . . . it's . . ."

"Will you slow down! And keep quiet!" Brady was standing now, hands on his hips. "My wife is sleeping!"

"My apologies. Sorry. Sorry again." Barry Seltzer dropped his voice so that he was nearly whispering as much as Sal had been. "Mr. Brady . . . I'm going to tell you what business I'm in and what I've got in mind. It's something that's going to benefit the whole of humanity and make us stinking rich besides."

And he proceeded to do so. Brady listened, and his eyes slowly widened as Barry outlined his plans. When he was done, Barry waited expectantly for Brady to say something. "Well, Mr. Brady?" he finally prompted.

A slow smile spread across Brady's face. "Call me Gene," he said.

CHAPTRE
THE TWELFTH

⸸

$\mathcal{E}$VERYTHING IS SWIRLING around Merlin. He has no idea where he is, or how long things have been spinning around him like this, or how he has gotten here in the first place. His past, present, and future . . . all matters which he usually has a fairly good bead on . . . are a jumble. It even takes him long moments to remember his own name or his status in the world . . . wherever the world has gone. He feels a dull aching in his chest, and isn't sure where the ache has come from or why he is being subjected to this apparently endless torment.

He cannot tell if he is breathing, or if his heart is even beating. His ears are filled with the howling sound of the ocean, a massive roaring of waves crashing like a violent storm happening, all in his head. His limbs wave about helplessly as he tries to get some sense of up and down, and fails utterly. He is as helpless as a leaf in a hurricane, with no more command over his destiny than that. He tries to shout for help, and that is not something that comes easily to him, for his pride is a vast and daunting thing. But cry out he does, to no avail. Not only isn't he certain whether he could make his voice heard over the beating of the waves, but he can't hear his own voice *at all. For all he knows, water has filled his throat and lungs and he isn't able to make a sound.*

He spirals down, down, or perhaps up, up, and suddenly he has a sense of the vortex beginning to let up. The thundering of the storm is receding. The water no longer seems to be pitching him around but instead easing him toward something, some ultimate destination. He calls out again, shouting for Arthur, cursing Nimue, and still neither is heard even by him.

And then, just like that, he is no longer moving.

The world of water has ceased moving crazily around him. He is not, however, remotely certain of where he is. He looks around what at first seems like nothing but water, then slowly starts to perceive details. There are columns surrounding him, tall columns towering high as far as the eye can see. No light is filtering through from on high, but the environment is benefiting from bioluminescence, casting the world around him in eerie blues and greens.

He feels neither warm nor cold, neither the iciness of frigid water nor the heat of a tropical current. He stands there for a long moment, then tries to take a step. He does not walk so much as float several feet before settling again. He considers this mildly odd, but not too much so. He has lived a very long life and it takes a good deal to get a reaction out of him that goes much beyond, "Well, this is interesting."

He says it aloud because, well, it truly is interesting, although he still doesn't hear his voice. Beyond that, he doesn't know for sure what to make of it, but he can take some reasonably educated guesses.

Nimue! Merlin calls out. The fact that he does still not perceive his own voice doesn't mean anything. She will hear it. Nimue, what have you done!

Saved your life, silly boy, comes Nimue's response. He doesn't hear it through his ears; instead he hears it within his head. The Spear Luin *impaled you. Did you truly think you would have* survived that without my intervention?

Yes, I would have! I didn't need your help!

Her laughing voice rings between his ears. And yet you stood there on the edge of the water and begged me to help you.

To aid you in finding the Spear. Well . . . you found it. Does that not warrant at least some token of thanks from the mighty Merlin?

Thank you, *he replies sourly. He studies the blood-soaked shirt, then pulls it up and aside to examine the wound. It is a fierce, gaping thing. It has, however, ceased bleeding.* How long have I been here? Hours? Days?

Time does not pass in this realm as it does in others, *she informs him.* I have no idea how much time has gone by in the outside world.

And where is here, this realm?

My home, sweet Merlin. The realm of the Clear. All water passes through here. Here I make my home, here is the nexus of all such realities. Time here is fluid, as are all other things. And you will reside with me here.

The hell I will! *Merlin rages.* You betrayed me! Betrayed me to whoever that spear wielder was!

I did not betray you. I was simply being loyal to my lover.

Lover, *he says in disgust.* You love him, and you would love me too? Don't you think that kind of diminishes the strength of your love?

Of course not. The tide flows two ways with equal strength. Does that make it any less the tide?

Merlin attempts to stalk back and forth, and does not entirely succeed as he once again floats from one area to the next. He feels that his annoying buoyancy does little to afford him the gravitas he feels he deserves. I don't understand how any aspect of you, tides or no, can possibly ally itself with someone who supposedly wants to annihilate the Earth.

He has no desire to do that. He just wants to annihilate the humans who walk the Earth.

That's the same thing.

No, it truly isn't, *she replies.* You keep refusing to understand that. He reveres the Earth. He believes that humans are infecting it, hurting it. And who am I to say he's wrong.

You're the Lady of the Lake, that's who!

She still has not appeared before him, but he can sense the pitying smirk that her tone of voice reflects. Yes, that's right. And how many lakes have become filled with garbage? How many oil spills or toxic dumps have found their ways into the oceans? How many fish have been hunted so thoroughly into extinction that it's upsetting the ecological balance? There were gods who . . .

Her voice trails off. The hesitation catches Merlin's attention where her ranting was simply annoying him. He tilts his head like a dog trying to pick up a high-pitched sound. Gods who what?

She makes no response. Gods who what, Nimue?

He hears the water, or perhaps senses it coalescing, behind him before he actually turns to see it. Sure enough, there is Nimue, or Vivian, or the Lady of the Lake, floating there with her arms out to either side.

Gods who watched humans when they first oozed their way out of the primordial slime and dragged themselves up to shore, *Nimue tells him,* and they looked upon those poor, pathetic, early incarnations of humanity, and said, "These are going to be nothing but trouble in the long run, mark our words." And lo and behold, they were right. They were as right as any gods could be. But they stood by and allowed mankind to grow and develop, because they saw how eventually they could be used. Your beloved Arthur is playing into that, and now, so have you.

You don't seriously think this place can hold me, do you?

She laughs lightly. I most certainly do. Your blood has touched a body of water, Merlin. That blood is all I need to keep you here for as long as I desire. In other words, forever, while my beloved attends to greater matters.

He pounds his fists against the blanket of water that envelops him. You can't do this, Nimue! By all the gods, you cannot! Arthur needs me! Even now he wilts under the awareness that I have disappeared again. I must attend to him, and to the backstabbing bastard who caught me in that cowardly attack.

Well, *says Nimue,* as it so happens, I have my reason and desires for keeping you right where you are. Get used to it, Merlin Demonspawn. You are going to be with me for a very, very long time. Or would you rather I'd have let you die?

It would take far more than one idiot with a spear to kill me!

Do not worry. *She smiles.* There is much, much more.

And with that comment, Nimue releases her hold on the attractive form she is presenting him. It dissolves around her as her body rejoins with the elements around her, and within moments she is gone.

Merlin endeavors to imitate her. He calls upon his abilities, tries to remove himself from her sphere of influence. But the forces that he calls upon to transport him away from this place do not answer him. He is cut off.

Isolated.

Trapped.

Nimue! *Merlin shouts in frustrated impotence, and her name echoes and echoes in the vast flowing void, but there is nothing now except his voice and the endless crashing of the seas.*

And somewhere far, far away, a hand with long fingers is staring at a globe in which the minuscule form of Merlin is visible. He pumps his tiny fists in frustration. The tiny Merlin does not see out, but the holder of the sphere can see him perfectly. The water swirls around like a snowglobe, and his face draws closer and studies the trapped mage with fascination.

The demonspawn is contained, *observes the man known as Cardinal Ruehl, while others in the darkness nod in agreement.* Now . . . to attend to his leader . . .

CHAPTRE
THE THIRTEENTH

✝

*E*NOUGH WITH THE *clanging!*"

Gwen thought she was going to go completely out of her mind. The sounds of swords smashing together had been a nearly endless thing in the castle. She had lost track of how long they had been there, although she suspected it had been a few months. It seemed like years and felt like centuries.

It wasn't simply that Percival was there along with them. Percival had actually been the model of propriety and sensitivity, making himself scarce when Arthur didn't require him or when Gwen and Arthur needed time just for themselves, but mysteriously at Arthur's right arm when the king sought his presence. Part of her wondered if this was any sort of remotely fulfilling life for Percival, but she had stopped worrying about it early on. She had stumbled across Percival alone one day and found him simply staring in blissful peace at the Grail. He looked as if he was communing with it on some level. It was a relief to her that the Grail was indisputably a force for good. If it had been something even the least bit evil, she wouldn't have been sleeping too well imagining what the thing was doing to Percival's mind. Indeed, she would have been constantly worried about waking up with the Grail transformed into its sword form, driving through hers and Arthur's sleeping bodies like a spit through a shish kebab.

Percival was so considerate about not imposing his presence upon Arthur and Gwen that she made a point of trying to include him at all times. He seemed pleased to be a part of things when she so desired, but equally happy to be off on his own, because it meant more time with his beloved cup. Honestly, it didn't seem much of a life to her, but certainly Percival had spent enough of his existence hanging around and accomplishing not a damned thing, so he was definitely entitled to spend the rest of eternity however he wished.

But the time was preying upon Gwen nonetheless, for she had no Grail to contemplate for hours at a time. It wasn't as if she didn't have diversions. This transdimensional castle, created by Merlin to be Arthur's home away from home, certainly had its amenities. TV screens that enabled them to keep apprised of what was happening in the world. A telephone that they could call out on, although how in the world Merlin had rigged any of this up she couldn't even begin to guess. Endless supply of food in a magical larder that was always well stocked whenever they opened it. Everything they needed to live . . .

"Not living," Arthur had said though, not too long ago. He had growled to himself while seated on the edge of the throne that had been set up for him. He looked like a brooding barbarian king out of a Robert E. Howard work, having withdrawn Excalibur from its sheath and leaning on the pommel. Gwen, happening by the throne room, glanced in at Arthur as he muttered again, "Not living."

"Arthur?" she had asked. He hadn't moved his head; his eyes merely shifted their gaze to her. "Arthur, what do you mean, 'Not living'?"

"We're not living," he had replied. "We're . . . existing."

Then he went back to his kingly frustrated musings, un-willing to say anything else despite all Gwen's prompting. But really, she didn't need to prompt him because she un-derstood perfectly what he was talking about.

They were not living in this castle, this hideaway, this re-treat. They were merely existing there, accomplishing noth-ing and waiting for a call to action that would likely never come. Because Gwen knew, as well as Arthur, that that call would very probably come from Merlin. It had always been that pint-sized bastard who had been the mover, shaker, and planner of Arthur's life, and now he was gone yet again. He had a nasty habit of disappearing: the forces of Morgan Le Fey had kidnapped him, and the Basilisk had transformed him into a life-size paperweight. Granted, the little shit had come back from those dire straits, one time with Gwen's help, an occurrence for which his gratitude had always seemed tepid at best. He had more lives than a cat, that much was certain. But the bottom line was that he had an annoying habit of not be-ing around when Arthur needed him the most, and this was definitely one of those times.

At least Arthur typically had other things going on in his life during Merlin's poorly timed absences. He'd had an elec-tion to win, or a country to run. Now, though, the time dragged as heavily for the ancient king as it did for anyone else. The first time that Gwen had mentioned the phrase "stir-crazy" to him, he had stared at her blankly, not understanding the term. Now, he'd come to understand.

One way he tried to deal with it was keeping his battle in-stincts sharp. There were other swords around the place aside from the unbeatable Excalibur, and Percival was perfectly happy to test the reflexes and power of his king. At first it had been once a day, or whatever passed for a day in this castle. But by this point, to Gwen, it seemed almost constant. Day and night, from somewhere within the castle confines, she could hear the crashing of swords as Arthur and Percival sparred with one another. Gwen had no idea who was truly the better swordsman, nor did she remotely care. As with any sound that is endlessly repetitive, all she knew was that she going nuts from it. If she was going to be required to spend the rest of her days listening to raging testosterone with accompanying sound effects, she was going to throw herself in between Arthur and Percival and hope that one of them inadvertently gutted her like a marlin. Anything was better than this.

She was seated in her study, trying to read a book, when the crashing of the swords finally took its toll, and she had screamed out, "Enough with the clanging!" To her relief, it had promptly ceased, the stone walls carrying her voice in a most efficient manner. As she knew would be the case, there were footsteps moments later, and Arthur appeared in the doorway of her study. He was frowning.

"Problem?" he asked.

"Not anymore," she replied without looking at him, staring at the pages of her book without making any serious effort to focus on them.

He remained where he was for a moment. He was wearing loose black pants and a simple white tunic that was sweated through. He wasn't holding a sword, although she assumed that Excalibur was hanging at his side as always. Then he crossed the room, rested his hands on the armrests of her chair, and leaned in toward her. To her surprise, there was barely controlled anger in his voice.

"Do you think this is easy for me? *Do* you?" he demanded. "Merlin has disappeared. We're effectively in exile, stranded in the midst of millions of people who could use our aid. I'm supposed to be a leader of men, dammit. *The* leader of men. And instead I'm here, hiding . . ."

"We're not hiding . . ."

"Then what the bloody hell is *it that we* are *doing?"*

She lowered her head and sighed. "We're hiding."

"Thank you for admitting that, at least." He turned away from her, hands draped behind his back. "This isn't like our being on the boat, Gwen. This isn't us sailing away into the sunset with our well-deserved happy ending. This is us with our tails between our legs, whiling away the time without the slightest hope of something better coming along."

"Merlin could still . . ."

"Could still what? We don't know that, Gwen." He looked back at her with pain in his eyes. "We don't even know if he's alive."

"He's alive."

"We don't know that," he repeated, and she knew he was right. "That concept alone is difficult enough for me to deal with. What makes it all the more stinging is the thought that we would waste away waiting for him, like Godot. Besides, I'm the damned king. Not Merlin. I shouldn't be lounging about waiting for him to tell me what to do. I should be taking the actions, initiating the strategies." He paused, then said with renewed vigor, "Perhaps we should do something at that. Are there still people lurking about the castle?"

"No." She sighed, looking relieved.

Arthur seemed a bit disappointed. "No?"

She felt her annoyance with him ebbing. Gwen reached over and placed the palm of her hand against his bearded face. "Arthur, there was no proof that you were here, remember? And people being the way they are, there were reports that you were sighted by people everywhere from Indiana to Istanbul."

Then Gwen jumped in surprise as Arthur turned quickly and slammed a fist into the wall in frustration. "People I'm letting down."

"Arthur, you can't help everyone in the world . . ."

"Why not?" he asked defiantly. "Why shouldn't I at least try?"

"Try going to every needy person in the world and giving them a shot of Grail ale? Arthur, you could spend a lifetime doing it and never get it done."

"As lifetimes go, don't you think it would be a better way to spend it than simply hiding here and waiting to be forgotten?"

"Maybe. But what about the healthy ones? Percival says that a healthy person who drinks of the Grail is granted immortality."

"We don't know that for certain," Arthur said. "We know it happened for Percival. Perhaps it was unique to him because he was the Grail Knight, destined for a singular relationship with the Grail. Perhaps other people will simply . . . I don't know . . . feel better."

"And what if you're wrong? Are you going to provide them with a ticket to immortality? Do you really think that's wise? Do you?"

He stared at her in annoyance. "You're starting to sound like Merlin."

"I'm not sure whether to take that as a compliment or not."

"That's all right. I'm not sure how I intended it."

He slumped against the wall, shoving his hands deep into his pockets, looking more like a dejected youngster than a king. "Of course we can't go around dispensing immortality," he muttered. "There is a natural order to things. Death is part of that order. If mankind knows immortality as a whole . . ."

"Overpopulation. A lack of striving. Hell, look what happened to Percival after a while, before Merlin salvaged him."

"I know. Still . . ."

"Still what?"

He looked up at her. "Jesus didn't have a problem going around healing the sick. He didn't feel compelled to go to everyone. He simply did what he could . . ."

"Yeah, well he didn't have to do it on CNN. And, by the way, they still crucify people, you know. They just do it without the cross, in the court of public opinion." She drew closer to him. "And Arthur . . . you're not Jesus. You're not the savior of humanity. You know that, right? You understand that?"

"Did Jesus know that as well?" Arthur asked her.

"Oh, Arthur . . ."

"Did he?" he insisted. "Gwen . . . I am . . . or at least was . . . as serious a Christian as anyone you could meet. And that's back when it was far more commercialized than it was now. I mean, you think that Christianity has become commercialized simply because they start tossing up decorations to celebrate Christmas right after Halloween? You've no idea what it was like when the crucifixion was far more recent history when I first started. I went to Jerusalem, did you know that? Traveled to the Middle East."

"No, I didn't know that," she said in wonderment. It was amazing to her that, even after all their time together, he could suddenly hit her with the most astounding reminiscences and make them sound almost mundane. Afterthoughts that he'd only just now gotten around to mentioning. "I never read . . . I mean, there weren't any stories about . . ."

"The stories didn't mention Percival was a Moor, did they? The stories don't cover everything, you know." Arthur got that faraway look in his eyes that she had come to know. "You'd walk through the streets there, or what passed for streets, and there would be peddlers, selling everything you could imagine. Pieces of the one true cross. Finger bones of Jesus, or one of the saints. Pieces of cloth from dresses worn by the Blessed Virgin. Holy Grails. Holy plates. Holy shite, all of it. Yet the suckers would grab it up, hoping that it would bring them that much closer to their lord. I watched them willingly subjecting themselves to the wiles of street peddlers and merchants. I'd see the hope in the eyes of the pilgrims . . . and the gleam of contempt in the eyes of the sellers. And here I am, with the genuine item in my grasp, and I can't say of a certainty whether it brings the supplicants nearer to God . . . or further away. I mean, Gwen," he said, and she had never seen him look more helpless, more confused, "I talked a good game with the Cardinal because, well, the man annoyed me. But what if the whole of Christendom really is based on a lie? What if the savior truly was no more of a Son of God than I? What if he is simply the beneficiary—as are you, and I, and Percival—of an ancient magic, the origin of which we can barely understand?"

"Well," Gwen said, trying to sound reasonable, "the magic had to come from somewhere. Could have come from God, right? With Jesus the intended recipient?"

"And what makes him any more or less worthy than any of the other recipients?"

"Well . . . I guess that's where faith comes in. I don't have an answer for you other than that."

Arthur rubbed the bridge of his nose. "Maybe I shouldn't have dismissed Ruehl out of hand. Perhaps I should be having this discussion with theologians. With the Pope."

"Sorry if I'm not up to the challenge."

He smiled at her wanly. "My dear Gwen . . . I know of no challenge that you're not up to."

"Why thank you, your Highness," she said, and curtsied in a majestic manner. Then a thought occurred to her. "If you drank of the Grail now . . . you being healthy and everything . . . you'd be immortal, right?"

"Even an immortal could be killed, yes, but I would effectively be so, yes."

"What's stopping you, then?"

"Percival."

She looked confused. "What do you mean?"

"I mean," he said patiently, "that I've given Percival instructions that if I should ever try it . . . he is to slay me."

Gwen could hardly get the word out. "W-what . . . ?"

"Or at least, he's to try. I have no desire to be immortal, Gwen. I've lived longer than, by any rights, I should. Percival is more than just the Grail Knight. I have given him the responsibility that the Grail never be abused. That immortality not be doled out, like sweets after dinner. He takes that responsibility very seriously, and he'll certainly try to take my head off if I endeavor to abuse the Grail's gifts. That is his responsibility. That's his curse as being the immortal of the Grail."

"Wow." She let out a low whistle. "I . . . had no idea."

"Well, it's not something that can be brought up in normal conversation." He tapped the side of a bookshelf thoughtfully. "I'm calling Cook."

"Cook? The Secret Service agent? Why?"

"Because I've endeavored to get through to Brady any number of times, and I've heard nothing. The number I have for him was put out of service temporarily . . . I've no idea why. And I want to know what happened with his wife."

"Arthur," Gwen sighed, "you know the odds were against its working. Why try to come up with something new to beat yourself up about?" Then she saw the look in his eyes and shrugged. "All right, fine. Do what you have to do."

Arthur nodded and headed for a different room, where there was a phone. Right before he left, Gwen suddenly said, "Arthur . . ." He turned around and looked at her expectantly. "If drinking from the Grail can grant immortality . . ."

"Yes."

"And Jesus was drinking from it at the Last Supper . . ."

"Yes."

"Then doesn't that mean that . . . maybe . . ." She was having trouble framing the words.

"Go ahead. Say it."

"That Jesus of Nazareth might still be walking around today?"

"That, my dear"—he smiled—"is entirely possible."

"Then . . . if that's so . . . why hasn't he said anything?"

"He may very well have," Arthur pointed out. "And if he made too much of a fuss about it, he's no doubt sitting in an insane asylum somewhere, committed by well-meaning individuals who were loath to let an obviously deranged individual walk the streets." He saw her blanch at the notion. "I wouldn't be concerned about it, my dear. I tend to think, if he's out there, and has lived twice as long as Percival or I, that he'd be wise enough to keep a low profile. After all, if anyone's learned the dangers of drawing too much attention to himself, it's him, wouldn't you think?"

"I certainly hope so."

He laughed mirthlessly. "If only I had learned the same lesson, eh?" And he walked out of the room, leaving Gwen to envision the Messiah in a straitjacket, shouting that he had returned and why the hell didn't anyone believe him.

ARTHUR, SEATED IN his study with the phone to his ear, listened to the ringing and was preparing to hang up upon receiving a voice-mail pickup. But then the phone was answered, and he instantly recognized the voice that responded with a brisk, "Cook here."

"Cook," said Arthur. "Are you free to talk?"

There was a pause, and Arthur could almost envision Cook's brain processing the voice that was coming through his phone. Arthur was about to speak again, to prompt Cook's recognition of him, when Cook spoke in a lowered voice. "Mr. President?"

"Once upon a time. If you need me to, I can call back at some later—"

"No. Good God, no. I've been hoping you would call."

Arthur detected a note of urgency in his voice. "Has something happened, Cook?"

"Yes. It's about Eugene Brady . . ."

"That's who I was calling about," Arthur said in surprise. "I . . . knew that his wife was ill, so I thought I would check up on her—"

"With all respect, sir, you don't have to pussyfoot around with me. I know what you did. I know about the water from the Grail. Brady told me. He told me everything because he knew that I was one of the last people to see you and was hoping . . . well, he was hoping that maybe you'd check in with me. He needs to see you. Something's happened."

"What's happened, Cook?"

"Long story short: His wife is fully recovered, and a businessman named Barry Seltzer wants to make you an offer that I, personally, think you should listen to."

"Seriously?"

"Mr. President, there's many things you can say about me, good and bad, but one thing I think we're all agreed upon is that I never joke, ever."

"And what sort of 'offer' does Mr. Seltzer care to propose?"

"I think you should hear it from him, sir."

"Cook, I'm not in the mood for this. Tell me what's going on."

Cook paused, then said, "He wants to bottle Grail water and sell it to people all over the world."

Arthur made him repeat it to make sure he had heard it properly, then let out a raucous, very unkingly laugh. "That," he said when he was able to control himself, "is the most ridiculous idea . . ." Then, after a moment's more consideration, he said, "Set up the meeting. This I've got to hear."

Chaptre
the Fourteenth

The diner was a real hole in the wall on the Upper West Side, one that had more than its share of disputes with the Board of Health. Handpicked by Cook for that very reason, it seemed unlikely that they would be disturbed there.

Naturally, Arthur could have simply had Seltzer come directly to the castle. But the king was suspicious of the circumstances and was disinclined to welcome just anybody into his unique home. So the unsuspecting diner was host to what was certainly one of the oddest, not to mention monumental, business meetings of the twenty-first century.

On one side of the table sat Arthur, Percival, and Gwen. They were not easily recognizable. Arthur, sporting an ensemble that no one would associate with him, was wearing a baseball cap pulled low and sunglasses, with a pea green army coat draped around him. Gwen was wearing a black wig that covered her strawberry blond tresses, an oversized hockey shirt, and shorts. Percival was wearing a black Kangol hat, jeans, and a short black-leather jacket.

Opposite them sat Cook, who introduced the fellow named Barry Seltzer. Seltzer, in turn, had his aide, who apparently didn't warrant a last name and was simply called Sal. Arthur didn't have the slightest idea what to make of them. Seltzer was doing everything he could to keep his voice down, but the sheer weight of his enthusiasm was making that a difficult proposition.

"This could be the greatest boon to humanity ever! Ever!" Seltzer was rhapsodizing. "I don't think you've even thought about the ramifications—!"

"Believe me," said Arthur, "we've been doing nothing but considering the ramifications, for months now. And I'm not entirely sure that you have done so."

"But we have! Look, your Highness, let me spell it out for you. Thus far, I'm a small-time operator. I run a water-bottling plant in New Jersey. Inherited it from my father. We sell bottled water. Jersey Springs. Maybe you've heard of it."

"Can't say as I have," admitted Arthur. "But don't take it personally. Keeping abreast of the latest advances in bottled water has never been one of my priorities."

"Don't worry about it," said Barry. "We have a market share that you can measure with an eyedropper." He made a loud, annoying, barking laugh, like a seal. "The point is, I have a vision. Can I tell you my vision?"

"Can we stop you?" asked Gwen.

"I am talking," Barry continued as if Gwen hadn't spoken, "about making Grail water available to the masses. According to Gene, you simply poured water into the Grail, then poured it out again, and poof. Magic properties of healing. Am I right?"

"That seems to be the case."

"So all we have to do is take the Grail, make it the centerpiece of our bottling and processing facility . . ."

"No." It was Percival who had spoken, and Arthur looked at him in surprise. "No, Highness," Percival repeated. "It's . . . it's demeaning."

"How is it demeaning if it's helping people?" Cook asked.

"It's demeaning because you're speaking of something that is soaked in ancient magiks," Percival replied. "You can't simply take an antiquity of such power and trivialize it by making it a part of mass production."

"Percival," Arthur said, and Percival looked at his king expectantly, "I think we should at least hear him out."

"My king, the Grail is in my charge to—"

"That was not a suggestion, Percival," he said sharply. "I'm saying I think we should hear him out."

If Percival was at all put off by the implied rebuke in Arthur's tone, he didn't let on. He simply nodded slightly, and said, "As you say, Highness."

"Look . . . Percival . . . would you prefer 'Sir Percival . . . '"

"Percival's fine. Just," and he winced, "not 'Percy.'"

"All right, then. Percival . . . do you seriously think that if Jesus had access to the resources that we can provide, he wouldn't have taken advantage of it? I mean, honestly!" He laughed. "What do you think his Apostles were if they weren't guys like me? Just hardworking, ordinary Joes who are trying to get the word out to as many people as possible. That's what I'm out to do, except I can get more than the word out. I can get the benefits of the actual Grail out there."

"There's a world of difference between words and what the Grail can provide."

"No argument. But let's look at that world of difference, Percival," said Barry, leaning forward earnestly. "These are difficult times we're living in."

"I think it's safe to say that, ever since the serpent kicked an apple Eve's way, they've always been difficult times."

"Fair point. But the difference is that, in the past, whenever people had troubles, it was . . . how to put it . . . their own troubles. It was the troubles of their families, or their immediate neighborhoods, or whatever. And sometimes those troubles would ease, and things would look up for a while before they turned to shit again . . . pardon my French," he said to Gwen.

"Actually, the French would be *merde,* but all right," said Gwen. "Don't worry about me. I've heard worse."

"Okay, fine." He smiled. Then he grew serious again. "The difference is . . . the world has shrunk."

"I've walked every side of the Earth. Trust me . . . it's the same size it's always been," said Percival.

But Arthur shook his head. "No. I know what he's talking about. Nowadays, everyone knows everyone else's business. We're certainly living proof of that, with that spy satellite taking pictures of us. I've had plenty of time to watch television in the past months that we've been holed up in the castle, and I have to say, there's a sense of constant disaster and calamity that pervades the airwaves. A sense that civilization is just barely holding itself together. And the press is so busy focusing on, say, people blowing themselves to bits in the Middle East that they're not telling us about genocides in even more remote countries. I was the president of these United States, I received daily briefings, and I can tell you that what you see on television is only the tip of the iceberg in terms of the horrors the people of this world are dealing with. And I think people sense that and they sense things are not only as bad as presented, but worse. They clutch faith like . . . like people from a sunken ocean liner clinging to life preservers. And the problem is, Percival, that although the faith can support you for a while . . . sooner or later, the freezing water, or sharks, or just simple exhaustion can still cause you to drown."

"Well said, your Highness," said Barry.

Percival looked at Arthur suspiciously. "Indeed, sire. You could almost be making Mr. Seltzer's arguments for him."

"I'd like to think you know me better than that," Arthur said with a mild remonstration in his voice.

"It doesn't matter who makes the argument," Barry insisted. "The point is, faith is all well and good . . . as far as it goes. And there are plenty of people for whom faith is enough. But there are also people—plenty of people—who could use more than that. Who could use some answers. Who could use some practical help. And that's what we intend to provide."

"By profiteering off the cup of Christ?" Percival said, and turned to Arthur. "Highness, what makes him any different than the peddlers shilling their wares to the suckers in Palestine?"

"Well, to begin with . . . the cup is genuine," Arthur pointed out.

"And what about the question of immortality?"

Seltzer looked from one to the other in confusion. "Immortality? What's he talking about?"

"If one is in perfect health, apparently," Arthur said, "the cup bestows immortality upon them."

Barry rocked back in his booth, looking amazed and stunned.

At that moment, the waitress came over to take their orders. She did so in a bored and detached fashion, although she did look at Arthur a bit longer than any of them felt comfortable with. They ordered quickly, hamburgers all around, and waited until the waitress was out of earshot.

"Now the truth is," continued Arthur, "we don't know that of an absolute certainty. We know it happened for Percival. And we know that it sustains life indefinitely while it's the Land and people are residing upon it . . ."

"The Land?" said Barry, looking confused.

"Never mind." Arthur waved it off. "The point is, we are

speaking of something ancient and, in many ways, unknowable. So it's something that has to be considered."

"Okay, well . . . this is a new wrinkle," Barry said after a moment. "I mean . . . obviously you don't want to go around turning the world's population immortal. That'd be catastrophic." Sal, seated beside Barry, simply nodded mutely.

Percival looked mildly surprised. "You understand that?"

"Well, of course I understand that."

"I'd have thought that, as a businessman, you'd try to turn that to your advantage."

"I'm a businessman second, Percival. I'm a smart guy first. And the smart guy in me says that providing people the water of the Grail in order to cure what ails them, or help them feel better about themselves . . . that's one thing. But death is part of life. Death is what gives life its juice. Its immediacy. To say nothing of the fact that we've got enough overpopulation problems as it is. Can you imagine if no one died and people kept getting born? It'd be insane! The world's resources couldn't handle it. People cannot live by water alone, even if it's water from the Holy Grail."

Percival leaned back and regarded Barry as if seeing him for the first time. "All right," he said slowly. "So how do you suggest we compensate for it?"

"I don't know. Maybe we can spike it."

"Spike it?"

"Water down the water," said Barry. "Have the average bottle of . . . I don't know what we'd call it . . ."

"Grail Ale?" Gwen suggested, with a puckish look thrown toward Arthur.

"I like that," Barry said, grinning. "We'll toss some carbonation in to give it some fizz . . ."

"But it's not real ale," said Arthur. "You can't name something after an alcoholic beverage if there's no alcohol in it."

The waitress came back with the drinks, and said, "Who ordered the ginger ale?"

"Me," said Cook.

"And the root beer?"

Sal raised his hand slightly.

She put out the remainder of the drinks and all eyes turned to Arthur as she walked away.

"Fine, I stand corrected." He sighed.

"Anyway, we'd have Grail water be only one of the ingredients," said Barry cheerfully. "With any luck, it maintains its curative and restorative properties, but doesn't pack the full punch of the undiluted water."

"How would we know that for sure?" asked Percival.

"Percival . . . I'm no ordinary schmuck."

Sal spoke up, and said, "He's an extraordinary schmuck."

Gwen covered her mouth so as not to laugh out loud as Barry looked over at Sal. "Whose side are you on?" Sal shrugged. Barry turned back to his audience. "I have lab facilities. I have lab animals. We can run tests on them. Determine speed of cellular degeneration versus preservation. I've got top scientists at my disposal who can study this to an absolute certainty. I can assure you that we would not remotely consider going wide with Grail Ale until we were convinced that it was giving us exactly the result that we're seeking."

"And what would that result be?" asked Percival.

Sal spoke up once more. "It's good for what ails you."

"That's exactly it," agreed Barry. "A health tonic, pure and simple. It's not intended as a medicine, so we wouldn't have to go through the endless testing that the FDA would require. It's something that would work on every level . . . both physical and mental."

"How 'mental'?" Gwen asked.

"That's easy. Doctors will tell you that the health of a person's body has direct correlation to the health of a person's mind. It's one thing for Catholics to go in for mass, eat the wafer, and believe that they're communing with their God. But to drink water that has come into direct contact with the cup of Christ? My God, that's got to put some extra spring in your step. The positive feelings alone that it's going to generate simply can't be measured."

"Not everyone believes, you know," Arthur reminded him. "I've been watching the television, as I said. There are people out there who are ready to believe in me, in the cup, and what it has to offer . . . but there are also people who believe that we're regularly being visited by aliens who are obsessed with administering probes in their captives' nether regions. In short, there are people who believe in the Grail because there are people who will believe in anything. What about those who reject the concept?"

"Maybe they'll even think that Arthur manufactured this whole thing as some get-rich-quick scheme," added Gwen.

Barry smiled. "They're welcome to deny reality if they want. I mean, you didn't have a hope in hell, Mrs. Penn, of recovering . . . until the Grail did its work. Plenty of people are aware of that. And they saw that reporter on television as well, and heard how the Grail cured him. There will always be skeptics. But you know what's even more powerful than skepticism? Word of mouth. People are going to be buying and drinking Grail Ale, and they're going to be healthier than they've ever been and feel damned good about themselves besides. And other folks are going to be saying to them, 'Dang, you're looking good these days.' And you can just bet that they're gonna credit Grail Ale for the fact that they've never felt better in their lives. Faith is great and all that, but people believe the evidence of their own eyes. If that evidence matches our claims, the skeptics are going to be the first ones in line. Trust me, there's no one who's more passionate about something than a converted skeptic."

"And if it's diluted, will it still cure the sick?" Gwen asked.

"We can't know that before testing. That should provide us all the answers we need."

"The poor," Arthur said abruptly.

Barry blinked in confusion. "I'm sorry?"

"The poor. I assume you're going to be charging money for this beverage? This Grail Ale?"

"Well, sure, of course. And it's not gonna be cheap, I can tell you that."

"Fine. But I want to make sure that a sizable quantity is made available free of charge to the poor. The starving. The downtrodden in countries that ordinarily wouldn't be able to acquire it."

His eyes widening, Barry sputtered, "Now . . . now come on, your Highness! That's going to be—"

"Expensive? Difficult? I've no doubt. But it has to be done nevertheless. If this concept is intended to fill the gap for my inability to go to every man, woman, and child who needs the help of the Grail . . . then the least you can do is everything possible to distribute the drink to those who need it most."

"Sire, I'm still not certain this is the wisest course," Percival said worriedly.

"Percival, I . . ."

"Here you go." It was the waitress, putting the burgers in front of everyone as briskly as she could. But when she got to Arthur, she placed his down carefully in front of him and Arthur noticed she wasn't taking her eyes off him.

"Is there a problem?" Arthur asked.

She hesitated, and then said, "My mother . . . she's got arthritis so bad, she can barely stand. And I thought, maybe . . ."

Gwen moaned, and Barry tried to shoo her off, but Arthur put up a hand that instantly silenced both of them. He stared into the waitress's eyes for a moment, then said to her, "Bring me a pitcher of water and a glass."

Not comprehending, the waitress nevertheless scrambled to do as Arthur had instructed her. "The Grail, Percival," Arthur said.

As always, when given a direct order, Percival offered no resistance. He handed the Grail over to Arthur. When the waitress returned, Arthur took the pitcher of water, poured half a glass of water into the Grail as she watched with wide eyes, then transferred the contents from the Grail into the glass. He then tilted the pitcher and filled the remaining half of the glass with the normal water from the pitcher.

"Take this to her and have her drink it in its entirety," Arthur said, picking up the glass with the water mixture in it. "I am going to return here in exactly one week so that you can report to me your mother's condition. You are to tell no one that I am returning. If you do, and I see people waiting here for me, you will never see me again. Is that understood?" She nodded. "I want to hear you say that you understand."

"I understand, sir."

"Good."

"What's . . ." She looked at the glass of water almost reverently. "What's going to happen when she drinks this?"

"Honestly? I haven't the faintest idea," he admitted. "I have to make that clear to you. We are dealing with strange, mystic forces, and I cannot absolutely guarantee that your mother will end up better off than she is. For that matter, she may end up worse. I mean, I doubt that she will drink of this water and erupt into flames . . . but anything is possible . . ."

She took the water from him and murmured something in Spanish that Arthur took to be some manner of prayer. "She's going to be fine. She's going to be cured. I know it."

"How do you know?"

"I have faith. God would not have brought you to me, to this time, to this place, for no reason. There has to be a reason."

"What if there's not?" Percival asked. "What if things happen simply because they happen, for no rhyme or reason."

The waitress shook her head. "I couldn't live in a world like that."

"If that's the way it is," said Percival, "then you're living in it whether you want to or not."

"But that's not the way the world is."

"That's circular logic . . ."

"Percival," Arthur said softly, and shook his head.

Percival sighed, then said, "Good luck with your mother."

"Thank you." She handed them a piece of paper. "Here."

Arthur picked it up and looked at it. "It's the check."

"Yeah."

Arthur looked at the others, then laughed. "You'd think that curing a woman's mother would be enough to get a free meal."

Barry reached over, picked up the check, and said confidently, "I've got it. Think of it as an advance on all the business we're going to do together." He handed a business card to Arthur. "Here's the deal: You take your time. Think about it. In a week's time, you'll check back with this young lady. And at that point, you'll call me and tell me whether we're good to go or not. Just to show you you can trust me, I'm not even going to ask you for a sample of Grail water for my lab boys to start working on."

"I doubt your lab boys would find anything useful," said Percival. "There's no test for the ineffable."

It was the mostly silent Sal who spoke up. "If there is, we'll find one."

The comment concerned Arthur, but then he saw the hopeful look in the waitress's eye and decided to let it pass.

CHAPTRE
THE FIFTEENTH

✝

ᴅERY LITTLE WAS said or discussed in the castle for the next week. Arthur became more and more absorbed in watching the various TV screens scattered throughout the castle. Despite the fact that he'd been gone for months now, he was still a hot topic of conversation. "Arthur Sightings" were a regular feature in all the news shows. Tonight reports had come in from Cairo, Guam, Chicago, Brazil, and New York City. That last report was a woman who swore that she'd seen Arthur, the first lady, and several others emerging from a run-down diner. Arthur grimaced. They'd been walking back from the diner, and when that infernal little yapping dog had started trying to chew on Excalibur hanging invisibly at his side, he'd known it was going to result in trouble. In for a penny, in for a pound: He should have just yanked out his sword and sliced the little mongrel in half. But that wouldn't have solved anything and just left evidence of his having been there. And the dog would have been a goner. No amount of water from the Holy Grail would put a bisected canine back together.

He watched reports of prayer meetings. He saw people gathering, dressed in medieval garb, holding up replicas of the Holy Grail. Every Renaissance Fair in the United States was having Arthur-oriented gatherings. He saw people actively praying that he would show up, Grail in hand, ready to dispense aid to the sick and suffering.

Nor could the newspeople get their fill of covering outraged men (and women) of the cloth who were complaining about the growing interest in Arthurism (as it was being called) and the growing number of people calling themselves Arthurians. No one could demonstrably prove that the Arthurians consisted of disaffected Christians or even Jews (although the Muslims seemed to be finding the entire thing tremendously amusing). From speaking to them, it seemed that most Arthurians consisted of people who had grown bored or fed up with most mainstream religions and saw Arthurism as offering something solid, practical, realistic, and down-to-earth. No praying to unseen deities. No worshipping a God that dispensed death through hurricanes, tornadoes, or tsunamis, and was content to let the good suffer and the wicked thrive. No, in Arthurism, there was simply a good and devoted head honcho with proven leadership qualities, capable of defending those who believed in him and performing indisputable miracles. As one Arthurian put it, "It's like getting into Christianity on the ground floor. It's like being there when it all first started. A thousand years from now, we'll be looked on as the lucky devils who basked in the presence of the true savior of humanity."

This, naturally, was the attitude that led to anger and protest from the representatives of various organized churches. Arthur sat and watched in frustration, shaking his head as everyone from Cardinal Ruehl on down spoke against him, calling him everything from a charlatan to a scam artist to the leading candidate as the Antichrist. The Pope had remained reserved and detached from the furor, settling only for saying (through spokespeople) that he was "disappointed" in the course of action that former President Penn was pursuing, and suggesting that perhaps he had never been quite right since his wife was fired upon by terrorists.

To make matters worse, every Arthurian gathering of any size could almost be guaranteed to find itself plagued by protesters who took exception to such get-togethers and considered them blasphemous. Thus far none of them had broken out into violence, as interviewed protesters would simply explain that they were concerned about the immortal souls of these poor benighted (no pun intended) individuals, and they were trying to put them back on the proper path before it was too late. Still, as far as Arthur was concerned, it was only a matter of time before violence did indeed rear its head. He felt, yet again, that growing sense of helplessness, expanding to such proportions that he wasn't sure how much longer he could stand it.

On one occasion, he became aware that Gwen was watching over his shoulder. She winced as an archbishop excoriated Arthur and his undoubtedly evil intent, and Arthur said, "You shouldn't be watching this."

"You're my husband. How could I not?"

"They're bastards, the lot of them."

"No, they're not." She walked up behind him and rested both her hands on his shoulders. "They're scared."

"Scared of what? Of becoming irrelevant? Useless? Scared that people will flock away from them and to me?"

"There's some of that, sure," she agreed. "But have you ever considered that maybe they're just scared of the notion of being wrong? I mean, they've pinned their entire lives, careers, faith . . . their belief in what will happen to them when they die . . . all on Jesus. And you come along and say, No,

Jesus wasn't divine, he just happened to acquire godlike abilities through drinking from this cup. If you challenge his divinity, you challenge the very center of their belief system."

"Well . . . maybe you were right. Maybe the two aren't mutually exclusive. Jesus could have been the Son of God, and his father led him to the Holy Grail so he could have abilities on Earth that would impress his followers."

"Yes, and I hear that evolution and creationism can also exist side by side," said Gwen, "so that should put that argument to bed once and for all, right?"

He laughed softly. "Yes, I hear tell that that dispute has been long ago dispensed with."

She watched the news unfolding on television, and commented, "It looks like there's going to be an Arthurian gathering in Central Park. Don't suppose you'd want to stick your nose in, say 'hi,' right?"

"That would be the height of folly, Gwen, and you know it."

"Probably. But that's never stopped me before."

"Nor I." He rubbed his eyes, suddenly feeling very tired. "I wish Merlin were here. He'd know what to do."

"Maybe. Or maybe he'd just tell you it's all your decision . . . which, by the way, it is."

"Yes, well . . . let's see what happens with the young lady at the diner. And then . . . we'll take it from there."

WHEN A WEEK had passed, Arthur decided to head over himself to the diner to meet up with the waitress. As far as he was concerned, it was simple math: One person was going to have an easier time of remaining unobserved than two or three.

The fact that it was a Sunday wasn't lost on him. He passed various churches where services were being held, and he thought for a moment about going in and presenting himself.

But he decided that it really would be a rather unseemly action for him to undertake. It was bad enough that people on TV were accusing him of being in league with the forces of Satan. He didn't need some pastor or minister on a pulpit waggling an accusing finger at him, and shouting, *"Begone, creature of evil!"*

It was bewildering to him that all this had developed simply out of his desire to help people and tell the truth. Then again . . . look at what Jesus had gone through.

There you go again! You're not him! You're not some god, or even son of same, to be worshipped.

Then again, maybe Jesus told himself the same thing, and look how that turned out.

Yes! Just look at how it turned out!

He mentally shook off the inner dialogue like a cocker spaniel shedding water and approached the diner. He briefly felt a flash of concern. What if the waitress had ignored his express wishes and summoned the media? He might walk in there to a bevy of flashbulbs and a hundred questions being hurled at him at once. Well, he just had to trust that she had done as he instructed.

He stepped in and spotted her instantly. She'd been waiting for him. The place was deserted, just as it had been a week previously, except for the waitress . . . and one other person. The waitress was seated at a booth opposite someone, and when Arthur entered, she gasped and pointed. The other person turned and Arthur saw it was an older woman. Not just any older woman, but the spitting image of the waitress twenty, thirty years from now. Obviously it was her mother.

The waitress's mother was immediately on her feet, and she was speaking in rapid Spanish. Now he was wishing he'd brought Percival with him, who was fluent in the language.

But the specifics of what she was saying were less important than the generalities of what she was doing. She was rapidly moving her hands and fingers, her arms, stretching out her legs in one direction, then the other. The waitress then chose to pitch in by saying, "My mother is demonstrating how the arthritis has cleared up, almost overnight. Before it was practically crippling her, so that her hands were little more than claws. And now she uses them with no problem. She says she thought she was going to have to move to Arizona or some such awful place to ever have this degree of freedom again. She is saying that you have released her from the curse of her own body. That you are a miracle worker, and she will thank you in her prayers for the rest of her life."

The older woman nodded, then reached out toward Arthur. Her hand froze a few inches away from him, and she looked at him nervously, as if afraid to make contact. "It's all right," he assured her, and reached out to take her hand between the two of his. She gasped at the contact, and tears began to stream down her face. She said more of the same that she'd been saying before, and then she threw caution aside and wrapped both her arms around him, holding him tightly.

"Thank you," she whispered. "Thank you, thank you."

He awkwardly patted her on the back. "You're . . . most welcome, I assure you. And thank you for being a willing test case . . ."

That was when Arthur started hearing sirens. Police cars were speeding toward the area, the red lights atop their cars blazing red and their sirens cranked up to maximum. Prying the mother off himself as he would a banana peel, he stepped out onto the sidewalk and watched as the police cars barreled into the nearest entrance for Central Park.

Naturally what occurred to him was that Gwen or Percival or both had gone out looking for him, and something terrible had happened. Quickly he called, "I have to go.

Sorry," and sprinted off without waiting for the waitress inside to translate what he'd said for the benefit of her mother.

As he ran through Central Park, he found that the sirens were confusing him, particularly insofar as the direction from which they were coming. They were in a park, granted, but there were buildings lining the perimeter of it, and he was getting echoes and rebounds that made it difficult for him to know exactly where the police were. Every instinct was telling him that he should retire back to the castle, to play it safe. But he was Arthur, King of the Britons, wielder of Excalibur. He was sick to death of playing it safe. It was a bad fit for him, like an ill-made jacket.

Then he started to hear voices. People shouting . . . a lot of people. Chants and profanities, and from the sounds of it it was one group hurling imprecations at another group. He wended his way through the trees and found himself standing on the edge of a large field. Off to his right was a baseball diamond that was, at the moment, unoccupied. All the people present were more toward the middle of the field, engaged in exactly the activity he had thought he was going to see.

It was a mob, a huge one. Several hundred people at least, by Arthur's estimation, and maybe more. A sizable portion of them were wearing medieval garb, and they were in direct, head-to-head confrontation with other people shouting, bellowing, carrying signs that denounced Arthur and everything he stood for. More police were arriving with every passing moment, trying to get between the two infuriated camps. It was clear to Arthur what had happened. There had been a get-together, a prayer meeting, whatever one would want to call it. And it had been transformed into a demonstration, and perhaps even violence, when aggrieved protesters had shown up to voice their fury over the perceived slighting of their lord.

"The amount of violence that's been done in the name of the Prince of Peace," Arthur muttered, shaking his head.

"Shocking, isn't it."

Arthur started from the voice speaking in a droll manner from practically at his shoulder. His hand went reflexively for Excalibur even as he turned and realized that it was Percival standing there, and he relaxed with an exhalation of air. "Damn your eyes, you could make *some* noise when you approach. How did you get out of the castle?"

"I pushed the door open," he said reasonably. "Gwen's waiting just inside to push it open for me if I couldn't find you and needed to get back in."

"Why are you here?"

"Gwen was getting nervous over your lengthy absence, so I went looking for you on her behalf. I heard the sounds of trouble and figured you'd be nearby, if not the central cause for it."

"Apparently, I'm both."

"And you're going to do something about it, aren't you."

Arthur glanced around at the last and greatest of his knights with a raised eyebrow. "Is that a challenge, Sir Percival?"

"No, your Highness. Just a prediction, knowing you as I do. Candidly, I'd much rather we head back to the castle. You throw yourself into the midst of this, and I don't stop you, your lady wife is going to want to smack me upside the head."

"And yet you seem disinclined to stop me."

Percival shrugged. "Honestly, sire? Men like you and I . . . we're not built for standing aside and doing nothing. If we're not in the midst of the fray, we're just not happy. And I think you deserve happiness as much as the next fellow. Besides"—and Percival grinned lopsidedly—"your wife hits like a girl, so I think I can take it."

The roar of the crowd seemed to increase. Despite the police officers' best efforts, punches were being thrown and connecting. The two groups were surging toward each other, and any minute now, things were going to get seriously ugly.

Arthur put out his hand, and said firmly, "Percival . . ." He didn't need to complete the sentence as Percival handed him the Holy Grail.

Without hesitation, Arthur started out toward the area of the empty baseball diamond. He remembered that when Excalibur and the Holy Grail—then in the form of its sword—had come together in combat, the impact that the two had made had been formidable, to say the least. Now it was, of course, in the shape of a cup, and Arthur had no intention of smacking it around with Excalibur. Nevertheless, he had the feeling that the mere act of the two coming in contact with one another might be sufficient to gain the mob's attention.

He stopped on the pitcher's mound since it was centrally located, pulled out Excalibur, and held it outstretched in his right hand, the Grail in his left. Percival hung back, wary, as Arthur swept Excalibur around in leisurely fashion, bringing the flat of the blade slapping hard against the cup of Christ.

The result, while not as cataclysmic as when the two arcane objects had come together in combat, nevertheless had the exact result that Arthur had been hoping for. It created an earsplitting "clang" that reverberated across the lawn, blasting through the surging crowd like a physical thing. People staggered, grabbing at their ears, looking around in bewilderment for the source. Then someone, or several someones, spotted Arthur. There were points and shouts, and the crowd started to thunder toward him.

"This was a bad idea," Percival said nervously.

"We've faced thundering hordes before," Arthur reminded him. "And at least this lot isn't armed."

"You don't know that. For all those times when we went charging into battle, one man on the opposing side with an

Uzi would have put paid to the lot of us. All it takes is a single lunatic with a gun to open fire on you. Excalibur is fine as far as it goes, but you're not Obi-Wan Kenobi with that blade, you know, deflecting shots hither and yon."

"I'm not *what* with the blade?" Arthur said, looking bewildered.

"Obi . . . never mind." Percival sighed.

The foremost of the crowd had drawn within about a hundred yards, and now Arthur brought Excalibur around and pointed the blade so that it was indicating a short distance away. He did not move beyond that position, but his gaze was fierce, and his mute instruction fully understandable.

Percival, braced and ready for anything, wasn't at all prepared for what he now saw:

The crowd was slowing.

More . . . the crowd was stopping.

Both the Arthur supporters and those who despised him. Whatever chants of fury and outrage they were prepared to level in his absence seemed to die in their throats when they were actually faced with him.

He had known the king for so long, known him of old, that Percival had forgotten just how much personal intensity and charisma Arthur was capable of displaying when he was so inclined. But it was on view now, as if Arthur had whipped aside a cloak to reveal a brilliant core shining with greater intensity than the sun. It cowed people into speechlessness, making them act like they were afraid they'd be struck down by a bolt from the blue if they took aggressive action or voiced hostility aimed at the modern miracle that was Arthur Pendragon.

Even the police officers were thunderstruck into silence as they gazed at the newly returned Arthur with the same sense of wonderment that the others displayed.

With the slightest tilt of Excalibur's blade, he bade them sit. They sat. Some on their backsides, many on their knees with their hands resting on their thighs or behind them and leaning back. All the noise that had filled the field before was in stark contrast to the utter silence that pervaded it now.

And then, there on the pitcher's mound in a Central Park baseball diamond, Arthur began to speak.

He would speak until the sun began to set. At the end of it, he would have little to no recollection of everything that he said. Subsequent accounts would differ from the listeners, each of whom would remember those aspects that struck home, that reached most directly to the very center of their essence.

He would speak of loving one's neighbor. He would speak of the great accomplishments that humanity could achieve if only they were willing to work together instead of kill each other. He would speak of overcoming whatever obstacles were in the way of humanity reaching its full potential.

He would speak of the incredible things that he had seen and done in his lifetime. Of a world that was long gone, a dream that had been snuffed out through the intervention of the forces of evil. A world of chivalry, of power being used for the goal of protecting the weakest members of society. For Arthur himself had once been one of those weak members, the lowliest of the low, held in contempt by all those around him. The weak had to be protected, not simply because they were weak, but because they were just as likely to serve society as a whole and better humanity's lot in life, and therefore needed that additional protection so that they would have the time and opportunity to contribute. "If the acorns are crushed into the ground, how can the oaks ever hope to touch the sky?" he would ask.

At one point one or two protesters summoned up enough nerve to shout out challenges to Arthur. Others tried to shout them down, but Arthur would not hear of it. Instead he welcomed their dares, spoke to them gently and calmly and with respect. Instead of shutting down their complaints, he answered them directly and fully, and soon even they were nodding.

That was how the entirety of the late afternoon progressed. And then Arthur noticed some among the crowd who were desperately in need: A woman who looked wasted and weary, her hairless head badly disguised under an abysmal wig that couldn't begin to hide the side effects her chemotherapy had upon her. A man whose eyes looked glassy as glaucoma exerted its devastating effects upon him. He ordered Percival to take the Grail to a nearby water fountain and fill it. As Percival did so, Arthur spoke to the crowd of the dangers of immortality. Of how he could not, would not offer it to them, because he cared about them and knew that it would be wrong and against the will of God, for why else would people have been born with a built-in self-destruct mechanism if there wasn't some reason for it? But he was willing to help nevertheless, as long as people remained exactly where they were and trusted him implicitly.

The Arthurians nodded. The protesters nodded. The police nodded.

He walked through the crowd unmolested as he went from one needy person to the next and ministered to them. The hairless woman drank of it. The man who was practically blind tilted his head back as Arthur gently poured some of the water directly on his eyes. The small boy in the wheelchair who had been paralyzed by a hit-and-run driver drank deeply.

The hairless woman cried out as heat ran through her body, incinerating the cancer cells. The man with glaucoma cried out as the filtered rays of the sunset were visible to him. The boy cried out as his hands began to respond to his mental commands, and his feet started to twitch.

And the crowd cried out. They cried out Arthur's name, for the miracle of the Grail, for the words that he had spoken that filled them for the first time in a long time with an expectation—not simply that they would be able to tread water in the great flood of life—but that instead the flood was going to recede and leave them standing there on dry land with hope and optimism for a better life, a better world, for them and their children and their children's children.

Finally, Arthur told them to go home. To go home to their friends and loved ones and spread the word of what they had seen and heard this day. To let the world know that the healing effects of the Grail would be available to everyone throughout the world and that a new day of hope was dawning.

Percival never expected it to work.

But it did.

The people nodded and rose. Some of them approached Arthur as if they wanted to touch him or hug him, but Arthur simply pointed and said; lovingly but firmly, that it was time to leave. And they did. All of them did, as if under a spell, and if Percival hadn't known better, he'd have thought Merlin was somehow responsible. But there was no sign of Merlin; merely Arthur Pendragon, Arthur Rex, Arthur, King of the Britons.

Finally, when it was just the two of them, and the last rays of the sun were disappearing over the horizon, Percival asked, "You realize what they're going to call this, don't you." Arthur looked at him questioningly, and Percival pointed downward at the pitcher's hill upon which he was standing. "The sermon on the mound."

Arthur closed his eyes and moaned softly. "Let us hope, Percival," he said, as the two of them headed back to the castle, "that you are completely wrong."

As it turned out, Percival was exactly right. By the time the waiting Barry Seltzer got the phone call from Arthur that he knew he was going to receive, the Sermon on the Mound was already the stuff of legend. Ten times the number of people who were in attendance would wind up claiming to have been there.

And within a month, the preliminary batches of Grail Ale were in production.

Within several months after that was when all hell broke loose.

CHAPTRE
THE SIXTEENTH

✝

PRESIDENT TERRANCE STOCKWELL was staring out the bay window behind his desk in the Oval Office when Ron Cordoba entered. It was ten o'clock at night, and it wasn't all that extraordinary for Ron to be working there that late. But he was exhausted, more so than he'd been for a while. His wife, Nellie, was entering her ninth month of pregnancy and she wasn't doing it in the most graceful manner possible. So the few hours of sleep he was accustomed to getting each night had been shaved back even more; as a result there were times he felt as if he were sleepwalking through the days. Which certainly wasn't the best way to be for someone in his position, but he was doing his best to deal with it.

"You sent for me, sir?" he asked.

"Sit down, Ron," said Stockwell, without turning to look at him and without sitting down himself. Therefore, despite the invitation to do otherwise, Ron remained standing out of courtesy. "I've been in briefings and meetings all day, Ron," he continued.

"Yes, sir. I know. I received a copy of your schedule, same as always."

"Notice anything about it?"

"Anything in particular I should have been looking for, sir?"

"I think you know."

Ron sighed and, despite himself, now took a seat. It wasn't a mark of discourtesy so much as that his legs were giving out on him. "Sir, it's been a long day. With all respect, if you could just . . ."

Stockwell turned and faced him with an expression that could have been graven from marble. "I think . . . you know."

Closing his eyes and trying to ease himself away from the headache that threatened to overwhelm him, Ron said, "Grail Ale?"

"Grail Ale," confirmed Stockwell. He walked over to the desk and slid noiselessly into his chair. "Arthur Penn . . . the Holy Grail . . . and Grail Ale."

"Sir . . . there's no more rioting. No more mobs or illegal assemblies. That's all been attended to. And former President Penn and his entourage are now residing in very luxurious guest quarters owned by one Barry Seltzer—a perfectly honest businessman by all accounts—in the same secured compound where the Grail Ale is being produced. Granted, the stuff is flying off the stands faster than any store can keep them in, and bottles of it have been going for five hundred dollars and up on online auctions, but still . . ."

"I know all that."

"And the water itself has been thoroughly tested and vetted by the FDA. They've studied it six ways from Sunday and all they find is water. Plain water."

"I know that as well. Why do you think that is, if this water has the sort of restorative powers people ascribe to it?"

"Well," said Ron reasonably, "I suppose because there are no lab tests for magic that we know of. And if magic truly is a component, then nothing we've got could possibly measure it in any way."

"Do you think Mr. Seltzer faces the same problem?"

"I wouldn't know, sir."

"I daresay you wouldn't. Would you like to know what else I know?" And he leaned forward, his fingers steepled.

"Yes, sir."

"Fewer people are going to the doctor. Far fewer. And there are fewer people going to hospitals as well. Oh, granted, there's still the major traumas . . . loss of limbs, that sort of thing . . . that require medical attention. But the day-to-day ills of humanity—coughs due to colds, sore throats, aches, pains, inflamed livers, enlarged hearts, high-blood pressure, diabetes, for God's sake—these things are becoming much fewer and far between."

"Well . . . certainly that's a good thing, isn't it? People feeling better, healthier . . ."

"Do you have any idea how much money the medical profession generates, Ron? Between doctors, hospitals, home care, insurance . . . remember when people not having medical insurance was a major crisis? Now people are canceling their medical insurance. They've invested their future health in the curative properties of Grail Ale. And don't think I'm not hearing about it. From the insurance companies. From the lawyers who specialize in medical malpractice. From everyone who has a financial stake in the illness of America."

"I have no doubt that you are, sir," said Ron. "But, reasonably speaking, what could you possibly be expected to do about it? No one is breaking any laws . . ."

"So?"

Ron looked at him askance. "So? What do you mean . . . so?"

"I mean that simply because laws are not being broken doesn't mean that actions cannot be taken."

"On what grounds? On the grounds that Arthur is making people feel better?"

"On the grounds of national security."

Ron was astounded, feeling as if he were having a conversation that had dropped in from Wonderland. And why not? He had been friends with King Arthur and Merlin and squared off against Gilgamesh. Who was to say that the March Hare and Mad Hatter weren't popping by for a mad tea party. "National security?" He laughed, because the entire thing sounded too ludicrous to be taken seriously. "How in the world is helping people a matter of national security?"

"Because we don't know how he's doing it," Stockwell said.

"Does it matter?"

"Of course it matters! If he were passing out specially grown plants that were giving people a sense of euphoria on a national—make that international—scale, wouldn't it seem reasonable for the Federal government to intercede?"

"If it's an unknown substance, of course! But this is water! You said it yourself. Plain water."

"It's obviously not just plain water, and we need to obtain the so-called Holy Grail so it can be subjected to extensive studies."

"But it's not ours to take!"

"It wasn't Arthur's to take either. Nor . . . what was his name? Percival's," Stockwell said reasonably. "Was it? I mean, it was an ancient artifact. According to you, they recovered it from someone fancying himself to be Gilgamesh, of all things. But that doesn't mean they're entitled to it. Something like that belongs to the world, not one person."

"And the world is reaping its benefits. May I point out, sir, that you didn't bring any of this up when Arthur was here in the White House with the damned thing!" Ron had never, ever lost his temper in the Oval Office, but he knew he was coming awfully close and did everything he could to rein himself in. "You could have tried to keep him here! You—"

As angry as Ron was getting, Stockwell was the exact opposite, the picture of calm. "With the whole world watching, the city on the verge of blowing apart, and, oh, by the way, I didn't really believe what the Grail was capable of accomplishing? Yes, Ron, I could have done that, but I didn't. I screwed up. I should have just locked him up when I had the opportunity. Does that make you feel better?"

"No, Mr. President, it really doesn't."

"Ron"—and Stockwell drummed idly on the desk with two fingers—"the simple fact is that there's every reason for the government to take a stronger hand in this matter. Something that is affecting so many citizens, especially when it possesses properties that we can only guess at, simply has to be under our control. And don't ask me what right we have, because you know the term 'eminent domain' as well as I."

"That's for acquiring property for public works."

"It's for acquiring whatever we damned well say is worth acquiring."

"And you have to provide just compensation, as per the Constitution," Ron reminded him. "Grail Ale is projected to rake in billions. You'll have to empty out the entire Federal Reserve and throw in the Air and Space Museum and the USS *Eisenhower,* and you still probably won't be able to offer him what the thing is worth."

"We'll find ways. I'm sure he'll take money on an installment plan."

"And what I'm sure of," replied Ron, "is that he'll take off the head of whoever tries to remove the Grail from his possession. And if he doesn't, you can sure as hell bet that Percival will. You don't know what they're capable of, and you don't know what the Grail is capable of either." He leaned forward intensely. "It can transform into a sword, did you know that?"

"A sword?"

"A weapon of such power and magnitude, that I don't know what it's capable of. The only thing that stood up to it was Excalibur. I don't know if anything else could."

Stockwell's eyes widened. "So you're telling me that an object capable of possibly unimaginable destruction is in the hands of several private citizens . . . and we're not supposed to do anything about it?"

That stopped Ron cold. He wanted to rewind time and take back what he'd just said. Failing that, he wanted to beat himself upside the head with a baseball bat for being so damned stupid as to mention the vessel's other properties.

"How does it change forms?" asked Stockwell.

Ron knew that Percival had developed a sort of rapport with the Grail and was capable of controlling its form. But he wasn't certain if telling the president that was going to make matters better or worse. Which left him in one hell of a position, having to sit there in the Oval Office and lie to the president of the United States. Still, he decided to opt for discretion, and simply said, "I'm really not sure."

"You're really not sure."

"No, sir."

Stockwell nodded, continuing to drum on his desk. He had elected to use what was called the Kennedy desk when he had taken office. Ron could almost imagine John John darting around under the desk while his father worked. What was it that they called those days again? Oh . . . right. Camelot. Ron smiled mirthlessly at the recollection.

"Ron," Stockwell finally said, "here's what I need you to do. You know Arthur better than anyone here. I don't need to send the army in to invade Seltzer's compound and take the Grail by force. I don't need the bad press; I don't need the lousy pictures that will certainly accompany it that will make us look like a police state. Long story short, I don't need the grief and, as chief of staff, neither do you. What I want you to do is contact Arthur, tell him to come here. Quietly. Under the table. No fuss, no muss. And he has to bring the Grail. Tell him . . . tell him whatever you want. Tell him there's a dying five-year-old boy here in the White House whose last wish is to see the cup of Christ before he dies, that he's too ill to travel, that they gave him Grail Ale and it wasn't getting the job done so he needs the real thing. Come up with something. I have confidence in you."

"And you figure he's going to bring the Grail here . . ."

"And we'll do the rest."

Ron stared down the president. "The rest meaning . . . ?"

"Ron . . . I assume you've been listening to what I said. Let's not take another two or three trips around the barn. You know perfectly well what I mean by 'the rest.' "

"You're going to take it from him."

"By force if necessary, yes."

"It will have to be by force, I would think," said Ron Cordoba, "and furthermore, I don't think you're going to be successful."

"Really. Well, Ron, I have a national security advisor, a secretary of defense, and armed troops with enough gas grenades to bring down a herd of stampeding yak, all of whom say you're very much mistaken. But I want this to go down with minimal problems, and you're key to that."

Ron took a deep breath and let it out slowly. Somehow he'd known—he'd always known—that it would come to this sooner or later. "Sir . . . respectfully, I cannot be your 'key' in this matter. I think this is an abuse of power, and I cannot be a willing party to it."

"Then you can be an unwilling party to it," Stockwell said, still sounding amazingly reasonable about the whole thing. "Do it under protest, I don't care. But do it. Consider that a direct order."

Ron stood, steeling himself, squaring his shoulders, and wondering how in God's name he was going to tell Nellie about this. He was certain she would respect him for this decision far more than if he'd served as the bait to coax Arthur and Percival into a trap. Certainly he respected himself more. "Sir . . . if that is the case, then consider this my official resignation as your chief of staff."

He braced himself, wondering what Stockwell would do. He'd certainly seen Stockwell lose his temper any number of times. It could be a truly frightening thing to see. Granted, not as frightening as seeing two epic titans battling to the death while the ground beneath your feet was breaking apart, but daunting nevertheless.

But Stockwell didn't seem the least bit put out. Instead he continued to seem unnaturally calm. "And if I refuse to accept?"

"Well, I think your refusal is going to melt in the face of the irrefutable fact that I'm not going to be in my office anymore. If you want me to stay on, sir, then you're going to have to drop this plan to ambush Arthur . . ."

"So you're dictating terms to me now, are you?"

"That is not my intention, sir. But if the price of my remaining as your chief of staff is betraying Arthur Penn, then it's too high a price to pay."

Stockwell considered this for a time, then— infuriatingly—he merely shrugged. "That's your decision, Ron. If you'd like, we'll issue a press release in which you simply explain that you want to dedicate more time to being with your imminent family. How's that?"

Ron felt as if a body blow had just been delivered to his solar plexus. All he did, though, was nod, and say, "That would be fine."

He had been standing the entire time. Now Stockwell rose and stuck out a hand. "It's been an honor working with you, Ron."

"I regret it's come to an end, sir," said Ron, shaking Stockwell's hand and feeling as if he were having an out-of-body experience.

He started to turn and head for the door that led to his office, his mind still reeling at the unexpected developments of the past few minutes. In retrospect, though, he realized that not only should they have not have been unexpected, they were practically inevitable. Before he could exit, however, Stockwell said, "Ron . . . one thing."

"Yes, sir," he said, without turning back.

"Everything I've discussed with you falls under the heading of National Security. You may have tendered your resignation, but you're still bound by the confidentiality agreements you signed. If I have reason to believe that you've somehow warned Arthur of our intent . . . if I have reason to believe that you've interfered in this endeavor in any way . . . if I have reason to believe that you've violated confidentiality and betrayed government secrets . . . the first physical contact you're going to have with your baby is when you shake his hand at his college graduation. Do I make myself clear?"

Ron looked over his shoulder at the president, who was staring at him with an unwavering gaze. "I said," Stockwell repeated, "do I make myself clear?"

"Abundantly, sir."

"This remains between us, then. You're not even to tell your wife the specifics of what's gone on here. If you do, we'll find out."

Unable to believe what he was hearing, Ron asked, his voice dropping to a hoarse whisper, "Are you saying that you have my house *bugged*?"

"No," said Stockwell coolly. "But I know women. She won't be able to keep it to herself. She'll tell Arthur or Gwen, and we'll run into the same problem."

"You threatening to throw her in prison as well?"

President Stockwell gave the slightest shrug. "I certainly hope not. I will say, however, that I've certainly made far more difficult decisions in my time as president." Then he gave a cold smile. "Good night, Ron."

"Good night, Mr. President."

Ron exited the Oval Office for the last time, pulling the door closed behind him.

Stockwell sat there for a time, staring at it, wondering if Ron wasn't going to throw it open, and say "Surprise!" or "Gotcha!" or beg forgiveness. But none of that happened. Ron did not return nor, Stockwell suspected, would he ever.

He reached over and tapped his intercom. "You can come in now," he said.

A door on the far side opened into a waiting area and a man in elaborate robes entered. "Well?" he asked quietly.

"He reacted in exactly the way you said he would, your Eminence," Stockwell admitted.

"It was to be expected," Cardinal Ruehl said.

"In a way . . . I'm jealous."

Ruehl looked confused. "Jealous, Mr. President?"

"I don't think I've ever commanded that level of loyalty from anyone." It was clearly not something that he was comfortable or happy admitting, but he did so nevertheless.

"You are a good man, Mr. President," Ruehl assured him. "People recognize that. His Holiness recognizes that. And he knows that you will trust me now to do what must be done. Unless, of course, you wish to send troops in . . . ."

Stockwell shook his head. "That, your Eminence, is the last thing we want to do. I can't even begin to imagine how that would play on CNN. No, actually, I can imagine it. They'll be howling for my head and my approval ratings will be subzero."

"Then do not worry about it," said Cardinal Ruehl, and he patted Stockwell's back in an avuncular manner. "As I've told you . . . my people will attend to this matter."

"And who, precisely, are your people?" asked Stockwell suspiciously.

Ruehl smiled thinly. "Mr. President . . ."

Stockwell put up a hand before he could continue. "Plausible deniability?"

"Just so."

"All right. I'm trusting in you, then."

"You don't have to," the Cardinal assured him, and he pointed heavenward. "Place your trust in Him . . . and all good things will flow from that trust and benefit you and humanity."

"And the Grail?"

"We're on it," Ruehl said.

CHAPTRE
THE SEVENTEENTH

✟

*A*RTHUR IS CASTING *about, surrounded by water. He is drowning. No . . . stranger than that. He is submerged, but doesn't need to breathe. He is somehow drawing oxygen from the water itself, as if he were a fish. Still, he feels a sense of utter disorientation, unsure of which way is up or down. He reaches out all around himself and discovers that he is hemmed in on all sides. The prison that is holding him is round, cylindrical. He wonders how this can possibly be. He brings his fist through the water in slow motion and thumps against the clear container, but he can't get any velocity with his fist. He is trapped, feeling frustrated and impotent.*

Then, drifting a bit, he suddenly realizes where he is: He is trapped inside a gigantic bottle of Grail Ale. He has no clear idea how high it goes, although from where he's situated, it seems to go on forever.

He doesn't know how he got in there, and isn't at all confident that he's going to be able to continue breathing or surviving or doing whatever the hell it is he's doing there. He reaches for Excalibur at his side, but it's not there. Desperately Arthur is grabbing at his hip and his belt, but there's no sign of the sword. He is alone. Alone and helpless. He calls for Gwen, he calls for Merlin, for Percival, for anyone who can possibly help him. He cannot see beyond the perimeter of the bottle. For all he knows, he's surrounded by people peering in at him, pointing and shouting in derision as if he were a zoo animal.

He brings his foot up and slams it against the bottle, but it simply propels him to the other side, and he bounces back and forth between them like a pinball. He shouts again for aid. None is forthcoming.

And then a voice sounds angrily in his head. It's a voice he knows all too well.

Is this what you're reduced to?

Merlin?

Of course Merlin, *says Merlin's voice.* Who else would it be?

Where are you? Can you help me?

Merlin's tone is derisive. How typical. You hear from me for the first time in months, and the first thing you do is beg for help.

I wasn't begging! I was simply asking for help!

You got yourself into this. Get yourself out of it.

Merlin! *Merlin!*

He thrusts about, tossing and turning so violently that he swings his arm around, only to be rewarded with a loud shriek of pain as Gwen sat up in bed, clutching the side of her head.

Arthur, still feeling disoriented and confused, blinked in the darkness of the room, his eyes stinging with pain from being forced open without sufficient rest. "What . . . ?"

"Arthur!" Gwen shouted. "You hit me!"

"I *what?*"

"You were shouting something about Merlin, and thrashing around like a crazy man. I was just starting to wake up when all of a sudden, you clocked me in the face."

"I was asleep, Gwen. I really don't think it's fair to be held responsible for something I did when I was borderline unconscious."

"I suppose." She lowered her hand and presented her face. "Is there a bruise?"

"It's dark in here, and my eyes are half-closed. I'm not the best person to ask. Hold on." He reached over and turned on the lamp on their nightstand. Then he reached over, took Gwen's face gently by the chin, and turned her right and left. "Nothing. You look fine."

"Well . . . you got off lucky," she informed him.

"I'll say. I certainly don't need people saying I'm smacking my wife around."

The bedroom they were in was nowhere near the opulence of their digs back in the castle, but it was reasonably hospitable. Gwen and he had become accustomed to it. It had been a necessity, since Percival would not leave the Grail unattended and constantly commuting to and from Central Park simply wasn't practical. Percival's relocation to the compound had been a necessity, and Arthur and Gwen weren't about to leave him alone to his fate. When Arthur had reminded Barry that there was no telling how long they would have to be there, Barry had cheerfully declared, "Stay as long as you want! Stay forever! My home is your home!"

He wasn't exaggerating: The vast, walled compound where his factory was situated doubled as his residence, with a large and respectively impressive Victorian house situated smack within its confines. Gwen had raised questions about zoning, but Barry had simply grinned, and said, "You'd be amazed how flexible the zoning laws can be when the right people become . . . convinced." He had been as good as his word when it came to Arthur, Gwen, and Percival having anything they needed at their disposal.

Best of all, Barry had a private beach, the compound bordering on the Atlantic Ocean. So from time to time, Arthur and Gwen romped in the surf and enjoyed time together, although it was occasionally spoiled by determined paparazzi sweeping by in helicopters.

Percival never joined them.

Percival stayed by the Grail. At all times.

During the ten-hour manufacturing cycle, he was always by the Grail's side. At the end of the day, the Grail was returned to him, and he kept it with him until the morning. Gwen was even moved to comment to Arthur that Percival was a touch obsessive about the cup, but Arthur had simply said, "He is the Grail Knight. It is his duty. His calling. Who am I to contradict him?"

"His king," replied Gwen.

But Arthur had done nothing about it, and so the situation had remained, week after week, rolling into month after month.

Now Arthur sat on the edge of the bed, rubbing the sleep from his eyes. "I was . . . dreaming about Merlin," he said.

Gwen propped herself up on one elbow and regarded him thoughtfully. "It's certainly not the first time."

"I know, but it was the most vivid. He was talking to me . . . scolding me, actually."

"Yeah, that sounds like him, all right."

"Don't joke," he said.

"Now *you're* scolding *me.*"

"I apologize. But you should know by now how frustrated and concerned I am about Merlin. It's a sensitive subject for me."

"I do," she said, putting her hand atop his. "Do you think he was trying to . . . I dunno . . . communicate with you somehow?"

"It's possible, I suppose. I'm not exactly schooled in the delicacies of sorcery. The problem is, even if he is trying to get in touch with me . . . what am I supposed to do about that? If he needs my help, how can I possibly rescue him when all he provides me are vague, enigmatic contacts . . . and ones where he's yelling at me for that matter."

"Maybe he's still trying to figure that part out."

"Maybe." He stood. He was bare-chested, wearing only pajama trousers.

"Where are you going?"

"To the loo. Is that acceptable to you?"

"Go ahead. Skip to the loo, my darling."

He rolled his eyes. She never tired of that joke. It had been barely funny the first time she'd uttered it, and hadn't improved with age. But it was simply one of those things that one either got upset over or chose to find charming. He elected the latter for the sake of their union, just as he was certain there were idiosyncrasies of his that she found annoying. Marriage, he had found, was about mutual tolerance.

So he simply nodded and headed for the bathroom. As he did so, Gwen pulled the blanket up around her shoulders. The bed was large and expansive, with wrought-iron headboard and footboard, and she liked it better than the one in the castle. She rolled over and proceeded to drift back to sleep.

Arthur shuffled into the bathroom, making no attempt to stifle a yawn. The bathroom was carpeted, and it felt comforting beneath his feet. He merely had to pass water, and so he opened the toilet and stood over it, preparing to relieve himself.

He looked down in the toilet water and gasped.

Merlin's image was staring back up at him from the water.

"Put that thing away, Arthur," he snapped. "There are children present."

Arthur let out an alarmed yelp and jumped back. From the bedroom, Gwen called, "Arthur? What's wrong?"

"Merlin's in the toilet!"

Moments later, Gwen was at Arthur's side, looking down. She stared right at the grim reflection of the young mage, and said, "I don't see anything."

"How can you not? He's right there!"

"Arthur," she said gently, "I know you've been worried about him, but . . ."

"He's right there!"

"She can't see me, Wart," Merlin informed him. "I'm in your mind, not hers."

Arthur was about to respond, but then he saw the way that Gwen was looking at him. "It's okay, Gwen," he said, trying to sound soothing and instead just coming across as sounding weird. "Everything's going to be fine. I was just . . . I was dreaming."

"Dreaming," she echoed, sounding unconvinced. "Dreaming about Merlin in the toilet. You look awake to me."

"I was starting to doze while I was relieving myself."

She stared at him for a moment. "Oooookay," she said finally. Then, after another pause, she added, "Arthur . . . do you need to go back to the castle for a while? Have some space to yourself . . . ?"

"I'm fine. I'm just . . . I'm fine. It'd probably be best if you left now . . ."

"Yeah, I'm thinking the same thing," she said, then cautiously backed out of the room while continuing to keep a wary eye on him. Finally, she closed the door, and Arthur turned his attention back to the toilet.

Merlin was still scowling up at him.

"Merlin . . . how . . . ?"

"The Lady of the Lake has me imprisoned," he said sourly.

"Nimue? *Again?* How many times are you going to fall for being seduced by that—?"

"She didn't *seduce* me," Merlin snapped at him.

"You always had a blind spot with her, and she with you," said Arthur. "I've never understood two beings so mutually dedicated to being wrong for each other. What sweet nothings do you say to her, what names of endearment do you speak, that make her love you so much that she draws you to herself in some sort of eternally selfish dance . . ."

"It wasn't like that, you great pillock! I was damned near fatally wounded and sort of . . . fell into her realm."

"Wounded! Merlin, what—?"

"Stop asking questions, Wart, and listen carefully, for truthfully I don't know how much time I've got here. Are you listening to me?"

"Yes . . ."

"I'm in a sort of . . . of fluid nexus that touches all aspects of water on earth. Nimue can manipulate it with more facility than I, and can come and go as she pleases. I'm not as fortunate. But mankind had its origins in the miasma of the world's oceans, and every one of us is mostly fluid for that matter. Which means that I'm connected to humanity through that aqueous commonality, at least to some limited degree."

"That dream I had of you . . ."

"That was me, yes, manifesting in your mind. It's taken me a while to insinuate myself sufficiently into your very being to be able to make my presence directly known to you in this manner. Thus far you've merely been benefiting from the side effects of my presence within you."

"Side effects?"

"I thought I told you not to ask questions," Merlin said in annoyance.

But Arthur ignored him. "What benefits? What sort of side effects?"

Merlin blew air in irritation through his lips. The toilet water bubbled slightly. "Arthur . . . no one's denying you're a great speaker. A leader of men. Charismatic and all that. But did you really think that, single-handedly, you could turn that entire crowd in Central Park around with merely the power of your personality? This isn't a Mel Gibson movie."

"Are you saying that you added . . . what? Some sort of charm or charisma spell to me that . . . ?"

"I'm saying I pitched in. It was ninety-eight percent you, two percent me."

Arthur, who had been singularly proud of the way he'd handled that day in the park, said in annoyance, "Two percent? How significant can two percent be?"

"The DNA of chimpanzees differs from human DNA by two percent, so you tell me."

Arthur didn't have a ready reply to that, so Merlin resumed speaking. "I'm going to continue to try and work my way out of here . . . but in the meantime, at least I've managed to find my way to a place where I can give you a heads-up."

"You spoke of being wounded . . ."

"Yes," Merlin said grimly. "By the Spear of Destiny."

Arthur was taken aback. "The Spear? I thought that was myth . . ."

"As many thought you to be, which shows yet again the danger of assumptions. Someone came in behind me while I was distracted by Nimue, and he damned near gutted me. It took every bit of puissance I had to keep me alive, which was how Nimue was able to work her watery magiks to bottle me up. I can help you in small ways, Arthur. Introduce aspects of myself, the smallest bits of arcane knowledge or influence to aid you. But until I break out of here, that's all I can do, and I have to warn you of what you're facing. There's a necromancer or alchemist out there, he's wielding the Spear, and I'm reasonably sure he wants the Grail as well."

"Why? For its healing properties?"

"No. For its destructive properties." He shook his head. "You think you know the damage it can cause? You think your sword-to-sword battle enables you to imagine it? You have no clue, Arthur. Not the slightest hint. For all the good that the Grail can do, its capacity for destruction is phenomenal. You know the saying about the Lord giving and taking."

"It's from the book of Job," said Arthur. "'Naked came I out of my mother's womb, and naked shall I return thither; the Lord gave and the Lord hath taken away; blessed be the name of the Lord.'"

"Very philosophical. The problem is that it's more than just an acknowledgment that we come into this world with nothing and leave whatever we acquire behind. It's a commentary on yin and yang, pushing coming to shoving. For every action . . ."

"An equal and opposite reaction. Merlin, what are you saying?"

"I'm saying, Wart, that for all the good that the Grail does, then the Lord, or Karma, or the laws of physics, or however you want to define it, builds up an account going in the other direction. For every positive, there's a negative, and sooner or later, the negative is going to be released."

"I still don't under—"

And then, in a flash, he did.

"Merlin," he said slowly, "the Grail . . . we've been using it to . . ."

"To make happy juice for the minions of Earth, yes, I know that. Do you think I could possibly not know that, considering where I am?"

"And what you're saying is that—"

"For every person who benefits, every person who has a better life, every person who is cured or helped or whatever . . . somewhere, an invisible tally board gets chalked up another mark for the inevitable reaction to the action," said Merlin. "The destructive capability of the Grail, by this point, is increasing exponentially even as we speak. Sooner or later, the Grail is going to reach a breaking point of stored negative Karma, like a volcano being bottled up and eventually exploding. And when it reaches that point, there will be a terrible psychic backlash against humanity. What's worse is that, if it's combined with the Spear of Destiny, the amount of damage it can unleash would be cataclysmic."

"How cataclysmic?"

"Final cataclysmic, Arthur," Merlin told him. "As in the end of everything. As in scorched earth, if the Spear's wielder has that kind of determination."

"But who is it? Who's got the Spear?"

"I've been thinking about that, and I have some thoughts along those lines. I think the greatest likelihood is—"

At which point, Merlin's image continued to speak, but the words were no longer audible in Arthur's mind. Merlin was instantly aware that something was wrong, because he was clearly starting to shout. It did no good as his image suddenly wavered and disappeared.

Arthur wanted to shout Merlin's name, but he'd been speaking very softly the entire time in order not to awaken or alarm Gwen, and so he restrained himself. "Damn," he said softly, staring down for the longest time, but the wizard did not reappear.

With a frustrated sigh, Arthur took care of the business he'd originally come into the bathroom for, washed his hands, and went back to bed. But sleep did not come to him that night as he stared in concern at the ceiling and wondered just what the hell he was going to do now.

*ℳ*ERLIN GLOWERS AT *Nimue, who waggles a scolding finger at him and speaks to him in a scolding, somewhat patronizing tone.* You have been a very naughty little wizard.

Get closer to me with that finger, and I'll shove it so far up your backside you'll poke your eyeball out from the back.

She laughs lightly at that. Oooo, how you do talk. And to whom you talk. You were speaking to Arthur, weren't you?

You know every damned thing in the world. You tell me.

She is around him then, encircling him. He feels the caress of her around his face, around his body. Merlin, *she sighs,* why do you torture yourself?

I don't. I have you to do it for me.

Why do you dally with the concerns of the outer world when I have so much more to offer you?

There's nothing you have to offer me that I could possibly want . . .

Her voice is whispering in his ear, and there is something terribly, terribly seductive about it. He feels a tingling that he neither wants nor needs, and yet cannot help but attend to what she says.

I can restore you to manhood, *she tells him.* You are aging backwards, true enough. But I can reverse the reversal, for the ebb and flow of the waters of reality are mine to command.

You can turn back time? Is that what you're saying?

In general? No. But you are a creature of mysticism, Merlin. The arcane is in your blood, and as such, I can help you—*and she swirls around to the other side of him*—and you can help me.

And what do I have to do in order to receive this boon?

Why . . . stay with me fore'er, of course. Who better to put to use your manly body than I . . . ?

He casts a glance at her and has trouble finding her, for she is so much a part of the waters that surge around him. I thought your interests had turned to the wielder of the Spear. Yet now you attempt to seduce me once more?

I am as vast as the waters of the world. I shift as the mood and tide take me.

And how do I know that you won't then shift away from me once more?

Ahhh, but if I do, *she purrs to him,* you will always be the one that I ultimately return to. Could you not take solace in that?

Get away from me, *he says angrily. He is not without resources, even in these circumstances, and he is able to push her away with the force of his will. She is startled by this display of power, is taken aback by it.* Merlin, how can you treat me so . . . ?

How can I treat you so! You . . .

He restrains himself then, tries to focus back in on what is important. And maybe, just a little bit . . . he seeks to understand some of the motivations that inspire this elemental creature. He thinks of the words of Arthur, of all things, and speaking names of endearment to her. He remembers when he first encountered her, when the world was just a little bit younger. Merlin, who was thought by many who encountered him to be either a god or, at the very least, demonspawn, found himself falling in love with a being who truly was divine. She had so many names, was worshipped by so many throughout her possibly endless lifetime . . . so many . . . he had taught her magic because it pleased her, and she pleased him, and she had needed it so desperately . . .

He whispers a name very softly, so softly that no one in the world could possibly hear it, and yet she does. Her impish dance around him slows, and she says, What did you say?

Coventina, *he repeats, for there is power in the speaking of names, and influences that the right name can have upon the so-named.*

She recoils in surprise. No one has called me that in . . .

Coventina, *he repeats, speaking the name that the Celts called upon when they were gathered in the midst of Stonehenge, seeking the blessing of waters upon their crops or their lives. And then the name uttered by the Romans,* Mnemosyne. Mnemosyne, look what you've done to me.

He hears a choking sound from her, and somewhere very far away, the creatures of the sea sense something wrong and do not know how to react.

Do not call me those . . . no one calls me those . . . it makes me feel . . .

Sad? *He actually smiles in sympathy.* Or nostalgic. Nostalgic for the days when your name lived on the tongue of so many people as a being who was genuinely relevant to their lives, rather than merely a fictional construct who serves as a plot means for Arthur to acquire Excalibur. You had a life before him, as did I, yet now you are bound only to him and thought of only in connection to him and me. Coventina, Mnemosyne . . .

She sounds as if she's pleading with him. Stop. Merlin, stop . . .

Mneme . . . Co-Vianna, Vivian, Nimue, I call upon you now . . .

Clapping her hands over her own ears, she tries to drown out the driving intensity of his voice, filled not with anger and frustration as it has been until now, but with patience, understanding, and worship. Please, no, Merlin, stop . . .

Niviene, Argante, *he continues implacably,* so many names once worshipped, so many fallen into disuse, with the actual worship of you confined only to desperate gamblers who call upon the corruption of your best-known title, Lady of the Lake—Dame du Lac—into Lady Luck. Once you were called upon by heroes such as Perseus or Arthur to provide them weapons . . . and now you're invoked by alcohol-besotted gamblers who are hoping you'll bless their dice . . .

WHY ARE YOU DOING THIS? *Her voice howls within his head, buffeting him with the raging intensity of the storm.*

I am doing nothing, *he replies,* except trying to get across to you the sense of loneliness and frustration I'm going to feel . . . by reminding you of what you must have felt all this time. When we found each other, centuries ago, interest in you was already waning, and your power with it. What a low and sad creature you were when we first encountered one another, and yet I loved you anyway. I taught you magic because I loved you so, then you imprisoned me, because it pained you too much to keep looking upon the face of one who had seen you at your lowest. You've used my magiks well, Nimue. If not for your influence in the memory of man, Arthur and I might well have been forgotten during our long imprisonment. You aided Arthur and me upon our return, I will always remember that. But now the legend of Arthur has spread beyond the dreaming mind of man and into reality, and you know that that is what truly angers you. So you attempt to imprison me, to dispose of Arthur . . . to bring an end to everything rather than risk becoming irrelevant yet again.

She has moved away from him, and her voice is becoming distant. It is not like that. It is not like that at all.

Yes, it is. It is exactly like that, and I have never been more disappointed in you, milady, than I am in you at this very moment. You claim to love me, but you are incapable of passing the one true test of love . . .

To let true love go? *Her voice echoes through the ether to him, and the disgust in her tone is palpable.*

Yes.

A vile and nonsensical notion, *she assures him.* And you know nothing of me, no matter how many of my ancient names you hurl at me. You do not wish to be restored to your maturity? Fine. Then remain here and rot for all I care.

There is a tearing of the water around him as if he were trapped in a riptide, and he feels as if his torso is going to be yanked in one direction while his lower half is hauled in another. For a heartbeat he really thinks he is going to be torn apart by the force of Nimue's departure, then she is gone, and he settles back onto the floor of the nexus of all vortexes.

THAT could have gone better, *he mutters to no one.*

CHAPTRE THE EIGHTEENTH

✝

NELLIE PORTER CORDOBA, former right-hand woman of Gwendolyne Penn, and carrier of the off-spring of herself and husband Ron, stared across the kitchen table at her husband with a face that had gone several shades of pale. Ron couldn't meet her gaze and instead became very focused on the table's shining wood surface. Not for the first time did he make note of the fact that their table was round. He found it comforting to know that, despite everything that had happened, he could still appreciate irony.

It had been difficult enough for him when he had come home the previous night and informed Nellie that he had quit his job. On the one hand she'd been upset since, naturally, mere weeks away from giving birth is not the time that a woman wants to discover her husband's out of work. On the other hand, it hadn't come as a total shock to her. She knew that Ron was becoming increasingly unhappy with the relationship between himself and the president. She wasn't stupid. She knew something was going to have to give sooner or later, and she'd been pretty damned sure it wasn't Stockwell who was going to be doing the giving.

So she had tried to find the bright side, to be a good and supportive wife.

However, she was not a stupid woman by any means and was soon able to figure out that there was more than what Ron was telling her on the surface, namely that he and Stockwell had disagreed over matters of national security. She had pushed and prodded as gently and insistently as she could, and finally an apprehensive Ron had brought her into the kitchen, turned on every appliance from the garbage disposal to the dishwasher to the blender, cranked up the radio besides, and drew her close to him at the table and spoke softly of the specifics of his and Stockwell's last conversation.

He had watched as her face had gone more and more pale, her vivid blue eyes widening and standing out in stark contrast to the sudden pallor of her skin. "You can't be serious," she whispered after Ron finished.

"I wish I wasn't."

"You *can't* be *serious*!"

"And again, I am. Did you take your vitamins today?"

She made a face over being reminded of what seemed so trivial a notion, but she resolutely got up, went to the cabinet, retrieved the little vitamin tray that she meticulously maintained with all the proper supplements the doctor wanted her to take during the pregnancy. Popping the appropriate medication into her mouth, she swallowed it with a glass of water and returned to the table. "Happy?" she whispered.

"Ecstatic."

"We have to—"

"No," he said, anticipating what she was going to say.

"—warn them . . ."

"We can't."

"Ron!"

He drew even closer to her until his lips were practically against her ear. "If they find out . . . they will put me in jail. Do you understand that? Stockwell wasn't kidding. Hell, they might charge me with treason, and I can't say for sure that it won't stick!"

"But what about Gwen! And Arthur!"

"Arthur's been taking care of himself for a thousand years. He doesn't need me to put my neck on the chopping block for him."

"Oh really," she said sarcastically. "Taking care of himself. Let's check the record, shall we?"

"Nellie . . ."

She started ticking off instances on her fingers. "Mortally wounded by his bastard son a thousand years ago. Almost died. Needed ten centuries to recuperate. Came back, ran for mayor, attacked and killed and barely brought back through medical science. Became president and his wife was nearly killed, and embarked on a quest to save her that almost killed him yet again and some other people as well . . . who were they again . . . ?"

"Look, I know you're concerned about—"

"Oh! I remember! You and me!" She slammed her open palms hard on the table, causing the cups to tremble. "Based on his track record, I'd say he needs all the help he can get."

"Well, he can't get it from us!" whispered Ron. "Not this time!"

"Arthur would do anything he could to help you if you needed him. And you won't do whatever you can to help him? Warn him?"

"That's right. And you know why? Because in the end, he's a legendary king, and I'm just some guy."

"He was just some guy too, Ron, at one point. He made himself a legend. And if you—"

Then she stopped, blinked, and put her hand on her stomach. "Wow."

"Wow what?" asked Ron, concerned.

"What a really hard kick," she said.

And then her eyes rolled up into her head, and she slumped sideways. Before Ron could catch her, she slipped out of her chair and crashed heavily to the floor. She lay there with her eyes still open, spittle trickling from between her lips, and he crouched over her, screaming her name, his shouts unheard over the cacophony of noise emanating from the kitchen.

CHAPTRE
THE NINETEENTH

✝

PERCIVAL SAT IN front of the Grail, as he had every day since they had come to the factory, and would continue to every day for as long as they were there.

He had to admit that the device Barry Seltzer had developed for siphoning water through the Grail was nothing short of ingenious. Nothing had been done to the cup itself: no holes drilled in, no intrusion on the surface. Percival would have fought to the death to prevent such a thing, and he doubted that Arthur would have requested it of him.

Instead Barry had developed a system of elaborate tubes that filled the Grail—which sat in the middle of a massive rig that occupied an entire large room—with water and withdrew it in a constant, steady stream. The water then moved to another section where it was blended with standard bottled water to create the appropriate mix. That was then pumped to another room where bottle after bottle with the label GRAIL ALE on it slid through on massive high-speed conveyor belts. Workers kept a careful eye on the entire process, steadily making adjustments so that everything moved along smoothly and in an uninterrupted manner.

At the end of the manufacturing day, the Grail would be returned to Percival, who then took it to his room and kept it safe. During the day, he sat and watched in a reasonably comfortable chair that Barry had provided him.

Most of the day, no one disturbed him. His Highness would stop by at least once a day, checking in with him, asking him the same sorts of questions every time. "Are you all right?" "Is there anything I can get you?" "Do you need to take a break?" Arthur never seemed to tire of asking those questions, and although it was frankly becoming a bit tiresome to Percival, he knew that the king was merely being solicitous. So he always remained respectful in addressing his liege, but firm in his certainty that he needed no special attention.

This day, though, he was mildly surprised when Barry showed up at his side. He said nothing to Barry, nor did Seltzer speak to him. They simply watched together the smooth processing of the machine.

"Don't you ever get tired of it?" Barry asked.

Percival looked up at him curiously. "Of what?"

"Of sitting here, day after day."

"I'm the protector of the Grail. I'm doing what I'm supposed to do."

"I guess," Barry said with a shrug. He didn't seem to understand, even remotely, Percival's dedication. Clearly he was just making conversation. "I guess we all do what we're supposed to do."

"Some of us. Some of us do what we have to do. And some of us do nothing at all, even though we should."

"Where do you think I fall into that?"

Percival frowned. "Why do you ask?"

"I dunno," said Barry. "I guess . . . well . . . I guess I just kind of envy you, that's why."

"Envy me."

"Yeah." Barry forced a smile, but there was pain in it. "I been around a bit, y'know? Had my hand in a lot of things. But I never had anything . . . not a woman, not a product, not anything . . . that I cared about a tenth as much as you care about that cup. I mean, part of me thinks you're kinda nuts because, hey, it's a cup for Christ's sake . . . no joke intended. You got this, y'know, obsession for it, and obsession for anything ain't healthy. But, I mean, honest to God, to care as much as you do . . . to have that kind of passion for something . . . for anything . . . that's where the envy comes in. I wish I could find something that I care that much about, the way that you do."

"Well," Percival showed his white teeth, "if you get to spend a thousand years or so thinking about something that slipped through your fingers . . . you'd probably care about whatever that is as much as I do about the Grail."

"I don't think I'll have that kind of time to devote to it," Barry laughed, "but in the meantime, I'm doing the best I can. And what we're doing here"—and he gestured to the machinery—"is good work."

"What we're doing here is playing God."

Barry looked taken aback at the tone of Percival's voice. "You got a problem with all this, Percival?"

Percival stared fixedly at the cup. "This is the Holy Grail, Mr. Seltzer. This is ancient magic. The miracles this cup can perform may well have given rise to one of the dominant religions in the world. A religion that may well break apart as the result of what we're doing here."

"Don't you think people are entitled to the truth?"

"I think people are entitled to whatever will get them through the day," said Percival.

"I had the impression you were no great fan of the Church."

"My feelings on the Church are mixed. But I'm a believer in faith. It almost doesn't matter, all the bodies that we are helping and healing with this . . . product. Think of all the instances of faith we may well have shattered with the revelations we've made."

"People bounce back, Percival. They're more resilient than you're giving them credit for."

"We're trivializing the miraculous, Mr. Seltzer." There was disappointment on Percival's face. "We're bringing the mystical down to Earth. We're taking the fantastic and making it mundane. Faith works because of so much that is unknown, and the mind fills in the gaps. The faithful make their belief work for them, and that gives it its potency. We've turned the Holy Grail into a health tonic. No different than sports drinks packed with electrolytes. We've bottled it and stuck a label on it, and we're sending it out to retail outlets throughout the world. How is that remotely honoring the greatness of the Grail's legacy?"

"I don't see that it's any different," Barry said, "from taking an ancient device of execution on which thousands of people died suffering, agonizing deaths, shrinking it down to this big"—he brought his thumb and forefinger close together—"and people wearing it around their necks to make themselves feel good. You tell me? How is it different?"

"Perhaps it's not," allowed Percival. "But is that, in the final analysis, the excuse to which we resort? That we do it because it's just the same as somebody else is doing? What's wrong with aspiring to be better?"

"You've obviously given this a lot of thought," said Barry. "Maybe too much."

There were footsteps behind them, and both turned to see Arthur approaching. "Barry," he said briskly, "we need to talk."

"When the king wants to talk, I obey," Barry said, bowing slightly. Gesturing in an "after you" fashion, he said, "In my office?"

"That would be perfectly acceptable."

* * *

"THIS IS UNACCEPTABLE!"

Barry looked as if his world was spinning around him. He was seated behind his desk, clutching his heart as if trying to prevent it from bursting out his chest. "Unacceptable," Barry repeated. "Mr. President, how can you do this to me?"

"It's not a decision I'm making lightly," said Arthur. "You have to believe me in that regard."

"I do, but . . . Jesus!"

"Arthur. A common confusion."

"I'm not making jokes here, Mr. President! The number of accommodations I've made in order to . . ."

Arthur put up a hand, stilling the protests. "No one is saying you haven't done your job or lived up to your end of things, Barry. But it's come to my attention that what we're doing here has a vast potential backlash . . ."

"See, I knew this was going to happen. I knew that once you heard about the lawsuits, you'd want to pull the product."

"That's not it at all, and you just have to trust . . ." Arthur stopped and stared at him. "Lawsuits? What lawsuits?"

"You didn't know?" Barry blinked owlishly.

"No, I didn't know. What are you talking about?"

Barry sighed as if he bore the weight of the world. "There are some people who are having adverse reactions—or at least claim to be doing so—to Grail Ale."

"What sort of 'adverse reaction'? Stomach cramps, rash . . . ?"

"No, nothing like that."

"What, then?"

"Dreams of eternal damnation, burning in hellfire, swimming in streams of molten lava, that kind of thing . . ."

"They're having *bad dreams*?"

"Yeah. See, my people are telling me these suits are completely without foundation . . ."

Arthur was appalled at the notion. "But . . . if it were true . . . why would water from the Grail be giving them bad dreams?"

"Ah. Well, see, that I have an explanation for," Barry said confidently. "See, my researchers checked into the ones who are suing us? Turns out each and every one of them is evil."

"Evil?"

"Yeah. Unrepentant sinners. Corrupt businessmen. People who committed violent crimes and walked away 'cause they had connections. Slimeballs, scumwads. Societal parasites, the lot of them. This is nothing that you should get your armor in a knot about. My people will manage to convince any jury we draw that not only are these claims without foundation, but if they *did* happen to be true, these bastards had it coming."

Arthur sank back in his chair, stunned over this latest development. "My God," he whispered. "Just imagine if they'd drunk of undiluted Grail water."

"They'd probably have spontaneously combusted. What can I say?" Barry shrugged. "God's a funny guy. Me, my guess is that if they cease drinking the water—which they have— then sooner or later it's going to work its way out of their systems. Like you said, it's not the same as drinking straight from the cup. So anyway . . . if that's what was bothering you, like I said . . ."

"It wasn't what was bothering me, but I can assure you it's going to be bothering me now. Barry . . . you have to trust me. It's over."

"Arthur," Barry said, and he looked so frustrated that Arthur felt sympathy for him. "We're doing incredible work here! Monumental work! We're helping humanity on a global scale, and you want to see it in the toilet! What would make you want to do that?"

"Something I saw in the toilet."

Barry stared at him uncomprehendingly. "What?"

"I told you, I can't explain it to you. You have to trust me when I say that we need to pull the plug. Not just on your operation. As much as I've entertained the notion of traveling the world with cup in hand, helping the poor and suffering, I can't do that either. There's simply too much danger involved. The water you're bottling right now must never leave the compound and has to be disposed of safely. The water that's out in the marketplace . . . If there's any left on the shelves . . . should be recalled. And the Holy Grail will never, ever be used to cure another person. You have my word on that."

"Arthur!"

Arthur turned in his chair and saw Gwen standing in the doorway. She looked upset, and her chest was heaving. Wherever she'd been before that moment, she'd run all the way to the office. Immediately Arthur was on his feet. "What's wrong, Gwen?"

"I just got off the phone with Cook, from Washington. It's Nellie."

"What's Nellie? Nellie Porter? Nellie, Ron's wife?"

She nodded. "She needs us," she said. "She's in some sort of coma. She needs the power of the Grail, or both she and the baby could die."

The King of the Britons felt a distant headache beginning to thud in his temples as, from behind his desk, Barry said quietly, "Well, well, your Highness . . . I guess we get to see what your word is worth, don't we."

R ON CORDOBA SAT in an uncomfortable plastic chair in Nellie's room at Washington Hospital Center. He didn't notice that it wasn't especially comfortable, though, as all his attention was upon Nellie, lying unmoving in the bed. The way her eyes were closed, it seemed as if she might awaken at any time. Were this a fairy tale, a simple kiss from her true love would do the job. Unfortunately, for all Ron's interactions with people straight out of myth and magic, a fairy tale this was most definitely not . . . if for no other reason than that "happily ever after" did not seem writ for their future.

The monitoring devices beeped steadily. He felt as if he were in one of those medical television shows and kept hoping that someone would yell, "Cut!" and Nellie would sit up and smile, stretch, and ask what was for lunch. But there was nothing. The doctors had no clue what had happened. They were running tests on her, but the results could take days, even weeks to return. They were monitoring the baby as well, and although life signs of both mother and child seemed steady, there was no telling when or if she was going to come out of this . . . whatever "this" was.

Except Ron was sure he did know what it was. Not specifically. Nothing that could help anyone. But he knew just the same.

He heard footsteps behind him and turned, expecting to see yet another doctor or nurse who was going to introduce himself to Ron and give him more of that attitude that made it seem as if they were on top of everything when in fact they were clueless.

Instead he saw a familiar figure. "Cook," he said. "This is the second time you've been here in . . . what? Twelve hours?"

"Something like that," rumbled the Secret Service agent. He walked over to Ron, who stood and shook his hand. Then Ron sank back into his chair, his head hanging low. "How's she doing?"

"Same as before."

"They still got no idea?"

"None."

Cook paused, as if he knew something that he was reluctant to broach. Then, in a low voice, he said, "And you do?"

Ron looked up at him listlessly. "What gave you that impression?"

"Things you said, or didn't say, when I was here earlier." He paused, then said, "Mr. Cordoba, I know what happened. I know you quit. I don't know why, but I know you're out. That doesn't mean that you can't trust me, just because I'm still in the White House."

"It's not simply you, Cook. I don't know whom to trust anymore. I don't . . ." His voice trailed off.

"Mr. Cordoba . . . Ron . . ."

"You know what? If I can't trust you . . . then screw it. Then all I'm doing is saying stuff you already know." The listlessness evaporated, and a boiling anger surfaced in his eyes. "They did this to her, Cook. I know it in my heart."

"They?"

"Yes."

"They who?"

"The mysterious 'they,' Cook. Whoever they are . . . they're behind this. For all I know, they've even got their tentacles into personnel at this hospital." He stood and his fist was tightly clenched and trembling. "She collapsed after she took her vitamins. I told them to check the vitamins out. They said they were normal, ordinary vitamins. Now maybe . . . maybe whoever they are simply substituted the vitamins for that specific day. So the rest of the vitamins are okay. On the other hand, maybe they've got people in the labs, or maybe the doctors are in on it as well, or—"

"Ron," Cook said firmly, gripping him by the shoulders, "your wife doesn't need you coming apart right now. She needs you to—"

"To what? Dust her off if she starts gathering cobwebs?" He paced the room as he said, "I know what they want.

They think I'm stupid. They think I wouldn't figure it out. They put me into this situation that no one in the world should have to face because they don't give a damn who gets hurt as long as they accomplish their goals . . ."

"Ron, what are you talking about?"

"Don't you see? Don't you get it?" His fist was still trembling. He knew he was spouting government secrets, and for all he knew, Cook was going to report back directly to Stockwell. But at that point, he simply didn't give a damn. "The president wants to avoid sending in his . . . his storm troopers to the Grail Ale compound. So someone, somehow—CIA, maybe, or a black ops guy—sends my wife into a coma. And Grail Ale is sold out in all local stores . . . hell, up and down the East Coast. It's damned near impossible to come by. If I had government resources behind me, I might be able to scare some up, but I don't and I can't. And even if it were accessible, he or they or whoever figure that I'll want to go straight to the source. Nothing but the best for my Nellie. So naturally I'll call Arthur, and he and Percival will come running with the Grail. And anywhere between the compound and here, they can intercept him, grab the Grail, and it'll be in the government's hands, which is what Stockwell wanted in the first place."

"Do you really believe all that? That the president's capable of such a thing?"

"Oh, I absolutely believe it," said Ron tightly.

"But . . . what if you're wrong? Then you're holding off on calling in help from Arthur for no reason. Have you considered that?"

Ron leaned back against the wall, thumping the back of his head gently against it. "Yes. Of course I have. Of course there's a possibility that I'm wrong. And Stockwell is probably hoping that that area of doubt, that margin for error, is where I'm going to pull the excuse from to call Arthur and get him out in the open."

"I don't understand. Why doesn't POTUS just pursue legal recourse, if he feels that the Grail is something that should be in his possession? Eminent domain—"

"We were through all that, he and I. He wants to keep this quiet. He wants to get his hands on the Grail and have it fly under the radar, because the bottom line is that the American people trust and believe in Arthur more than they do Stockwell. And Stockwell's approval ratings are nothing to write home about right now. If there's a square off between Arthur and him in the public eye, Stockwell's numbers are going to go down faster than a two-dollar whore. He doesn't need that." With a woebegone expression, he looked at Nellie. "So instead he needed her."

"And you're not going to call President Penn."

"I can't. I can't take the chance. I . . ."

"Ron, she's your wife . . ."

"Don't you think I know that?" Ron said in a hoarse voice. He sounded as if he were strangling from within. "She's my wife. That's my child. They're both in danger. But what happens to Arthur if the government's waiting for him? What happens to the world if the wrong people get their hands on the Grail? I'm dying inside, Cook. With every beep of that damned monitor machine, I die a little more, and if Nellie and the baby don't make it, chances are you can drag the Potomac for my drowned body because I'm not gonna see the point of continuing. But I can't do it. I can't call Arthur or Gwen and tell them that—"

"I did."

Ron stared at him. "You did what?"

"I called." Cook squared his shoulders as if prepared to take a punch to the face. "I called Gwen. I told her what happened. By this point, she's probably told President Penn. They're likely on their way right now."

"No," whispered Ron.

"Mr. Cordoba, I felt that—"

"Oh my *God*!"

"Sooner or later, it's going to be in the newspapers," Cook said reasonably. "Sooner or later, they were going to find out. It's a miracle the story hasn't broken yet. But it will, and if it's going to be sooner or later, then it might as well be sooner—"

"How could you *do* that? You had no right—!"

"I had every right," Cook shot back. "I had every right because we're in this together."

"In *what*?"

"This! This situation! This story! This . . . this grand adventure . . ."

"What the *hell* are you *talking* about?"

"We're walking alongside myths, Mr. Cordoba," said Cook. "You went on a quest. You think this stuff doesn't rub off? You hang out with people of legend, and you wind up getting pulled into the legend. Fate is writing the story of King Arthur, and we're part of it whether you like it or not. And I don't see that fate lets it be that an innocent woman and baby die while the king hides in a compound. If the story needs a kick in the right direction, and you won't do it, then I had to."

"You're insane!"

"No. I just read a lot."

Ron buried his face in his hands. "You don't know what you've done."

"I'll grant you that," admitted Cook. "But I got a funny feeling that, in pretty short order, we're gonna find out."

A T THAT MOMENT, Arthur was in a posture identical to that of Ron's. He hadn't moved from Barry's office as Gwen filled him in on what Cook had told her. Barry watched the two of them with singular intensity, clearly fascinated by what Arthur was going to do.

It didn't take the king long to render his decision. "We have to help her."

"Aha!" Barry started.

Arthur immediately interrupted him before he could say another word. "Yes, Barry, I know. I had that coming. I have coming everything you no doubt want to say. And, frankly, I'll be ,taking a chance using the Grail to heal Nellie. But it's a chance I'll take, a calculated risk. One last healing with the Grail. I cannot stand by and do nothing."

"Well, that's the question, isn't it, sir," said Barry. "Is it about helping someone in need? Or is it about your ego, that you don't want to feel helpless yourself?"

Arthur had no immediate answer, but then Barry gave a dismissive wave. "You know what? I take it back. You want to help her, you feel the need . . . so you'll help her. That's what you're made of. Look . . . I'm sorry if I gave you a tough time." He stood and extended a hand, and Arthur shook it firmly.

"I'm glad you understand . . ."

"Oh, I don't remotely understand," replied Barry. "But you gotta do what you gotta do. You guys get ready to go; I'll go tell Percival that he's going to be knocking off early today."

"Thank you, Barry."

"Eh." And Barry shrugged. "It was fun while it lasted."

Moments later, Barry was heading toward Percival's station and found the Grail Knight there, as always. Inwardly, Barry sighed. He'd grown to like Percival in the time that he'd been there and regretted the notion of losing his company. He was in so many ways an admirable individual. There weren't enough of his type around.

"Percival," he called, "we're shutting everything down."

Slowly Percival turned and looked at him, puzzled. "Is this because of whatever it was that Arthur wanted to talk to you about?"

"It's because of a number of things. What it comes down to is, we've made some money, we've had some laughs. And now it's time to put an end to it."

Percival stood up, uncoiling from his seat with the smoothness of a dragon. "I have to say . . . I don't know the reasons for it, but I'm relieved. I was never happy with this. Never."

"But you didn't tell Arthur that."

"Wasn't my place." Percival shrugged. "He's my king. I'm his knight. That's just the way it goes."

"Well, I guess that's simply a divide that we're going to have to agree to disagree on. Go get the Grail out of the machinery, then go meet up with Arthur at the main entrance. I'll have cars waiting there for you; he'll explain what's what." Barry stuck out his hand. "Godspeed, Percival."

"You too, Barry Seltzer . . ."

Percival reached out to shake Barry's extended hand, and at that moment, something punched through Percival's chest.

He looked down in utter confusion and saw that there was a wooden staff sticking into him . . . no.

No. Not a staff.

A spear.

He staggered and saw that the spear went down the sleeve of Barry's extended right arm. It had snapped out of his sleeve like a spring-loaded magician's cane, had driven through Percival's torso as easily as a hot poker through tissue paper, and had come out the other side.

Barry's expression was cold and distant, completely unlike the pleasant demeanor that he now set aside like a useless mask. When he spoke again, his voice sounded different, tinted with an accent that sounded vaguely Austrian.

"The name," he said softly, "is not 'Barry Seltzer.' It's 'Paracelsus.'"

Percival gasped, tried to pull away. His hand reflexively went for his sword, but he had none. He hadn't been going around armed. He did, however, have a knife in his boot, and he tried to reach down for it.

He didn't come close.

Paracelsus twisted the Spear of Destiny, and Percival staggered as blinding heat started to radiate from him. He was on fire, and the only thing that prevented him from going up in flames was the power of the Grail that had run strong in his blood for centuries. But the power of the Spear of Destiny was vicious, and Percival—who had been determined not to scream, not to give his newfound enemy the satisfaction—screamed now. He gripped the Spear, gritted his teeth as his lips began to burn away, and fixed a look of utter hatred upon the man holding the Spear.

"I really do regret this, sir knight. I truly have enjoyed our chats," said Paracelsus.

And then, to the obvious shock of Paracelsus, Percival yanked with a degree of strength that would have seemed impossible, and tore the spear out of his chest. Blood flew everywhere and Percival collapsed with a gaping wound in his chest, but he was still grasping the weapon.

Paracelsus pulled as hard as he could. Had he been up against an uninjured Percival, he wouldn't have had a prayer. But the Grail Knight had used the last of his great strength, and Paracelsus yanked the spear out of his grasp even as Percival hit the floor and lay there in a spreading pool of blood.

The few employees who were a witness to the battle simply stood there, blank-faced. From across the room, Sal came running up, his red hair blazing brighter than ever. "Problem?" asked Sal.

"It's been attended to," Paracelsus replied. He crossed quickly to the cradle in which the Grail was sitting, ripped open the glass door that gave access to the relic, and pulled it out. He smiled as he gripped the Grail firmly. "It's almost ready. I can sense it. One more person, I would

think . . . and I know the perfect recipient, down in our nation's capital, for—"

"*What the bloody hell—!*"

Paracelsus spun just in time to see, at the far end of the
room, Arthur and Gwen. There was utter shock on Arthur's
face as he saw Percival spilling blood and organs out of his
body. He saw Paracelsus standing there with the Spear in
one hand and the cup of Christ in the other.

That was all he needed.

"*Bastaaard!*" howled Arthur, and Excalibur was in his
hand, glowing and angry. He started to charge.

"Sal," Paracelsus said as casually as if he were asking for a
cigarette, "torch the place, would you?" He pointed at
Arthur. "Start with him."

Sal nodded as Paracelsus, the picture of calm, turned his
back on the oncoming king and headed for the far door. Sal
stepped directly into Arthur's path, and Arthur stopped in
his tracks, stunned, as Sal's head erupted into flame. His body
followed suit a second later, and Sal rose into the air, his form
changing as he did so. He became elongated, lizardlike, and a
corona of fire danced around him. Arthur brought up an arm,
shielding his eyes. Gwen had been trying to get to the pros-
trate form of Percival, but she was likewise driven back by the
heat.

"*A salamander!*" Arthur cried out.

The fire elemental let out a triumphant hiss and threw
wide its arms. Fire lanced out in all directions, enveloping the
factory. Employees—minions of Barry Seltzer, presumably—
scattered out of there as fast as they could. Having dropped
its human guise, it didn't seem remotely interested in trading words with Arthur. Instead it unleashed its elemental
fury in all directions.

Arthur charged forward as Gwen screamed a warning,
and the salamander unleashed a blast of flame—not at

Arthur—but at Gwen. The king realized what the creature was doing the second before it did so, and he leapt in front of Gwen a split instant before the flame got there. He brought up Excalibur in a defensive position, certain that it was going to be the last thing he ever did, and as he did it he muttered something that he himself did not fully understand.

To the shock of not only the salamander but of Arthur himself, the flame split around the sword on either side, as if the great blade was cleaving it in half. The ramp ways on either side ignited, but Arthur, Gwen, and what was left of Percival were all unharmed.

The salamander tried again, this time bringing its hands together and letting loose a fireball that could have been spat out by the sun. Yet again Excalibur barred the way, and yet again the flame did not hit its desired target.

Growling in fury, Arthur advanced on the salamander, and the creature backed up, suddenly daunted by the gleaming blade. It didn't take the time for large fireballs this time, instead throwing several smaller ones as fast as it could. Arthur batted them aside with the flat of his blade, continuing to advance, and suddenly Gwen's cried out, *"Arthur! We need to get out of here!"*

He glanced behind him and saw that Gwen was struggling mightily to haul Percival out. Then smoke began to rise, the suffocating heat getting to him. He remembered the last time he'd been in an inferno; it had taken the timely arrival of New York's Bravest to hose him down and get him through it safely. No such arrival seemed likely now. Gwen was coughing violently. Her lungs would likely collapse if she was in the place much longer, and God only knew what was going to happen with Percival.

Arthur looked back at his foe and saw that the salamander was gone. Scarpered off, the cowardly monster had. Knowing that he was running out of time, Arthur quickly sheathed Excalibur and ran back to Gwen and Percival. He scooped up the fallen knight in his arms and only at that point did he see the horrific wound that Percival had suffered.

He glanced around desperately, but the entire place was alive with flame. It was hitting the treated water from the Grail and all of it was quickly evaporating in clouds of hissing steam rather than slowing down the spread of the fire at all. Arthur let out a choked sob even as he staggered forward, cradling Percival in his arms. Gwen followed directly behind. Overhead there was the cracking of roof supports. Arthur wanted to shout for Gwen to hurry, but he was afraid to draw a breath and inhale smoke. Besides, it wasn't necessary: Gwen couldn't have been moving faster if hellhounds were barking at her heels.

The specifics of the next confusing minutes were a blur to Arthur as flames seemed to spring up in their path wherever they went. Arthur saw the automatic sprinkler heads set into the ceiling, but they weren't raining down water; Seltzer had undoubtedly disabled the system.

It was Gwen who took the lead. "This way!" she called out, as they staggered into corridors filling rapidly with smoke. He didn't know how she knew, and chalked it off to the fact that women always seemed to know where they were going. They headed down a hallway, and suddenly the doorway in front of them blew open, a sheet of flame blocking their way.

There was a large window to their right, but it was reinforced glass, unbreakable. But not to Arthur . . . except he was carrying Percival. *"The sword! Grab Excalibur!"* shouted Arthur, indicating the window with his head.

Gwen understood instantly and reached for Excalibur. Even though it was invisible, she knew right where to grab at the hilt, and a second later she was wielding the legendary blade. She didn't hesitate, but instead braced the pommel against her stomach, brought the sword level, and charged toward the window like a rhino. The sword blasted apart the glass, shattering it in all directions. Cool air blew in through the window.

"*Go! Go!*" Arthur shouted, and Gwen practically flung herself through the opening. She let out a pained shriek, upright shards of glass tearing right through her skirt and ripping her legs as she fell through the opening. Then she was out, and Arthur threw himself through it as well, holding Percival close as he did so.

Seconds later they were clear of the building and putting more distance between it and themselves with every passing moment. They ran toward the large gates at the front of the compound. Gwen didn't wait to be told by Arthur what to do. She let out a roar that would have been worthy of a barbarian queen charging the gate while swinging Excalibur as she went. The blade sliced easily through the locks and the massive gates swung open. Arthur and Gwen ran through the opening, heading toward Barry Seltzer's private beach. The water was lapping gently against the shore, the peace of the ocean in stark contrast to the conflagration they were leaving behind.

Arthur fell onto the sand and Percival tumbled out of his arms. "Gwen! Call for help!" Arthur shouted. Gwen laid the sword down, pulled her cell phone out of her pocket, and dialed 911.

Arthur looked helplessly at the abominable mess that had been Percival's chest. He knew to apply pressure, but there was so much bleeding, so much damage, he didn't know where to do it. "Just hold on, Percival! Everything will be—"

Percival reached up and clawed at Arthur's shirtfront, grabbing the material in his blood-soaked hand and pulling Arthur down toward him. "Para . . . celsus," he whispered, blood trickling out of his mouth with every syllable. "It was . . . Para . . . celsus . . ."

"That . . . that can't be . . ."

"It is. It was . . . I think . . . he's going to . . . to DC . : .
to help . . . Nellie . . ."

"*What?* Why in God's name would he do that?"

"Said . . . Grail   needed . . . needed   more . . . don't
know . . . don't know more what . . ."

Everything fell into place for Arthur. "I do," Arthur said,
everything suddenly becoming clear . . . or, at least, clearer.
"We've got to stop him."

"Stop him?" Gwen said. She had closed her phone, and
now she was crouched near Arthur. "I don't understand. I
thought you were going to help her yourself! Now we're not
helping her . . . ?"

"It's complicated . . ."

"*Y'think?*"

There were sirens in the distance, although whether they
were ambulances or fire engines, Arthur couldn't be sure.
He turned away from Gwen, his full attention on Percival.
"Steady, Percival. Just a few more minutes . . ."

Percival was shaking his head, his body trembling.
"Used up . . . all my few more minutes," he said softly. "It
has been . . . my honor . . . to serve you my liege . . ."

"Percival, you're going to be—"

". . . in this long . . . long life . . ." And his voice drew
fainter and fainter still. ". . . and perhaps . . . in the next . . ."

"*Percival! I order you to live!*" Arthur fairly shouted at him.

His gaze looked as if it was drifting away, then Percival
forced it back to Arthur. "By your leave . . . sire . . . don't
make your last order . . . one I cannot obey . . . please . . . I
beg you . . ."

Arthur clutched Percival to him and choked back a sob.
Gwen, several feet away, brought the back of her hand to her
mouth, her eyes wide and brimming with tears.

"I . . . beg you . . ." Percival whispered, barely audible.

"Very well," Arthur said, holding him even more tightly.
"You have my leave to go . . . brave sir knight . . ."

"Thank you . . . Highness . . . an honor . . . as al . . . ways . . ."

His breath rattled in his throat one last time, in a way that Arthur knew all too well.

Thus passed Sir Percival, variously known as Parsival, Perceval, and Peredur, son of Pellinore, brother of Dindrane, both long gone to dust. Percival, beloved of Blanchefleur. The Grail Knight whose role in fictional accounts had been supplanted by Galahad but was, nevertheless, truly the knight who had encountered and healed the Fisher King, who had brought the Grail to Arthur and completed the last great deed associated with Camelot before its collapse.

Percival, the last surviving knight of Camelot, had fallen, slain by the same holy lance that had pierced the vitals of a man of peace two thousand years earlier . . . and, unbeknownst to him, had also slain the King of the Unicorns quite some time before that.

Of the brave and noble men who had sat at the Round Table . . . only King Arthur remained.

He had never felt more alone.

ERLIN IS SLEEPING.

Even the endless wizard does not have unending amounts of stamina. Even he must rest from time to time.

He does so now, floating. He sleeps a dreamless sleep; Nimue sees to that.

She watches him, enraptured, so many thoughts floating through her mind that she has difficulty keeping them all straight. It is a difficult business, this endeavor upon which she has embarked. She feels as if she no longer is certain of where to turn or whom to trust.

A voice resounds, a brittle voice, rippling through the water.

He lives still? It is the voice of her lover, of Paracelsus, and he does not sound happy. What game is this you play, Lady?

My game. My waters. My rules, she replies airily. She speaks softly lest she awaken the mage.

As long as he lives, he remains a danger. You must dispose of him now, lest he or Arthur, under his guidance, ruins everything.

If you are so determined to wield death, why do you not kill him yourself?

I endeavored to, *he reminds her.* Or have you forgotten your own intercession?

I forget nothing, *she lies, for she had indeed come close to forgetting it. Nimue is very much a creature of the present, her memories governed by what most interests her at any given moment.* I think it has nothing to do with me, and everything to do with the idea that you simply do not have the stomach to attend to the business of killing with your own hands.

Say that to the corpse of Percival, dead at my hands.

The news surprises her. Despite her memory, as inconstant as the moon, she recalls Percival, with skin as smooth and sleek as darkened marble. He had been very pretty. She had fancied him. She had fancied him so much that, many centuries ago, she had had a dalliance with him, calling herself Blanchefleur and lying with him on a distant shore. He had awoken and found her gone, and had mourned her abrupt departure for he had desired her more, but she had other interests to attend to. But she had watched him from a distance, and when he had returned Excalibur to her after the sore wounding of Arthur, he had not recognized her for she looked very different.

She had desired him for one night of passion, and having attained that, desired no more, but for that night she had loved him greatly and would always think of him fondly.

And now he was gone. One lover . . . slain by another.

Now slay Merlin, milady, *Paracelsus says to her.*

I do not fancy your attempting to order me about.

It is no order! You promised, and now I am simply holding you to your promise.

She smiles to herself, hearing the childlike frustration in his voice. And if I have changed my mind? If I decide it suits my fancy that he live . . . what will you do then? Will you try to slay me as well? Shove your pointy cursed little stick into me? An endeavor in which you would have as much luck, I might point out, as you would stabbing at the ocean.

There is a long pause, and there is no petulance in his tone as he says to her, I do not need to stab at the ocean. All I need do is boil it away, along with the rest of the water that covers this pathetic globe.

You could not do such a thing, *she laughs, but she feels uneasy, and rightly so.*

Yes. I can. And you do not want to tempt me or challenge me, milady. Slay him now.

It would not be all that difficult. She merely has to have the water crush itself upon him. Bound as he is by her magiks, he could never resist the crushing weight. It is a small matter, truly.

She senses him waiting.

Come here and do it yourself, *she says defiantly.* He is pretty and I fancy him, and I shall keep him for myself, unless you choose to take his fate in your own hands.

She hears his low grunt of frustration. You had best decide, milady, *he says finally,* whose side you wish to be on when the end comes. I thought you knew. At the very least . . . you would be well advised to keep yourself and your little wizard out of my way, lest it end badly for you.

His voice withdraws.

She waits for him to speak again.

He does not.

She looks at Merlin. He is hers. He will remain hers, to do with as she wishes, until the oceans all burn away . . .

Which, she realizes, just may be sooner than she could have expected.

YE OLDE SECOND
INTERLUDE

†

May 2, 1945

"I LIKED IT better during the Blitz."

That was the conclusion to which Paracelsus had come as he walked around the streets of London late that night. The Blitz had ended some four years earlier, and he was waxing nostalgic for it. There had been something about the relentless destruction, the shattered buildings, the shattered lives . . . that appealed to the love of chaos that pulsed deep in the conjurer's chest. The prospect of peace descending upon the world, of the people being able to relax and breathe deeply the air of freedom from terror . . . what fun was that, really?

Word was already spreading through London that the Allies had overwhelmed Berlin. That Hitler was on his last legs, on the run. Some were even claiming that he was dead, which seemed too good to be true. There was talk that, in a few days, there was going to be an official declaration of the defeat of Germany. When that happened, London would practically explode in an orgy of celebration. Paracelsus had no intention of being there.

As a matter of fact, with any luck, London wouldn't be there either.

Or Paris. Or Berlin. Or anything.

As he walked along the bank of the River Thames, Paracelsus told himself that he was really doing the world a favor. After all, it wasn't as if peace would last indefinitely. Certainly sooner or later, war would break out again. That was simply the nature of things. The so-called Great War had been termed "the war to end all wars." So what had happened? The Great War had been demoted merely to World War I, while this latest conflict was World War II. The only reasonable conclusion to be drawn was that there would be a World War III, and IV, and however many World Wars it took until there was no world anymore.

Why drag things out?

Paracelsus walked to the edge of the Thames and stood there for a long moment, holding the Spear of Destiny casually in one hand. He reversed it and stuck the point of the Spear deep into the water as it flowed past.

"Come to me, milady," he called. "Come to me, Nimue. I've done it. I've done that which you said could not be done. Now keep your promise. Give me what I need in order to accomplish my goal."

There was no immediate movement in the water. Paracelsus felt a quick flash of annoyance, and said sharply, "Lady of the Lake! I've come to you at the appointed time and appointed place! Now present yourself, my love!"

Still there was nothing, and Paracelsus was about to lapse into an annoyed string of profanity. But then the water began to roil a short distance away. He drew back the Spear and waited with a smug expression. Seconds later, the water of the Thames split wide, and the Lady of the Lake rose from it, her arms hanging loosely to either side and a pleased smirk upon her face. Her eyes flashed in delight upon seeing him . . . or perhaps it was the Spear that prompted the reaction.

"My, aren't you clever!" called out Nimue. "You truly did find it. From the vague clues I provided you, I never thought you'd accomplish it."

In the distance, Big Ben sonorously chimed out the hour. Paracelsus ignored it. "Yes," he said, smiling thinly. "The clues you provided me—"

"Were all part of the game," Nimue replied, laughing lightly. "Oh, now look at you, getting all scowly. How serious you are." She stuck out her lower lip in a pouting manner. "Such a handsome face you have, to malign it so. You know . . . I think I may take you as a lover sometime."

"That would be my honor, milady," he said. "And now . . ." He held out his hand. "You promised me that you would present me with that which I need to accomplish my final goal."

"Did I?" she asked.

"Yes. You told me that the Holy Grail was in your keep. And that if I managed to get my hands on the Spear of Destiny, then you would tell me its location. There are far too many fake Grails out there for me to waste time going from one to the next to the next. Now . . . where is the Holy Grail?"

"The Ancient King has it," replied the Lady of the Lake airily. "Find him, and you'll find the Grail."

"Ancient King?" said Paracelsus. He was confused. "Which ancient king?"

"Which one do you *think* I mean?"

Paracelsus gave it only a few moments' thought, then the answer burst into his head, so obvious that he couldn't believe he'd needed to think about it at all. "Arthur? Arthur Pendragon?"

"Certainly that seems obvious, does it not?" replied the Lady of the Lake, as she said to herself, *I am of the sea, and I am deep, so deep. That which is upon the surface means nothing. You must look below the surface if you are to see the truth of things, my dear. Does the tip of the iceberg inform you of what lies below? Do smooth waters give a hint of the predators that lie below?*

"Where is Pendragon?"

"You wish to find Arthur?"

"Yes! Of course!"

"Would you like me to tell you where you can find him?"

"Of course!" His patience was beginning to fray. Obviously the Lady knew where the remains of Arthur were, and apparently the Grail was there with him. "And no riddles this time! No vague clues! I want specifics!"

"Very well. Go to the northwest corner of St. James's Square."

"What?" Paracelsus frowned. "He's buried at the northwest corner of St. James's Square?"

"Of course not, silly. He's very much alive. And he's in there. Go to the northwest corner of St. James's Square. A fellow named Geoffrey will take you to him, and there you will have words with him."

"Are you serious?"

"Absolutely," she replied. "I swear on the purity of all the world's water: There will you have words with him. And now farewell, mage. We will not see each other again for some time, if ever."

Before he could say anything to stop her, the Lady of the Lake dissolved back into the River Thames with a soft splash.

Paracelsus could scarcely believe it. Was it going to be that simple? Could his plan, after all this time, finally be on the verge of completion?

His mind was racing faster than his feet as he sprinted

toward St. James's Square. He felt young, far younger than his years could possibly have reflected.

He skidded around a corner, nearly fell, righted himself, and dashed across Piccadilly Circus toward Buckingham Palace. Soon he was panting, his chest heaving with exertion, and his legs were becoming heavy. It didn't slow him.

Finally, he reached St. James's Square. Dead center of it was the private garden, with a statue of William III on his horse. Paracelsus scarcely glanced at it. Instead he got his bearings and headed straight for the northwest corner.

And as he approached it, he began to slow, then eventually he stopped. He stood there, slack-jawed, staring at the building in front of him.

There was no person standing there by the name of Geoffrey, or with any other name.

Instead there was a building, with signage that was visible even in the darkness. There, big as life, were the words, LONDON LIBRARY.

You will have words with him . . . Geoffrey will take you to him . . .

"Geoffrey," said Paracelsus slowly. "Geoffrey . . . of Monmouth . . . who wrote the first history of Arthur . . . which is undoubtedly in the London Library . . ."

Fury began to take shape deep within him, like a black cyclone, and build and build, and when he threw open his mouth he expected a howl of indignation to emerge. Instead, to his utter amazement, laughter exploded from him. *"Well played, milady! Very well played!"* He laughed and laughed, and when a London bobby showed up and demanded to know who he was, what he was doing out long after curfew, and what was so bloody funny, Paracelsus turned, jammed the Spear through him, and killed him where he stood while continuing to laugh.

And somewhere deep within his head, the Lady of the Lake was laughing as well.

It was the true beginning of the bond that Paracelsus believed would continue to the end of the world . . . whenever that would finally be . . . and whenever he could make it happen.

PARTE THE THIRD:

The Sword
in the Stones

CHAPTRE
THE TWENTIETH

✝

THE CAR HURTLED down I-95 toward Washington, DC, with Gwen at the wheel. Night had fallen and she was maneuvering as quickly as she could, deftly threading through the traffic. Arthur sat silently in the passenger seat, staring out at nothing.

They had grabbed a car from the nearest rental place and were getting down to the nation's capital as fast as possible. She had tried using her cell phone to get in touch with Ron, to warn him that something was up, that an extremely bad man armed with a Spear was on his way to the hospital. But Ron's cell phone had simply rung, leading her to believe he didn't have it on him. When she tried calling the hospital or Cook's cell phone from his business card, she was met with a blaring busy signal and buzzing noise, so loud and annoying that it made her wonder whether someone or something was interfering with her signal. That was the problem when dealing with aspects of magic; it made you paranoid about everything, including things that could easily be ascribed to everyday screwups of technology.

So she stopped at one point and tried to use a pay phone, and hit the same obscuring busy signal . . . at which point all concern about paranoia was gone. Something or someone was screwing with her, and she could guess who.

Except . . . the name didn't mean anything to her.

With all that, it was still several hours before she could bring herself to try and pry information out of Arthur. She had never seen him colder, more distant. Part of her said that this was certainly not a new experience for him. He'd commanded armies. He'd lost men before. But this was Percival. Her heart ached, for Percival had been strong, brave, and at once the most proud and most tragic individual she had ever known. And now he was gone, and she knew that whatever grief she was feeling couldn't begin to touch whatever Arthur must be enduring.

She knew he loved her. She knew he valued her. But Percival was his comrade in arms, his good right arm. She wondered if, in the future, Arthur would have ghost sensations of Percival there beside him, tingling in the same way as when an arm has been lost and yet you still believe it's right there because you can feel it.

Finally, though, as the steady stream of oncoming headlights gave her the initial stirrings of road fatigue, she began talking—if for no other reason—as a means of keeping herself awake.

"Who is Paracelsus?" she asked.

No answer was immediately forthcoming, which wasn't exactly a surprise to her. But she persisted, asking every couple of minutes because she wasn't entirely sure whether Arthur was even hearing her.

Finally, he stirred himself to speak. "An alchemist."

"Alchemist." She frowned, searching her memory. "One of those guys who gets all hot about changing lead into gold? There are really guys like that?"

"There's a guy like him," said Arthur, continuing to stare

out the window, as the conversation had no real importance. "He's one of the most famous of that breed. He was born Philippus Aureolus Theophrastus Bombast von Hohenheim, in Switzerland—sometime toward the end of the fifteenth century . . ."

"Well, naturally," said Gwen. "Because, y'know, you can't possibly find yourself facing off against someone who was born *after* the dawn of the Industrial Age."

"Do you want to know this or not?" he asked sharply.

She was taken aback by his tone although to some degree she was relieved to hear a bit of fire in his voice. She simply nodded.

"Celsus was an ancient Roman physician. Von Hohenheim came up with the name 'Paracelsus' to mean 'superior to Celsus.' He was raised in Austria and, from the very beginning, he was an egomaniac. If he had contented himself with his intense study of the human body, he might have simply been remembered as a brilliant doctor, because he did pursue some theories that were then radical but now commonly accepted. But he became obsessed with the occult in general and alchemy in particular. Traveled the world seeking to expand his knowledge into things best left unexplored."

"And this is that guy? That same guy?"

"It's hard to say for certain," Arthur admitted. "Paracelsus is recorded to have died five hundred years ago. But there have been others who have purported to be him over the centuries. The facts of Paracelsus have been inextricably mixed with the legend, and it would be difficult for me to say whether what we're dealing with is the original item . . . or some individual who has either assumed his identity or even believes that he really is the alchemist of legend. The problem is, if he has the Spear of Destiny—which I have every reason at this point to believe he does—it doesn't matter whether he goes by Paracelsus or Mickey Mouse. Between having that and the Grail in his possession, he is unspeakably dangerous."

"Because the Spear is such an awful weapon?"

"It's more than that. There's apparently some way of combining the power of the Spear and the Grail that will bring about unparalleled destruction."

"Who told you that?"

"Merlin. He was in the toilet, and he told me."

Gwen stared at him and almost forgot to put her eyes back on the road. "He told you this one day while he was sitting on the toilet?"

"Not on, in. He was looking up at me from the water." He glanced at her. "I suppose that requires some further explanation."

"I'm thinking so, yeah."

So he told her all he knew, which, as he realized upon the retelling, wasn't as much as he wished. "Why didn't you tell me any of this earlier?"

"Because I knew how insane it sounded."

"Arthur," she said slowly, "when one looks back at the history of my life since you and I first met, I think it's safe to say that there's nothing you could tell me that would sound more insane than what's already happened."

"Fair enough. I'll try to be more forthcoming."

"And you think he's going to try and cure Nellie with the Grail . . . so he can then turn around and destroy the world?"

"Well, if you can't develop a sense of irony in the course of six centuries, when can you?"

She nodded, then said softly, "I'm . . ."

"If you're going to say that you're sorry about Percival . . . I'd rather you didn't," he said, not ungently. "Honestly . . . I'm not entirely certain I can discuss the matter while keeping my eyes dry, and tears over such a matter would be . . . what's the word . . . ?"

"Lugubrious?"

"Unmanly."

"Oh. Well . . . I wouldn't want that."

There was silence for a time, then Arthur said, "Gwen . . . when I catch up with Paracelsus . . . I . . . don't want you to be there."

"What are you talking about? Of course I'll be there. I don't pretend to be a knight of Camelot, but I'm not slouch when—"

"Not because of that. Because of me."

"I don't understand."

Gwen had known Arthur for many years . . . in some ways, she felt as if she had known him her entire life and before that even . . . but there was something in his voice now that she had never heard before. Something dark and terrible that caused her spine to chill. "There are aspects of me that you've never seen . . . that I've never had need to show you. I fancy myself a . . . a civilized man, Gwen. But I hail from a very uncivilized time, and the forces that influenced me in that time remain in me still. And the standards for civilized behavior have changed over the centuries. Once upon a time, it was considered civilized to parade a prisoner naked through the streets . . . to castrate him, disembowel him, draw and quarter him . . . it was considered justice. Even . . . even entertainment."

"So . . . so it was entertainment back then," she said, trying to keep her voice light, trying to keep the shakiness out of it. "So you didn't have cable and had to make your own fun. I . . . I get that, okay? It was a long time ago . . ."

"Not to me. To me . . . it was practically yesterday. I have done . . . terrible things in my life. Terrible things. Things that if you saw them, by today's standards . . . you would think them barbaric. And more . . . you would be repulsed by not only the actions I took against my enemies . . . but the satisfaction, bordering on glee, that I displayed while taking them. The historians tend to tidy things up. Gloss over the more unpleasant realities of life back then in the greater pursuit of presenting tales of chivalry. Geoffrey of Monmouth didn't make mention of it, Tennyson gave it a pass, and God knows Malory wouldn't touch it with a ten-meter cattle prod."

"Arthur, I don't understand why you're telling me this," she said. "I mean, it's all in the past . . ."

"That's the point. It's not. It's in the future."

"What?"

"I will catch this man, Gwen," he told her, and his voice became even lower, "and there will be no mercy for him. For what he has done—for the magnitude of his crimes—I will kill him, oh yes. But that will not be immediate. I will kill him slowly. I will make him suffer with every small, meticulous stroke of my blade. I will have him begging for death, and I will withhold the boon and continue to torment him and torture him until his soul runs screaming from his body. No judge and jury trial for him; I will be both, and I have already decided his guilt and his sentence. I will be brutal and terrible and civilized only in the sense of what passed for civilized eleven centuries ago."

She knew it was her imagination, but in the back of her mind she could hear the screams of past victims of Arthur's wrath as he spoke.

"And because of that," he said, his voice coming from deep within the darkness of not only the night but his very being, "I don't want you there because it is a side of me that I don't want you to see. I am concerned it will repulse you. Turn you away from me. That you will no longer be able to love me because of it."

"Arthur, that's ridiculous. I love all of you . . . even the aspects of you that you're ashamed of. There's nothing you could do or say that would ever—"

"Gwen . . . when you . . . when an earlier incarnation of you . . . betrayed me by sleeping with Lancelot . . . I sentenced you to be burned to death for your high crime."

"I know," she said easily. "I saw *Camelot*. But you knew Lancelot would come and rescue—"

He shook his head.

"What?"

"No," he said softly. "Lance was under siege. He had no way of getting to Camelot. There was no ulterior motive on my part other than revenge over my humiliation, wrapped in the comforting cloak of justice. There was no expectation of rescue, and none was forthcoming. I stood there in the window of my castle, looking down upon you, and you begged me. Gods, you begged me for forgiveness, and there was none in my heart. I watched from on high, like a vengeful deity, until you were a charred corpse. It took a long time, as burning always does, and I monitored every agonizing minute. To this day, I can still smell the burning of your flesh, like roasting rancid meat, the—"

Gwen pulled the car violently over to the side, skidding onto the shoulder of the highway and almost hitting the guardrail. She threw open the door, leaned out, and vomited violently onto the pavement. When she was done, she simply hung there, holding on, gasping for breath, her hair hanging down around her face.

Finally, she hauled herself back into the car and pulled the door shut. She slumped back in the seat until her breathing returned to normal.

Very softly, he said, "I told you the historians cleaned things up. What you see in movies, in plays . . . it's romanticized. It's . . . entertainment, except real people aren't being tortured to death for public consumption."

She sat there a moment more, then started the car up again.

"For what it's worth, I spent every minute of my subsequent thousand-year captivity regretting what I had done . . ."

She speared him with a look. "It's worth shit, Arthur."

He sighed and leaned back in his seat. "Yes. I rather thought it would be."

The car moved back out onto I-95 and continued its path toward Washington, DC.

CHAPTRE
THE TWENTY-FIRST

✟

HE HOSPITAL'S SMALL chapel was deserted at three in the morning. It wasn't as if the lateness of the hour was a contributing factor; there had been other instances where the chapel had been fairly crowded with individuals praying for the recovery of their loved ones.

Then again, since the introduction of Grail Ale, there'd been a general rise in health and fewer supplicants for the favors of God. This was not lost on Paracelsus. But it didn't surprise him all that much. Why, after all, should one throw out cries for divine intervention that might or might not be heard, and might or might not be answered, when one could go down to the local convenience store and—if they had it in stock—plunk down money for a much surer thing?

He stood in the doorway of the chapel for a long moment, then walked in and up to the image of Jesus on the crucifix. Paracelsus paused a moment, then crossed himself and picked up one of the votive candles. He lit it, murmured a prayer, and put the candle in its proper place.

"Offering up a prayer, my son?"

Paracelsus glanced over his shoulder and raised an eyebrow. "Hello, your Eminence," he said. "I'm a bit surprised to see you here, of all places . . . and somewhat underdressed, as it were."

"Why not here, of all places," asked Cardinal Ruehl. As Paracelsus had observed, Ruehl was not attired in his normal, elaborate robes. Instead he was dressed in the dark brown cassock of a monk. The hood was dropped back so that his face was easily seen, but his hands were tucked into the copious folds of the sleeves. "I am wherever God's work is required. And why are you here, my son?"

"Just . . . paying my respects," said Paracelsus, nodding toward the icon.

"Indeed. And are you not concerned about the crisis of faith that has been occurring lately in the world?"

"It's not lately, Eminence." Paracelsus shook his head, looking discouraged and frustrated. "It's been centuries now. Centuries of a slow, steady decline into decay and squalor."

"Oh, I don't know about that . . ."

"I do. There used to be . . ." His voice trailed off.

"Used to be what?"

"There used to be . . ." Paracelsus sought for the right words. "There used to be grace in the world. There used to be a sense of personal responsibility. Mankind used to celebrate that which was the greatest in all of us. Now we've become obsessed with that which is the lowest. There is no greatness because we can't wait to tear down that which is great. No matter who our heroes are, we keep searching and searching until we discover their feet of clay, so that . . . what? We can feel better about ourselves and our own inadequacies? Do you know," he continued, "that the vast majority of the country had no idea that Franklin Roosevelt was in a wheelchair? It's true. Even as recently as that, there was a sense of—at the very least—dignified distance.

Now we want to know the type of undergarments our leaders wear, and television cameras are going up people's rectums. What the hell is it all coming to? What's the purpose?"

"You sound very disappointed with the state of humanity."

"And you're not?" Paracelsus smirked. "I mean, are you really going to stand there and tell me you're not disappointed with the state of humanity?"

Ruehl inclined his head slightly. "I . . . wish for better. And I figure it's my job to try and work for better."

"How can you?"

"Because I have faith."

"Ah. Well, see, that's the difference between us, then," said Paracelsus. "I don't. I've seen too much. Become too disgusted. If there really was a divine presence that put us on this planet, either we've totally failed to live up to our potential, or if this was truly what He was expecting of us, then it was just a bad idea to begin with and we're not worth the planetary resources we're consuming."

"You say you have no faith, and yet you light a candle. You pray to our savior."

"Professional courtesy."

"You fancy yourself a savior?"

"Yes." Tears began to well in Paracelsus's eyes, and he wiped them away with the back of his arm. "Because I loved humanity so much . . . and I see what it's become . . . and sometimes, that which you love, you have to be willing to let go. It's the only way that it can be saved."

"Saved . . . by destroying it?"

There was a silence then, and slowly something changed in the atmosphere of the chapel as Paracelsus turned to face Cardinal Ruehl as if truly seeing him for the first time.

"So," said Paracelsus, sounding amused and regretful, "we see each other plainly. Not just happenstance in the selection of the ensemble, I see. The monks of Montserrat in Catalonia?"

Ruehl inclined his head slightly. "That is where our society had its origins, yes. Since then Montserrat has cast its influence in a far wider net than Catalonia . . ."

"To Sainte Chappelle, perhaps?"

Ruehl smiled. "You know your history, I see. Your holy orders."

"My enemies."

"We have no enemies, except the enemies of mankind."

"It's amazing," said Paracelsus, his hands draped behind him as he walked back and forth, as if studying a museum painting from different angles. "The Holy Order of the Monks of Montserrat. The Secret Society of Sainte Chappelle. All dedicated to holy relics that you don't have in your possession."

"We had them. We lost them. We intend to regain them, then keep them safe."

"Been searching for quite a while, haven't you. So let's see if I have the time line straight. After an indeterminate origin, the Grail came into the hands of St. Luke, who carved a statue eventually called *La Moreneta* or *The Black Madonna*. An interesting color for the mother of the savior, don't you think? Black?"

"That's simply the way the wood has discolored over the centuries."

"So you say. In any event, the real intention of the statute was to hide something in plain sight, namely the Grail. The statute depicted the Virgin holding her infant, and the Grail was in her upraised left hand, affixed there by St. Luke in such a way that people simply assumed it was part of the statute. There it sat, in a grotto beneath what would eventually become the monastery, until it was discovered some centuries later." Paracelsus smirked. "Except what Luke had not anticipated, or realized, was that the Grail can change shape.

So it became something else . . . the belt, perhaps, or the sword. The shepherds who found the statute had no idea that the Holy Grail was lying next to it. They doubtless thought it some relic left behind by an errant pilgrim. So the two became separated, although the statute still had enough of a touch of the divine—thanks to its lengthy contact with the Grail—to perform the occasional miracle for the truly devout."

"You've learned a lot about these things," said Ruehl.

"Well, I've had plenty of time. Now the Spear . . . ah, that bounced around even more, and had even more pretenders to the name than the Grail. Especially with the staff going in one direction and the head going in another. Except the true Spear never became separated but remained in one piece. Vanished from Saint Chappelle around the, what? Eighteenth century?"

"Thereabouts."

"And then the Nazis got their hands on it." He shook his head. "I think . . . it was at that point that my faith first began to crack. I mean, all these holy orders running around, spending centuries searching in futility for these holy relics, and who gets his hands on the Spear of Destiny? A demented little hanger of wallpaper who rose to power on the backs of millions of innocent people. What does that tell you about the way of things?"

"It tells me that we cannot question God's plan."

"Of course not, any more than you can question the master plan of the dodo. You can't question what doesn't exist."

"My son—"

"So anyway," said Paracelsus, as if Ruehl hadn't spoken, "the Nazis had the Spear of Destiny in their possession, until . . ."

"Until the Allies reacquired it."

"Except you know that's not true," Paracelsus said quietly. "Because I acquired it first. I went down into Hitler's bunker, and I took it away from the Nazis, for which you might want to bloody well thank me. My removing it from their possession guaranteed the fall of the Third Reich."

"So it was you who made the switch. We always wondered."

"Well, wonder no more. Of course, carrying a Spear around can be a bit . . . noticeable. But as an alchemist, I've learned a few tricks. Not just transmutation of elements, but also tinkering with size. Watch. Nothing up my sleeve . . ."

He extended an arm and Ruehl stepped back quickly as the Spear of Destiny snapped out from Paracelsus's jacket sleeve and into his hand. He held it there at its full length, and now in his other hand was the Holy Grail.

"Looking for these?" he asked calmly.

Ruehl's face could have been carved from stone. "They are not yours to possess, Paracelsus."

"Ah, so you do know me."

"Think of it as an educated guess. Although, frankly, I was expecting former President Penn to be in possession of the Grail. To come down here and cure Mrs. Cordoba . . ."

"Cure her of an illness that you inflicted upon her." Ruehl didn't answer at first, and Paracelsus prompted him, "Come on. You can admit it to me. I hear confession is good for the soul."

"We did what we had to do," Ruehl said tersely. "Our concern is for the greater good. We needed to get the Grail away from Arthur. It belongs to the Church. To the world."

"Not anymore. Too bad your plan didn't work."

"Obviously, though . . . it did."

Six more men slowly entered the Chapel. They were clothed identically to Ruehl, and two were holding shields with the sign of the cross upon them. The rest were carrying truncheons, which they slid out of their sleeves, as Ruehl also did. "For whatever perverse reason, you came here instead with the cup to complete Arthur's mission," said Ruehl. "Why, we cannot begin to guess. But you are here, and we are here, and you will turn both the Grail and the Spear over to us . . ."

"Well . . . in answer to your question," Paracelsus said, "I came here with the cup because I killed Percival, the Grail's previous protector." He was pleased to see the slightly ashen tint that Ruehl's face took on. "But the Cordoba woman doesn't matter to me. She can lie there in whatever coma you bastards induced in her until the end of time, for all I care. No, I came here because I'm not stupid. I sensed the fine hand of your society or order or brotherhood or whatever you call yourself. I need to have the Grail work another miracle or two, you see, and I knew you'd be waiting for me. I didn't come here to cure Mrs. Cordoba." And he smiled. "I came here to slaughter the lot of you."

He whipped the Spear around as the Holy Order of the Monks of Montserrat charged.

There were no screams, not because the monks were inured to pain, but because in one, fast sweep, Paracelsus brought the Spear around and severed their vocal cords.

When the blood really began to fly, it spattered on the statute of Jesus. He stood there, looking on in silence, as crimson tears flowed down his face.

RON CORDOBA SHOULD have been at home. The middle of the night was hardly the time for visiting hours. But he was who he was, and that certainly carried some degree of influence with the hospital staff, thus allowing an exception to be made. They'd brought in several chairs of the nonplastic variety, and Ron had managed to fashion a makeshift bed that he was certain was still going to destroy his back. He was drifting in and out of sleep when he looked up, convinced he was dreaming, to see Arthur staring down at him. He half smiled at the comforting sight and closed his eyes once more.

"Ron?"

The speaking of his name startled him to full wakefulness, and he almost fell out of the chairs. Arthur reached down and steadied him before he hit the floor. His vision clearing, Ron saw Gwen standing directly behind Arthur.

"My God," he whispered, as Arthur helped him to his feet. "I . . . I thought I was dreaming."

"No." He glanced toward Nellie. "How is she?"

"No change in her condition . . . Arthur," he suddenly said, "you can't be here. The Grail . . ."

"We don't have it."

That brought him up short. "You came without it?"

"It was taken from us."

"Where's Percival?"

Gwen spoke up, her voice hollow. "He's dead."

"Dead?" Ron laughed nervously. "He can't be dead. He's . . ."

"He was killed, Ron," said Arthur. "By Barry Seltzer . . . who, as it turns out, is an alchemist named Paracelsus."

"Para . . . what the hell are you talking about? Percival can't be dead—"

"*Ron!*" Arthur said sharply, gripping him by the shoulders so hard that Ron gasped from it. "This really isn't the time to discuss it. We think he's coming here for Nellie. Thank the gods I got here first."

"But . . . why for Nellie? I don't understand . . ."

"You explain it to him, Arthur," Gwen said, and she headed for the door.

"Where are you going?"

She glanced over her shoulder at him. "You said you

didn't want me around. So I'm going to find the chapel and pray. I figure we need all the help we can get."

CARDINAL RUEHL, HOVERING in blackness, felt something liquid and burning being forced between his lips. He was so disconnected from everything around him that he didn't remember at first where he was, nor did he have a clue what was happening. Then it slowly began to dawn on him. He remembered that he had eyes, and he forced them open.

The cup of Christ was just within his sight line, and he saw Paracelsus's face hovering just beyond it. Paracelsus was actually smiling at him gently, and he was upending the contents of the cup into Ruehl's mouth. "Excellent," he whispered. "There you go. Come on back. Don't try to sit up. It's going to take you a little while to get fully up to snuff."

Ruehl found that he indeed couldn't move. His mind was telling his body what to do, but it refused to obey. He turned his head slightly, then gasped, a low moan of distress.

His brethren lay scattered about the room, unmoving. There was blood everywhere. It was like something out of a horror film rather than a chapel.

"It's a mess, I know," said Paracelsus sadly. "But . . . what can you do? You fought. I had superior weaponry. That's all there is to it."

"You . . . monster . . ." At least, that's what Ruehl tried to say. But his voice was a hoarse whisper, and a sharp stabbing pain lanced through his throat. He moaned in pain.

"I wouldn't suggest talking. Your entire breathing apparatus is going to take a little while to mend. But it will mend. I brought you back." And he held up the Grail. "It's ready. Isn't it beautiful?"

Ruehl's eyes widened in confusion.

The Grail looked completely different than it had moments before. Earlier, the wood of the cup had been dark brown. Now it was ebony, as if carved from some sort of solid black wood. The gold lamination that had lined the edges had turned bloodred.

"Isn't it beautiful?" said Paracelsus, and he sounded as if he was going to cry with joy. "You have no idea of the lengths I've had to go to in my studies . . . the places I've traveled . . . the people I've sacrificed, the demons I've summoned . . . to learn what had to be done. It was just rumors . . . faint rumors . . . but I learned the facts of it. I learned how to accomplish my goal."

"What . . . what's your goal? What are you going to do?"

Paracelsus stared at him pityingly. "Do I *look* like a comic opera villain to you? What, I'm going to tell you everything while chortling, 'I wanted you to know everything that will happen so you can die feeling helpless?' And then have it come back to bite me on the ass? To hell with that. I much prefer that you die without knowing a damned thing. You've spent your life living in ignorance. Die the same way."

He drew back the Spear, prepared to plunge it into Ruehl's chest.

An abrupt scream drew his attention.

GWENDOLYNE PENN HAD walked into the chapel, so lost in thought that she noticed nothing until she was already a few feet in. Then she stopped, frozen in place, as she saw the bodies on the floor, a couple of shattered shields nearby them, the guy from the Vatican sprawled not far from her, and "Barry Seltzer" astride him, about to drive the Spear of Destiny into the Cardinal's chest.

Understandably, she let out a startled scream.

Paracelsus looked up, and he grinned. "My, my. Mrs. Penn. You look a bit more singed than last I saw you."

"G-get away from him!" Gwen managed to say.

"As you wish," said Paracelsus. "Is your husband still with us?"

"Yes," and her voice grew cold, regaining her nerve, "and he's going to kill you for what you did."

"Really. Then allow me to send him a message through you."

Without hesitation, Paracelsus stepped around Ruehl, gripped the Spear with one hand while clutching the Grail in the other, and shoved the Spear forward right at Gwen's chest.

Reflexively, Gwen stepped back, choking on sudden terror, her eyes fixed on the spearhead driving toward her chest. The only thing that saved her was blood. A pool of it had formed behind her, still seeping from the fallen body of one of the monks, and her foot hit it. She slipped, her foot going out from under her, and she fell flat. As it happened it was what she needed to do to save her life, for the Spear went right past where she'd been standing a second before. Paracelsus staggered, thrown off-balance, and this time Gwen didn't hesitate. She drove both her feet up and forward, and Paracelsus let out a shout as Gwen made solid contact with his crotch.

Paracelsus staggered back, the wind knocked out, pain exploding behind his eyes. He managed to hold on to the Spear, but then he tripped over the fallen form of Cardinal Ruehl.

Instantly, Ruehl was atop him. Acting entirely on instinct, Ruehl grabbed Paracelsus by the throat, squeezing as hard as he could. Paracelsus spear arm was blocked by the weight of Ruehl's arm, but he brought the Grail up and around as hard as he could. It was solid, ancient wood, and it struck Ruehl in the side of the head with the impact of a brick. Ruehl moaned but didn't let go, and Paracelsus struck him a second time. This time Ruehl couldn't hold on, rolling off to the side, and Paracelsus yanked the Spear of Destiny clear.

Gwen had clambered to her feet and was in a crouch, grabbing at a fallen truncheon from one of the monks. She brought it up just as Paracelsus—not moving especially fast since there was still pain lancing through him from where she'd kicked him—stabbed at her with the Spear. She batted it aside with the truncheon and whipped her fist around fast enough to slam Paracelsus square in the face. She felt the satisfying crunch of his nose breaking under the impact, and suddenly she let out a shriek as the spearhead slashed across her right thigh. Her leg bent, and it was just enough for Paracelsus to bring the Spear around again. She almost got out of the way, but not quite, as the point slashed across the upper part of her right breast. Gwen fell back, sprawling into a pew, blood welling from the two places where the Spear had sliced her.

Snarling in fury, Paracelsus gasped out, "I'm going to carve out your liver."

"Go ahead," said Gwen. "I hate liver."

"Murderer!"

It was Arthur. He was standing in the door of the chapel, and there was fury in his eyes and death in his heart. "Now . . . now you will die . . ."

"Oh, to hell with it," said Paracelsus. He shoved the Grail into his belt and, just as Arthur started to reach for Excalibur, Paracelsus pulled a gun out of a holster under his jacket. He aimed and fired in one smooth motion.

It was that exact moment that a young orderly, attracted by all the ruckus, came practically out of nowhere and stepped directly in front of Arthur. He said angrily, "What's going on here? This is a hospital! What's all the shouting about?"

At least, that's what he started to say. He didn't actually get much past "What's—" before the bullets slammed into his body. One of them went completely through, continued through, and glanced off Arthur's rib cage. The rest were stopped by his muscular form, and the orderly—without ever knowing what he had wandered into or what was going on—sank to the floor with a vague whimper and a confusing desire to call his mother. He was dead before his head struck the ground.

With an outraged cry of grief and fury, Arthur yanked Excalibur clear of its scabbard and came right at Paracelsus, shouting, "You'll die slowly, Paracelsus!" Gwen realized that, seized with a warrior's fury and desire for blood and punishing his enemy, Arthur didn't care if she was there to see it or not. In fact, she wasn't even sure he knew or remembered that she was there at all.

And what frightened her even more . . . was that Paracelsus didn't look the least bit concerned.

He pulled the Holy Grail out of his belt, held it up, and suddenly the Grail was no longer a cup. Gwen's eyes widened as she saw it had transformed into a sword. A solid black, glowing sword. She had known that Gilgamesh had wielded it as such; Arthur had told her, although she'd been unconscious at the time. But he'd said nothing about it looking dark and menacing and slightly evil. Even Arthur looked taken aback by what he was now witnessing.

"I hope this works," she heard Paracelsus mutter as he brought the Spear of Destiny around and crossed it with the Grail sword in front of him, holding it up as if he were warding off Dracula.

The response was instantaneous.

A wave of force ripped out of the intersection point of the two ancient weapons. Arthur tried to deflect it with Excalibur, and almost managed to do so. But he wasn't properly braced for it, and the force lifted him up and off his feet, slamming him back into the far wall of the hallway.

The only thing that saved Gwen was that Paracelsus wasn't completely prepared for what he was unleashing either. In the same way that Arthur was flung in one direction, Paracelsus was hurled in another. He smashed into the large figure of Jesus, which was sent crashing off its fixture in the wall. Paracelsus sat there for a moment, stunned by the impact.

Gwen clambered to her feet, started for him, and Paracelsus saw her coming and brought the relics together once more. Yet again a powerful force erupted, and this time it struck Gwen directly. It was like being bitch-slapped by God as Gwen tumbled through the air ass over teakettle.

But it was more than just the force that hammered through her. When it struck her, there were images slamming through her mind. Images and sounds that she didn't understand. Flames licking at the walls of a castle, and people screaming, and a loud whinnying sound like an agonized horse that sounded like more than a horse . . . that sounded almost human. She didn't know where it was coming from; it wasn't her memories at all. She knew though, instinctively, that she was bearing witness to something terrible, some ungodly, horrific sin that had been committed at some distant point in the past; a sin that mankind was still paying for.

All this went through her mind while she was still airborne, and then she thudded to the floor barely a foot away from Arthur. Arthur was still trying to shake off the effects of the impact.

There was a crash from within the chapel, the sound of glass breaking. Gwen tried to haul herself to her feet, but Arthur put out a hand firmly, and said, "No. Stay here," and pushed her back down. Excalibur gripped firmly in his hand, he staggered back into the chapel. Gwen braced herself, waiting to hear screaming or another blast of force, or the general sounds of battle, or something. But there was nothing, and a moment later, Arthur reappeared, hauling Cardinal Ruehl out with him. Ruehl looked ashen and weakened, but at least he was still alive.

"He's gone," Arthur said. "Out the window. Take him." And he passed Ruehl over to Gwen, who prevented the Cardinal from slumping to the floor. By that point, hospital personnel were running up from all directions. By the time they got there, Arthur had already gone out the window after Paracelsus.

"

CHAPTRE
THE TWENTY-SECOND

✝

ARTHUR RAN SEVERAL blocks, looking around desperately, trying to pick up some sort of track. But there was none to be had.

He circled the area, desperately wishing he had the forces at his command that he'd once had. Once upon a time, he could have had an entire phalanx of knights fanning out, sweeping around the area. If Paracelsus was anywhere on foot, they'd have had him in no time.

But there was no sign of him. He might simply have vanished into thin air—which, for all Arthur knew, might be within his abilities—or he might have done something as simple as find a cab or even steal a car. Hell, maybe he'd just driven himself there. There were any number of possibilities.

"Dammit," he muttered, and then louder, *"Dammit!"* He pictured Percival's corpse, a mute testimony to Arthur's failures, and he brought Excalibur slamming down onto the sidewalk shouting, *"Dammit!"* one more time, shattering the pavement beneath his blade.

Frustrated, Arthur started back to the hospital, but as soon as he drew close, he stopped.

The place was swarming with TV cameras and police cars. Arthur was still a good distance away. No one had spotted him yet, and he meant to keep it that way. He didn't need to go wandering into the middle of the situation; there was every likelihood that he would be detained for extensive questioning, perhaps even arrested. And what was he supposed to say under questioning? That a centuries-old alchemist was out to destroy the world and he, Arthur, was the only hope of stopping him? They'd probably want to lock him away . . . possibly next to the hypothetical fellow who claimed to be Jesus.

Arthur, having sheathed Excalibur, walked quickly away from the hospital. It took him a few minutes but he found a pay phone in the middle of a small park and called Gwen's cell phone, half-expecting not to be able to get through. Instead she picked up on the first ring.

"Gwen . . ." he said.

She let out an annoyed sigh. "Mom, for God's sake, you can't keep calling me every time you're having a bout of insomnia."

He paused, then understood. "You're not alone."

"That's right, Mom."

"Police? Government agents?"

"All that and more."

"And my coming back there . . . ?"

"I wouldn't really suggest it."

He moaned and sagged against the booth. "How's Nellie?"

"Same as before. Mom . . ."

She stopped talking abruptly, and Arthur pressed his ear against the phone. It was a strain to hear, but he was positive that he was hearing different breathing on the other end. It was obvious what had happened: Some agent had grabbed the phone out of her hand and was waiting for Arthur to say another word.

Pitching his voice as high as he could, Arthur—hoping he sounded sufficiently womanish—said, "All right, dear, obviously you're busy. Bye-bye," and he hung up. He knew he had to get out of there quickly, though. Her phone had caller ID. It might come up blank, or it might peg the call as having come from a nearby pay phone, which would have the area crawling with agents in no time at all.

He drew his coat tightly around him, the wind whipping it up against him. His mind raced as he went, trying to think of someone, anyone in DC that he could seek out for aid. He couldn't think of anyone; certainly no one that he trusted.

Only one name came to mind: Cook, the Secret Service agent.

But even as he started to reach for his wallet to pull out Cook's business card, he hesitated. He realized that he was in a hideous position of not knowing whom to trust anymore. For instance, he had written off Cardinal Ruehl as simply some officious oaf from the Vatican, and yet he had apparently fought valiantly against Paracelsus . . . and in the company of similarly clad monks, leading Arthur to think that Ruehl was part of some sort of secret society. He had been fighting Paracelsus to . . . what? Safeguard the Grail? Retrieve the Spear of Destiny?

And Cook had been the one who had put Arthur together with Paracelsus in the first place. It could have been an honest mistake, with Cook being taken in by the alchemist. Certainly Arthur, Gwen, even Percival had been. But what if Cook was actually a compatriot of Paracelsus, working with him to bring about the end of the world? By seeking Cook's help, Arthur might be delivering himself right back to the forces of his enemy.

His enemy, who could at that moment be anywhere, doing anything.

Arthur sensed that the world was running out of time, and he didn't know what to do or who to turn to.

For a man of action and determination to feel that indecisive . . . it was agonizing. Frustrating. Humbling.

And then slowly . . . reluctantly . . . Arthur looked up.

Clouds had moved in, blocking the moon, with the streetlamps of downtown DC as the only illumination. Arthur stared up at the clouds for what seemed an eternity, although it might just have been minutes, or even seconds.

"Hello," Arthur said, continuing to look up. "It's, uhm . . . it's me. Arthur Pendragon, son of Uther, King of the Britons. You can, uh . . . tell I'm a king because I haven't got shit all over me." He paused, then cleared his throat. "That was sort of a joke. People love to say it in regards to me. It's related to a film. It's also, well . . . it's not all that far off from truth, when you get down to it . . . except in this case, I really am waist deep in shit, and perhaps it's rising or perhaps I'm sinking, but either way, it's going to be over my head in short order and there doesn't seem to be anyone else around, so I thought perhaps I'd give you a go.

"We haven't chatted in a while. A good long while. Not at length. I admit, I offered up some fast and frantic prayers to you when Gwen was shot, but somehow I knew there wasn't really all that much you were going to do. I mean, someone put bullets in her, and you weren't about to make them vanish. So I set out to find my own way, and I found the Grail, except according to both Merlin and Gilgamesh it had nothing to do with a messiah or a savior, but instead some sort of ancient magic that predates any link to . . . well, to anyone claiming to be your son. So I hate to say it, but that sort of diminished you somewhat in my eyes.

"And there's so much evil in the world, and I saw so much of it in the old days, and there's more and more nowadays, and I know there's free will involved, but for crying out loud! If you see a sheep about to wander into a pond and drown itself,

you don't just stand there, and say, 'Free will.' You make personal intervention and you stop the stupid creature. And perhaps mankind is smarter than sheep, but a good number of us
aren't, especially in our group efforts, and how are we supposed to keep saying 'The Lord is our shepherd, I shall not
want' when so many are in want and there's no bloody sign of
you while we keep wandering into ponds and drowning! And
whose free will ever summons earthquakes or tidal waves!
They don't call them acts of God for nothing! You're like a
shepherd who picks off the flock with a bazooka when he's
bored. It . . ."

His voice trailed off, and he put his face in his hands.
Then he laughed ruefully. "Piss poor prayer, isn't it. I mean,
honestly. Lack of practice is showing, I suppose.

"All right, then. It comes down to this." He put his hands
palm to palm, fingers to fingers, and interlaced the fingers
and closed his eyes tightly. Then, speaking as fervently as
he could, he said, "I need help, God. There's a man down here
who wants to put an end to your creation. I'd like to make
sure he doesn't do that. So if you like me or despise me, either
way, it certainly seems that at this particular juncture, our interests are intertwined. And I'm telling you right now . . . I
need some help. That's not an easy thing for me to admit. I'm
a proud man, sir. Very proud. Almost too proud. And perhaps
I . . . I don't deserve your aid. I've done things in my life that
I'm not proud of. Terrible, barbaric things. And I'd like to say
that I'm sorry for doing them, and I am for some of them. But
for others, no. Definitely not. They were bloody bastards who
had it coming, and I'd do it again if I had the chance. But I'm
going to go out on a limb and say that you're not going to descend from on high with trumpets blowing and the firma-
ment shaking beneath the wheels of your golden chariot
being drawn by great golden horses. I'm suspecting that
you're going to be up in your heaven, but all is not going to
be right with the world.

"I mean . . . all right, yes. My faith has been taking a beating lately. But that's going to happen when people start worshipping me the way they used to worship you, isn't it? It's difficult to keep one's perspective. I mean, as a king, I was used to people bowing down to me, but this was something . . . more. I had to become a recluse for a time. I literally couldn't go anywhere without people asking me to produce miracles to help them or improve their lives. Perhaps," he said thoughtfully, "that's why you stay up in heaven. If you walked about down here, you wouldn't get two meters without being accosted by people wanting things from you. It'd be inevitable, what with you being God and all . . ."

He stopped talking for a time, then continued, even more introspectively, "I know that you place a great store on worship. On people worshipping you, I mean, and having faith in you. I don't know . . . maybe with people turning away from you and worshipping me . . . and my causing all this controversy . . . perhaps it hurt your feelings. I figure your feelings *can* be hurt. After all, it's said you made us in your image, and we can get our feelings bruised up rather handily. So why not you? And if that's the case . . . if you're angry because some people turned away from you, or sought a quick way to improve their quality of life . . . I suppose that's understandable.

"They made mistakes. I made mistakes. We're human. We do that. But now there's a human who's planning to make the biggest mistake in the history of humanity . . . by trying to annihilate the world through means I can't even guess at.

"And if you care about that . . . if you'd rather I put a stop to it, rather than every man, woman, and child dying . . . then I could use some help. I'm not saying I need some divine weaponry. I have my right arm and Excalibur at my side, and that's all I require on that score. But I could use some guidance. Point the way. A . . ." He sighed deeply. "A sign, as clichéd as that sounds. I need—"

There was a crack of thunder from overhead, and lightning lanced across the sky. Arthur was startled by the sound, and squinted as the lightning yet again violently illuminated the night.

If this is for my benefit, it's damned impressive, Arthur admitted to himself.

Then several large raindrops hit him in the face, and more, the quantity increasing rapidly with each passing second.

"Oh, you right bastard," said Arthur.

Within moments, a downpour was hammering down upon Arthur, who now wished that he had a hat to go with his coat.

Arthur sprinted across the street, splashing through quickly forming puddles, and ducked under the overhang of a closed office building. He stayed there, huddled, cursing himself for his stupidity in thinking that if anyone on high was listening to him, they were going to give him help of any sort whatsoever.

"Great. Just brilliant," he snarled, wringing out his hair to get the water out. He stared up at the skies, watching the rain continue to pour down, and couldn't help but think what a fool he'd been. He'd been humbling himself, pouring his guts out, and this was the response he was getting.

The rain continued, and he watched it collecting, pooling at the curbside and in cracks in the sidewalk right in front of him, all the time grousing to himself over this latest development. If he knew where to go, if he'd gotten some guidance, then he'd run through the water and simply deal with the inconvenience. But there had been no sign, no nothing, and now he was just . . .

. . . just . . .

He stared at his reflection in the dirty water of a puddle.

"Bugger me," he said, using coarser language than he normally would employ. "Water . . . of course . . . how could

I not have been thinking about . . . how could I . . . there was so much on my mind . . . *damnation*!"

Things that Merlin had said to him, quickly, hurriedly, that Arthur's mind had not fully processed because he was too busy trying to deal with the new reality of Merlin speaking to him from within a loo. But now it all came back to him with crystal clarity. *"Water!"* he shouted, and sprinted through the rain.

He splashed through the puddles and one time even slipped and sprawled hard upon the rain-slicked asphalt. His hair was soaked through, plastered onto his head, but he paid it no mind. He was totally focused upon his destination, cursing himself that he had not thought of it earlier. Who knew how much time he had wasted while being oblivious to the most obvious place he could go, and person to whom he could turn, for help. Not that he was certain he would receive that help; there was every possibility that he wouldn't. But that wasn't going to deter him.

Running through the darkness, he sprinted across a deserted street and started running out onto the Capitol Mall. Suddenly he skidded to a halt, literally, as a light flared up directly in front of him. "Hold it, sir!" came a voice, and Arthur immediately realized that there was no mystical attack here but rather a flashlight being shined in his direction. And from the tone of voice and the general outline he was able to make out in the dark, he was reasonably certain he was face-to-face with one of DC's finest. "Little late at night to be wandering out . . ."

"I have to get to the Reflecting Pool," Arthur said.

The cop was obviously about to give a canned reply, but then he stopped and Arthur knew without having to be told that the cop had recognized his voice. The flashlight now shone straight into his face, and the cop gasped. "Mr. President . . ."

"Yes, right, now that you know, step aside like a good lad. I have places to go, things to do. Busy time of the year." He was babbling. He must have sounded like he was Santa Claus on a hurry to get on with his errands.

"Sir," the young police officer said, "I'm going to have to ask you to come with me."

"Tragically, I'm going to have to refuse." Arthur started forward, angling so that he would go around the officer. The cop tried to head him off, stepping directly into his path. Arthur had neither time nor patience to deal with the situation any further. His fist lashed out and clocked the officer squarely in the middle of the head. The cop collapsed like a bag of rocks, and Arthur kept going.

He made his way across the darkened Capitol Mall. He saw the Washington Monument standing erect in the near distance, looking not unlike a giant sword itself. The rain was tapering off, thank God for that, but it was still lightly coming down. The surface of the Reflecting Pool was a steady ripple of falling droplets.

Arthur got to the edge of the Reflecting Pool and hesitated for a moment. The impression he got from Merlin was that Merlin had been attempting much the same thing as he was endeavoring to do: summon the Lady of the Lake. And for his troubles, he had been caught unawares as someone— Paracelsus, most likely—had attacked him from behind. Well, Arthur had no intention of being caught by the same maneuver.

Without hesitation, Arthur stepped down into the Reflecting Pool. The fortunate thing about already being soaked to the skin, thanks to the downpour, was that he really didn't care whether he got wetter. Granted, the shoes were probably going to be a total loss, but he had bigger things to worry about than the condition of his footwear.

He strode out toward the middle of the pool. As he did so, his thoughts turned to the notion that perhaps the rainstorm had been the message he'd been seeking. It had, after all, prompted him to think along the lines of water, and thus come to this current course of action. So perhaps, he further reasoned, God might get some points for steering him toward help after he'd asked for it so intensely. He decided to reserve judgment until he saw how the whole thing worked out.

"Lady of the Lake!" he shouted, and he pulled Excalibur from his scabbard. "You recognize this, I assume! From your own hand did I take this and, with it, my destiny! I was supposed to return at the time of mankind's greatest need, and now I summon you, at the time of my greatest need! Come and face me!"

Nothing. Not the slightest stirring in the water.

"Milady, I implore you! I, Arthur Pendragon, summon you hence, lest the world itself face its end."

Nothing.

Annoyed, Arthur shouted, "Right! That's it! I don't have time for this, you . . . you moistened bint! You watery tart! Get your aquatic ass up here, now!"

That was when he heard the warning sound of hammers being cocked, and saw that policemen were ringing the Reflecting Pool.

"Shite," muttered Arthur.

CHAPTRE
THE TWENTY-THIRD

✝

THE HOSPITAL WAS lousy with cops, Secret Service men, everyone with a badge or a gun that Gwen could possibly imagine within the confines of the District of Columbia. Every one of them that she encountered was solicitous of her, but by the same token, she sensed a collective look of suspicion from all around.

She supposed she couldn't blame them. There'd been two of them sitting with her when Arthur's phone call had come in, and she doubted it had been terribly convincing when she'd pretended that her mother had been phoning her up. The agent who had taken the phone from her and put it to his ear had made a curious face, and then had simply handed the phone back to her without comment. She suspected Arthur had figured out what was happening, and she could only guess what he said to confuse the poor devil.

No one was letting her leave the hospital. Because of what had happened there, between the presence of the former president, the former chief of staff, and one of the

Pope's most visible representatives lying in a hospital bed, a lockdown had been put on the entire hospital. She'd been barraged with questions and, after the first round was over, she was pretty sure there was going to be a second, third, and any number of others.

Nevertheless, with all that going on, she managed to get herself over to the Cardinal's room. An agent was standing there, taking notes, and the Cardinal was being as oblique as possible. No, he had no clear notion of what had gone on. He and several religious compatriots were merely visiting the local hospital chapel. Yes, three in the morning might seem curious, but God's work knows no time constraints. And so on, and so on.

When she walked in, the agent looked up at her and nodded politely. "If you don't mind," Gwen said, "I'd like to have a few minutes with the Cardinal in private."

"You can speak to him, ma'am," said the agent, "but I'll have to remain here."

"Why? Do you think he's planning a breakout? For that matter, is he under arrest?"

"No, ma'am. But—"

"Then a little privacy, please," she said with gentle insistence.

"Ma'am, I don't . . ."

"If you must know, I want to make confession. Do you have to be here for that, or are we stomping on church and state separations completely now?"

The agent rolled his eyes. "No, ma'am. We certainly are not."

With that, he got up and strode out of the room. Gwen made sure the door was securely closed, then walked over to the Cardinal and sat down near him.

"Let me guess," said Ruehl. "You don't want to make confession."

"No, but you do: right now. Tell me what the hell is going on, or I'll give these guys more than enough reasonable cause to keep you here until Judgment Day."

He glanced once at the door, perhaps to make certain there was no one there, then said softly, "I suppose you deserve to know. God knows we're all in the same boat."

THE LADY OF the Lake moves toward Merlin, and she appears annoyed. What is it, *she asks,* about you people and my ass? You called it flabby. Arthur demanded I produce my aquatic ass . . .

He always did have a weakness for alliteration.

Honestly, Merlin, he sounded so much like you just then.

Well, *Merlin says with indifference,* I am the teacher and he the student. So some influence isn't totally out of line. *Then his tone becomes serious.* Help him, Nimue. You see he's in dire straits. The police are closing in; the end of the world is nigh. You owe no allegiance to Paracelsus.

He did slay my lovely Percival, *she recalls with a hint of sadness.* On the other hand, he shares my frustration with humans for their polluting, careless ways. Why must it be this way, Merlin? Why must there be something wrong with everyone? Why can no one and nothing be exactly what I want it to be?

Merlin is silent for a moment. He knows the correct answer to give. He knows he is running out of time to provide it. Finally, with a heavy heart and frustrated sigh, he tells her, It is possible for it to be that way. For someone to be that way.

She regards him with intrigue. Speak, fair demonspawn. Tell me your heart . . . and I will know if you speak truly or not.

*G*WEN LEANED BACK in the plastic chair, shaking her head in disbelief. "So you're telling me that this whole . . . this whole 'society' of yours . . . was on Arthur's side?"

"We are on the side of humanity," Ruehl said. "We have been for centuries. And we knew the difficulties Arthur was in for, the forces that were converging upon him. One of our members is a mystic, a very powerful one. His necromantic globe saw the young Merlin Demonspawn being stabbed by the Spear of Destiny. With Merlin taken out of the equation, we knew we had to attend to Arthur's safety ourselves. Arthur's . . . and the Grail's."

"And you did it by poisoning Nellie Cordoba, you bastards," she said angrily.

"We intended to use the power of the Grail to revive her. We did not . . ." He paused, then, sounding full of regret, admitted, "We did not know the full difficulties of the Grail. The full threat it posed. We had some inkling, but . . . not everything."

"A little knowledge is a dangerous thing."

"That's pretty much right." He frowned. "You don't have to look at me with such anger. We're not the villains of the piece."

"Yeah, well, that's because you had Paracelsus to displace you for that title. The only reason you're not the villain is by reason of comparison. And what the hell are we supposed to do now, huh?" she demanded. "Arthur's gone, the Grail's gone, the bad guy's gone . . . do you have anything to offer now? Any suggestions? Any thoughts?"

He lowered his gaze. "None, I'm afraid."

With an angry snort, Gwen headed for the door, and just before she got there, Ruehl said, "Thank you . . . by the way."

"For what?"

"For saving my life."

She stared at him blankly for a moment, then remembered. "Oh. Right. I did do that, I guess."

"Paracelsus was about to kill me. He would have, if you hadn't stopped him. Perhaps God put you at that place, at that time, for a reason."

"Yeah. Well . . . did you ever consider that maybe he put me there to watch you die for your sins, and I screwed up his divine plan?"

"I doubt that very much."

"Really. Well . . . next time you speak to him, ask him. Who knows? His answer may surprise you."

She opened the door. The Secret Service man was very much in evidence, clearly having not gone very far. Just before she stepped out, Cardinal Ruehl called, "Go and sin no more, my daughter."

Gwen forced a lopsided smile, and said, "You too, Eminence. You too." And she walked out of the room.

SHE HAS A sense of what Merlin is about to say, and Merlin knows that she knows as well. Nevertheless, there is a moment of crackling anticipation, like the instant at the beach just before a wave strikes you and lifts you off your feet, propelling you toward the shore.

You cannot hold me forever, Nimue, *he tells her.* You know this to be true. I've lived too long, learned too much. Sooner or later I will devise a means of escape, whether it takes days or years. However . . .

However . . . *Nimue prompts.*

However . . . should you provide aid to Arthur, then I will make myself yours in all things. I will never try to depart. I will love you and none other, and if you wish to work magik to make me more . . . adult . . . then you have my full permission and cooperation. I will be yours, Nimue . . .

Body and soul?

He considers that. I am not entirely sure that I still possess a soul. I may have lost it a long time ago. Thousands of years of experience and memory . . . a few minor things slip away.

But whatever I have that passes for a soul is certainly yours, if you desire it. I will be the love of your endless life, Nimue, and never try to escape. I promise this to you, on my honor, on my life, on everything that I hold dear. I pledge myself to you, forsaking all others.

She swirls around him, thoughtful, considering.

You love me that much? *she asks.*

No.

Ah. You love the world that much.

No. I love Arthur that much, *Merlin gently corrects her,* and I would be most obliged if you didn't mention that to him. After all, I have an image to protect. So . . . what say you, milady. Have we an agreement?

Let me . . . consider it.

Milady, *he says nervously,* we are running out of time.

Are we? I'm not accustomed to such concerns. The water, you see, has all the time in the world. So . . . let us go over the specifics of this proposed agreement one more time . . .

RON CORDOBA, SEATED near his unconscious wife, looked up and smiled to see Gwen standing next to him. She put a hand on his shoulder and he put his own hand atop hers, squeezing it affectionately.

There were no agents inside the room, since Ron hadn't been a witness to anything. Nevertheless, the agents were keeping a cautious eye on matters because of Ron's rank in government, no matter how recently abandoned it was. Since they were standing outside, Gwen leaned forward so that she and Ron could speak as softly as possible.

"How you holding up?"

"Better if I had a clearer idea of what the hell was going on."

Gwen resisted the urge to look toward the door as she spoke even quieter. As quickly as she could, she gave Ron

the bare bones of what was going on . . . or at least as much
as she understood, since there were still pieces that she felt
as if she were missing. Ron took it all in and, since this was
not his first time at the rodeo with the adventures of
Arthur, he actually took it in reasonable stride.

Still, his eyes narrowed when Gwen got to the part about
Cardinal Ruehl and a number of others leaping into the fray
with Paracelsus. Ron waited for her to finish her narrative,
then he said, "You've seen Ruehl? I mean, since the attack?
Talked to him?"

She nodded. "He's well on the mend. Probably the only
reason it's taking a little longer for him is because the
damage was inflicted by the Spear of Destiny. They're
probably keeping him here for a day or so for observation.
I figure—"

"I don't care about that," he said curtly. "I just want to
know one thing: Was he involved in doing this," and he
pointed to Nellie, "to my wife?"

She saw a look in his eyes such as she had never seen in
him. A look of cold, hard fury. And in seeing it, she saw
something else: She saw Ron waiting until there were no
agents around, going into Cardinal Ruehl's room, covering
his face with a pillow, and holding it over him as the holy
man kicked and fought and screamed noiselessly into the
smothering cushion. When the Cardinal finally stopped
thrashing about, the enormity of what Ron had just done
would hit him, and he would come unraveled. Either that or
he would simply stand up, adjust the knot in his tie, and go
about his business. Gwen honestly couldn't say which
would be worse.

"No," she said.

He eyed her suspiciously. "Are you sure . . . ?"

"Ron," she told him with utter conviction, "he may be
kind of a prick . . . but Ruehl is one of the good guys, okay?
I asked him. I asked him point-blank. And he swore in the

name of the savior and everything, and you know how seriously guys like that take that kind of stuff. He wasn't involved. He . . ." She paused so she could say it without her voice cracking, "He told me to tell you . . . that he is praying for Nellie."

It seemed endless, the amount of time that he was just staring at her, staring, and she felt as if his eyes were boring straight into her brain, excavating the lies with a spoon and tossing them aside so that he could gaze upon the truth, pink and quavering and vulnerable.

Then he lowered his gaze. "Me too," he said. "Now I just wish that someone could remind me of why."

CHAPTRE
THE TWENTY-FOURTH

✝

PUT THE SWORD down, Mr. President!"

Arthur stood squarely in the middle of the Reflecting Pool, trying to watch in all directions at the same time. He didn't think they were going to open fire on him, but at this point he couldn't be certain of anything. The water was just over his knees, and every police officer had flashlights out and shining in his direction. He didn't know which one had warned him to lower his sword, and it didn't matter. This was no time to surrender.

But what was the alternative? Try to slice up several peace officers? Not only would it set him irrevocably on a path that he had no desire to tread, but it was hardly a sure thing considering he wasn't bulletproof. Parting mystical flame with Excalibur was one thing. There was nothing magical about a bullet, much less a fusillade.

Would be a hell of an ending, wouldn't it. Facedown, floating in bloodred water. Thus ends the future of the once king, with the Earth's end following him shortly thereafter. Not much of a triumphant quest, eh, Arthur?

"Gentlemen," Arthur said, "I'm not going to put down this sword. I need you to understand that. I need you to understand—"

"Mr. President, don't make us—"

"Don't try to make *me,* lad. Don't try to make me surrender, because I won't. Because if I surrender, then believe it or not, as pretentious as this will sound . . . the world will not survive. So for me to give up now means that I'll be giving up on my world. And I'm not about to do that."

"Mr. President," said one of the cops. "Mr. President, put the sword down and keep your hands where we can see them."

"We'll compromise. Keep your eyes on the hilt of my sword, and you can see my hands all you want."

"Mr. President, I'm going to come in there, and you're going to hand me the sword . . ."

"I appreciate the respect, son," said Arthur, and he brought the sword around. "But I swear to God, you try to put a hand on Excalibur, and you lose the hand."

"Sir, threatening a police officer—"

"It was no threat. Nothing happens if you do nothing. *Merlin!*" That last was a desperate shout to the mage, who he knew was with the Lady of the Lake. "I could use a bit of help here!" This was a vastly different situation from the Sermon on the Mound. These were armed police officers trying to decide whether or not to shoot him, and all the charm in the world wasn't going to make the slightest difference. He knew that he sounded like a madman to these police officers, but nevertheless he shouted, "Nimue! I call upon you now! You—"

Suddenly he heard something that sounded like a gunshot, but different. Instinctively he pivoted, twisting out of the way of possible bullets, and he saw one of the police officers holding an odd-looking, streamlined black gun. There were wires extended from it that were in the water, attached

to leads that had landed just inches shy of Arthur because of
his quick movement.

What the bloody hell is that . . . ?

An instant later, Arthur was staggered as electricity from
the taser sizzled through the water and hammered through
his nervous system. Excalibur dropped out of his numbed
hand as Arthur pitched forward, hitting the water face-first.
He could barely see, then he spotted Excalibur lying a foot
away from him. But it might as well have been a mile. He
tried to move his arms; he sent mental commands to them.
They did nothing.

He heard the police officers splashing through the water,
coming for him. *It doesn't end like this! I won't let it!*

It should have been impossible for him to get to his
sword. There was simply no way that his arm should have
done what he was telling it to do. And yet it did as Arthur,
with sheer force of will overcoming the determination of his
muscles to ignore him, propelled himself sideways and
grabbed the hilt of his sword . . .

. . . and fell sideways and off the bottom of the Reflecting
Pool.

The police converged on where they saw Arthur go
down. The fact that he had been shocked insensate didn't
make them act rashly. All of them were perfectly aware that
something could have gone wrong. They'd seen guys flying
on angel dust who were hit with full-strength taser blasts
and kept right on going. For that matter, from the way that
he was ranting and waving a sword and shouting about the
end of the world, it seemed that the former president was
high on something. It made as much sense as anything, and
a lot more sense than some things.

And this was not a full-strength blast by any means. The
proximity of the leads to Arthur had sent a jolt through
him, yes, but not quite comparable to what he would have

received if the barbs had struck him directly. Even a full-strength jolt would only paralyze for a limited amount of time, so it was entirely possible that Arthur could come up swinging. Thus, even as they made their way toward where Arthur had fallen, they did so very slowly and carefully with their guns out.

"Guys, we gotta pick up the pace! He's gonna drown!" said one of the young officers.

"You wanna risk getting your foot chopped off with that pigsticker of his? Fine! *You* pick up the damned pace!"

The young officer looked in annoyance at the other cop, and then did exactly that. The others continued to shrink their cautious circle a bit at a time, but the young officer went straight to where Arthur had fallen.

He splashed around, looking confused. "He's not here."

"What the hell do you mean, he's not there! He's gotta be there!" The lead officer looked around. "Did he get past . . . ?"

There were shouts of protests and "Hell no!" The protests seemed valid, because the ring of officers had been too tight and focused in the first place. It would have been difficult enough for Arthur to get past them underwater if he was at full strength. Slowed to a crawl from a taser, probably even having trouble breathing . . . it was impossible.

Tossing caution aside, the police now started moving quickly and noisily through the water. They had called for backup upon seeing Arthur with the sword, and now more cops were showing up. They looked everywhere, splashed about through every square foot of the Reflecting Pool.

Nothing. No sign of him anywhere.

"I don't believe this shit!" one of the older cops shouted in frustration. "He can't have just disappeared! It's ridiculous! It's impossible!"

"Yeah?" said the young officer. "Well, I'll tell you what. His whole thing about the world coming to an end was ridiculous and impossible too. And now he's gone and we're here, and maybe what he was saying was true! You think of that, maybe?"

"So what are you suggesting, huh?"

The young police officer splashed to shore and started to walk away. "Where the hell are you going?" demanded the older officer, as every other member of the assembly watched him depart.

The cop turned, and shouted, "I'm going home, and I'm praying. And I swear to you, man, right now I'm not sure who I'm praying to. Maybe God. Maybe Arthur. Maybe both. 'Cause I'm thinking that the world might just need all the help it can get."

He left. The other cops looked at each other, then, slowly, one by one, they each headed off to their respective homes to pray . . . and to determine who indeed should be the prayers' recipient.

ARTHUR HAS SEEN tornadoes once or twice in his lifetime. Most vividly recalled is the time in his youth where one of those terrifying wind funnels dropped to the ground barely five hundred feet from where he was standing. He had sprinted madly across a field, the tunnel howling after him as if God himself was screaming for his life. Just when all had seemed lost to him, he had stumbled upon a cave and taken refuge in there. The tornado had passed directly over the cave, and he had even fancied that he could hear it calling Aaaaaaaaarrrrrthuuuuurrrrrr as it passed by, as if it were searching for him and was imploring him to come out and face it . . . or perhaps simply venting its frustration over having lost him.

Now it seems to Arthur that, after a thousand years' delay, the tornado has found him once again. This time he is not fleeing from it. This time it has captured him, and he is within the heart of its funnel. But it is not simply keeping him stationary, or even whipping him around in a manic circle. Instead he is being propelled through

*it, like a cork from a bottle or a bullet through the barrel of a gun. It
stretches out before him endlessly, and as he hurtles through, he feels
himself brushing against . . . he doesn't know at first. He can't process it. Millions of voices, of passing thoughts, of whispered secrets
that he cannot begin to understand or remember. He feels both outside
and inside of himself, connected to the whole of humanity . . .*

Of course you are, Highness. That's how this works. We
come from the water, we mostly are water, and the water is
the great link between all creatures. You cannot live without
it . . . although your efforts to befoul your own waters would
almost indicate that you don't understand that simple truth.

*He senses his headlong whirl through the funnel of water slowly,
just enough for him to get his bearings. He speaks but no words
emerge, and yet he hears his own voice.* Nimue!

Of course.

Where is Merlin?

He cannot help you, *she says with both a touch of sorrow and
a touch of triumph . . . emotions flowing in opposition to each other.*
He is mine, now, promised only to me.

I don't believe you! What is he, besotted by some sort of
love spell—?

Interestingly . . . yes . . . although it's not what you think.
In any event, it matters not. He is pledged to me in exchange for my helping you. *She adds with a sense of amusement,*
Or did you think that I came to your aid because of the al-
luring way you demanded the presence of my aquatic ass?

I want Merlin! Now!

Since you are alive at this moment owing to my good
graces, you're not exactly in a position to be making de-
mands, Highness. Listen carefully, before my good humor
fades . . . along with the protection I'm providing you as I
speed you through the Clear . . .

*He wants to struggle fiercely, but he doesn't know how to go
about it. Excalibur remains clutched in his hand, but it is not as if
he can start chopping at the water.*

Paracelsus, *she continues,* is heading toward the henge of Wiltshire. It is a place of vast magic. It is, in fact, one of the origin points of magic. But it is destructive magic. Magical blood was spilled there. A great sin of magiks was committed there. Dark forces, dark memories, have lain dormant there for thousands of years, gaining strength. The Spear and the Grail were both present at the time . . . and so was what you hold in your hand. What the Spear and Grail can channel into destruction . . . that which you hold can reverse.

You mean Excalibur?

What else do you hold in your hand? *Nimue asks matter-of-factly.* You will arrive at the henge of Wiltshire at about the same time as Paracelsus. I have seen to that since, in the final analysis, I believe in fairness.

Please! Lady! Let me speak to Merlin! *He hates the sound of his own voice. He hates the sound of begging. But he does it nonetheless, because he senses there is information Merlin has that could be of great help to him.*

The Lady confirms that with her next words. He very likely could help you, Arthur. But he is mine now, and I am a very selfish lover. I know that because I've been told it repeatedly, by a variety of men whose opinions I respect. But I am what I am, and cannot change that. So instead I will simply embrace it. You cannot see Merlin, nor hear him in the way that you briefly were able to earlier. I've seen to that. He is mine, all mine, not yours. Understood?

All too well, *Arthur says grimly.* For I was once like you. A selfish, self-centered bastard, especially in matters of love. And I destroyed my great love with my selfishness. You will, too, milady. Mark me. Everything about Merlin that you may have loved, which makes him special to you and great and wonderful . . . your self-obsessed love will cause it to wither and die. It is a terrible and rapacious way to be, milady, and it is unworthy of you.

And what is unworthy of you? *Nimue asks.*

You don't see poets celebrating that aspect of me in their epics or madrigals now, do you. I can believe that mankind came from the seas, Lady Nimue, because we aspire to the heights of great, crashing waves . . . but truly, we are all filled with darkest depths into which we frequently sink.

There is a pause, a long pause, during which time the only noise Arthur hears is the spinning of the great funnel of water around him. He sees a literal light at the end of the tunnel, and suspects the end is near . . . in more ways than one.

Merlin is mine, *her voice finally says resolutely.*

Then try not to drown in him, milady.

And suddenly, faster than Arthur thinks possible, he has reached the light and passes through it and Arthur came up coughing, splashing to the surface. He was soaked to the skin and through, and the sun was just coming up over the horizon.

He coughed once more, expelling water from his lungs, and realized that he was in a slow-moving river. All around him was flat, green countryside.

Arthur splashed about, then his feet suddenly and violently struck the riverbed beneath him. He landed ignominiously on his backside and realized that he was standing in a fairly shallow section of the river. He gathered his wits and stood. The water surged to just below his waist.

"Brilliant," he muttered.

"Here now! What's all this?"

Turning around carefully so that he didn't lose his footing, Arthur saw an older man and a young boy seated on the shore. Probably grandfather and grandson. They had fishing lines dangling in the river. It had been the grandfather who had shouted out at him, and continued, "You're scaring the fish!"

"Sorry. Where am I?" asked Arthur, splashing toward the shore.

"You've got a bloody great sword in your hand!" said the old man. "I'm not telling you a bleeding thing until you put that away!"

"Right. Fine," said Arthur, sheathing Excalibur. "Now would you please tell me where I am . . ."

"Don't you know?"

Arthur closed his eyes, having trouble believing he was dealing with such idiocy. Perhaps the world really did deserve to end after all. "Of course I don't know. Why would I ask if I already knew?"

The old man considered it. "Perhaps you were just making conversation."

"Oh, for the love of God . . ."

"Grampa," the boy spoke up. "I've seen him on the telly. I think he's the king."

"The what?"

"The king," the boy repeated.

"Yes, he's right," Arthur said, hoping against hope that it would speed things along. "I am the king."

"Well, I didn't vote for you."

"You don't vote for——!" Then Arthur caught himself. This was beginning to sound eerily familiar, and he knew he didn't want to let himself get pulled any further into this ridiculous conversation. "You know what. Never mind. I'll figure out where the henge is myself."

"Henge?" said the boy.

"Yes. It's a large circular area with a ditch around it, usually, used for rituals in ancient times. It usually is surrounded by wood posts or——"

"Stone."

"Yes, they can be——" Then Arthur's eyes widened and he realized. "Wiltshire! She said it was in . . . bloody hell! Stonehenge, Pendragon, you great bleeding idiot! This is, what, the Wylye River? The Avon . . . ?"

The boy nodded, looking pleased. "Yes, the River Avon."

"Which way is——?"

The youngster pointed off to the right. Arthur had no idea how far Stonehenge was, but it didn't matter. He had to get there as fast as he could and couldn't risk any more time chatting. He sprinted off in the direction the child indicated, and it was five minutes later when it occurred to him that he was staking the fate of the world on the directional instincts of a boy who appeared to be no more than eight or nine years old.

And a little child shall lead them.

The words from the book of Isaiah came to him unbidden. And what else did it say? A child shall lead them, and some things about snakes—well, certainly he'd encountered enough snakes in the grass in his recent encounters. And . . .

They shall not hurt or destroy in all my holy mountain: for the earth shall be full of the knowledge of the Lord as the waters cover the sea . . .

Arthur didn't know if he was going through the motions of actions dictated in scripture, but he did know one thing for sure: He knew nothing for sure.

I suppose, he said as he ran up the small mountain leading toward the holy area of Stonehenge, *I'll just have to have some faith.*

CHAPTRE
THE TWENTY-FIFTH

✝

PARACELSUS HAD LOST count of how many times he had circled the interior ring of Stonehenge. He kept running his fingers over the surface of the megaliths, studying them with awe and fascination. Even Paracelsus, for all his endless studying and all the sources that he had investigated over the years, had not been able to determine to an absolute certainty the stone ring's origins. There were theories: Celts, Druidic cults, an assortment of ancient sorcerers. But nothing definitive.

He knew, though, that it was a focal point of dark and forbidding magic. Magic that was somehow tied in to both the Grail and the Spear of Destiny. Even if he'd had any doubt of the veracity of his investigations, he was certain of it the moment he stepped inside the ring of stone with the two weapons in his hand. The Grail sword, black and eerie, did not glitter in the filtering rays of the sun. Instead it was as if the weapon was absorbing the light. If it had been nighttime, the sword would have been invisible. And the Spear . . . Paracelsus might have been imagining it, but he was quite certain that he was getting a sense of building heat from within the Spear's shaft. The head of the Spear was likewise beginning to glow. Not a lot, but enough to get Paracelsus's notice.

Sal was situated in the middle of the circle. Having tossed aside his human disguise, he was curled in his flaming-lizard form, idly drumming his fiery claws on the ground. "What the hell are we waiting for?" Sal demanded.

"The sun to come fully up." He watched with fascination as the orb slowly ascended upon the horizon. "I wonder," he said softly, "how many people are watching the sun come up right now . . . while at the same time, others are watching it set. And in both cases, they're watching it for the last time. I wonder what's going through their minds? What are they thinking about? Their little lives . . . the things that they need to accomplish in this day to come, or what they didn't accomplish in the day just past."

"I don't understand. You're planning to wipe them out. Why do you care?"

Paracelsus shook his head in a pitying manner. "I'm wiping them out . . . because I do care."

"Oh, well, that makes sense."

He ignored the sarcasm. "Yes. It does make sense." He turned his attention back to the rising sun, and his voice quavered with pent-up emotion. "We reached for the stars, Sal . . . We reached for the stars, and instead we continue to eat dirt. Whatever grand hope or scheme or design there was for humanity . . . it's gone off the rails. It's not working. We're killing each other, starving each other, annihilating each other. And there's still such . . . such continued hope for a paradise that will never, ever come. They know it, deep down. They lead lives of quiet and not-so-quiet despair, and cloak themselves in tattered cloaks of belief in higher powers and a greater destiny, and it's all nonsense. It's fairy tales. They deserve better, and they're never going to get it.

"The Norse had their legends, you know. Tales of Rag-
narok, and the end of the world. And you know what happened? The last, cleansing act after the final battle of the
gods? Surtur, the fire demon, with his great flaming sword,
reduced the earth to a great floating cinder.

"Eventually, though, there will be a rebirth. Life does
have a way of reinventing itself."

"Yeah, well," said Sal, "one can only hope that whatever
the next species is that rises to dominance, they do a better
job than this lot."

"Indeed." Paracelsus yawned and stretched. It seemed an
age since he'd slept. "The thing is, Sal . . . in the end, I'm
simply a scientist. I understand the concept of experiments.
More . . . I understand the concept of failed experiments.
That's what humanity clearly is. When you're faced with a
failed experiment, you don't linger over it. You don't stand
around wishing that it had turned out better. You simply
dump it and move on. That's what I'm doing. It was not an
easy decision to make . . . but, in the end, I was the only one
who could make it."

Sal nodded, then he stood. "Sun's up," he said. "So . . .
what happens now?"

"Well," said Paracelsus, "there are specific steps that must
be followed. What we're standing in . . . it's more than just a
center of mystic power. It's a gateway."

"Through where?"

"Through time and space, actually. Through to the actual point when the great sin against magic and humanity
first occurred. I use the power of the Grail sword and the
Spear of Destiny to traverse that gateway . . . not go back in
time myself, actually, but simply open the path that will
summon the energies. Energies that will create a giant vortex, if you will. And that vortex"—he smiled—"will then
draw the power of the sun to me."

"And that will actually work? You can tap into that?"

Even Sal, who always appeared blasé about everything, looked impressed.

"It's not as if it doesn't happen all the time. Lesser mystics—with similar aspirations but without the tools, resources, and research—make such endeavors all the time. Why do you think that, every so often, great tongues of flame lash out from the sun into space? The sun's power heeds the summons of the lesser mystics. One fellow in the mid-1800s almost got one all the way out here, but it fell somewhat short. For me, though . . . it will be different."

"It sounds amazing."

"It will be. I will require, however, a means of 'jump-starting' the process, if you will. A way of channeling into the primal forces of power that will open the gateway for me."

"Don't you have enough power when you cross those two weapons of yours?"

"Power, yes. The right kind, sadly, no."

"So how are you going to 'jump-start' it."

"Funny you should ask," said Paracelsus.

He pivoted on the ball of his foot and brought his arm through with perfect precision. The Spear of Destiny sailed through the air and lanced directly through Sal's body, pinning him to the ground. Sal let out a horrific scream and clawed at the Spear, trying to pull it loose. He did not succeed.

Paracelsus walked toward him slowly, a look of sad amusement on his face. "I truly regret you won't be along for the ride, Sal. It's going to be . . . magnificent."

He gripped the staff of the Spear, and he felt energy beginning to churn around him. The stones of Stonehenge trembled slightly but remained in their places, serving their ancient role as containers of unleashed magic.

Sal continued to struggle, but the Spear could not be resisted. It steadily drained away the elemental forces that were part of the creature's physical essence. Overhead the clouds began to churn, turning dark and threatening. The sun was blocked out, but it didn't matter; Paracelsus knew it was there, and knew that he would be able to tap into it as needed.

The salamander faded more and more, then with a final, agonized shriek, the fire demon flared out of existence. Eldritch power began swirling furiously within the enclosure of Stonehenge. Paracelsus watched, fascinated, captivated. He was clutching the Spear, taking care not to cross it with the Grail sword. He wanted to wait until the right moment. Everything had to be perfectly in place.

"Explain it to me," he whispered. "Make me understand."

The arcane winds whipped around, faster and faster, and Paracelsus stood there in the middle of it, unscathed, the eye of the hurricane. He watched, fascinated, and images began to play out before him. Ghost images, moving slowly through their paces and beginning to accelerate, like a movie getting up to speed.

And one of the images . . . one of them was drawing closer toward him, heading right for him. Paracelsus spread wide his arms, and cried out, "Give me knowledge, being from a time long past! Shade and shadow, reveal your secrets to me now! Show me the first sin against—"

The figure drew closer still, and that was when Paracelsus realized it wasn't one of the flickering, phantasmic images of a bygone age advancing on him. It was real, it was solid, it was from modern day, it was armed, and it looked extremely pissed off.

"Oh, shit," muttered Paracelsus as Arthur Pendragon came straight at him.

ARTHUR SPRINTED ACROSS the greenery, watching the sun come up and knowing—without knowing how he knew—that the sunrise itself was some sort of deadline.

Excalibur's invisible scabbard kept slapping against his leg. *Let me be in time, please let me be in time,* he kept thinking.

As he came up over a rise, he suddenly felt the ground beneath him begin to shake. It was at that moment he realized that he wasn't going to be in time.

The clouds began to blacken, and the power of ancient magiks sizzled through the air. He knew the scent all too well, like the ionization following a lightning strike, except that it stirred ancient and unknowable feelings and gave you nightmares for three days.

Stonehenge was now in sight, except Arthur couldn't say for certain exactly what it was that he was seeing. A virtual cyclone of eldritch energy was swirling within the confines of Stonehenge, heading straight up into the sky, where the black clouds were churning around it. It looked like a great gaping hole had been torn straight into heaven.

The hairs on the back of Arthur's neck were standing up, and his greatcoat was flapping furiously in the wind that was building up. He shucked the coat since it was weighing him down, leaving him only in black pants and a white shirt. He would have killed to have had some armor at that moment.

He staggered forward, pushing against the fierce resistance, until he was almost to the edge of Stonehenge. But when he tried to cross the divide, he found it an impenetrable barrier. He slammed against it with his shoulder, but it was as if the wind was solid brick.

"All right, then," growled Arthur, and he drew Excalibur. The sword seemed to hum with eagerness to join battle, as if it were attracted to this time and this place. He shoved the great sword forward, and Excalibur cleaved through the whirlwind as he had hoped it would.

Gaining strength and speed with every step, Arthur managed to penetrate the vast gyrating obstruction that was the wind funnel created by the arcane forces Paracelsus had unleashed. He gripped his sword tighter than ever; for the instant he was within the sphere of influence, all reality around him seemed to go completely mad.

He was seeing a place from long, long ago. A castle, and people within, but their clothes were like nothing worn during Arthur's time. They predated Camelot by who-knew-how-long, and it was difficult for Arthur to understand what he was seeing because the images were overlaying each other. There was no sequence, no progression of this happened, then this happened, then this happened. Instead everything seemed to be transpiring at once.

He saw people feasting, and there was a fire, and there was some sort of white horse hanging upside down, and people were running and screaming and exploding and dying, and there was a young man whose back was to Arthur, and he appeared untouched by all the insanity unfolding around him . . .

And slowly the reality dawned upon Arthur. This place . . . this place had not simply been selected at random, some rocks thrown up and that was that. This henge enclosed an area that had once been this grand throne room, this place of power for some ancient ruler whose name was long forgotten. The slaughter of the white horse was some sort of momentous event, and people had died for it, and . . .

He spotted Paracelsus, and it took a moment to register that he was very real and very much there. Arthur started toward him, clutching Excalibur in a death grip, fighting his way toward the alchemist. He had to fight the impulse to dodge the figures that hurtled past him with increasing fury and speed, and there was the white horse again, except—

Oh my God. Oh . . . my God . . .

It was a unicorn. It had a horn of pink and purple protruding from its head, and for half a heartbeat, Arthur was able to make out its deep, limpid eyes.

They killed a unicorn here . . . perhaps the last . . . perhaps the only one that ever was . . . oh my God, how could they? How dare they? How can anyone forgive such brutality? Sometimes their knowing not what they do is simply not an excuse.

And the young man was there again, moving through the flames that were consuming the bodies of the others, and this time he turned toward Arthur. It seemed as if he were looking straight across a barrier of time, directly into Arthur's eyes, and there was something about him . . .

And suddenly Paracelsus was just a few feet away. Arthur had become so absorbed in watching the images around him that he'd been moving forward automatically, giving no thought to his struggle. He drew back his sword and charged the intervening distance.

Paracelsus turned and saw him coming. The alchemist spat out a profanity and started to bring the Grail sword up to crisscross with the Spear of Destiny.

"No you don't!" shouted Arthur, and with a sweep of Excalibur, he slammed the Spear of Destiny aside. Excalibur, which could cut through anything, should have sliced through the Spear with ease. Instead all he managed to do was shove it to one side.

It should have been enough as he stepped quickly forward, reversed the sword's arc, and sliced it around with the full intention of knocking Paracelsus's head clear of his body. But Paracelsus was faster than his unassuming appearance had led Arthur to believe. He brought the Grail sword up just in time, and the two blades slammed together. When last they had done so, the results had been seismic. But they were within an area that was containing the magiks being unleashed, and so the swords came together merely as two weapons of devastating power meeting in battle once more.

Arthur shoved forward, the hilts of the swords engaging, and he snarled in Paracelsus's face over the howling of the power around them, "You don't win. Not this time. This time . . . you pay for your foolishness!"

"Startling coincidence that I was about to say exactly that," shot back Paracelsus. He tried to bring the Spear of Destiny around, to drive it through Arthur. But the king lashed out with one hand and miraculously caught the Spear just under the head.

The two men struggled against each other, and slowly Arthur pushed Paracelsus back, back, until he had the upper hand as he started to push the point of the spearhead directly toward Paracelsus's throat.

"In the name of Percival . . . die," he said through clenched teeth.

And then, just before he drove the spear home, Arthur suddenly saw the young man again . . . the young man from a long-ago time, picking up the fallen horn of the unicorn from its incinerated body, looking once more directly at Arthur.

He had seen those eyes . . . that face. He had seen them much older and much younger.

"Merlin . . ." whispered Arthur in shock.

It was exactly the wrong time to be distracted, even for a moment.

Paracelsus seized that instant to twist suddenly and cross the Spear of Destiny with the fearsome power of the Grail sword.

Instantly a fireball of monumental power erupted from the intersection point, a fireball in the unearthly colors of pink and purple. It lifted Arthur, knocking him back and sending him flying across the circle. Excalibur flew out of his hand as Arthur crashed into one of the megaliths. His teeth rattled, his bones were jarred, and he was reasonably sure that his brain was slammed around inside his cranium.

He tried to stagger to his feet, and he saw Paracelsus coming toward him quickly. He had the two weapons crossed once more, and another ball of fiery energy was building up. Arthur looked around desperately, trying to spot Excalibur.

It was lodged in one of the stones. When it had been sent flying, it had been driven into one of the megaliths and penetrated almost up to the crossguard of the hilt.

Oh, now this is just too ironic for words, thought Arthur as he lunged for Excalibur. He grabbed the sword by the hilt and yanked.

It didn't come out.

Arthur pulled a second time, and then a third, and fear started making his heart pound double time.

"*Don't you get it, Arthur!*" shouted Paracelsus as shades of time long gone continued to move around him. "*You're no longer rightwise king of all England! You're nothing! You're no one! Nothing except a pawn in my game! Hell, whose satellite was it do you think took the pictures of you and Gwen that set all this into motion, eh? Me, baby! All me!*"

He unleashed the ball of flame at Arthur, and it was nothing short of miraculous that Arthur dodged it. He flung himself desperately to one side, and the flame sizzled through the air just over him.

The dirt churning under his feet, Arthur scrambled back for the embedded Excalibur as Paracelsus advanced upon him. He could sense the intensity of the mystic vortex building up, and as he lunged for the protruding hilt, he thought desperately, *This is a test! A test of faith! If I believe I can pull it out—just as I did with the first sword in the stone— then I am worthy . . .*

He grabbed the sword once more and this time, with ferocious intensity, thought, *I believe in my power . . . in my place in the world . . . I believe in the triumph of might for right . . .*

"*I am Arthur Pendragon, lord of Camelot, and I shall be victorious!*" he shouted as he yanked with all his strength. Paracelsus was coming right at him, and the mighty Excalibur slid gracefully out of the stone as Arthur brought it down and around and right at Paracelsus.

Paracelsus sidestepped it.

For half a second, Arthur was off-balance, the blade at full extension, and Paracelsus brought the head of the Spear of Destiny down from one direction and the Grail sword up from the other. They slammed into Excalibur at precisely the same second.

Excalibur shattered.

CHAPTRE
THE TWENTY-SIXTH

✦

THE LADY OF the Lake screams.

She had to know this outcome was possible. But she had forgotten it, because she is who she is. So now, when the reality presents itself, she is caught off guard and reacts with horror.

And because she is of the Clear, she is connected through the delicate latticework of human consciousness to all human beings. Her horror, her scream, echoes through every living human mind in the world. Those who are sleeping wake up screaming; those who are awake instantly stop whatever they're doing and gasp in horror without actually knowing what it is they're reacting to. There have never been so many car accidents at one time in the history of the world, and it is nothing short of miraculous that airplanes don't come tumbling out of the skies as pilots struggle to process what has just been seared into their minds.

And in short order, everyone is going to come to several understandings without the slightest notion of how they know it. But know it they will, and what they will know is this: The end of the world is nigh; Arthur Pendragon is fighting for the life of the world; the mighty Excalibur has just been destroyed.

The world will join the Lady of the Lake in mourning, and howls of prayer and begging from the world over will wash over the consciousness of humanity. They pray to God, to Buddha, to the Prophets, to Jesus, to Arthur, to Ra, to Thor, to Shiva, to everyone and everything that they can think of.

And above all . . . they pray it will be enough.

INSULATED FROM THE collective mourning of the world, Arthur stared in shock at the shattered pieces of Excalibur. The useless handle slipped from his numb fingers.

"It's time, Arthur!" Paracelsus called. *"Time for you to die! Time"*—he brought the two weapons up and over his head. Instead of crossing them in front of him, he held them high and brought the tips together, forming a triangle—*"for everyone to die!"*

The unleashed magic of the two weapons stretched up, up and out of Earth's atmosphere, creating a vortex of energy that Arthur realized was more powerful than anything he'd ever seen before. He shielded his eyes, trying to make out what in the world was happening.

Paracelsus, in grand style, was feeling expansive. *"It's reaching up toward the sun, Arthur! Reaching toward it to generate a solar flare, such as humanity has never experienced,"* Paracelsus shouted above the increasing power enveloping him. *"It will leap from the surface of the sun and strike straight here. And I will harness it and spread it out all over the world. Here, from the heart of magical darkness of Stonehenge, the final, blinding light will blossom forth! It will be glorious!"*

Having no idea what else to do, Arthur came at Paracelsus with his bare hands. He didn't even get close. A shield of intense heat had grown around him so vicious that it drove Arthur back. He fell to the ground a short distance right next to the shattered remains of Excalibur. Desperate beyond measure, he grabbed one of the broken pieces of Excalibur and flung it at Paracelsus. Paracelsus never saw it coming. It didn't matter. It melted in midair before it got to him.

"*It's on its way, Arthur!*" shouted Paracelsus. "*In fifteen minutes, the solar flare will be here!*"

He had no reason to doubt. Paracelsus had moved beyond any need to confront Arthur. He was reveling in his power. "*Lucifer means 'light bearer,' did you know that, Arthur? I am like unto a god! An opponent of God! Am I not terrible in my wrath? Bow down and worship me! Every god should have his worshippers, after all!*"

Arthur felt like butter on a skillet. His skin was starting to redden. The air around him was becoming superheated. Fifteen minutes? Perhaps even sooner.

He had nothing.

He had no weapon.

He had no hope.

He saw the younger Merlin, shimmering as he moved through another time like a swimmer through water, holding the unicorn horn, tucking it in his belt.

Merlin, why hast thou forsaken me, he thought miserably.

And then he took a closer look at the horn.

He saw that it was tucked in Merlin's belt.

He saw the length of the horn. The right length for two hands to grasp firmly.

And the words of Nimue echoed in his mind:

The Spear and the Grail were both present at the time . . . and so is what you hold in your hand.

He didn't hold the sword in his hand. He never had.

He held the hilt.

ALL OVER THE WORLD, *weather stations are going insane. They have detected the incoming solar flare. Word goes out far and wide, every television program is interrupted, people are told to seek shelter, to get to low ground, to bomb shelters if they have them, to tunnels if they can be near them, because when this thing hits, it's going to be bad.*

They have only minutes left.

The world panics.

The world sobs in despair.

And somewhere, amidst the hand-wringing and howling for divine intervention, is Merlin. He's paying no attention to any of that. He's watching Arthur.

He's got it, *Merlin says softly.*

ARTHUR GRABBED UP the fallen hilt and swung the pommel toward one of the megaliths. The hilt was feeling brittle in his hand, a result of the steadily increasing heat. He slammed the pommel repeatedly, furiously, desperately, and suddenly it shattered.

He turned it upside down, shook it as the solar flare cut through space.

The horn of the King of the Unicorns slid out and dropped into his waiting hand.

"Son of a bitch," he muttered.

He had always simply taken for granted the magic of Excalibur. He had just assumed that the magic stemmed from the blade.

It hadn't. It had stemmed from the magic of the unicorn horn embedded within the hilt.

A grim smile on his face, he turned and sprinted toward Paracelsus. Paracelsus, his weapons still held in a triangular position, grinned at Arthur's approach.

Arthur lowered his head, closed his eyes, held the horn straight out in front of him, and charged. His legs pumped furiously, and when he entered the heat barrier that was protecting Paracelsus, he felt it rippling around him, crisping him, but not killing him, as the unicorn horn protected him from the worst of it.

Paracelsus saw it coming. His mouth a surprised "O," he tried to bring the weapons down to defend himself. He couldn't. His arms were locked into position; the forces holding the mystic energies in place were so powerful that Paracelsus was no longer in control of them but merely the means of completing a sorcerous energy circuit.

Arthur was barely feet away, and Paracelsus, trying to gather his bravado, shouted, "You . . . you can't hurt me with a unicorn horn! All the books say that they only possess healing power! The power to give life, not take it!"

And Arthur slammed the horn squarely into Paracelsus's chest. Paracelsus screamed as Arthur drove it into his heart, and his snarling face inches away, Arthur said, "Don't believe everything you read."

Paracelsus trembled violently, screaming, his life's blood seeping out through the mortal wound. And the burning thread of eldritch flame that was leaping from the tip of the Grail sword to the head of the Spear of Destiny was drawn irresistibly down to the small portion of the unicorn horn that was still protruding. Instead of Paracelsus projecting the power heavenward, the horn caused the energy to be drawn directly into Paracelsus himself. Arthur stumbled back, trying to put as much distance between himself and Paracelsus as he could.

Paracelsus barely had time to let out one final shriek as his entire body erupted into flame. He was no longer anything remotely human. Instead he was himself a gigantic fireball, with flames so intense that Arthur had to look away. He covered his head with both arms and curled his legs up protectively as he heard a thunderous explosion and release of energy. It washed over him in waves, blast after blast of heat, and Arthur let out a most unkingly scream, certain that this was it, and he was going to be with Percival in moments. And the scream was not random; instead it was the name of his wife, howled at the top of his lungs, because he wanted her name to be the last sound to escape from his lips.

And then, slowly . . . slowly . . .

. . . everything subsided.

Arthur lay there for a long moment, his clothes little more than tattered and charred rags, barely decent. There was smoke rising from the ground around him. He started to lean against one of the megaliths in order to stand and yanked his hand away because it was so hot. So he managed to stagger to his feet and slowly turn toward where Paracelsus had been standing.

There was nothing left of the man himself.

The Spear of Destiny had been incinerated. The head itself was melted.

Lying next to the remains of the Spear of Destiny was the Holy Grail. It was no longer a sword. Unfortunately, it was no longer much of a cup, either. It had, likewise, been incinerated. The wooden cup was completely charred. Arthur tried to pick it up, and the vessel collapsed in his hands, falling apart into blackened shards.

He thought of Nellie, lying in a coma.

"Damn," he murmured.

CHAPTRE
THE TWENTY-SEVENTH

†

$\mathcal{A}$RTHUR'S TRIP HOME took considerably more time than the one over to England. He had walked until he'd found a major road, and from there thumbed a ride to a local police station. The constabulary had recognized him instantly, of course. All Arthur had hoped for was some simple cooperation to get him back home. Instead representatives from Her Majesty were immediately dispatched. Given appropriate and less-tattered attire, Arthur was escorted to Heathrow while being questioned intensely by Her Majesty's representatives. By the end of the conversation, Arthur was astounded and flattered to learn that the queen was prepared to offer permanent quarters to Arthur and Gwen in no less a residence than Buckingham Palace itself.

"Her Majesty," the envoy said politely, "felt it was the very least that she could do."

"Extend her my thanks," replied Arthur, "and tell her that I shall very seriously consider it."

As the private plane winged its way over the Atlantic, Arthur pondered the notion. It did seem attractive, that much was true. Still, there was little chance that Britain was going to universally proclaim him their king. Which meant that he would be perpetually puttering around Buckingham Palace like an elderly uncle, observing his surroundings and yet knowing they would never be truly his.

Of course, he could try and press the notion of being declared King of the Britons yet again. But he wasn't sure that was what he wanted either.

"What would you like?"

The stewardess who was working on the private plane smiled at him graciously, having just spoken. "Have you given it any thought?" she inquired.

"Yes, I have," he told her. "I would like the Round Table back. More than anything, that's what I miss the most. What most people don't realize is that my knights were not merely among the bravest men to walk the Earth. They were also some of the greatest intellects, the most probing minds. We didn't just spend day after day waging war. Many was the time we would just speak of our hopes, our dreams . . . our thoughts on how to improve the world, to better mankind in general. The most powerful men around, trying to determine how to improve the lot in life of the weak and downtrodden. Seeing images of bygone times parading right in front of me . . . it makes me think of how much I miss those days. That, good woman, is what I would like. Thank you for asking."

She hesitated, then said, "Okay, but . . . I was asking about your drink order."

"Ah. Scotch, neat."

"Yes, sir."

HE HAD TO admire the efficiency of the British. When the private plane touched down in Washington, he had half expected the press would be all over the place. But the plane landed at a small, private airfield, and there were no journalists within miles. A car from the British embassy was waiting for him, the driver instructed to put himself at Arthur's disposal for however long he required.

Arthur directed him to take him straight to the hospital where, to the best of his knowledge, Nellie was still lying in a coma. He couldn't begin to imagine what he was going to tell Ron. On the entire ride over, he kept going over possibilities in his head, different things he could say. None of them seemed especially promising, and all of them ended exactly the same way: with Arthur admitting that he didn't know what to do. The Grail was gone, and with it, Nellie's best chance of recovery.

When he arrived, he was relieved to see that the various police cars and their ilk had departed the area. Still, he couldn't be entirely sure of what it was he was going to find. He stepped out of the car, asked the driver to wait for him, and entered the hospital. The hospital personnel, upon seeing him, looked at him with mixtures of reverence and awe. Patients were coming up to him and thanking him. It was at that point that Arthur first began to understand that everyone in the world knew, deep in their souls—even if they didn't know all the details—that Arthur had fought to save humanity. And since the world was still turning on its axis, obviously he had won.

"It appears you're their savior. Nice feeling, isn't it."

He turned and saw, to his surprise, that Cook the Secret Service agent was standing behind him.

His instinct was to shake his hand, to be happy to see him, but then Arthur held back, cautious. Cook, sensing a difficulty, said, "Problem, sir?"

"Yes, well . . . you *were* the one who put me together with the fellow that turned out to be the villain of the piece."

Cook shrugged. "Never claimed to be infallible. Besides, it all wound up turning out for the best, didn't it? One might think there was a divine plan at work."

"Perhaps," Arthur said, bitterness in his voice, "but I don't exactly think much of a plan that ground Nellie Cordoba in its cogs."

"Go see her," said Cook.

There was something in his voice that caught Arthur's attention. He tilted his head slightly, and said, "What do you mean . . . ?"

"I mean, go see her. Then come back and we'll talk some more."

Cook turned and walked away as Arthur, uncomprehending, went to the ward that Nellie was in. Reaching her room, he found the door closed, and so he gently knocked on it. Ron's voice called for him to come in.

He entered, and his spirits leapt at what he saw.

Nellie was sitting upright in the bed, and she was cradling an infant in her arms. It had a tuft of black hair on its head, and its face was round and pink and scrunched up in a very serious manner, as if it was giving a great deal of thought to matters of vast importance. Ron was standing near her, and he grinned as he said, "Well, well . . . the man of the hour. Or maybe the millennium."

"She's . . . she's all right," Arthur said, his heart soaring with relief. "And . . . she had the baby . . ."

"See, that's why he's king," Ron told Nellie. "He notices the small details."

Arthur crossed the room and embraced Ron fervently. Then he turned toward Nellie and sat gingerly on the edge of the bed. "He's beautiful," Arthur said.

"How did you know he was a he?"

"He radiates manliness."

She smiled down at the baby and ran a finger along his cheek. "Ron and I have been discussing it, and we want to name him Percival . . . on one condition."

"Condition?"

"Yeah," said Ron. "See, we're concerned with a name like

Percival, he's going to wind up getting into a lot of fights as a kid. So we'll need you to teach him self-defense."

"I would be honored," Arthur told them gravely. "But . . . I still don't understand. This is miraculous. Did you just . . . come out of it . . . ? Or . . . ?"

"It was the damnedest thing," Ron said, still looking bewildered over it. "I was sitting here, just being depressed over the situation, and suddenly I look up and Cook is looking down at me."

"Cook?" echoed Arthur.

"Yeah. And he says that the hospital administrators need to see me. So I go, except they don't. So now I'm wondering what the hell is going on, and I head back here . . . and when I come in, Cook's gone, but Nellie is looking up at me with her baby blues, and telling me she's having contractions, no less. I'm figuring that's what brought her out of it."

"Yes, well . . . that certainly makes sense." But Arthur's mind was racing . . . things that Cook had said, other things about him. "Excuse me a moment, would you?" He ran quickly out of the room, leaving a puzzled Ron and Nellie looking at each other and sensing that something had just occurred that they weren't quite getting.

He started down the corridor, and stopped.

Gwen had been coming in the other direction, and she looked stunned to see him. For a moment, neither said anything, all the harsh words and anger a barrier between them.

And then the barrier shattered as Gwen, with a choked sob, ran to him and threw her arms around him. She kissed him fiercely, and he returned it, both of them speaking words of love and apologies that tumbled over one another in their determination to be heard.

"Gwen," he finally managed to say, "this . . . this isn't going to sound good, but I have to go."

"Go? Go where? Oh God, what's trying to kill us now . . . ?"

"Nothing, it's nothing like that," he said. "I just have to talk to someone. It will only take a few minutes, then I swear to you, I swear to the heavens above, I will be back, and I will never leave you again. I promise."

"All right. All right, go." She smiled. "I'll be waiting."

Arthur emerged from the hospital, looking around for the Secret Service man, and didn't have far to look. Cook was standing across the street, and Arthur jogged across to meet him. He stood there for a moment, arms folded. "Divine plan?" he asked.

Cook smiled slightly. "Something like that."

"You cured her. You brought Nellie out of it."

"Yes," said Cook.

"You drank of the Grail."

"Yes."

"A long time ago."

"A *very* long time." Cook sighed.

Arthur chuckled softly to himself. "Your skin is darker than I would have thought."

"Indeed. But the dark skin isn't what a lot of people want to see. Unfortunate but true. And the painters tended to . . . oh, how to put it . . . ?"

"Clean things up?" suggested Arthur. "I know exactly what you mean. Still . . . I don't claim to understand everything that's transpiring here. I mean . . . why a Secret Service agent, of all things?"

"Why not?" asked Cook reasonably. "A way to continue to serve the cause of humanity in my own small way. Protect the president, and those with him, including various world leaders. Plus, you know, the dental's great."

He said it so seriously that it took Arthur a moment to realize he was joking. He chuckled, then said, "I'm sorry the Grail didn't survive."

Cook shrugged. "It wasn't unexpected."

"So the magic it possessed . . . it and the Spear of Destiny . . . both stemmed from a dying unicorn?"

"That's correct. Merlin had them both in his possession for a time. He built Stonehenge as a way of both memorializing the site of the great sin against magic . . . and trying to contain the potential powers therein. But eventually he decided that keeping the both of them together was far too dangerous. If nothing else, it served as a temptation to him. So he separated the two of them. Gave the chalice to one group of holy men, and the Spear to another, each at opposite ends of the Earth. He kept the unicorn horn . . . until he encountered the Lady of the Lake and, besotted with her, gave it to her as a gift. She was the one who fashioned Excalibur from it. Unfortunately"—Cook sighed—"the two sects ran into their own troubles. They lost possession of the two mystical artifacts, which remained drawn to each other . . ."

"And eventually both wound up in Jerusalem?"

"Two thousand years ago, yes," said Cook. "Where there were certain . . . difficulties . . . and then eventually they became separated again as the waves of events carried them in two different directions."

"Impressive how much you know about all this."

Cook shrugged. "Merlin and I met once, centuries ago. Before the fall of Camelot. We had a long discussion about many things."

"He never told me."

"And this surprises you?"

Arthur considered it and then smiled. "No. I suppose not. So . . . what happens next?"

"I suppose, my son," Cook said, "we'll find out together."

Cook started to walk away, and Arthur called after him. "Doesn't it bother you?"

Turning and regarding him oddly, Cook said, "Doesn't what bother me?"

"That it's all a sham. The entire concept of divinity and all . . . when, really, it all came from the magic contained in a unicorn."

"Well, yes, but . . ."

"But what?"

"Who do you think put the magic in the unicorn in the first place?"

"Hunh," said Arthur. "My wife said something along those lines."

"Smart lady, your wife." Cook cocked an eyebrow. "Anything else?"

"Come to think of it, yes, one other thing. Why 'Cook'? I mean, Joshua I understand. It's your name. But 'Cook'?"

"Because," he said with a grin, "I thought 'Carpenter' might be too obvious."

And with that, Joshua Cook headed off to the White House to begin another miraculous day.

THE LADY OF the Lake studies Merlin thoughtfully. Here, in her place beneath the waters, she watches him explore his new surroundings. They are much nicer, much more luxurious than the limbo she had been keeping him in. She has asked him if he likes it, and he has said all the right words.

But she knows. In her heart, she knows.

And she dwells upon what she has seen, and what has been said to her, and how it has made her feel.

I believe, *she announces,* that I am bored with you.

Merlin turns, confused. Pardon?

Well, *she says carelessly,* I have simply come to realize that . . . that the pursuit of you was far more attractive to me than the having of you. Now that you are here, and all mine, and none can take you and you will never leave . . . well, the fact is that you are something of a bore, Merlin. I am tired of you.

A bore? *Merlin sounds outraged.* How dare you! I am the greatest wizard of—

Honestly, Merlin, who cares? You are so full of yourself, when you should be full of me. You're much better suited to be at the side of your beloved Arthur. Away with you, then.

Before Merlin can offer a frustrated protest, she gestures casually and, just like that, he is gone, hurled through the Clear, up and out.

Nimue looks at the empty space that Merlin had, until recently, been occupying. And then she sags, and puts her hands to her face, and sobs copiously and in mourning for her sacrificed love, and has never been happier in her existence that—underwater—tears are an impossibility.

C OUGHING AND SPUTTERING, Merlin emerged from the middle of the Reflecting Pool in front of the Washington Monument.

Passersby gaped in confusion as Merlin slogged his way over to the shore and pulled himself out. Wringing out his shirt, he muttered, "I'm really starting to hate this damned pool."

And with that, he stood, tried to determine what the hell had just happened, decided that he would never, ever figure out women, and headed off to find Arthur. He would try not to be too demonstrative in the reunion, and there were several things that he would make sure to let Arthur know he could have handled far better in the Paracelsus business.

The worst thing he could do would be to let Wart get a swelled head about saving the world.

Ye Olde Epilogue

†

ARTHUR LOOKED AROUND the assemblage of the Round Table and nodded with grim satisfaction. "We've done some solid work here today, gentlemen," he said. "You have reason to be proud. By the interaction we have here, I am hoping—praying, really, if one can accept that notion— that we are not only going to put forward ideas that will be embraced by the leaders of our world . . . but that we will raise the level of discourse in our society. Thank you."

There were nods and murmurs of "Thank *you*, Arthur." "Thank you, sir." "The same to you."

Then Arthur swiveled in his chair, faced another direction, and said, "Next Sunday . . . the poor and downtrodden. How best to help them and yet let them maintain their sense of dignity. We will have a new panel of experts, including the return of Cardinal Ruehl . . . who regularly presents some very spirited controversy . . . and, as always, we're anxious to hear your input via our website at double-u, double-u, double-u, Arthurs Round Table Tee Vee dot com."

He leaned in toward the camera, keeping his shoulders

squared as Merlin had drilled into him, and smiled that smile that had prompted *People* magazine to dub him "Mr. Charisma." "These past thirteen weeks have been elevating, energizing . . . and the response we've received from you, our audience, has been nothing short of stellar. And I'm pleased to say that the fine folks here at PBS have renewed our little chat fest for the remainder of the year and well into the next. I couldn't have done it without my executive producer, Merlin . . . my beloved director, Gwen . . . and, of course, viewers like you. And so, until next week, this is Arthur Pendragon and the denizens of Arthur's Round Table, seeking to raise the quality of life in general and television talk shows in particular, wishing you a just and chivalrous good night."

"Aaaaaand we're out," called Gwen.

THE ULTIMATE IN FANTASY!

From magical tales of distant worlds to stories of those with abilities beyond the ordinary, Ace and Roc have everything you need to stretch your imagination to its limits.

Marion Zimmer Bradley/Diana Paxon

Guy Gavriel Kaye

Dennis McKiernan

Patricia McKillip

Robin McKinley

Sharon Shinn

Katherine Kurtz

Barb and J. C. Hendees

Elizabeth Bear

T. A. Barron

Brian Jacques

Robert Asprin

penguin.com